SHATTERED DYNASTY

AVA HARRISON

Shattered Dynasty
Cover Design: Hang Le
Editor: Editing4Indies, Tamara Mataya
Proofreader: Jaime Ryter, Marla Esposito

"I am not what happened to me. I am what I choose to become."
~Carl Jung

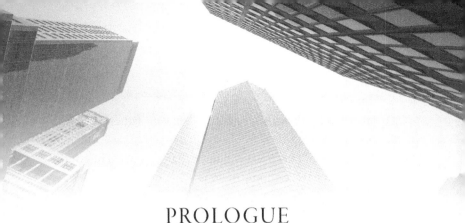

PROLOGUE

Trent

MY FINGERS DRUM AGAINST THE SURFACE OF THE DESK. THE sound echoes throughout the space, low and steady. A peaceful rhythm at this hour of the day.

It's quiet this morning. Dark, ominous skies loom outside my large windows overlooking New York City.

I'm the first person here.

Not unusual, though.

I do a lot of my business overseas, so naturally, I am always ready to work when the UK market opens.

Despite the time, the phone on my desk rings. The tone is a blaring contrast to the surrounding silence.

Its shrill sound reminds me of a fire alarm that takes you by surprise.

Without my assistant here, I'll have to answer. That's the only way to be sure it's not a business emergency. Few people know I get here this early.

Only my most important clients.

And family.

Still knowing this, I don't answer.

It stops ringing for a brief second, only to start up again.

Must be important.

Letting out a sigh, I grab my office phone.

"Speak," I respond.

"Mr. Aldridge."

"This is."

"Hi, Mr. Aldridge. This is Larry Baker, your father's attorney."

"Not interested."

I lean forward in my chair, about to hang up when he continues. "If I could have a minute of your—"

"No, you may not."

Nothing my father could say would warrant having a conversation with him. After what he did to my family, he's lucky I haven't put a hit out on his ass. His days are limited, though. My dad isn't cut out for jail. Orange is not the new black for that man. I have no doubt that he is currently trying to figure a way out.

Either by appeal or a prison escape.

Knowing the type of men he used to be associated with, neither would surprise me.

Because if he doesn't get out of there, it's just a matter of time before he gets himself killed.

He has too many enemies.

The Russian mafia wants him dead.

Cyrus Reed wants his head.

And I can't think of a better way to spend my day than at his funeral.

How the hell has he lasted this long?

"Your father called me yesterday, frantic. He wishes to see you," the sleazebag drawls out. I have never met the guy, but anyone who would represent my father has to be the scum of the earth.

"I don't give a crap what he wants," I hiss.

"Please—"

I hang up the phone . . . okay, more like slam it back down onto the receiver.

No matter how often this guy calls me for my father, I have nothing to say to the ass. Moving forward, I'll screen my calls better.

My dad lost the privilege to speak to me when he tried to sell my sister off in a game of high-stakes poker.

There's no coming back from what he did.

No apologies. No actions could ever make it okay.

There will be no redemption for him. No amount of money is worth his unforgivable sin. The bastard should have offered his own life first.

I'll never understand how he could do it. Not just how he could leverage and lose all our assets. No. That's just money, and in the grand scheme of life, that doesn't matter. The part that keeps me up at night is how the hell he could do what he did to my sister. He put Ivy on the chopping block. How was that even an option in his head?

But it doesn't matter because that man, my father, died that day. As far as I'm concerned, I haven't had a father in the past two years. I haven't spoken to him since we had him arrested.

The "we" being myself and Cyrus Reed. My brother-in-law. His associates helped, too. Men who've become my clients.

We didn't give the bastard any warning. Stacked evidence of his crimes like they were bricks, and we were looking to build him a new home in hell. We ruined him.

It'll be a hundred fucking years before he takes a step as a free man unless he pulls strings, which we've made nearly impossible. Stripped away any power he possessed—and his willpower in the process.

If by some miracle he manages to get out, we will be here waiting for him. Waiting to strike him down like the scum he is.

The phone rings again.

I ignore it.

A part of me wonders if he is reaching out to me to help him on his quest. He can try all he wants. I wouldn't help him if the fate of the world laid in his hands. So, regardless of whatever bullshit he intends on spewing, my father is dead to me.

Fine by me.

Swiveling my chair to face the windows, I stare outside.

At five o'clock in the morning, darkness still bathes the city.

The only lights that illuminate the sky comes from the buildings. There are no stars.

Which throws my mind into high gear. Why would my father's lawyer call me this early? The thought weasels past my barriers before I can stop it.

Don't read into it.

It's the same old bullshit, just a different day.

Dad knows this is the best time to reach me, and he told his lawyer that.

He knows no one is here but me. Not much has changed since I used to work for him.

The phone rattles again. There's something desperate to the sound of a call while the city sleeps. Almost eerie.

This time, I unplug the cord to the landline. The ensuing silence blankets me. I pretend, for a moment, my father never sold his soul. Or try to. The past is so far removed from where we're at, and I can no longer grasp it.

In his glory days, my father ran one of the most successful hedge funds in the city. Fuck city—he ran one of the largest funds in the world.

He made a lot of men very rich.

Made a lot of people very poor, too, as a direct result.

I'm not sure how it happened. One day, he could hop on a private jet to Saint Tropez for a quick dip in the ocean. The next, he couldn't even afford an economy-class ticket to Florida. He lost it all.

Not just his money, either. Desperate to refill his coffers, he entered an underground poker game, sold his soul to the devil, and became a monster.

Raising my head, I pull at the roots of my hair and force the thought out of my head. The bitter aftertaste lingers, lacing with the scent of the office. Where traces of his betrayal seep into every inch, every second, every decision.

I still run a hedge. But instead of just getting money from trust-fund babies, I also house money for the scariest mother-fuckers out there.

In the end, I ended up being no better than the man I hate.

Unlike him, I can sleep at night with my choices.

Which is ironic, since at the moment, I can't relax, no matter how hard I try. The phone call from his lawyer stirred the pot I have long tried to forget.

I push up out of my chair and head to my private bathroom to throw on sweats, a T-shirt, and sneakers.

Going for a run will clear my brain.

This always happens whenever my shit of a father reaches out.

And like clockwork, he always does.

I take the private elevator that leads to the ground floor and nod to the doorman on duty on my way out of the building.

My feet hit the pavement, each step leading me farther from my office. Once they cross over Fifth Avenue and into the park, I'm off to a sprint, pushing myself at a speed that can't be healthy.

The air against my face steadies me.

The adrenaline surprisingly calms my nerves.

I'm not sure how long I run, but my feet finally stop moving. The moment has come that I need to deal with the shitstorm that's probably waiting for me. I turn to head back. The sun has risen past the horizon.

The only priority should be to make some fucking money and forget how this day started.

I'm only a block away from my building when my cell phone vibrates in my pocket.

Now it's my mother.

"Mom," I answer.

I should probably be nicer. It's not like I'm in the habit of being a dick to my mother, but I have a good feeling I know why she's calling, and I want nothing to do with it. Nor do I understand why she even bothers trying after everything.

My mom did divorce him, thank fuck.

But for some reason unbeknownst to me (and trust me, I've tried to understand for the sake of my sanity), she kept his last name, sends him gift baskets in jail like he's there for a fucking birthday party, and still goes to bat for him when I refuse to talk to him.

Life is too short to hold on to animosity.

Her words. Not mine. And a big, fat lie. Inevitably followed by the same cheesy we-are-the-world bullshit.

"Give yourself permission to move on. A flower can only bloom if it feels the warmth of the sun."

Fuck that.

I'd take a part-time job as Charon just to ferry my father into the depths of hell. And even that wouldn't be enough to redeem him. An eternity of punishment is still not adequate for his crimes against my family.

"Hi, sweetie." Her voice is clear, but it lacks her normal, cheerful tone. It sounds somber.

At one point, I didn't expect to hear any joy when she spoke. That was when life had beaten her down. Guess that warmth-of-the-sun shit worked because she blossomed, gardening in her spare time and harassing me with the rest of it.

"Are you calling to talk about Dad?"

"Trent—"

"Let me stop you and tell you the same thing I told his lawyer. He's been dead to me since he tried to sell off Ivy. There is legit nothing you can say that will make me speak to him. It'll never hap—"

"Trent!" she yells. She *never* yells.

I halt. Maybe even cease breathing altogether. My pulse thrums against my neck, the long run catching up with me in one fell swoop. I wait for her to finish.

"Your father is dead."

CHAPTER ONE

Payton

M Y FLIP-FLOPS SLAP THE PAVEMENT WITH MY QUICK steps. Not a good choice for footwear, but I was running late this morning, and they were still out from the weekend beach trip.

Lucky for me, it's only a few blocks to school.

It's the reason Ronald picked it for me to rent. That and its beauty were the deciding factors when we signed the lease.

Four years ago.

Most freshmen at Ludlow University lived in the dorms the first year of school, but not me. My sister's boyfriend at the time, Ronald, would never allow that. He insisted on renting me the perfect house.

Erin's dating history could fill a yearbook. Jocks, goths, rockers. She'd done them all, shuffling through men faster than a deck of cards. But with Ronald, it lasted longer than most. They were together for what seems like forever. About nine years. Until something happened and, like the rest, he was gone.

I still love him like my own brother. Father, actually. He's way older than Erin, who's way older than me. Unlike the few before him, he has his shit together and has always been good to me, which is why I humored him and let him rent this palace.

Because that's what it is.

A beautiful home close enough to the school that my commute never impedes my studies. Something I'm grateful for given the heavy coursework in business.

I never want to go back to the way my life was before Ronald.

At the crosswalk, I palm my phone, type out a message, then delete it. My teeth sink into my bottom lip. I stop when I realize I'm pacing. Erin is an adult. Thirteen years older than me. I shouldn't be worried about her, but ever since Ronald cut her off, she's been needier than usual.

The air is warmer than I expected for this time of year.

Despite being fall, it still smells of summer. Of barbecues and freshly cut grass. New Yorkers are trying to squeeze the most out of the lingering weather. That will change soon. To cold air, burning leaves, and roasted nuts that will invade my nostrils on my walk to school.

The light signals me to walk. I do, forcing myself to shove my phone back into my pocket and readjusting my jean jacket around the crook of my elbow. I need to forget about my sister. Erin can take care of herself.

I graduate at the end of spring. That's over nine months away. With the way the past few years have kicked my ass, it may as well be a decade.

I can already envision this school year. More sleepless nights on the phone with Erin. She'll be frantic like she always is now that money has gotten tight. She'll ask me what she's going to do. I'll tell her it's going to be okay, but she won't believe me.

It's the same call each night, followed by a cram session of homework and studying I pushed aside to calm Erin.

And every morning, I wake up and do it again.

Assuming I sleep. Lately, I don't.

My life boils down to two things—Erin and school. In that order. Unlike my sister, once I get my degree, I'll get a job and support myself.

I stop at the next crosswalk. The urge to baby my older sister wins over, so I pull out my phone again.

Me: Have you eaten? Are you okay? You should get some rest. Please take care of yourself.

The message stays in the text box, unsent. I'm not supposed to encourage this level of codependency. Not with me, and not with Ronald.

It's not that I don't love him, but it's painfully obvious Erin can't live without him. *Or his money.*

Regardless of what drove them apart, he's always done right by me, and the truth is, he deserves better than her. She used him for his money. For his status. For his safety net.

Without him, she is hanging by a thread and so close to snapping. I used to feel like she was the baby of the family, and I replaced her not only as the older sister, but also as her mom. Like I was raising her.

Then Ronald happened.

That's when her fairy tale started. He moved us out of the small home we shared and into a beautiful mansion on the water.

When I was old enough, he sent me to school, bought me a car, and rented me a house.

Everything was perfect.

Until he left.

Erin is back to being a wreck now.

From the little I gathered from her, he stopped paying her bills. Odd, since mine are still being paid. She won't tell me what happened between them or where he went. All she said is he was gone. Her exact words were, "That asshole left us. If you really didn't do anything wrong with him, something to convince him to pay for you instead of me, you'll respect me and not hit him up. 'Kay, Payton?"

Which should've been the end of that. After all, she banned me from contacting the only father figure I can remember having. But nope. To top it all off, my sister calls me every night, making sure I haven't tried to contact him, and then accuses me of sleeping with him.

Why else would he have cut her off yet still pay for my college? Why else is my life still perfect when hers is now shit?

Her words, not mine.

We are still very fortunate.

We both have roofs over our heads. Food in our mouths. There was once a time, before him, when we had neither.

Still, regardless of all of that, I can't help but think something is wrong. That something bad happened to him. Why else wouldn't he reach out to me? Maybe he's sick? Hurt? The what ifs don't leave. No matter how hard I try to distract myself, I can't. The nagging feeling never goes away.

I finally cave, deleting the text to Erin and replacing it with one for Ronnie.

Me: I know it's been a while since we've talked. I'm sorry. I should have contacted you sooner. Are you okay? Erin asked me not to reach out, but I'm worried.

Okay, narcing on my sister is peak immaturity, but it isn't like she is winning any trophies in the maturity department, either.

I tried to respect her wishes as long as I could. *I really did.*

The text bounces seconds after I send it. I worry my bottom lip as I resend it.

Bounced.

Again.

With my heart heavy and my mind confused, I make it to my class.

Heather gives me a wave. She's not in her usual seat.

Instead, she's closer to the window. I look over to where we normally sit and see those seats occupied. I guess I'm not the only one running late today.

I head in her direction, taking the spot beside her.

"What's going on?" She narrows her eyes at me.

"Nothing." I shrug.

At my word, she shakes her head. "Nope. Something is wrong. Because it sure doesn't look like you're fine."

Of course, she noticed.

Heather and I have been friends since freshman orientation. She lived in the dorms and was my lifeline to a social life. After watching my sister overindulge for years, I was too driven to screw it all up by going to house parties, so she dished all the dirty details to me secondhand.

I touch my hair.

"What do you mean?" My eyebrow lifts as I pat the loose strands down. "Am I a mess?"

"Not a mess, per se. But it did look like you were thinking really hard when you walked in here."

My chest expands as I inhale deeply. "I was thinking about Ronald," I admit on a sigh.

Her large brown eyes continue to scrutinize, but she puckers her lips. "Still no word?"

"Nope. It's kind of weird. Why would he vanish like an asshole? My sister is tough to love, and I get it. Still . . . why not cut ties with both of us?"

"Maybe he wants something from you." She raises her brow.

"Gross."

"Gross, yes, but maybe he thinks you're like your sister. Men can be dicks sometimes, Pay. Maybe he's going to pop back up and be like, I paid your bills . . ."

"No way. It has to be something else."

"Like what?" She lifts her closed pen to her mouth and

starts to tap her lip. "I got it! Maybe he did something awful to Erin, and paying your bills is his penance."

"That makes no sense. Because then he would be paying her bills."

"True . . . Okay, what if she did something awful, and he feels guilty for leaving you in the lurch?"

"But wouldn't he call to tell me that himself? It's been years and still, no contact."

Tap. Tap. Tap.

"He's on Mars." She shrugs.

"That makes the most sense, to be honest. Or he's in the CIA, and we were his cover story."

We both laugh at that.

"How's your sis?"

Tilting my head, I give her a look that says, *are you kidding me?*

"A mess, as always." I roll my eyes.

"She drinking?"

I shake my head.

"Using?"

Again, I say no, but then I shrug. "Honestly, I don't know. I don't go visit her that often."

"I can understand that. Even without seeing her, she calls all the time."

"Yeah, plus, what's the point of asking her? She doesn't answer any of my questions. And I ask a lot. She isn't telling me something. Something huge. I know it. And because of that, I just can't bring myself to hear her lie to me. For years, before Ronnie, I dealt with this behavior. He made everything better. But she's regressing. She's as flighty as before, and I can't deal. Plus, the guy she's dating right now . . ." I shiver.

He gives me the creeps. The way he looks at me like I'm a piece of meat. Which in and of itself is not okay, but seeing as he's dating my sister, it makes him a real lowlife.

Heather goes quiet as the door swings open. Our professor steps out and crosses the front of the room to the podium. Her heels click on the wood floors as the room goes quiet.

She demands respect, and we give it.

When she begins the lesson, I lean forward to make sure I don't miss a word.

I'm so engrossed in the lecture that I don't notice Heather whispering to me, or that the teacher has stopped speaking and every eye in the classroom is on me.

Heather bumps my arm, and I snap out of my trance.

"Please, Ms. Hart, don't let us keep you." The professor points at my bag, and the sound registers.

My phone is ringing. I forgot to silence it.

"Please answer the phone." Her tone is harsh.

This isn't good. The semester has only just started, and my professor already hates me. She made a speech on the first day of class, warning us to silence our phones or live to regret it. Now I understand precisely what she meant by that.

That's the problem with taking a class in your major. The classes are smaller, so the professors know you.

Especially here at Ludlow, a small, private college. Everyone in the department knows me.

The phone keeps ringing, and I have to hit the little button. I don't want to, but I also know I have no choice.

"On speaker. So everyone can hear who so rudely interrupted my lecture."

I pull it out and instantly cringe when I see the word Erin on the screen. This is going to be bad. There is no telling what she will say.

"Answer it."

So, I do.

I press the button.

The sound of my heartbeat drums in my ears.

Then I hear the familiar sound of Erin sniffling, and I want to melt into the chair.

Erin is about to go on a crazy, dramatic rant for my class to hear.

I look up at the professor, imploring her not to make me do this, trying desperately to convey that I've learned my lesson.

But she only smiles at me. One that says I sealed my own fate.

I don't interrupt my sister.

Instead, I wait for her.

But the words she says are not what I expect.

And as she says them . . .

My hand opens. My fingers slip. And the phone crashes to the floor.

"Ronald is dead."

CHAPTER TWO

Payton

I CAN'T BELIEVE RONALD IS DEAD. AFTER FINALLY LEARNING what happened to him, the sense of relief I thought I would get isn't there. It hurts.

I never expected this reaction.

A part of me always assumed he left us because my sister did something to him. That she hurt his pride, but eventually, he'd lick his wounds, come back, and apologize. But that wasn't the case at all.

Instead, I found out everything was a lie.

That's the hardest part about sitting here. I'm grieving for him, but I'm also having a hard time reconciling all the truths that have come out since Erin's phone call.

I'm out of place.

I know absolutely no one but my sister.

From where I sit in the back of the church, I watch the front row. People who I assume are his family sit side by side in the pew closest to Ronald's coffin. They must be related to him since they always reserve the front row for family. Not the back row. The back row is reserved for people like us.

People who sneak in, hoping no one recognizes them for what they are . . .

Homewreckers.

There is no way to sugarcoat what we are.

The truth stabs me in my chest.

The lie my sister kept from me all these years is finally out in the open for me to fully understand.

Ronnie was never *our* Ronnie.

He was their dad.

Someone else's husband.

I stare at the people I assume are his daughter and son.

A blond woman and a handsome man are sitting in the front row. Beside them, an older woman weeps into a handkerchief.

The person he promised to share a life with. That's the part I have a hard time reconciling. Watching them hold each other is a dagger in my heart.

He said he loved us. He said he loved me and he'd take care of us.

It was all a lie.

That voice in my head hasn't shut up all week.

Beside me, I hear my sister huff. The sound grates on my nerves. It's like nails on a chalkboard.

She knew.

I might have been ignorant, but she always knew.

She's staring at his family too, but instead of remorse over the part we've played in their lives, she's shooting daggers at them.

"They can cry all they want. Wait until they find out the money is mine," she mumbles to herself. I turn to face her, shocked by what she just said, and she shrugs. "What? I put up with that man for almost ten years of my life. It's time to get my money."

I wish her bitter words shocked me, but they don't.

We shouldn't have come.

I told Erin we should just go to the reading of the will, but she insisted on being here for this too.

But Mr. Baker, Ronnie's lawyer, told us we had to be here after the service, that we were all to meet down the block at his office to discuss the provisions of the will in person. But that didn't mean we had to come to the funeral; this is all Erin. Probably a way to hurt his family even more than she already has.

I only came because, despite the truth of the situation, I know in my bones Ronald Aldridge loved us, and we should pay our respects.

What that means for our future is the question.

Last night, Erin sat me down and told me Ronnie had another family. That he was estranged from them.

Ronald Aldridge was not the man I knew. He was a criminal, apparently. For these past few years—the ones I spent worrying about him—he was in jail for murdering someone. Erin claimed he was innocent, but after all the lies, how could I believe her?

She squeezed my hand, acting like a sister for the first time in years. "He didn't want you to know."

So, she'd accused me of sleeping with someone I considered a father instead of telling me the truth? But it got worse.

Her hand retracted. She swiped at her hair, then stared down at her nails. "He said if I told you the truth, he'd stop paying our bills."

Something must have happened between them when he was in jail because he stopped paying hers. Cue the freak-out and daily calls to me these last few months.

At the time, I tried to piece the puzzle together. Now I finally know the truth.

I will never see him again.

Ronald died in prison.

Someone got ahold of a knife and killed him.

The police have no suspects, but from what Erin told me, Ronald didn't lack enemies.

My stomach turns every time I think of how he died. Yet, despite everything I found out, I still love him.

Which is why I'm here, paying my respects even though no one wants me here.

The service goes on, and I'm surprised no one in his family speaks. It's short and lacking emotion. It feels sterile, and I want to get up myself and speak of the man who was the only person to put me first.

I don't, though.

It's not my place.

By the time they conclude, my sister is standing and walking out the door before anyone can see her. I'm quick to follow, adjusting my glasses.

"Go to Mr. Baker's office." She points at the building a block away from where we are now standing. "I'll be there shortly."

"Okay."

Mr. Baker instructed us to meet him in one of the meeting rooms in the building. Apparently, things wouldn't take long.

I'm surprised we are doing this now. Surprised we aren't going to a cemetery first. But I guess the shock of the location isn't enough. The speed of the cremation and service and now, the reading of the will have my mind swirling. Is there no burial because his family found out about us and are still angry? Did they care about him? They went to the service, but no one spoke . . .

I make my way down the block, my black dress clinging to me in the heat. My legs don't want to move. Now that I know Ronald is dead and has a family, a whole slew of questions arise inside me. I don't want to think them, but I can't help where my brain goes.

What does his death mean to me? To my bills? To my school? I hate myself for thinking of this as my heels click on the pavement, but what if that's why I'm being called to this meeting? What if I am ten seconds from finding out that I'm about to lose my dreams?

When I step into the lobby of the building, the cool air hits me and makes me shiver. Or maybe it's just the nature of the day.

Of losing him.

I make my way to the fourth floor, where Mr. Baker told Erin the meeting room is. Last door on the right.

I'm not looking forward to this. Having to meet the eyes of his family will be hard. How can we look at them after what Ronald did? I know I didn't see the truth, but they don't know that. They have every right to hate us. To hate me.

If I were them, I'd hate me, too, for being here.

In the elevator, the music is low and depressing, matching my mood.

The air is too still.

It's hard to breathe.

As I ascend, I try to calm my fragile nerves, but it's useless.

Eventually, the elevator chimes, and the doors open.

In life, things get thrown at you—crazy batshit things—and you just have to adapt. Either that or die. I choose the former.

Pushing back my shoulders, I muster the strength to face this head-on. It doesn't take long before I reach the door Mr. Baker told my sister was his.

The cold metal knob bites my palm as I turn it. There's no going back.

I swing open the door.

A squeak escapes my mouth.

In the far corner of the room is a desk, where a handsome man sits behind it.

Is this Mr. Baker?

It would make sense, seeing as he's working behind the desk.

Did my sister know he's gorgeous?

No, not gorgeous. That's too simple a word for the man sitting there.

Then, as if it couldn't get any worse, he lifts his head, and his gaze meets mine.

Jeez.

My stomach feels like a dozen butterflies have exploded inside me. Their wings flutter rapidly with excitement.

I have never seen eyes that blue.

Deep blue. Like the depths of the ocean. Bottomless. I shouldn't be swooning at a time like this, but Lord.

I need to stop staring, but I can't pull my gaze away.

"Hi," I say nervously. "I'm here for the reading."

He doesn't answer me. Just continues to stare from where he's perched.

"I'm here before my sister, I guess? I'm so nervous. I don't know why I'm here. I—he never told me"—I shuffle my weight between my feet nervously—"about them. About . . . *you*?"

The air feels heavy with Mr. Baker's silence. Uncomfortably, I look around the office and take a seat in a chair as far away from the desk as I can.

This lawyer is much more intimidating than I thought he would be.

"You're not who I pictured," I say before I can stop myself. I can feel my cheeks turning a shade of red I'm sure makes me match a tomato.

"And what did you picture?" When he finally speaks, I am not at all prepared for how gravelly his voice is.

Heat sweeps across the exposed skin by my collarbone, melting me into a puddle.

What is wrong with me?

Drooling over a man is not why I'm here.

"You're younger than I thought—from your voice on the phone." His lips tip up, and he smirks at me.

If I thought he was handsome before, he is downright deadly with that smirk.

Not why you're here, Payton.

"Anything else?" he probes.

"Um . . ."

By now, I'm sure I could pass out. I want to fan myself. It's like I have never met a man this handsome, which is ridiculous. But not really.

I'm used to college boys. He is definitely not that.

Nope.

He's all man. An attorney. And apparently, Ronald's attorney.

I shake my head to right myself.

"I can't believe I'm here. I told my sister we shouldn't come. That we should honor him privately, but she insisted. I can't imagine his family will be happy to see us." I bury my face in my hands at the thought of more private proximity to them. It was easier for some people to be civil in public. "Do you think they know about us? I don't think I can face them. Imagine finding out your dad has another family."

When Mr. Baker doesn't respond, I move my palms away from my eyes and look at him.

The playful look is gone. In its place is a look I can only describe as pure hate.

A look I don't understand at all.

A fine line appears between his brows, and his lips are no longer turned up. A scowl wears them down.

But that's not what makes my back go ramrod straight.

What makes my body shiver are his fists, I can now see, balled by his sides with white knuckles showing.

I'm about to ask him what I said to upset him, but the door swings open, and in walks a man closer to Ronald's age.

He strolls up to me and extends his hand.

"You must be Payton. I'm Larry Baker, Ronald's attorney."

I look from him to the man who I now realize is not him across the room. I shake Mr. Baker's hand, but my eyes never leave the blue-eyed stranger who stalks over to us like an angry beast.

"Trent Aldridge. And who the fuck is this girl to my father?"

His father?

Shit.

CHAPTER THREE

Trent

I KNOW. DICK MOVE.

But I'm not one to stand on principles.

I guess when I got into business with the underworld, some of their scruples rubbed off on me.

Oh, who am I kidding? I've always been a dick.

Letting this girl think I was an attorney was low but worth it to watch her ogle me. Not that I need the ego boost. Mine is already large enough to fill a football stadium. Still, it was fun fucking with her, regardless.

The real question is, who is she? And why the hell is she at the reading of my father's will?

"Hello, Trent." Larry Baker wipes the sweat off his palms and reaches into his inner suit pocket, fishing for something. "I have a letter from your father that he wanted you to read."

The short, bald man I know to be my father's attorney hands me an envelope. I have no desire to take it, but I do anyway. I won't read it now. Nor will I probably ever read it. Nevertheless, I put it in the inside pocket of my suit jacket.

"Can we get this over with?" I scoff. On a list of things I want to be doing today, this rates right below getting a root canal.

"We need to wait for a few more people," he says, and the urge to pace out my aggravation kicks at my legs.

Instead, I stride to the window and pretend to stare out, studying the two of them in the reflection without them knowing.

"What's the point? He had nothing," I mutter under my breath. The man was broke.

"Trent, can you please just have a seat? As soon as your sister and mother get here, we can proceed." Mr. Baker turns to the girl cowering in the chair in the corner. "Payton, is your sister coming?"

She nods.

"Who are you?" I ask her, knowing full well this girl is probably my illegitimate sister.

Fucking Dad.

Literally.

Of course, he knocked up some woman behind my mother's back. Nothing this dead bastard did should surprise me anymore.

The fact that, only a few minutes ago, I was checking her out makes me want to vomit.

"I-I'm," she stutters.

"My sister?" I lead, fixated on her reflection with an intensity that should worry me.

"No. Yes. Well—"

"It's not a tough question. Either you are, or you're not." Her large blue eyes stare into my back, and I swear she looks like she's going to cry. "It's not hard." When she still doesn't speak, I poke a little harder. "Here's how this works. You open your mouth . . . or even better, bob your head."

"No," she mutters back and looks down at the floor. As if she is praying it will swallow her up and save her from me.

Spoiler alert: It won't.

"Now that you've proven you know how to have a conversation, tell me why you're here."

"Trent, there is no reason to be hostile to the poor girl. I'm sure Mr. Baker will inform us."

I turn to the owner of the voice. My sister, Ivy, is the picture of serenity beside her husband, Cyrus. They entered silently, a tell-tale sign that his bad habits have rubbed off on her. My mother walks in behind them. Her stride is slow as if weighed down by a physical burden. Deep lines stretch across her forehead. In the past day, her eyes have grown due to the swelling from crying so much over the trash of a man she was married to for so long.

She's been broken for so many years. Mom was finally starting to come out of her shell-shocked being.

And now she must face more lies from the bastard.

"We are only waiting for Erin now." The damn lawyer needs to get this over with already.

And who the fuck is Erin?

"Who the fuck is Erin?"

As I echo my thoughts, the door opens, and as if she's been summoned, a very attractive woman, who looks almost as old as Payton, walks in. The resemblance is uncanny, despite the fact that her face is obviously stretched tight from years of Botox and fillers.

I peg her as Payton's older sister. Her head is held high as she strides into the room. As if her arrogance isn't bad enough, as if her mere presence isn't an insult, she's also dripping head to toe in diamonds.

Diamonds, I don't have to guess to know how my father funded.

The gambling problem.

He fucked away his empire to finance his affair with his side piece, giving up his own daughter in the process. Good fucking riddance. If someone hadn't beaten me to the punch, I would've killed him myself right here for his bullshit.

"This must be Erin." I scoff, not a question but a statement. Turning my back to her, I look back at the attorney. "Now that everyone is here tell me why I had to miss my meeting to deal with this shit."

"Your father wanted to go over his assets."

"My father had no assets."

"Well, that actually isn't the case." The lawyer looks down, sheepish.

"I don't understand," Ivy whispers. "Dad had nothing." Her voice cracks on the last word.

So much has gone down in the past few years. Even speaking about Dad makes my fists clench.

Everything, including his jail time, stemmed from his lack of funds and what he was willing to do to get some.

If he had money, what was it all for? And, better question, why didn't we know?

Cyrus moves closer and places his arm around Ivy's shoulder. He leans in and whispers in her ear. I can't hear what he says, but it seems to calm her.

"Can everyone please sit?" The lawyer smiles uncomfortably. Uh-huh. What the fuck are we here for?

"I'd rather stand as I hear how Dad fucked us over one last time."

"Trent." My sister's soft voice should calm me. Unfortunately, it doesn't.

Instead, I stalk toward the door, putting myself between the exit and every person in here. My feet punctuate the wood floor with my steps, delivering my intentions. No one can exit unless I move. Until every fucking secret is spilled here and now.

"Very well." Dad's lawyer clears his throat. "If everyone else is ready, I'll proceed." He looks around the room, and everyone else nods. "Ronald had a considerable estate when he passed away. We set the estate up in an offshore account."

My teeth grind together. That fucking bastard. "How much are we talking?"

"Millions."

"How many?" I hiss. "Tell me just how much Ivy's life wasn't worth when he hung his daughter out to dry."

"Twenty-two million."

Before I know what I'm doing, my fist connects with the wall.

Plaster breaks away as I hear a scream from my mother, followed by Ivy's soft voice in trying to calm down Cyrus.

I turn back to the lawyer, knowing full well the picture I painted with blood dripping down my knuckles. "How long . . . ?" Cyrus asks.

His lawyer at least has the decency to look uncomfortable.

"Long enough that he could have spared Ivy," I mutter. "There's no point in arguing. It's obvious."

When the lawyer doesn't speak, Ivy lets out a strangled cry as she puts her head in her lap.

"If he weren't dead, I would kill him," Cyrus says.

Him and me both.

"Well," I spit out, "now that we know with no measure of doubt—and mind you, this topic was never up for discussion—that my dad was an utter piece of shit, what do you have to tell us? I can only speak for myself by saying I have much better things to do."

"Just sit, Trent," my mother says.

I look over at the woman who used to be a shell of a human.

It's remarkable how far she has come. She's strong now. That's what having my father away from her did.

His presence made her a shadow, and now that she's stepped out, she's bloomed. Maybe there's hope for us all. But my eyes linger on the signs of her heartbreak, and I'm reminded of how useless feelings can be.

I let out a sigh and take a seat at the table.

From my position, I can see the girl.

Payton.

If she and her sister are here, it means he left them something, too. This should be interesting.

The money is blood money, and I want none of it, but I'd rather burn it than give it to them. Ivy will want to donate it somewhere.

She's too good for this family.

Always has been, always will be.

Definitely too good for Cyrus, the sadistic fuck.

But, regardless, he's good to her.

Loves her. That man would never let anything happen to her. In my book, that makes him a better man than me because he's capable of that kind of love.

"Spit it out, Baker," I growl. "Who gets the money?"

The woman I assume is Payton's sister sits up. As if she knows the answer to this question.

I watch her with narrowed eyes. If what she thinks is about to happen happens, there will be hell to pay.

Regardless of what she knows, Ivy deserves the money. It was her life that was almost sacrificed.

Mr. Baker produces a thin folder, pulls out a sheet of paper, and addresses the room, taking painstaking care to avoid looking me in the eyes. "I hereby bequeath the entirety of my estate to the one person who loved me unconditionally."

Erin's smile broadens.

Ivy wilts.

Mom sighs.

Cyrus scowls.

And me? I envision Dad's murder.

Over, and over, and over.

It doesn't help.

"You were my daughter," Mr. Baker reads.

Erin's face falls.

Ivy's eyes mist.

Payton stares at the floor.

"Not by blood but by bond."

And then Erin's eyes gleam. A wicked gleam as I realize what is happening.

"Payton. Everything is yours."

CHAPTER FOUR

Payton

S UCKER PUNCH.

That is what it feels like.

When my name rings through the air, it feels like someone punched me in the stomach.

I can barely breathe.

Shards of glass have broken off in my lungs.

Maybe I'm dead.

Yeah. That's it.

I'm hallucinating . . .

Or maybe when I was walking to the lawyer's building, I got hit by a car. I'm having an out-of-body experience, and none of this is real.

That would make more sense than what the lawyer just said.

Because there is no way he's right.

It can't be right.

No way did Ronald, aka Ronnie, aka the only man who has ever been a father figure to me . . . No way did he leave me his entire estate when he had a family.

As I struggle to breathe, taking deep inhales of oxygen, I re-member I'm not the only person in this room.

Surrounding me is not just my sister, but his family, and as they glower at me, hate filling their eyes, I know this isn't a dream.

My gaze pulls to where my sister sits. There is an odd look in her eyes.

One that says, although she is smiling, she's anything but happy. I know her too well. I know she is pretending—putting on a good show, the actress she is—but her eyes are slightly narrowed, meaning she did not expect this, and she is about to snap.

I move closer to Erin, ready to calm her when she grabs my arm forcibly. Instead, her sharp nails grasp my skin. "What did you do?" she hisses, and here it comes.

I have become accustomed to her accusations.

What'll it be this time? Cheating? Blackmail? Sex? I don't know, but I do know my sister's flair for the dramatic will rear its ugly head. When she's hurting, she doesn't know how to do anything but transmit it to others. Something I'm not looking forward to at all.

"I knew you were a slut. I should have dropped you off at Social Services."

These are the words of someone lost. Someone beat down by the world and lashing out. I know this; it hurts. I clench every muscle inside me, forcing myself to exhale. I will not let her words hurt me. It's time to stop letting *her* get to me. I tolerate her because of the past. What she did for me. Not just in raising me, but in truth, she saved me, but at some point, enough is enough. There is a line, and right now, she just crossed it.

I will deal with this later because Erin is the least of my problems right now. After the bomb that just went off in this office, I have bigger problems to deal with.

Namely, the blue-eyed stranger whose glower sends a chill running up my spine.

Pure venom.

He hates me.

It's a weird feeling to see such hatred in someone's eyes, especially when they don't even know you.

I haven't felt this way in a long time. Not since my life became more stable. He stares at me, and I refuse to break the contact. I won't cower.

No matter how I feel at this moment, I won't allow this man to see my feelings.

Sure, I'm shocked by what I just learned, but instead of showing it, I take my hands and dig my nails into my thighs to regulate myself.

Slowly, I take a deep inhale and pull my eyes away from him to look back at the lawyer, whose name I cannot wait to forget.

"What does this mean?" I ask.

"We still have a lot to discuss in regard to all of this. There were stipulations put in place before he died."

"What the fuck does that mean?" Trent barks. He's not even trying to be civil.

If he could burn this place to the ground, I think he would.

"There's a lot to go over."

"Then you better get started because some of us have places to go. Like work. We are not all gold diggers." He stands and begins to pace.

I shake my head and do my best not to pay attention. He has no idea who I am. He's grasping at straws to intimidate me. Nothing this prick says is going to make me question who I am.

You can bring it, Trent, but I know who I am.

His eyes narrow on me as if he can hear my thoughts. A lump forms in my throat. My mouth dries, butterflies ping-ponging around in my stomach in full force. He leans against the wall, kicks one foot over the other, and stares me down as if he knows exactly what kind of effect he's having on me.

I feel like I've just lost a game before it's begun.

Congrats, Payton. You may know who you are, but your body needs a memo, a postcard, and a freaking billboard to learn it can't react to him like this.

Mr. Baker slides the letter back into his folder, though it looks way longer than what he read. He must've memorized it.

"Normally, we would have a lot of paperwork to do over this with the estate tax and death tax, etc., but this is different. The money has always been in Payton's name. Ronald started this account years ago. It's been accruing money and interest over the years."

"What are you talking about?"

Finally, something comes out of my mouth. It flies out. Trent, whose eyes have never left mine, studies me harder. I refuse to wilt under the intensity of his gaze. I tip my chin up, hoping my message is delivered.

You don't intimidate me.

He does.

You may hate me, but I've done nothing wrong. Not knowingly.

Doesn't seem to matter.

Neither of us has a clue what's going on.

Three seconds pass. I avert my eyes, redirecting them to Mr. Baker, whose only ability to elicit reactions from me comes from the will he just put away. How is it possible that all the money has been in my name this entire time? It makes no sense. Is that why my bills are always paid? Because technically, it has always been my money?

No. I would have known.

Wouldn't I?

"Why would he do that?" I hear my sister say. Well, she mumbles it under her breath, but it's not low enough for no one to hear it because then he speaks. The one whose full attention is still pinned on me, and there's no hiding the storm of hatred brewing inside him. His voice sounds like he's chewing on gravel.

"I know exactly why he did it. He put it in that little girl's name, so we couldn't touch it."

Little girl.

He spits it out like I'm beneath him. If I were any less secure in myself, the words would claw at me. As it is, I find my fingers curling inward, nails pinching the sensitive flesh of my palms.

"But why not put it in my name?" Erin stands and whines.

"Because it's obvious." He moves away from the wall and into the middle of the room; his focus is now on her, and it's lethal. So lethal, my shameless sister staggers back. On the other hand, Trent's sister reaches out to stop him, but the man she's with holds her back.

"You were just a whore," Trent says as if he's reading the weather. He circles her like a predator at the top of the food chain. "And if you think he gave a shit about either of you, you're wrong. Whatever promises he gave you are lies." This time, he stares at me. Steps closer. Steals my freaking breath with the bloodthirst leaping out of him. "He didn't give a shit about anyone. Only himself. You are nothing. You are no one."

"Trent," his sister begs.

"Stay out of this, Ivy," he warns, but for her, he pulls back the bite from his voice. For me, it reappears in full force. He jerks his thumb at Erin. "This home-wrecker and her sister were his way around giving us his money, Ivy. This was in place just in case Mom divorced him—which she eventually did—and couldn't touch this money because she didn't even know about it." His laughter is a dry rumble. He peers down at the floor as if he has a direct line to hell. "Good work, Dad. Point to you, fucking bastard."

No one corrects Trent.

Not his sister.

Not her man.

Not their mother.

Certainly not Erin, who looks unapologetic. Actually, she looks furious at me. I can't wait to hear all the accusations she'll hurl my way after this meeting adjourns.

Not.

Mr. Baker clears his throat. "There's something else you should know."

Jeez. The more tidbits he imparts on us, the more fucked up this situation gets.

"Great." Trent throws his hands in the air, releasing a scoff. "Now what? What else did that asshole do?"

"As I was saying before, we set the account up before his death. He controlled the money. It pays for Payton's college and cost of living, but your father saw to managing it. She can't access the funds. When he was in jail, I served as his proxy. He gave me directions, and I made sure everything he wanted was taken care of."

Trent's eyes narrow. "You knew. This whole time, you knew."

It's obvious. As his lawyer, Mr. Baker had to know. Trent isn't just now coming to this realization. He's putting the accusation into the air as a warning. For later.

The sharp edge to his words may as well hold a blade because it cuts through the thinly held peace like a dagger.

And like an idiot, Erin doesn't heed the warning. "I don't understand. My sister has the money, but she can't touch it?" Mr. Baker nods, eliciting a gasp from Erin. "Then how can she use it?"

"Mr. Aldridge set up the funds in a trust. Originally, she never had access to it. But recently, when he went to jail, he had it amended."

"How?"

"He set up provisions and a contingency plan."

"Such as?" Trent presses, looking like he needs ten years of meditation to undo the shitstorm from the past ten minutes. Or someone to release his pent-up anger on.

That is starting to seem like me.

Lovely.

Mr. Baker edges behind me, putting space between him and Trent. "We set the account up to pay for her lifestyle until she turns twenty-two, then she can control it."

"And how old is she?"

I wave. "I'm here, you know. You can ask me yourself."

He looks me over like I'm the dirt beneath his shoe.

"As I was saying, how old?"

"Twenty-one," Mr. Baker says, still hiding behind me.

Coward.

The beginnings of a smirk form on Trent's lips. He has the glistening, devious eyes of a viper and the behavior to match them. "Interesting . . ."

I still.

"That's why I called this meeting," Mr. Baker says, and I know things are about to get very bad for me.

"Who is in charge of the estate until that day?" Trent asks.

"You are."

Trent's eyes meet mine, and if I thought the last look he gave me was terrible, this one is like the devil rose from hell and took form in his body. A sinister smile slices across his face. It downright frightens me.

"So . . ." He stalks toward me, slow and measured. "I am in charge of the money."

"Until she is twenty-two," Mr. Baker clarifies, taking refuge behind Erin this time as Trent closes in on me.

"For the next year," Trent follows up, another step closer.

"That is correct."

The smile widens over Trent's face. It makes him look a bit maniacal, and I don't know what it means. I just know that I have three massive problems on my hands: a twenty-two-million-dollar fortune I have no access to, Erin's wrath, and the full force of this stranger's hatred.

"Is this all?" Trent asks the lawyer.

"In a nutshell."

"Very well."

The room falls eerily quiet.

If a pin dropped, you could hear it.

I can hear my sister breathing. Hell, I can hear my own heart beating. That's how silent it is as we wait for Trent to do something.

By the look he just gave me, it will be deadly, that's for sure.

Trent shifts.

We suck in a collective breath.

He steps in the direction of the door.

None of us dares to exhale.

He's almost out of the room when he stops.

His head turns over his shoulder. There's an odd look in his eyes. The blue is nearly gone, replaced by black. Almost like he's been possessed.

"You will be hearing from me," he says.

It's a promise.

A promise of what? No clue. But when I return home to the house Ronnie rented me, I tuck myself into the bed he bought me. Beneath the sheets he gifted me, I curl myself into a ball and finally let the truth slip past my lips.

"I'm scared."

CHAPTER FIVE

Trent

J AIL AND DEATH WERE TOO EASY FOR THAT BASTARD.
The thought—and the accompanying desire to destroy something—bounces in my head as I exit the room, wishing for the first time that my father hadn't keeled over in prison, and I had the opportunity to deliver the pain myself. I don't stop walking until I'm outside. It's only when the fresh air hits my face that I take a deep breath and try to calm down.

What the fuck was that shit?

I can't even wrap my head around what just happened.

It feels like a fucking bomb just exploded. I walked into a landmine factory, and they all fucking detonated at the same time.

Not only was my dad a lying prick who had real money, but he set it up so even if we found the account, we wouldn't be able to touch it.

The worst part, which feels like I'm being stabbed from within, is that he was still willing to sell Ivy. He always had the money. He just didn't want to spend it.

I stare down at the pavement, a snarl forming on my lips.

You listening down there in hell, Dad? I'm taking your money. Sit back and enjoy the show.

Yeah, it technically belongs to that girl now, but I hold those damn purse strings. And I intend to tighten the hell out of them.

Maybe the idiot thought he was untouchable in jail.

Maybe he thought his appeal would go through.

Maybe he thought I'm a more forgiving person than I am.

Fuck.

Who knows what he thought? It doesn't matter now. All that matters is figuring out a way to take the money from that girl. Payton.

It's not that I need it. Nor do I want it. It's that she and her gold digger sister are the reason Ivy was in a situation that hurt her. I don't believe for a second they didn't know about my family. It's evident in Erin's body language. The way she gloated beside Mom as if she'd been waiting years to meet her.

Usually, I'd at least try to be the bigger man, but I can't.

Ivy is a good soul, my mother a better one.

This gold digger and the little girl hurt my family, and for that, they will pay.

Someone must take the brunt of my anger.

My eyes fix on a weed sprouting through a crack in the concrete. Most of it has died, the other part halfway to hell.

"A bill is due, and someone must pay it." I grind my heel against the weed, snuffing out the remaining life and putting it out of its misery. And they say I'm not capable of mercy. "Since you aren't here to face the consequences of your actions, Dad, you've limited my options. What happens next is on you."

It didn't matter that he died. Evil lasts forever. I have no doubt he's in hell, watching this unfold. His fault for loving the girl. His fault for wanting her to be taken care of after he was in jail. His fault for leaving her here for the wolves.

For me.

Instantly, I know who to call.

Reaching into my back pocket, I fish out my cell phone, swipe the screen, and hit number two on speed dial (Ivy is number one. I love my sister. Sue me).

"Aldridge," Jax answers. "How the fuck are you? I haven't spoken to you in forever."

"Apparently, you're too busy to call back your old friends."

"You're one to talk. When was the last time your sorry ass picked up the phone to call me? You use me for my resources and then crickets. Some friend you are." His signature sarcastic chuckle fills the line.

"Fine. You're right," I admit, forcing myself to loosen up. "I'm just as bad, but I like to fuck with you."

"So, what's going on? As much as I'd like to believe this is a social call, you sound off. Talk to me."

"Not over the phone."

"Come on, Trent. You know my shit is locked down."

"True. If anyone's is, it's yours."

I run a palm down my face, making my way to the car. I feel like I'm leaving behind a crime scene. The weed is lifeless behind me. Strong enough to break through concrete but not strong enough to survive the heel of my Kitons.

"But hell." I sigh. "You never know."

With some of the shady shit I get myself involved in these days, I can never be too careful.

"Fine. Where should we meet? The usual?"

"That works for me. Time?"

"Same old time. Once I finish work."

"Should we hit up Cyrus's after?" I chuckle, sliding into my Aston Martin DBX.

There's no way Jaxson Price would show up to a card game these days. The man is too busy hacking foreign governments.

"Shut the fuck up," he barks out, not missing a beat, making me laugh even harder. "See you at six."

When I hang up, I drive to the office, park in my spot in the structure, and head out onto the sidewalk instead of into the building.

I'm later than normal, but it's fine.

Technically, I should probably call Ivy and see if she wants to talk.

I'm sure this shit is hurting her.

If my brain is this fucked up, I can't imagine hers is okay. This shit has got to remind her of a past she wants to forget.

Be the big brother you're supposed to be and check on her.

I should call her. But no matter how much I know I should, I can't bring myself to. Guess being a bastard runs in the family.

Instead, I find myself walking.

Anything to distract me from my thoughts for a little while longer.

New York City has a way of calming me.

The sounds. The smells. The chaos. They force me to stop thinking about everything else. Immediately.

I allow myself to become immersed in the hustle and bustle until all thoughts of this morning are gone.

There is no point in thinking of something I can't fix right now anyway.

It takes me twenty minutes to get back to the building.

Once inside, I take the private elevator up to my floor. My assistant, Allison, sees me, but I must look like I do not want to be disturbed because she says nothing as I walk past her and into my office, closing the door.

Stacks of notes pile on my desk. She must have left them here. She's the only person allowed inside this space, other than the cleaning crew. I'm sure I have a shit ton of emails waiting for me too.

I fire up the computer, and just as I suspected, there are hundreds.

This is why I come in at five o'clock in the morning most days.

Now I'll get nothing done today but answer emails.

By the time my assistant finally walks into my office, it feels like my eyes are going to melt from staring at the computer.

I lift my hand and scrub at them.

"You haven't left that spot all day."

I lower my hand. "I know."

"Are you caught up?" she asks, standing in front of my desk, a stack of folders in her arms.

"I am. Thank fuck. I take a few hours off, and it's like the world has gone crazy."

"Well, luckily for you, you have me. I would have answered all of them if you had asked." She smiles, steps forward, and places the stack of work she completed in front of me.

"I wouldn't give that job to my worst enemy. Actually, maybe I would."

He just happens to be too dead to do it.

She chuckles. "Are you going to work late tonight?"

"Why? You have places to go that are better than this?" I gesture around.

"I actually do."

"Of course, you can leave. Enjoy your night, Allison."

"Thank you, Mr. Aldridge." She turns to leave before stopping and looking over her shoulder. "Don't forget. Tomorrow you are meeting with Lorenzo."

"Thank you. I won't."

Once she leaves the room, I close out my computer and stand.

My father should have treated Ivy like he treated Payton, putting her first. Instead, he protected a stranger while throwing Ivy to the wolves. Unfortunately for Payton, my father is no longer around.

Time to plan how I'm going to ruin Payton Hart.

Jaxson Price is waiting for me when I arrive.

He's sitting at the same table he always sits at. Drinking the same drink he always drinks.

It's almost like no time has passed.

Yet . . .

Years have passed. Things have changed.

Jax met a girl. Fell in love. Got married.

And me . . . ?

I basically got married to the mob. Now my entire life is based in the underworld.

A series of unfortunate events led me down this path.

At first, I hated the cards they dealt me.

Pun intended as it all stemmed from a terrible game of poker. But now, after all these years, I'm content.

Or at least I *was* content.

Sure, before that fateful day, I would have taken over a family dynasty. I would have followed in my father's footsteps.

But then it all shattered.

Everything was a lie.

Like glass, all that was left were sharp, jagged pieces. Pieces that cut your finger to the bone if you didn't play your hand right.

The past forced me to become the man I am today.

And now I will have to change again. Because that's the shit I do. I fucking adapt.

That option or die.

I choose the former.

"I ordered you a scotch, neat," Jax says.

"Rather presumptuous of you." I move to take a seat. "It might be too strong for a Tuesday."

"And here I was, thinking even that isn't strong enough. Should we skip right to drinking straight rubbing alcohol?"

"With the way I'm feeling, that's a good idea."

Jaxson chuckles. "Spit it out. What's going on, man? This is obviously more than Cyrus getting on your ass over his returns."

"Cyrus's issues seem like child's play right now."

Jaxson leans in, placing his elbows on the small wooden table. "What's up?"

"It seems I have a stepsister."

That statement has his eyes widening. "What? Really? Are you shitting me?"

"Fuck yes, I am. Jeez. No, I don't have a stepsister. Thank fuck. My father didn't even have the decency to make her legit, but I have a thorn in my side."

"That sounds more like something I'd believe. Start from the beginning."

And I do. With a drink in my hand, a large gulp, and a desire to unburden myself, I tell Jaxson all about the wonderful benefactor that my father was to people who weren't even his family.

A family he supported without us knowing.

How he lived a double life for years and how every word out of his deceitful mouth was a complete fucking lie.

After Jax leaves and I'm left at the bar alone, I pour a single drop on the floor.

"Hope you enjoy watching her suffer, Dad. After all, fair is fair. You were the one who taught me that."

CHAPTER SIX

Payton

Two Months Later . . .

WHERE DID THE DAY GO?

My stomach chooses that second to growl. Not only did I sit in a cold and drab library all day, my eyes basically bleeding from looking at the books I had to read, but it dawns on me that I also didn't eat.

I'll make something and crash for the night.

I need my energy to finish the research on my paper due at the end of the week.

I can't wait to be done with school.

I can't wait to be far away from all of this.

As I walk back into my house, after grabbing something from my car, there's a crunch under my shoe. Little shards of glass litter the floor.

Slowly, I take another step, careful not to crush any more.

I bend over and pick up one of the pieces. It's blue. It reminds me of the Moreno glass trinket holder I have in the living room.

Turning on the hall light, I head toward the table next to the couch where I usually keep it. That's when I notice a few things.

One: It's missing.

Two: And this part makes my back go straight. The window is open.

Did I leave it open?

No. That doesn't make any sense. Even if I left it open, it wouldn't explain the glass all over the foyer.

Maybe I left it open, and a gust of wind blew it over.

That is the dumbest thing I have ever thought. There's no way. But if it didn't, if it wasn't my fault, that would mean . . .

A chill runs up my spine.

Someone was here.

Someone broke into my house.

But I was only gone for fifteen minutes.

All the nerve endings in my body become hyperaware. I tilt my head, straining to hear. It's silent, but I can't shake the possibility that someone might still be in my house.

Am I being robbed?

Goose bumps break out across my arms.

My phone's vibrations echo through the house.

"Hello?"

Nothing.

"Hello? Is there anyone there?"

No sound.

I hang up, fully on edge now.

A phone call. A break-in.

I need to call the police.

This sounds far-fetched even to me.

Plus, I might have left the window open myself.

Which reminds me, I need to close it. Then I need to make sure it's locked. Or maybe I'm just being paranoid. Either way, I can't seem to control the heavy beats of my heart.

Reaching my hand out, I try to shut the window, but the lock won't click no matter how hard I push.

I'll have to get that fixed. For now, I grab some duct tape and fix it over the window, taping it up like I'm sealing off the house for fumigation.

I really should call the police, but maybe it was me that left the window open. Why would anyone break-in? I have nothing of value.

Before I can think better of it, I bolt up the stairs to my bedroom, needing to double-check nothing is missing.

Once in my room, I take stock of the space.

My heart pounds. I glance around.

I let out a long, audible sigh. Again, nothing is out of place. I approach my desk next, slowly. Nope. All the papers are still in their usual spot.

But the lid of my laptop is open.

Did I leave it open?

I can't remember. Why is it you can never remember anything when you need to? But I think I closed it this morning.

I must have

Right?

The following week goes by, and I never find anything out of the ordinary in my house. Still, I can't shake the feeling that something is wrong. Even this morning, it felt like I was being watched on my walk to school.

An unspoken presence floats over me like a spooky ghost. That, coupled with the endless wrong phone calls I keep getting . . . it's starting to feel like I'm in a bad '80s horror flick. I've been cast as the idiot girl, walking into the dark house, ready to be murdered.

Every morning, like clockwork, my phone rings, but there's never anyone there.

It's making me angry.

Today, a song played. Which was creepy as hell.

A thought hits me.

Shit.

Is this Trent Aldridge?

I've waited months for him to show back up in my life. Every day that passed, I expected the call from Mr. Baker, informing me Ronald's family is taking me to court.

Are the calls from him?

Did he break into my house?

No.

That's ridiculous.

He wouldn't get his hands dirty.

Unless . . . this is part of a bigger plan.

But what can that plan be?

To make me look unhinged?

If he's as smart as I think he is, this goes beyond scaring me. That's too juvenile. If I go to the cops, looking as paranoid as I do, I become the unhinged lunatic in their eyes, just in time for Trent to serve me with papers. It's a damn good way to ruin my character. It also pushes me into a corner.

No cops.

No reprieve.

I'm out of options.

When I take a seat in my chair in the classroom, Heather is already there.

"Any word yet from the dickbag?" Heather asks. After the showdown in the lawyer's office, I mentioned that I was scared he would be a thorn in my side. I didn't go into details because I don't want to drag her into this mess with me.

Every day that has since passed, we started class with a mini-meltdown. She pries me for info while I give vague answers, unsure whether Trent Aldridge would stoop so low as to come after my friend.

"Well?" Heather follows up, watching as I take out my laptop for notes. A gift from Ronnie.

The answer is no. I haven't heard a word from Trent or Mr. Baker in over two months.

What does that mean for me?

I would be lying if I didn't admit that I'm getting nervous.

Too much time has passed.

It feels like one shoe has dropped down on me, and I'm waiting for the other one to hit me in the head. With my luck, it'll crash down, weighing a million pounds, and cause a nuclear fallout in destruction.

Yep. That's me. Forever the optimist. Watch out for my TED talk.

"Come on, Payton." Heather edges closer. "You're killing me here."

I sigh, finally bringing myself to answer. "It's kind of crazy, but I still haven't heard anything."

The muscles in my body hurt. Too tight for comfort.

Sitting with my friend should relax me, but I can't help the tension in my back. It's been there for the past couple of months. I'm a hot mess of distress. A punchline for a bad joke.

I walk around looking over my shoulder, waiting for him to approach.

I'm so uptight it's like I'm a piece of glass, bound to smash to the floor, shattering into a thousand tiny pieces.

"Then what's the problem?" Heather nudges my shoulder. "That's a good thing, right? Why the scowl on your face?"

Lifting my hands to my eyes, I scrub away the exhaustion. "That's the problem," I admit, lowering my arms back down in my lap.

"That you haven't heard?"

I nod.

"That has to be a good thing. If something were to go down, it would have already, right?"

My teeth lower, biting my lip. "No. It's not a good thing. The longer I wait for his next move, the sicker I get over it. I feel like someone is fucking with me. Or at least, I can't be too sure it's not the case."

"Maybe there is no next move. Maybe he'll let you live your life. Maybe he'll respect his father's wishes."

I roll my eyes at her comment. If only it were that simple. "You didn't see the look in his eyes. The malice and hatred. This isn't over. If anything, this is part of the game."

"How so?"

"He's making me squirm. He's basically an angry lion, playing with his food. He might not have killed me yet, but eventually, he'll pounce."

"That sounds oddly sexual. And he is smoking hot." She smirks.

"What? Stop. How do you even know that?"

"How does anyone know anything in this modern age? I googled him, Payton. Duh." Heather rolls her eyes as if I should've assumed she'd google him. "You really thought that wasn't the first thing I did?"

"You never mentioned it."

"Ronald just died. I thought it would be insensitive to mention his son is hot as fuck!"

"Shh. Can you be any louder?"

I look around the room, but it is still relatively empty, and no one appears to be paying attention to us anyway. I shake my head.

"Plus, he's not that hot," I say lamely.

I'm not fooling her. Not with how warm my cheeks feel. Like he's grazed a red-hot poker against my skin, ready to brand.

"Yes, he is, and even your frigid ass knows it, honey."

Her voice is way too loud this time, and the student sitting next to her giggles. Sam. I hate Sam right now.

"Can you shut up? Someone will hear you."

Sam is actually playing on her cell. That's why she is laughing, not because of me. No one is listening. No one cares.

"Oh, shut it. Look at this man," she chides as she unlocks the home screen of her cell and starts to google Trent. When his picture is on the screen, she flashes it at me. She's like a dog with a bone when she wants info, and she won't give up asking until I give it to her.

"Fine."

"Go on . . ."

I shrug. "He's not bad on the eyes."

"Getting warmer. Cut the shit. Just admit it."

"Jeez." I exhale. "Fine. I think he's hot. Like smoking hot. Nuclear hot. The hottest man I have ever seen. Hot." I let out an audible, dramatic-as-hell sigh.

She giggles. The smirk on her face is enough to make me place an ad in a newspaper: *accepting applications for a new best friend.*

"Yes, maybe he's hot, but he's also a total douche canoe," I follow up.

"Douche canoe? Really?"

"Dick. He's a huge dick."

"I wonder if McHottie has a huge dick." She completely ignores my distress. Typical Heather.

If I wasn't embarrassed before, now I'm really cringing.

"Totally off-topic," I mockingly scold. "How hot or big his dick is," I whisper, "is not the point."

"Then what is the point?" Her eyebrow raises, and again, I'm totally second-guessing this friendship. Too bad I love her ass and could never replace her.

"The point is, I'm afraid he's coming for me."

"With his big dick?"

"Yes."

She bursts into laughter, and I realize what I've just said.

"What?" I backtrack, chanting, "No. No. No. No."

"The lady doth protest too much."

"Really? You cannot use Shakespeare when I'm talking about Trent Aldridge. The man is the devil incarnate. And I don't want him like that." I use my stern voice.

I don't know whether he's behind the break-in or the phone calls, but I suspect he is. I don't trust that man. When I met him, he was way too smug and full of himself for my taste.

She takes a deep breath and straightens her back, then drops her voice. "Do you really think he'll come after you . . . ?" Her voice trails off as if she finally realizes how scared I am.

I'm about to answer and finally tell her about all the strange stuff that's happened to me when the door opens and our professor walks in. I turn my attention toward the front of the class.

"Ms. Hart," she says, looking straight at me. The muscles in my neck tighten. She just said my name, and I have no idea why. "Can you stay after to speak with me?"

I nod.

"What's that about?" Heather whispers.

So wrapped up in Trent-stress, I lift my shoulders before remembering I applied for a position in the department for next semester. After this year, I plan to continue my education and get my master's. The program is super competitive, so working with the department will help my chances of getting accepted.

"Maybe it's for the position."

Her eyes light up, and she smiles broadly.

Both of us know this could be huge for me.

The class goes by, and for the first time in months, I'm not thinking of how Trent Aldridge will reap his revenge. Instead, I'm thinking about what I can do to get far away from my sister.

Erin has been so difficult.

That's an understatement.

Between yelling, crying, and accusing me of sleeping with Ronnie for his money, it sucks being near her. Then there's her new boyfriend.

My body shivers uncontrollably.

But if I get this recommendation, I can get any job I want.

One even hundreds of miles away. Coupled with the money Ronald left me, the future looks bright.

Once the class ends, I stand from my chair and approach my professor.

"This is a little unorthodox, but I've been asked to deliver a message to you on behalf of student services," she says without looking up at me from her slideshow notes. It's clear she thinks I've inconvenienced her and that, whatever this is about, she thinks it's my fault. "They'd like you to visit their building the first chance you have."

I deflate like a torn balloon. Would it kill her to smile? She knows I want this position. The woman has hated me since day one.

"Okay, thank you."

Turning back the way I came, I make my way out the door to the student services building. My throat feels clogged. I've never heard of student services calling a student to their building. Everything is done online. The building is staffed with students, run by a single adult, which isn't a power dynamic I'm interested in thrusting myself into.

I feel like I've been called into the principal's office as I wait my turn in a row of students who've missed tuition and have questions on how to get more financial aid. When it's my turn, I step up to one of the sophomores running the station, slipping her my student ID. She whistles then turns to flag down her supervisor, who takes over.

"Hi, Ms. Hart." His name tag reads Happy, but he looks anything but. "We processed your tuition for the semester on the card on file, but it bounced after the hold period."

"Bounced?" I echo, curling my toes inward. This cannot be happening.

"There seems to be a problem with your payment method, and you don't have an alternate one on file. We've issued several alerts on the campus's portal system, along with dozens of dunning emails. Since all of them went unanswered, you are currently showing up as an unregistered student."

Impossible.

Dozens of emails?

I check them daily. Hourly, as a matter of fact. I'm sinking inside, unable to accept this reality.

"I don't understand." My hands are shaking. "This makes no sense. I didn't even get an email! My portal looks fine."

I pull out my phone and log in to the school's app. Sure enough, there's a little red exclamation point on the messenger icon, which wasn't there when I checked this morning. I immediately palm my phone, stuttering out a lie about forgetting my password.

Any sympathy this dude has for me is wiped out in a second. "Until we straighten this out, you're not an active student."

"Who do I have to speak to?" I ask in a daze.

"I strongly suggest you pay the tuition as soon as possible. None of your problems will be solved otherwise. As for reinstating your student status for the semester, it may be too late, but in case it isn't, you need to speak with the registrar."

"Fine."

I don't bother saying anything else as I dash for the door. The sooner I get this finished, the faster I can move toward my future.

It doesn't take me more than five minutes to reach the registrar's office.

That's the beauty of a small, private university.

"I need to speak with someone," I say to anyone in the office who will listen. It's a little grandiose and super dramatic, but it works.

"Do you have an appointment?" the lady behind a desk says.

"No. But it's an emergency. The supervisor I talked to at student services said I need to speak with someone in the registrar's office."

"What is your name?"

"Payton Hart."

I hear her hands typing on her computer. Then she nods to herself.

"Oh. You're the student with the unanswered dunning emails."

The student.

As in one.

Guess that's the bad thing about small, private universities. When shit happens, there's not really company for the misery. Only an audience.

"We tried to call you," she continues, "but it says your line was disconnected, and they couldn't get in touch with you."

"I didn't get a call."

"Like I said, normally, the registrar would call you, but they couldn't get in touch with you."

"But—"

I shake my head. There's no use in arguing. In fact, it only seems to make the stern lines of her face deepen. Does everyone hate me at this school?

I reach into my bag, pull out my phone, and scroll through the contacts, hitting the button for Heather's number.

The phone doesn't ring.

The phone doesn't do anything.

What the hell?

My phone has no service. It's as if the number has been shut off, but that makes no sense. The bills are on autopay. I used it to scroll through Dog Instagram this morning. It's functioning. It's on. It just has no service.

How can that be?

How long has it been since I accepted a call?

The only person who ever called me or texts me off a messenger app is Erin, and I just assumed she preferred to duke it out face-to-face.

The registrar lady nods. "Forget to pay your bill?"

I never paid my bill—didn't even know when it was due.

My sister does. No, not my sister.

Ronald.

He pays my bills.

This is the first time since he disappeared that there's been a problem. Erin told me that while he was in jail, before his death, his lawyer took care of everything.

Trent.

The name ping-pongs inside me, rage building with it. He's the one in charge. Maybe it's a simple mistake. Or maybe I'm a dumbass with a penchant for underestimating assholes. Either way, I'd rather double-check with Mr. Baker to see if he can help straighten things out for me before approaching the devil himself.

I need to call Mr. Baker.

It feels like I'm floating up above myself, but the woman in front of me is still talking. Only a few words flood through my brain.

No tuition.

No class.

I can't take classes until I settle my account. And if I don't settle my account in time, I'll be ineligible to complete the semester. There's no way I'll graduate in time if that happens.

With my shoulders hunched forward, I know where I have to go.

Home.

I have no doubt in my mind that Trent is a part of this somehow. That he's chosen to come after me. How else would the silent calls come through and no one else's? It sounds crazy just saying it, but there's no other possibility.

Now that Trent's chosen to come at me, I need to know what my options are. Will there even be anything left at the end of all this if he gets petty and steals the money? One thing's for sure—he's up to something.

I walk the three blocks to my house and find a tow truck in my driveway.

The car Ronnie gifted me is already halfway lifted on the back.

"What are you doing?" I scream from the street as I run toward where a man is stepping into the truck my car has been rigged to.

Shit.

"Stop!" I shout.

The door closes. The ignition turns. I'm now at the driver's side, hitting the door.

"What are you doing?" I yell between pants. "Get my car off this thing."

The window rolls down. "Sorry. No can do."

"What do you mean no can do? What kind of answer is that?"

How can they take my car?

"Listen, little girl. No. Can. Do. I have one job. That job is to collect the cars at the address provided to me by my boss."

"And then what? I don't understand how you can take my car as if it's yours."

"I just take 'em." He shrugs. "I don't keep them for myself. I can't tell you much, but I have to assume not paying your bill will do this."

"But I did—"

"That's what they all say." He shakes his head. "I wouldn't be here if you did."

Before I can say anything else, he shifts the truck in drive, and I step back.

Nothing can be done.

Another bill hasn't been paid, and I have a sinking feeling I know why.

Rearranging my bag over my shoulder, I tentatively walk toward the door.

My heart hammers in my chest as I make my approach.

There is no way that, from where I am, I can read the writing on the paper. It isn't clear, but I already know what it will say.

I don't need to read it. I know I'm being evicted.

And the worst part?

I now know for sure that my hunch was right. I know who is behind this.

Trent Aldridge.

He threw down the gauntlet.

I have no choice but to play the game.

Then I hear a chirp from my pocket.

Great. *Now* the phone is working again!

Grabbing my cell, I scroll my texts that are showing up again. Then I go to the contacts and dial her number, holding my breath to see if it even rings. It does. Again, I have this stomach-churning feeling I'm being watched. My eyes skim my surroundings and find nothing. I hunch my shoulders as if it'll protect me from prying eyes.

Erin answers after the third ring.

"Fancy of you to call me after ignoring my hundreds of calls. What do you want? To ruin my life some more?" She scoffs. "Maybe steal something else from me?"

"Erin, you know that's not what it's like," I say softly.

How can she think I did this on purpose?

"Do I? Because from where I'm standing, that's exactly what this is. My boyfriend left you all his money. Do you know how bad that looks?"

"Erin—"

"No, don't Erin me. After everything . . ." She pauses, letting her rage consume her. It's so palpable, I can feel it through the line. It forces me a step back. "I gave up my life for you, and you get the money. That's fucking bullshit, and you know it."

"Erin," I say again, trying to calm her.

"Unless you are signing over the money to me, I have nothing to say to you," she spits out.

"That's why I'm calling," I tell her, hoping that's enough for her to listen to me.

"To give me the money?"

"Not exactly . . ." I wince. "I mean, yes, some of it, of course. He was your boyfriend, after all. That was always the plan."

"Save me the stutters. I don't want to hear it—"

"I will give you money," I rush out, "all of it. But first, I need access to it. Seeing as none of my bills have been paid, I'm not sure that's ever going to happen."

She lets out a large, angry growl. It sounds like a pissed-off animal. Of course, she is angry. She wants to be the one in charge. I, on the other hand, felt relief at first. If Erin were in charge, there would be no money left by the time I hit twenty-two. It never dawned on me I might have the same problem with Trent.

I don't need all the money, but I need enough to pay for school and start over somewhere else. Somewhere far away.

"So, why are you calling me?" Erin hisses. "It's not like I'm the one in charge of the money."

"I need you to tell me where Trent works, lives, and where you think I can find him. What he's doing is bullshit."

Time to stand up to the ass.

CHAPTER SEVEN

Trent

B Y NOW, THE LITTLE PRINCESS HAS PROBABLY RECEIVED MY gift. The gift of being totally fucked.

Not fucked—self-reliant in ways she hasn't needed to be in years, at my family's expense.

A smile spreads across my face at the thought. I wonder which one she received first . . . Jax tends to hold his cards close when he delves into shady shit, but I trust him enough to get the job done.

Did she find out about school first?

Or maybe her car got towed as soon as she woke.

Maybe she walked out the door, only to realize she no longer has a ride.

I start to laugh as I think about the piece of paper taped to her door.

The eviction notice. The boarded-up house.

The home I bought out from under her.

I wish I could see her as she found the little envelope placed on the mat at her front door. The one that told her that her belongings had been taken to a certain address.

Best part . . . The address is mine. Not that it matters, seeing as I've had her car repossessed, but it should be interesting if she tries to get here.

Today is going to be the first good day I've had in years. I might not be able to seek my pound of flesh from my dad, but Payton and her sister are the next best thing. After years of my father's betrayal, I'm seeking my vengeance on the family who put mine on the chopping block.

Dad forever altered my family's life in order to give these princesses the luxuries they never deserved. Taking it away from them, making them feel even an ounce of the pain and suffering Mom and Ivy did for years, will be my vengeance.

The icing on the cake? It will also be entertaining.

All of Payton's belongings are currently stored in the basement of this building.

If she's lucky, I'll let her rummage through the boxes. If she's not, I'll let the incinerator do the work, and she can rummage through the ashes.

I lean back in my chair, waiting for the knock on the door. I have instructed my staff that we might be having a guest today.

There's no telling when she will come.

But I know she will.

I reach my hand out and grab the tumbler on my desk. The amber liquid slushes across the surface of the crystal.

Will she beg a friend for a ride, or will she take a train?

I canceled all her credit cards.

Who knows if she will even have enough cash to get here?

A train, then a cab from Penn Station.

Yeah, that will set her back, too.

Victory tastes sweet.

I lift the glass to my mouth and take a swig. Then I pivot my chair to look toward the computer.

There's an email on the screen.

A confirmation.

Her car is now in my possession.

How long have I been staring at my computer? All I know is that my glass is now empty. There is a knock on the front door.

I don't need to stand to know it's her. Now I just have to wait for Martha to show her to my office.

"Where is he?" I hear her scream.

Feisty. I wasn't expecting that.

"If you could please calm down, I'll show you to Mr. Aldridge—"

My door flies open.

Payton Hart storms into the room like a tornado.

Wild and unpredictable.

Her eyes are wide. I allow myself to watch her. Stare, really.

This is the first time my anger has subsided enough for me to really look at her.

She's fucking magnificent.

If she were anyone else, I would allow myself the brief distraction from my work to fuck her right here on the desk.

But she's not someone else. She's a means to an end.

A final "fuck you" to my dad.

But nothing, not even her pert-as-fuck tits, can distract me from that fact.

What was so perfect about them that he'd sell my sister like an object?

"Payton." I fill my glass halfway and raise it to her in greeting. "How nice of you to visit me. Is there something I can help you with?"

"Are you kidding me right now?" she fires back. Her back is ramrod straight, and her hands rest on her hips.

A warm heat begins to spread inside me. It's a feeling I haven't felt in a long time.

Excitement.

I'm excited to ruin this girl's privilege, built on my family's pain. Crushing her every dream is a fantastic aphrodisiac.

"What the hell are you smiling at?" she hisses at me. Her tone only makes me smile wider.

"Just you. Why? Is something wrong?"

Her hand drops, and she begins to cross the space that separates us. Her sneakers slap the hardwood floor with purpose. When she is standing directly in front of my desk, she stops.

"Why did you do it? What did I ever do to you?"

"You are going to have to be more specific." I settle my features, making my face serious as if I have no clue why she's pissed.

Her lips pucker. She is ready to burst. This is not just normal pissed. She is ready to blow.

I can't wait.

"You know exactly what I'm talking about."

"Why don't you take a seat?" I lift my hand and gesture to the empty chair beside her. "It seems like you had a rough day."

"Seriously?"

I let my lip twist up into a smile again. "Yes. Seriously."

"You really are an asshole."

I shrug, casually sipping my drink. "I've been called worse. So, what can I do for you, Ms. Harlow?"

"Hart. My name is Hart. And I want my stuff back."

She stands tall, trying to make herself appear strong. Too bad she doesn't realize I have only just started with her.

I tsk at her. "You really shouldn't get so attached to material items. It's not good for your well-being."

At my words, her eyes go wide. "Are you fucking kidding me right now?"

I stand from my desk, rising to my full height, over a foot taller than her, if I had to guess.

"No. I'm not fucking kidding you. Being dependent on items isn't good for the soul. You should be thanking me."

"Thanking you? Thanking you! You're ruining my life."

Cue the smile.

Cue the smirk.

Cue the devil inside me who wants to swallow her whole.

"Not yet."

"What?"

61

"I said, not *yet*. Your life isn't ruined *yet*." I wink, and the hands at her sides fist.

"Why are you doing this?"

"Because I can."

She starts to pace the room. She reminds me of an old cartoon I watched as a child. The one where smoke came out of the characters' ears because they were so mad.

"You won't get away with this."

"I already did."

With that, she storms out. The door slams behind her, and the sound of the force she exerted echoes through the space.

For the first time in a long time, I feel anything is possible.

This will be fun. I pour another drop of liquor on the floor for Dad, watching it splatter across my expensive wood flooring. "Checkmate, bastard."

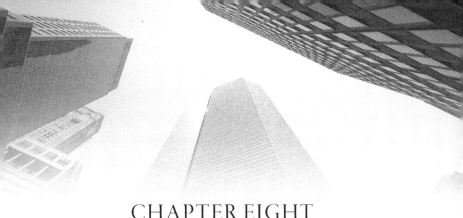

CHAPTER EIGHT

Payton

THE TREK BACK TO LONG ISLAND IS LONG AND TEDIOUS.
One: Without a car, I must take the train.

Two: My cash is limited, so I couldn't even spend money on a cab to get to Penn Station since I'll need all my money to get back to campus once I'm off the train.

The worst part . . . my cell is temperamental as hell. One minute it's on, the next minute it's off. It's like someone is manipulating the phone line just to mess with me. Which is ridiculous because there is no way Trent has the power to do that. *Right?*

My plan, which isn't a very good one, is to break into my house and sleep there. It can't be legal to kick me out without notice. Tomorrow, I'll speak to the lawyer, but tonight, I just need to crash.

Yep, add criminal to my list of problems.

And lord, are the problems piling up.

It feels like the world is spinning out of control, and I'm going to topple over.

Deep breath in.

Exhale out.

A coping mechanism I learned long ago but haven't used in years.

Deep breath in.

Exhale out.

I'm fine.

Everything will be fine.

And at least I'm in sneakers and not impractical heels.

When the cab from the train station finally drops me off, I pull out my cell and turn on the flashlight.

It's dark outside, but at least my cell is charged.

Something tells me once inside, I'll need it. The bastard probably didn't pay the electric bill either.

It's pitch-black other than light coming from my phone.

What the hell am I going to do?

Where will I sleep?

And my things. I need clothes, a toothbrush, my schoolwork.

Wait.

The back window in the family room isn't locked.

Holy crap! I almost forgot. It's broken. I have a way in.

My body shakes, and tears prick my eyes.

Finally, something is going my way. It might have no electricity, but at least I'll have a bed and my things. At least I'll be safe.

As I jimmy it open and hoist myself through the window, I realize my assessment of the situation is spot-on.

It's pitch-black inside. All the lights are off. Even the one I have set on timers, so it always appears that someone is home.

My feet hit the floor, and they echo. It sounds like an angry stampede of elephants. It's not.

It's just me.

There is nothing.

I want to fall over and sob.

One lone tear escapes my eye, but I wipe it away fast and stand up straight. There is no time to allow myself to fall apart. Instead, I take another step. Again, it echoes.

Without furniture, nothing absorbs the sound.

Goose bumps break out across my skin as I move through the room. It feels like someone is here.

Watching. Staring.

I chalk it up to my paranoia this time.

Trent has me wound up and seeing things.

No one is here, obviously. It's all in my head, but I have that feeling. The feeling you have watching a scary movie. When you know something terrifying is lurking behind the door.

I start to pace the room. I love this house. It was the start of something amazing.

Something solely mine.

And now it's gone.

No. Not true. Tomorrow, I will regroup. I will find Mr. Baker and figure a way out of this mess.

He'll probably tell me to move back home with my sister, but I won't do that. Not ever. Last I spoke to her, she was living with that creep.

That's what she does.

She latches on to a man. Well, that was how it was before Ronald. He was our second chance. Also, my sister's longest relationship.

He loved us and took care of us, and when he was around, I thought anything was possible.

As a little girl, I envisioned him as a prince. He rescued us. The fact that it was all a lie doesn't sit well with me.

I'm having a hard time reconciling the two stories.

The one that Trent Aldridge yelled about and the man I knew. The man I knew would never have abandoned his family.

But at the same time, the man I knew would never have had a secret family, so I guess what do I know?

Nothing, obviously.

I start to walk around the house, looking to see if he left anything behind.

A blanket?

Clothes.

Anything that can help make tonight more comfortable.

I don't have a bed. Maybe I should just go to Heather's apartment. It's not that far of a walk. Plus, she would take me. She would kill me if she knew I was planning to sleep on the floor with no blanket.

The problem is, I can't ask for help. A level of pride has been ingrained inside me since I was a small girl.

Since back in the day when we lived in my sister's car rather than ask for help.

That was before . . . but I can be that strong girl again.

The hard times don't kill us. They teach us how to adapt. How to grow thick skin. How to become resilient. And even now, after all these years of wanting for nothing, the feeling of asking for help is still hard.

I shake my head.

No.

Every once in a while, you have to table your emotions and lay yourself bare. I can ask for help. It's not the end of the world. It won't undermine my growth as a person. I allowed Ronald to help me. I didn't ask for help, but he gave it.

My stomach drops. He always helped me, yet it seems he only caused his own family pain. Reconciling the man I knew from Trent's father is hard enough but doing it while standing in a house cloaked in darkness due to his son is impossible.

I continue to search the house for anything I can use. With my phone's flashlight, I go from room to room. Nothing. Not a damn thing.

Garbage can: Gone.

Toilet paper: Gone.

Hell, even the light cans in the ceiling are stripped of the bulbs.

Gotta hand it to the jerk. He left nothing. Even the bag of recyclables I left by the back door is gone. On the off-chance I managed to convince the electric company to turn the lights back on the bastard stole the light bulbs like he was the Grinch.

He was thorough. A complete ass, too. Can't forget that part.

There should be a rule that jerks come with a warning label on their forehead. That way, people know to stay clear of them. It should be mandatory the same way it is with food labels.

Someone with a peanut allergy knows not to eat a Snickers bar.

The outside should match the inside. However, I know that is not to be the case. My sister is the perfect example of this. It isn't fair for the façade to hide the truth. Someone should come up with a device to remedy this. Like beer goggles but for character.

I shake my head at my ridiculous thought. There are bigger problems right now than this dumb invention.

Like which floor I should sleep on.

In the bedroom? Living room? Definitely not on the kitchen tiles or the bathroom floors.

It's still warm out for the next few hours. With the central air off, the heat will rise to the bedroom.

Downstairs it is. Lucky me.

Tomorrow I'll ask for help. But tonight, I'll suck it up on the floor.

I explore the place for the coolest room, crossing into the family room.

I sit so my back leans against the wall and close my eyes. There is no way I can stay like this. I'll never fall asleep. I have no pillow.

Nothing to sleep on.

I look down at the sweatshirt that I'm still wearing from school. It's way too hot to be wearing it, but it gets so cold in class. And by the time I knock out, the temperature will drop, then I'll need a triple layer.

But for now, I succumb to the fluff and decide to use it as a pillow.

Once the cotton is off my skin, I feel much better.

My skin cools.

I ball it up and prop it beneath my head, resting on my make-shift bed. I bring my knees into the fetal position.

The level of power Trent Aldridge yields is unmeasured.

He could use this power to better people. To build them up. To be safe and kind. He could use this strength to protect, not crush.

I won't allow him to crush me, though. Nor will I shed a tear over him. I haven't allowed myself to cry since I was little. Since my parents died. Since we lost everything.

Now is no different.

I refuse to let myself fall to pieces.

My eyes close, and I take a deep breath.

Nothing can be worse than that.

A creak wakes me up.

I'm not sure how much time has passed or how long I've been sleeping, but I'm groggy, and my eyes struggle to adjust to the darkroom.

There is no light, and I can't risk the sound of searching for my phone, but a small sliver of the moon reflects into the home. Not enough to see anything. I gamble, reaching out to find my phone to use as a flashlight.

Not fast enough.

"Isn't this cozy?" a familiar voice says.

Well, maybe something can be worse.

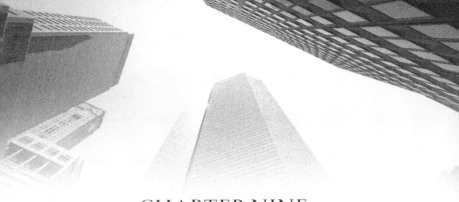

CHAPTER NINE

Trent

S HE'S CURLED UP ON THE FLOOR.
Head on what looks like a worn-out sweatshirt.

Sleeping tight after her nice, long walk.

I'm light on my feet as I move closer. A trait I picked up from the men I do business with.

Never let your enemies see you coming.

Or, in this case, hear you coming.

I'm standing a foot away from her before I speak.

Darkness bathes the room. Only a few slivers of light stream in from the window.

The very window she shimmied in through. Cyrus's man, who loaded her furniture, was right. He predicted her point of entry through the window with a broken lock. I watched it in full definition on the large screen in my bedroom, my A/C on full-blast, and a thousand-dollar comforter sprawled over half my body.

I'm a sick bastard because my comfort only makes her discomfort sweeter. I felt like diving into hell just to take a victory lap around my father.

How'd that secret trust work out for you, Father Dearest?

"Isn't this cozy?" I scold, my voice dripping with sarcasm.

"What the—" She sits up abruptly, and that's when I notice her big mistake.

She hasn't realized it yet.

But I can't wait until she does.

My lips spread wide.

But she will. Because I am currently fishing my phone out of my pocket to show her.

"What are you doing here?"

"One could ask you the same question."

"I live here!"

"No, Payton . . . You *lived* here. Past tense. Now you are trespassing."

"You don't know what you're talking about." She huffs.

My phone's light flickers on, and I shine it on her.

"You ass—" She blinks, the new brightness making her squint.

"Hole," I finish for her with a smile. "Yes. I am. And you, my dear, need to put clothes on."

She looks down, and a loud gasp rings through the air. Her hands jet up to cover herself, and although I'm an ass, I'm not big enough of an ass to watch, so I turn and give her a moment of privacy.

However, I'm not above using the moment—any moment, really—to taunt her. "I'm not here to collect you next. Don't fear. You're not up to my usual standards, though I am impressed," I chide.

"Shut the fuck up."

She's a mouthy one. Even half-asleep.

Too bad she's dealing with me.

"Not likely."

I walk around the room, taking in the empty space I left for her to find. The men I sent to empty it did a good job. There is not one thing in the house but Payton. Even the art is gone.

"Then get gone," she snarls.

"Again, not likely."

"Why are you doing this?"

"Would you like the long answer or the short one?" I ask. She shimmies to put her shirt back on, so I keep talking, "Short answer. This is my house. I own it. So yes, dear sweet Payton, you are, in fact, trespassing. And, as you've noticed, you have zero possessions here. No reason to return. As for the long answer . . . I really don't feel like telling you."

"You are such an asshole."

"We've gone over this already. Nothing new here."

"Let's add creep to the list then. You came in like a creeper while I was asleep. What is wrong with you? Also, can you stop shining that flashlight on me?"

"Sure thing, princess."

"Don't call me that."

"Oh no. You don't like that? It seemed fitting. I mean, who else was left an inheritance so large she can buy a small country?"

"I don't think I can buy a small country," she mutters.

"Oh . . ." I pretend to sound sorry, drawing a hand to my chest. "Twenty-two mil is not enough for you . . . your highness."

"That is not what I meant, and you know it. I just meant—"

"I think you mistake me for someone who gives a fuck."

"What I am trying to say is—"

"Again, doesn't matter. All that matters is you're in my house, and you need to leave."

"What? Are you serious? I can't leave. Do you know what time it is?"

"It's 3:02 a.m. I'm sure you can crash on your friend's couch. What's her name again? Oh, yeah, Heather."

Her eyes widen. I also don't miss the way her jaw trembles. "How do you know her name?"

I won't dignify the question with a response.

She looks pathetic.

Huddled on the floor like a little mouse.

As if she can hear my thoughts, she lowers her hand, straightens her sweatshirt, and stands.

Rising to her full height.

She's still smaller than I first thought. Now barefoot, I peg her at five foot three.

I'm still almost a full foot taller at six-two.

"I will see you out," I offer, though it's more like a warning.

Her arms cross over her chest. "I'm not leaving."

"What part of 'you are trespassing in my house' did you not understand?"

"All of it, I guess. But you are the one not understanding. It's three o'clock in the morning. You will not tell me to go out on the street at night."

"You have two choices." I hold up a finger. "Stay and get arrested." I hold up a second finger. "Or leave." I point the two fingers at the door, highlighting her only real option, though watching her get arrested could become a fun memory.

Her eyes narrow, and she rights herself even further.

"I can't believe you're his son. You're nothing like him."

"What do you know about my father? You think he was a saint," I grit out. "He was a monster."

"Takes one to know one."

"Never compare me to that man."

She shrugs. "Feels the same right now."

"I don't care what you think of the great Ronald Aldridge. The real Ronald sold his daughter to the Russian mob."

Her eyes go wide.

With only my phone for light, it's hard to see her face clearly, but I can see the shock. She didn't know. Ever since I found out about Payton, I pondered her involvement in this mess. Wondered if she'd known about what my father had done to Ivy.

Did Dad tell her? If he loved her so fucking much, if they were the family he chose, the one he really wanted to be with, did he protect them from the truth? From us. Were we the other family? Or were Payton and Erin?

At this point, the answer wouldn't do me any favors.

But it's obvious right now she didn't know about the Russians.

Good.

She should see the truth.

Feel it, too.

That's what I want.

I want her to feel fear. Feel helpless.

To feel it, even if it's a small sliver of what Ivy and I felt . . .
Hopeless. I can't make him pay. When I'm done with her, she will
have assumed that emotional debt for him and her part in Ivy's
misery. Even if I now know she didn't know that he sold her to
the Russians, I will make her life hell until I find the proof that she
knew about us, and then I will take all the money away from her.

*Are you watching this, Dad? The illusion you crafted is crum-
bling. Your favorite "daughter" is about to see you for who you are.
This is just a taste of the ugly and cruel world you made me create
from the broken pieces of your shattered dynasty.*

After I burn his legacy to the ground and force her to realize the evil of the man Payton idolizes, leave her poor, then, and
only then, will I walk away.

"I—" she starts, but I stop her.

"Don't want to hear it, princess. Get out of my house. Go
somewhere. I can't stand to look at your face for another second."

"I have no place to go . . . you took everything."

"They were never yours to have." I stalk toward her, enjoying
the emptiness of this place. "And frankly, not my problem. Leave,
Payton. But know this isn't over."

"I have nothing left for you to take."

"That's what you think. It wouldn't be fun to just tell you my
plan, now, would it?"

She doesn't respond, and I'm happy about that.

Instead, she storms out of my house.

The house I bought just to fuck with her.

Mature? No.

Fun? Hell yeah.

She is right about one thing; I am a dick, but I'm not about to let this girl walk alone at this time of night. I wait a minute before heading out. As soon as she has a reasonable head start, I follow her.

This neighborhood is safe, but you still can't be sure.

After what happened to my sister, I wouldn't do that to anyone, even if I hate everything she stands for.

She walks in the direction I expect her to—toward her friend's place—and knocks on the door.

Her body is pressed up against it as if she is afraid.

A few seconds pass, but then it opens, and she throws her arms around her friend, holds her, then pulls away.

A single moment of weakness.

Because once she's a few feet away from her, Payton stands straight. Her actions make her uncomfortable.

Interesting.

I file that away in my brain.

Another thing I have learned about Payton.

She doesn't want to appear weak in front of her friend, not just me.

Good to know.

This I can use.

I smile to myself as I watch the door close.

Soon, she will be exactly where I want her to be.

Begging for mercy.

Unfortunately, she won't get that from me.

CHAPTER TEN

Payton

RUBBING MY EYES, I SEE I'M NOT ALONE IN THE LIVING ROOM. But this time, unlike last night, the eyes are friendly and don't belong to anyone who wants to kill me.

"Morning."

"Good morning to you. How did you sleep?" Heather raises an eyebrow.

"Great." I smile. "Thank you for letting me stay here."

She rolls her eyes at me. "Of course, I would let you stay here. You know you never have to ask, right?"

I nod, knowing full well I'm going to have to come clean about everything that happened last night.

"I made coffee. It's in the kitchen," she says.

"Wait. There's no room service or, in my case, living room service? What kind of place are you running here?" I say sarcastically.

"The kind of place that opens the door at three o'clock in the morning with no questions asked."

She does have a point. I wryly smile, nod, and stand from the couch, pushing down my sweatshirt that has risen. I follow her into the kitchen.

Just as promised, my coffee is in a mug and ready for me at the table. Something tells me this will be a serious chat, and Heather isn't going to let me off the hook about last night.

Pulling out a chair, I take a seat. Then I lift the mug to my mouth. If we have a long talk, I'll need all the caffeine she's offering.

Heather sits in the chair opposite me. She's not drinking her coffee, just waiting for me to get enough fuel in me to hold a proper conversation.

"Why didn't you come to me in the first place?" she asks as I place my mug back down on the table.

"It was late."

She shakes her head, not buying what I'm selling. "That is no excuse, and you know it."

I try again. "I didn't want to wake you . . . ?"

"Again, not a good reason. Plus, eventually, you did anyway." She has me there.

"I know." I look down toward my bare feet. "I was embarrassed," I admit.

A long-drawn-out sigh escapes her mouth. "Payton, we have been best friends for years. There's no need to be embarrassed in front of me. We all have been in a bad place before."

"Thanks for not asking questions when I showed up at your door."

"One look at you, and I knew you wouldn't have been able to answer anyway. But now that I know you need help, it's a different story. Tell me. Tell me everything you have managed to leave out up to this point."

And then I do. I start from the little bits I now know and fill her in up until last night.

I tell her Ronald left all this money to me, Trent is in charge of releasing the funds, and that shoe finally dropped like a lead weight.

Everything is gone.

Will he have me declared dead next? I think I saw that in a movie once.

Just like that, everything is gone in an instant all over again. How many times can that happen to a person in a single lifetime?

The rug completely swiped out from under me, all because of whatever Trent has in his mind that I've done wrong to him and his family.

After I finish, I let out a sigh. "I just don't know what to do."

"It's your money. He shouldn't be able to do this."

"Technically, it's not my money until I turn twenty-two."

"Not too far away. But doesn't Ronald's estate have to pay your bills?"

"Well, technically, they do. The problem is, Ronald never stipulated how much that means. It's not written anywhere how much I'm allotted to live off. Basically, it's up to Trent's discretion how much I need until my birthday. I should have realized he wasn't just going to be fair. I should never have deluded myself that he wouldn't let me live my life as is."

"This is ridiculous."

"Agreed." I lift my mug and take a sip. My throat is dry, but despite the heat, I need something to help.

"What are you going to do?"

Swallowing, I place the mug back down. "I don't know."

"You can fight it."

"I don't have the funds to fight it until I'm twenty-two. And no attorney is going to take my case out of the kindness of their heart. I can't afford a retainer, and Trent is likely going to be successful in screwing me out of my inheritance."

Heather reaches her hand out and gives mine a squeeze. "I'm sure you can find one."

"Yeah. But is that the attorney I want? They'd be no better than an ambulance chaser."

She giggles at that. "You're right. Okay, no crappy lawyer. So, then what?"

"I guess I have no choice. I'll have to take a train and meet with Ronald's lawyer to see what my options are. It's ridiculous, if I'm being honest. I got the inheritance, and he needs to suck it up."

"I'll drive you."

"You have class. And you've already helped me so much."

"This is more important. I can't have you sleeping on the floor again."

"I could go to my sister's place."

"No way. You said your sister's new boyfriend is a creep."

"He is."

"Then you can't go there. You have to stay with me. It's really not a big deal."

"It is to me."

As much as I love her, and I do, she's my only friend, the best friend a girl could have, and I can't put her through that. This drama is my drama, and I need to sort it myself. I can't have her in front of me while shots are being fired.

I sigh. "For now, I'll take you up on the offer to drive me to the city, if you don't mind."

"Of course, I don't mind."

"Thank you so much. You have no idea how much I appreciate it. I really don't want to ask my sister for anything."

She reaches her hand out and takes mine, giving it a little squeeze. "Anything you need, all you have to do is ask."

I know she's not lying to me. I know she'll do anything to help me, but I need to settle this by myself. I need to stay on my own two feet. I can't risk her getting involved. I would never be able to live with myself if Trent came after her too. I need to walk into that lawyer's office on my own.

We both finish our coffee, and then we are in her car and driving toward the city.

It's much faster this way, and I curse Trent Aldridge for what I had to do yesterday. When we pull up in front of the tall building that houses Mr. Baker's office, I step out of the car.

"Do you want me to wait?" Heather asks.

"You don't have to."

"I know, boo. But I got you."

"I don't know how long it will be, plus, you have class. Go."

"Let me at least give you money."

"I can't take your money."

"Sure, you can. And you will. It's not much. But at least with fifty bucks, you can get back to my place."

"I promise to pay you back."

"Oh, honey. Forget about it."

"I won't. Nor will I ever forget your kindness, Heather."

"Fine." She sighs dramatically, making me laugh. "But no rush."

I nod my head in agreement and chuckle, stepping out of the car with the fifty tucked into my front pocket. As I'm closing the door, I force out one last smile. The air in the city is warmer than normal at this time of year. It's fall, but it doesn't feel like it. I know this heatwave won't linger for much longer, but I'll take it.

Last night, for example, sleeping without a heater, I could've frozen to death if this was winter.

Something tells me after Trent's warning, freezing to death will be the least of my problems. Today, there is no question he will have the locks on all the windows fixed. I'll probably have to take Heather up on her offer.

It's only a few steps to the door of the familiar building, but I welcome the air-conditioning once I step inside. I walk toward the same elevator I got in two months ago, and then I'm riding it up back to the place where it all started. Where my fate was sealed.

When the elevator opens, I walk down the dark hallway to the office. I open the door, and no one is there. I expect a receptionist or someone to be milling about in the reception room, but it's empty.

"Ms. Hart?" Mr. Baker calls out from the room in which we held the meeting.

I start to walk toward the room.

"Yes."

"Show yourself in."

I'm about to open the door when I hear another voice inside the room.

It's the very distinct raspy tone that haunts my nightmares.

I don't know how or why he's here, nor do I want to know. If it were up to me, I would never see that man again, but something tells me I won't like today's turn of events now that I know he's attending this meeting.

I open the door tentatively, but it doesn't matter how slow my movements are. It still squeaks in the silence that has descended around me, taunting me. The sound reminds me of nails on a chalkboard, scratching as I enter the space.

"Look who finally decided to join us. Rough start today? Need a bit of extra coffee?" Trent winks.

He's such an incredible ass.

A myriad of choice words grows heavy on my tongue. It takes everything inside me not to holler back at him.

Inhaling deeply, I will myself to calm.

My hands are by my sides, and I tuck them behind my back as I fist them so no one can see.

Unfortunately, the sharp curve of my nails digs into the fatty skin of my palm, making me hiss. My jaw is tight, my teeth grinding as I suck in my cheeks to stop myself.

Nothing good will come if I lash out.

I take a deep, long inhale and school my emotions.

"Oh. It's you, Mr. Aldridge. I didn't know you would be here. What an unexpected and pleasant surprise." My voice is sugary sweet. Like syrup being poured on pancakes.

If the confection was laced with poison.

I'm so damn sweet that a root canal will probably be necessary.

His smile broadens, and there is a gleam in his blue eyes. He's enjoying this.

"Always happy to surprise," he retorts, beaming at me.

I turn my attention to Mr. Baker, who takes it as his cue to begin.

"Please sit, Ms. Hart. It seems we have some things to go over."

"You think?" I mutter before I can stop myself, and Trent chuckles.

Bastard.

Also, if I wasn't scared before, now I'm positively terrified. His laughter screams of a promise to hurt me. I look back at him, and just as I suspected, he's leaning up against the wall. Legs crossed casually. Arms folded across his chest.

But that's not the frightening part. It's more than the laughter. It's the look he's giving me. He is downright ecstatic. He's gleaming in pure triumph.

He won.

He knows it, and now I do as well.

CHAPTER ELEVEN

Trent

I LOVE WATCHING HER SQUIRM.

She does this little thing when her brows furrow and her nose scrunches. A dozen thoughts flash behind her eyes. No doubt, fantasies of my murder. Replayed in a gruesome fashion. She wants me gone. Out of her life.

It's a wish I'll never grant.

If not for the fact that I'm dead set on ruining her, watching her get pissed is a bonus. It's better than playing poker. Almost better than when a stock tip pays off big, too.

Almost.

She looks like she barely slept.

Dressed in old sweats and a ripped hoodie, it looks like she pulled an all-night drinking bender. Dark circles line the bottom of her eyes. The skin is puffy, like she was crying.

I don't know her backstory. I don't know her struggles. There had to be some for that fire inside her to build. She's the feistiest woman I've ever met. So, princess may not be the most accurate term to describe her, but it's what she was to my father.

Bonus points for driving her insane, which is fun and why I have no intention of giving it up.

That would be too easy.

I don't do easy.

"Come in," Mr. Baker says, scrambling to pull out a chair for her.

I stay silent and continue to stare at her, wondering what my father saw in her. Not that she's not gorgeous. She is. With brown hair and light-blue eyes, she has a forbidden and exotic look to her.

Was my dad banging her, too?

It's the only scenario that makes a lick of sense.

My father wouldn't have left everything to her over a fatherly relationship, considering he didn't have a paternal bone in his body.

Payton looked shell-shocked when her sister accused her of fucking him at the will reading, but she could be a good actress.

What else could it be?

I'll find out the truth.

I'll get to the bottom of it.

I don't care what it takes. This is my new goddamn mission.

Payton stays by the door, even as Mr. Baker returns to his seat, nodding to the empty chair he pulled out.

My gaze scans over her, followed by the scumbag lawyer.

Maybe she's working with him?

They could have concocted the plan together.

Finally, she steps into the room. There's a question in her eyes. Something like rage and fear twisting in one hailstorm within them.

If anyone knew the shit I'm thinking of doing to her, they would say I'm crazy.

It's not about the money. Sure, it sucks to lose something that's rightfully my family's, but that's not why I'm doing this. We have more money than we can spend in ten lifetimes.

It's the principle.

Payton might not have technically fucked with my family's life, but she's the reason for our pain. She is the only one I can hurt. And I will.

Revenge is a dish best served cold.

And I am about to serve her up with extra fucking ice.

"What do we have to talk about?" she asks, making me want to roll my eyes at her, but I'm not some prepubescent teen, so instead, I glare.

"So much," I deadpan. "Now, Payton, please make yourself comfortable. I know this isn't my office, but I also know we will be here for a long time."

"I don't understand why," she mutters under her breath before finally taking a seat and turning her attention back to the weasel shit lawyer.

If I was unsure of his involvement, it's looking clear to me now. He definitely has a hand in this, so that's why my plan is in place.

"Don't look at him," I order. "He has nothing to add. He is merely the moderator."

"Isn't there anything you can do?" she asks him, ignoring what I just said to her.

I can feel my skin heating.

She is infuriating.

"Ms. Hart, other than advise you, there is nothing I can really do regarding the late Mr. Aldridge's will. As I said before, the trust doesn't revert to you until your twenty-second birthday, which isn't that far off. Maybe—"

"There is *no* maybe!" She jumps to her feet.

"Sit down," I fire, and I watch as she stumbles as if she's not sure what to do.

Her confusion on how to approach this lingers in the air.

"Sit down, now."

She does what I ask and sits back in the chair. She's obviously nervous. My voice probably scared her, but I'm sick of this shit.

Her knee bounces while her nails sink into the skin of her palms.

After a beat, there is a tightness to her jaw that wasn't present before.

She's angry.

It's not just the look that she fires off, nor is it the lines that furrow around her eyes that give her away. No. Her hatred seeps out of her like an intoxicating perfume.

I want to sniff it up and wear it.

Fuck.

As much as I hate her, and I do, she's irresistible when she's angry. I love the challenge her strength brings. She's a raging inferno, and I'm tempted to touch the flame.

A small part of me wants to forget this feud and kiss her, which is the craziest fucking thought I've had since I met her. I put it in park and tell myself to cut this shit out.

There is no time for that now. No time for it ever.

Not with her.

Not after what I'm about to say.

"I own you," I tell her as if I'm discussing a recent acquisition in the stock market. My eyes lower to my nails. I bring my hand to my face, pretending to examine it. I'm well aware she is fuming across the table, and it takes everything in me not to smile.

Her palms slam down. "The hell you do—"

I like her fire. It's refreshing. It's also useless.

There's no way she's winning an argument against me.

I blow on my nails and polish them against my dress shirt, sparing her a cursory glance. "Actually, until you turn twenty-two, I own you."

"You have to pay for my—"

"Stop right there . . ." I lift a finger, treating her as I would an untrained dog. "I only have to pay for necessities, and I don't think a house to yourself and a fancy car on top of that expensive private university is a necessity."

"It's not your place."

"But that's where you're wrong, princess." My lips part and spread. "It is. My father, your benefactor, for whatever reason, decided to leave you this money for services rendered."

My smile drops, replaced with a look of disgust.

She pauses, taking her time to digest my words. "What the hell is that supposed to mean?"

"What do you think it means?" I lift my right brow.

Payton's mouth drops open. "It wasn't like that. He was like a father to me—"

"Okay. If you say so," I say in a tone that obviously implies otherwise. "Doesn't matter what he was. What matters is he put you in this position. You think I want to deal with you, princess? Spoiler alert—I don't. I don't want to see or speak to you. But my father was a dick. He didn't care what I wanted. If he cared at all about me, or you for that matter, he would have put your sister in charge of your finances, now, wouldn't he?"

Wide eyes.

They consume her face, staring back at me in silence, beginning to realize just how fucked she is.

Welcome to reality, baby. Check your expectations at the door.

"My father didn't care about anyone," I continue. "Never did. The man you thought he was . . . that was all a lie. You probably think I'm wrong, that I'm being too hard on him. I'm not. He was a grade-A asshole. I should know. I'm his son . . . and the apple didn't fall far from that tree."

Everything I learned about hatred, I learned straight from the source.

Her teeth bite over her lower lip, and she starts to nibble as if she's trying to stop herself from saying something that she won't be able to take back.

Knowing that I have control over her keeps her in check.

I like it.

But as much as I want to celebrate this win, I can't think

about that now. I need to tell her why she's here first, and when I'm alone, I can savor the moment.

"What do you want from me?"

"Patience, princess. I'm about to tell you." I lean back in my chair, getting comfortable. I'm already pretty comfortable, but I like to make her wait. "I'll pay for your college. Well, my father technically will, but I'll free up the funds—"

"You really do think you're God, don't you?"

I watch as her shoulders drop in relief. Her reaction to my next news will make the following part even more fun.

"No. God has nothing to do with it. This is a deal with the devil you'll be making."

"Delusions of grandeur are not an attractive personality trait."

"Can you shut up for a minute and listen? There are stipulations."

"What kind of stipulations?"

"Stipulations for the money to be freed up for you to go to your fancy university. A university, I might add, that had my father not paid for, you would never be able to afford, but that's neither here nor there. My point is, I will allow you to attend your school, but you will need to follow a few rules."

"Rules? Seriously. Do I look five?" Her voice is strong, but the way her hands shake by her side, I peg that as fear.

"You need to prove that you deserve such an education. And before you ask how you'll do that, I'm just going to tell you." I wait for a beat to build the suspense. "One, you will move into my loft. I know what you're going to say, that it's too far from your college. But before you can ask, I'm going to save you the time . . . not my problem." My demands are ridiculous, but I need her under my roof to find out just how much she had to do with what happened to my family.

"You can't be serious."

"Oh, I am."

"You can't make me live with you." She turns to the lawyer as if he can save her. "Can he?" she asks him.

"Legally . . . no. But—"

"No buts, he can't force me to live with him," she fires back.

"I can, and I will. Also, don't get too excited about your new living arrangement." I wink. "There's more."

"More? How can there be more?" She shakes her head. "Doesn't matter because living with you is not going to happen, so I don't know what more you could want to say."

"Again, for some reason, you think this is up for debate. There are not going to be any negotiations here. Do you want to finish college? Fine. You wanna graduate? Fine again. Hell, you want some fucking spending money? That's cool, too. But . . . and there is a huge but. In order for any of this to happen, you will live with me. You can try to fight this"—I shrug—"but just so you know, it will take you years, and it will still leave you in exactly the same position. You'll have nowhere to live because your money will be tied up in probate. You can go to court, but again, your money will be tied up until it's gone. Do you understand me?"

"No." She huffs, her face red with anger. "That is not going to happen."

"Really? You're going to go against me." I smirk. "Do you know who I am?"

"A pretty rich boy who had everything handed to him on a silver—Nope, make that a gold platter."

I stand from my chair and step forward until I'm standing beside her, looking down.

"No, princess. That's not who I am. I'm a man you should fear."

"What are you going to do? Have you ever gotten your hands dirty? Have you ever been desperate, wanted for anything . . . ?" She levels me with her stare. One that says she won't back down, not without a fight.

If I didn't hate her, I would probably respect the fuck out of her. Then want to literally fuck her. But this is the hand we were dealt. One where she will be on the permanent end of pain, just like she'd done to my family.

Dad's hack of a lawyer clears his throat.

"May I have a minute with Payton?" he asks.

"No," I respond, making his mouth drop.

"But—"

"I don't have time for this shit. Whatever you have to say, say in here."

He nods at me before gesturing for her to move over to the other side of the room. They think that will give them privacy, but whatever he has to say, I'll hear anyway.

They migrate to the corner of the small office, and I watch with a smile on my face as a very angry Payton places her hands on her waist.

"What?" She scoffs.

"You need to be careful," he tries to whisper. Not well, I might add.

"I don't need to do anything. I'm not scared of a rich trust-fund kid."

"Ms. Hart, please keep it down."

"Why bother? We all know he can hear, so spit it out already. Tell me what's so damn important about this man that I have to listen to this shit."

"It's not about him . . ."

"Stop with the damn riddles."

"His clients, Payton. Do you know who his clients are? If he wanted to, he could have Lorenzo Amanté take you out. Or Cyrus Reed. Do those names ring a bell? Cyrus basically runs the underworld. Should I keep going? Mafia, drugs, arms dealers . . . you do not want to get on this man's bad side. If he wants to just take the money and set you up for murder, he could. The money would be the least of your problems."

That makes Payton shut up.

From where I'm standing, I can clearly see how wide her eyes are. Couple that with her mouth hanging open, and I think she has finally grasped her precarious situation.

I move forward. "Are you done? Because I'm ready to tell her the other stipulations when we get home."

"I—"

"Stop."

With that, I make my way toward the door.

"Wait. Wait. Just . . . I need to speak to Mr. Baker for a minute. Alone," Payton asserts as if I would try to stop her. She can talk all she wants. It won't change anything.

I shrug. I'm done with this anyway. "Go ahead, but know that he can't do anything to change what's about to happen."

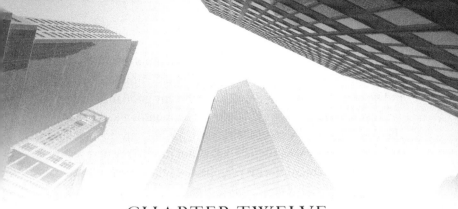

CHAPTER TWELVE

Payton

WHAT. THE. ACTUAL. FUCK. JUST. HAPPENED.
I'm supposed to just follow Trent and move in so he can "monitor" me?

I pinch myself, double-checking this isn't a dream. Or to be completely accurate, a nightmare.

Mr. Baker has the spine of a wilted flower. On its last legs before a snowstorm. He's so useless it truly makes me mad.

"I'm just supposed to go along with all this?" I ask him.

No matter what Trent just said, he must be able to do something to help me. He's a lawyer. The one who probably drafted the will. Do I even believe him about the mafia ties? That excuse sounds completely ridiculous. None of this popped up on Google; wait, would that show up on a basic search? No. It wouldn't.

"Unfortunately, yes," Mr. Baker mumbles before walking to the door and opening it.

He's done with me. I'm not surprised. The man is a weasel.

When I step out of the office, I look at Trent, who has a smug look on his face. He's been enjoying every last second of this whole exchange.

Basically, I have no choice.

He stripped away my autonomy.

There's nothing pretty about it. I won't take it lying down, but for now, I'll move in, recuperate, and map out my options. One thing's for sure—he is about to get a roommate from fucking hell, and he better believe I'm not going to do any goddamn dishes.

If you told me this would happen two months ago, I would've offered to buy you a coffee to sober up. Now, not only do I not have the money to buy you a cup of coffee, but it's also my new reality.

"I'm late," Trent informs me, checking his expensive watch.

The command is clear. Follow him.

I have a sinking feeling it's one in a long list of orders to come, and I don't see a way out of this.

Not without asking Erin for help.

I'm not sure which is the lesser of two evils. My sister is volatile, and her scumbag boyfriend gives me complete hives. I am a hundred and ten percent sure Brad is a criminal. The last time I was there, I witnessed him dealing to teenagers down the block from their apartment. And even without Brad, Erin is convinced Ronald and I shared a sordid relationship.

The very thought of what she implied is sickening.

It absolutely hurts.

The thing is, even if she believed me, I still wouldn't be able to live with her. There are always strings attached to her help. I have too much on my plate to deal with that.

"That's unfortunate for you," I tell Trent. "Sorry, but I'm all out of fucks to give. Maybe you'll find them in the house full of things you stole from me."

"Cute," he deadpans.

"Must be what good ole Ronnie found so special about me."

It's a low blow.

But I don't regret it. They say revenge is throwing piss in a strong wind. If this asshole is picking bones with his late father by making my life a living hell, the least I can do is bite back. And I can bite. Fucking hard. Not in the way men usually like.

There's a reason Ronnie left his money to me. Sure, he should have told me. But he was in jail. It wasn't like he could hit me up without alerting everyone else the money existed. Unlike my sister and Trent, I trust Ronald and need to believe he wanted to make sure I would always be taken care of.

That's the thought that helped me get through the pain of losing him right after his death.

Trent narrows his eyes. He eats up the space between us in three large strides. I'm pressed against the wall, shaking with something I'm shocked to realize isn't fear. It's excitement. His body pressed close to mine. His cologne. His eyes and how they burrow into me. This game we're playing is dangerous. Addictive. I never craved adrenaline until Trent Aldridge, and nothing about this burgeoning addiction is healthy.

"Silly, silly girl," Trent murmurs so low I strain to hear. "Ronald Aldridge was incapable of love, but if he wasn't, you are the last person who would be on the receiving end of it."

I flinch.

I cared for Ronnie deeply, but the more I hear the venom in Trent's voice, the more skeptical I get.

Trent has spewed poison, and it's killing off all the good feelings I have. A part of me, growing larger by the day, questions why the money was left to me. It's obvious why it didn't go to Erin. She'd blow through it faster than a virgin popping his cherry. But me? When he had a wife, a daughter, a son? Could it really be because Ronald thought of me as his daughter?

"He knew the truth would come out," I tell Trent, just to throw him off balance. To even our hand. "After Ronnie died, Erin told me he was planning an appeal on his sentence."

"Let me guess," Trent drawls out, the sarcasm as thick as the humidity. "Ronnie thought by placing his money in your name, it'd sit in limbo until he was released."

Well, yeah.

That was the theory I was running with.

But he made it sound like a stupid idea. As if I had a part in this grander than I was capable of. With all the things I've learned about Ronnie, I don't think he ever intended for me to know about the money. He probably put it in my name solely to hide it until he got out of jail. He probably intended to transfer it to himself after he was released.

But I don't tell Trent this.

That would mean letting him win.

The only thing that seems to dent his ego is the idea that Ronnie loved me as a daughter. The idea to use that to hurt Trent gains speed inside me. It's a horrible thought. Alas, I'm dealing with a horrible person.

I can't let him walk over me like this.

"No," I tell Trent, following him out of the building at breakneck speed. His strides are so long, and he gives no fucks about my inability to keep pace. "It's just a theory, but it makes more sense that he gave it to me because I matter to him. He considered me as his own daughter. Told me so himself."

Trent walks straight to a car parked on the street, ignoring me. I think he's reached his bullshit quota for the day, but I'm not done.

"He'd buy me ice cream, take me textbook shopping, and help me with my homework when I needed special insight."

Trent nods to his driver, sliding past the door the hatted man holds out for him. I didn't peg Trent Aldridge as the type of man who'd relinquish control behind the wheel, but then again, I don't know anything about him. All I know is he's the asshole I'm now living with.

A very rich one, by the looks of this Mercedes.

The driver bows a little, motioning for me to enter after Trent. So much for ladies first. Not quite the gentleman, but I guess I can't expect much from someone hell-bent on making my life insufferable.

"Money can't buy class," I say as soon as my butt touches the leather seat. "Ronnie used to tell me that. Guess I see where he first observed it."

No answer.

I reach forward for the A/C at the same time Trent does. Our fingertips touch, and it feels like I'm being electrocuted.

It's like the anger built with each word from me dissipates, but whatever replaces it is intense. So intense, I cave first, snatching my hand back and cradling it in my lap.

What the hell was that?

The uncertainty of it is almost enough to make me retract my taunts. Almost.

He was turning the A/C toward me, which is the polite thing to do, but it doesn't mean he is a nice guy.

That is the last description I'd use on a man actively trying to make my life a living hell.

I scurry to the furthest edge of the seat, staying as far from Trent as possible. The cabin is small. I can smell him everywhere. His presence, his scent, *him.*

My fingertips feel like they've been singed. I brush them against the seat. Soft leather touches the skin of my palm.

It feels like butter.

This car is officially the nicest car I've ever been in.

A Mercedes Maybach.

I guess whatever he does, he does it well. Judging by his Olympic capabilities at being an asshole, I believe it.

"Nice ride," I mutter.

"It gets me from point A to B." He shrugs, and it may be the most civil conversation we've ever had.

Living with him is gonna be hell. But I'll make sure it's hell for both of us.

"Any car would do that," I volley back, unable to help myself.

"Maybe, but not every car has a back seat that reclines." He points at the button beside me.

"That must come in handy after a long day of work. What is it you do again?" I ask, making simple and easy conversation. If I'm going to be stuck with him, I need to learn to talk to him without wanting to flee.

"Oh, I thought you would know . . . Being Daddy's pet and all."

The insult brushes off my shoulders at this point.

I shrug. "Can't say that I do. Why don't you just tell me? Or does everything have to be so complicated?"

"Just tell you? What would be the fun in that?" He smirks.

That smirk is dangerous.

It's deadly.

What could I do to make him genuinely smile at me? I shouldn't want him to look at me that way.

I turn my attention away from him and stare out the window instead. Anything is better than losing myself.

It sounds cliché.

No man should have any power over me, and he doesn't. Not really. But when he smirks like that, I forget for a second. I forget that he is pure evil incarnate.

I forget he is the reason I have lost everything and that, because of him, I am a pawn in a game I never intended to play.

The car starts to move. It weaves its way through city traffic.

I'm lost in the vision; I'm lost in the sights of the city. It's been a long time since I lived here with my sister.

For the past ten years, I've lived on Long Island twenty minutes outside of the city. Nestled far away from Ronald's web of lies. In hindsight, that seems by intentional design. After all, he'd been the one to suggest Ludlow, insisting on covering tuition after I balked at the price. He even wrote me a letter of recommendation.

Despite the sounds of the honking horns and traffic, it's eerily quiet in this car. I can hear every time Trent taps his hand on his phone, firing off text after text.

I pretend not to notice, but from the corner of my eye, I can see him.

"Like my father, I run a hedge fund."

I was willing to let it go, but apparently, he wants to talk now. On his terms, of course.

"Sweet. A field full of gentle souls," I say sarcastically.

"You asked."

"And you supplied, yet again making me feel underwhelmed," I deadpan.

"Is that how you're going to start this tenure?"

"What do you mean?"

"The attitude. Do you think this is going to work for you? You think it will bode well? I said I would pay for college if you lived with me, but what about all those other expenses?"

"What other expenses?"

"Living."

"What else do I need if I'm in your apartment, asshole?"

"Again, with the asshole thing. Well, you do need to eat every day, right?"

"You wouldn't," I seethe, making a mental note to keep a log of anything that may violate a legal definition for the standard of care.

"Yet you know nothing about me because if you did, you would know I totally would."

I take a few deep, audible breaths, trying desperately to calm the anger bubbling up inside me. "What exactly am I going to have to do to get *living expenses* from you?"

If he says sleep with him or anything sordid at all, I'm out of here. I'd rather be homeless again than be his toy.

"All in good time," he answers cryptically.

It isn't long before we pull into a garage under a building.

We are at his place.

Where Trent Aldridge lives.

Where I am about to live.

The last time I was here, I didn't pay much attention to where I was. I knocked on the door of the address my sister gave me and was let in. Well, I barged in there.

Now, I look at it with fresh eyes. The building looks somewhat like a loft or warehouse and stretches a whole block.

A shiver runs up my spine as we get closer to parking.

I know nothing about this man, and now I'm being forced to stay with him. Where will he make me sleep?

Shit.

A thought pops into my head. I try to shoo it away, but I can't . . .

What if he expects something from me that I am not willing to give?

It feels like a bucket of ice is dumped over my head, and the shivers intensify at the thought.

No.

He wouldn't expect that.

Would he?

Then there is the story he told me about his father. A father who sold his own daughter.

Shit.

What have I gotten myself into? Maybe the apple didn't fall so far from the tree like he previously stated.

Maybe this is all a ruse to get *me*.

I could be in real danger.

I bite down so hard on my lip that I can feel the pinch of pain right before I taste the coppery liquid that leaks into my mouth.

"What do you want from me?" I ask quietly, and he ignores me.

The car pulls to a stop, and then it's shut off. His driver steps out and moves to open the door for me. No point appealing to him for help . . . from his boss.

I step out.

"Come with me," Trent says, breaking through my haze. He starts to walk toward the door that enters the building. I don't move.

"No. First, tell me about your expectations."

He stops, reluctantly. His back is still to me. "For you to shut up and do as I say?"

"No can do."

"Just get upstairs, and we'll talk."

"I'd rather do it here."

"I'd rather not be in this situation." He swivels, pinning me with a look. "And before you embarrass yourself—no, I don't expect any sexual favors from a college kid. Now, get the fuck upstairs."

I follow him inside like a lost doe.

The last time I was here, I didn't notice how big and open the space was.

I just barged into the first door I saw, which, by chance, happened to be exactly where he was. The room, I've come to realize, was his home office. Now, I'm calm enough to look around.

The space has huge high ceilings, white walls, and exposed beams.

Normally, I assume this type of building would probably hold multiple apartments, but I imagine with the endless amount of money he has, he bought them all up and knocked down all the walls.

It's huge.

Artwork decorates the space. Dark black-and-white photos bring contrast. It's beautiful. Void of emotions, but beautiful, nonetheless.

"This way," he says as he leads me down a hallway. "Your room is over here."

"My room?"

"Yes. Your room, Payton." He says my name with pure disdain. As if he hates that I'm here as much as I hate to be here.

Then why am I?

He swings the door open, and my breath hitches.

The room is huge.

Again, all white.

White bed.

White sheets.

White walls.

It's perfect.

No . . . it's sterile.

As if it has never been used before.

I'm almost afraid to walk into the room.

The thought of making it dirty is giving me anxiety already.

No wonder the guy made fun of me when I was lying on the floor.

Besides the fact he's a complete dick, he must also be a clean fanatic.

"As you will soon see, living here doesn't have to be all bad." I roll my eyes. It doesn't matter how beautiful and pristine this place is. It's still a prison. I didn't choose any of this.

"Why am I here? All this BS and you still haven't told me why you are doing this to me."

"Because despite what you say, I don't fucking believe you're innocent in all this. Maybe you didn't know about what happened to Ivy and the Russians, but no way you're ignorant about everything else."

"I didn't—"

"Your word means nothing to me. I'll find out the truth, and until I do, you will live in my house and do as I say." He walks across the room, and his finger points at a door. "Your belongings have already been put in the closet."

"You went through my stuff?" I hiss even though I'm admittedly shocked and pleasantly surprised he didn't throw them out.

"No. I didn't go through your stuff. A member of my staff did." He says this like it's normal for someone else to unpack. It's not. Even when my sister was with Ronald, my life wasn't like this.

"How many people do you have employed here?"

"You will meet them later, and you can count for yourself."

"Why do you have to be such a dick all the time?"

"Because I'm my father's son. And if you knew the real him, my sunny personality wouldn't be such a shock."

"Just get out."

I storm into the room and start to slam the door. But just as it's about to close, Trent steps into the doorframe. "I expect you downstairs in my office in thirty minutes."

"Why?"

"To go over the rest of the rules and stipulations of my house."

"Seriously?"

"Yes. Seriously." With that, he turns on his heel and leaves, slamming the door behind him on his own.

I guess it could be worse. At least I still have a pulse.

It's not a convincing pick-me-up, but it'll have to do. I don't have the energy to pretty-up my situation.

The sound of the slam echoes around me. Which isn't surprising, seeing as this room is barren.

If I'm to live here, I'm going to have to spruce it up.

Add a color or two.

Maybe an area rug to help make it feel warmer.

Like a home.

Home . . .

The word makes my heart lurch.

I miss my home.

I wish I lived with Heather.

If I could tell Trent to fuck off, move in with her, live on her couch, and figure out a way to pay for the tuition without his help, I would.

Maybe I can take out a loan with a bank and use the will to show the bank that I'm good for the money. That's if Trent doesn't blow through all my cash. Knowing him, he would buy that small country just to spite me.

Probably wouldn't work, though.

Plus, I don't want to put Heather out.

She doesn't need to be mixed in with my personal drama.

Now that I'm alone in the room, I take a minute to look around. I open all the cabinets and the closet.

Just as he said, all my clothing and personal belongings are here.

After I sort where everything is, I go into the bathroom attached to my room and freshen up.

I'm thankful I have a bathroom. I can't imagine what I would do if I had to go out into the hallway and see him every time I had to pee.

That would be a nightmare.

With only a few minutes to spare, I find my toothbrush and brush my teeth. Something I haven't been able to do since yesterday.

Sure, I used toothpaste and my fingers at Heather's, but that's not enough.

I wish I had time to shower, but . . .

Actually, I might have time.

As long as I'm very fast.

I spit into the sink and turn to the shower.

My hand opens the glass, and then it's coming to life.

Once I step in, I allow the scalding water to wash away the past few days.

It feels incredible.

Exactly what I need right now.

"I guess it could be worse," I repeat. "At least there's a state-of-the-art shower."

And this time, when I say the positive affirmation, I don't feel totally doomed.

I can do this.

CHAPTER THIRTEEN

Trent

W HEN THE MINUTE HAND OF THE CLOCK HITS THE TIME I allotted and Payton doesn't show, my anger bubbles.

Clearly, her situation hasn't sunk in.

I'll just have to break your will, Miss Hart. Then you will confess all your sins and the part you played in Ivy's kidnapping.

The irritation fades in an instant. I'm looking forward to our game of cat and mouse. I admire her audacity. The fire that lights in her eyes drives me wild. Fucking sue me. I'm an asshole.

I stand, walking to the side of my office with a built-in bookcase. My finger brushes against the spine of a book. *War and Peace.*

I consider my options of punishment to dole out for this infraction. They say the punishment should fit the crime. She stole my time; I'll steal her money. With the book in hand, I sit back down. This time I set a timer on my phone, noting my net worth increases about two grand a minute.

By the time another ten minutes pass and she's out twenty large, I decide to inform her of her predicament.

She's lucky I'm even giving her this solution to her problems.

With the friends I have, I can easily remove all traces of the money, especially now that I have the account number. Before she realizes what I've done, she would be broke.

This—*me as her controller*—is mercy. Jaxson Price would

destroy her identity. Cyrus Reed would ruin her financially, reputationally, and mentally. My other friends and clients? They'd just not bother with the effort and kill her outright.

If she had to pick a ruthless bastard to piss off, she's lucky it's me. She's still breathing. I won't go as far as ending her life. Not my style.

See, Dad. Take notes: Some of us have scruples.

That doesn't mean I'm opposed to introducing a heavy dose of fear into her life.

I stand from my chair, pushing it back. The wood scrapes against the floor.

Another five minutes have passed, and she's out a total of thirty grand at this point. A drop in the water when you consider the twenty-two-million-dollar pot. But if this continues, she'll be bankrupt before she turns twenty-fucking-two.

I am dead set on ruining her day and possibly her life. First, she needs to know the money she has happily spent all these years is blood money.

Would she even care?

I exit my office, walking down the hallway in large strides.

Another minute.

Another two grand out the door.

I continue until I'm in front of her room. I lift my hand to knock but decide against it.

One, this is my house. I don't need to knock to enter my room.

Two, she was supposed to be in my office seventeen minutes ago.

Three, I don't owe her a damn thing.

I fling the door open.

As soon as I do, a scream rings out through the air. My eyes immediately pivot to the entry points, taking inventory of potential threats.

Windows, empty.

Vents, intact.

The amusement is hard to smother, so I don't bother, letting my lips tip up when I realize *I'm* the threat.

Payton is standing in the middle of the room.

Right in front of me.

Mouth open.

Eyes wide.

Then I look down and see why she is screaming.

Her brown locks are pitch-black now. The strands cling to her skin.

Her hair is wet.

My gaze travels farther down her body over her exposed skin. She's standing in front of me in a towel.

It does little to hide her. Although, it's wrapped tightly, glued to her body. Her cleavage spills out of the edge. Little droplets of water caress the swells.

She showered, and I barged in.

For the third time, I note that she's gorgeous.

Three times too many.

"Do you mind?" she hisses at me. "I'm trying to get dressed!"

I lean against the doorframe, kicking one foot in front of the other. "Seeing as you can't seem to bring yourself to show up to our appointment, I can't seem to bring myself to give a fuck about what you're wearing." My eyes lower, one brow lifted. "Or, in this case, *not* wearing."

"Get out!"

"No."

"I can't get dressed if you're in the room." She's clearly angry, and that just makes me want to fuck with her more.

"You don't need to be dressed for what I'm going to tell you."

I let my words hang in the air until I see her scowl deepen, shoulders visibly shaking with rage. She takes a step toward me, remembers her situation, and eases back, tightening the towel around her chest.

"But first . . ." I trail off, lifting my phone and making a show of typing something in it. "You were seventeen minutes late. At two grand a minute, that's thirty-four thousand dollars I'll have to garnish from your inheritance." I tsk, pretending to be saddened by the idea. "It's only fair. But you should know, if you keep this up, there will be no money left to inherit."

"What the fuck!"

She starts for me, reaching for my phone. It brings her body against mine. Her bare thigh slips between my legs as she lunges up for the phone, which I hold above my head. I'm almost a foot taller. She'll never win.

But damn, does she try.

And damn, do I enjoy it.

"You can't do this!" she cries out.

"Who's going to stop me?" I raise a brow, staring down my nose at her. "You?" I laugh. Loud and in her face.

"Two thousand dollars a minute! That's insane." She's seething.

Her eyes shutter before she takes several calming breaths, pushing her chest against mine with each inhale. She moves to step back before realizing her towel has slipped. It puts her in a precarious situation where she's using my body to shield hers from me.

Glare heavy on my face, she reaches between us to adjust her towel. The back of her hand presses against my chest. There's no helping it. There's no helping the fact that I'm hard as a fucking rock, either.

This is not what I had planned when I moved her in here.

Not even close.

If anything, it's an inconvenience I'll have to overcome. Because I have no intention of letting her leave. Not until I get my revenge.

"Are you done with your tantrum?" I ask after she finally steps back. "Because there are more stipulations to cover, and you're eating up quite a bit of my time." I pause. "And *your* money." The way I say "your" implies I think it's anything but.

Payton shakes her head, her eyes narrowing. "No. That's unfair. You said all I had to do was live with—"

"That was for college tuition," I cut her off.

"What do you mean?" Her voice breaks as she speaks.

"There are other incidentals. There are other things you'll need. Do you truly think you're going to live in my house, and I'm going to pay for everything? News flash, princess, I'm not a good person." I level her with my stare. "You're going to have to work for it."

Her mouth drops open, and her eyes are as wide as saucers.

She looks confused and defeated at the same time.

It's a cute look on her.

Does it make me sick that I'm enjoying this?

Probably, but I don't care.

With a twist of her jaw, she recovers. Rather quickly, as I expected her to be in shock a little longer, but nope. Instead, she narrows those big blue eyes and scoffs at me.

"I am not a prostitute," she replies sharply.

I continue to smile, loving the anger, hoping to further piss her off. The way I stalk forward has her on edge. I circle her, watching her stiffen.

"I will not sleep with you to pay for my food," she adds, her nostrils flared.

"Calm yourself. You look like you're about to have a brain aneurysm." I stop behind her, whispering into her ear. "You are the last thing I'd ever want. Unlike my father, you mean nothing to me."

"Then why am I here?"

I continue walking again until I'm standing in front of her, an easy foot away. "You are here because I deem this to be the place that you deserve to be."

"So, I'm here so you can make my life a living hell."

"Ding. Ding. Ding. You finally understand. I could easily give you the inheritance. But I won't." I shrug, making light of her situation, knowing it pisses her off more. "It's not about the money. It's about you."

"What did I ever—"

"I don't have time to listen to you complain, princess," I interrupt. "There are rules to the house that need explaining."

She glares at me. Her head tips down at what she is wearing, or in this case, not wearing. "Can I at least put on clothes?"

"No."

"But you just said—"

"I know what I said, but my time is valuable. I don't have time for you to get dressed." I pause. "Well, at two grand a minute, I suppose it doesn't matter to me how you spend it." I gesture toward her closet. "Go ahead."

She doesn't budge. Her eyes sparkle as if she is playing at something.

"Very well." She smiles.

A coy smile.

What are you up to, Payton?

"Speak," she prods when the silence lingers for too long.

And with that, she drops the towel.

Fuck.

Yep. There she is. Standing in front of me . . . naked.

If that's not bad enough, little droplets of water hug her body.

Lucky bastards.

I allow myself a minute to appreciate the sight.

Might as well enjoy this moment.

I allow my eyes to rake boldly over her body. My gaze drops down from her eyes to her collar, across her breasts, down her navel until I'm almost . . .

"Yes?" Her voice cuts in through my perusal. "What are those rules, Mr. Aldridge?" she asks, her voice low and seductive. This little shit is purposely trying to get a rise out of me.

If she's not careful, she won't like the type of rise she'll get.

I shake my head and realize I have been standing here for lord knows how many seconds, just staring at her.

Well played, princess.

I cough and right myself. Shifting my weight.

"You'll need extra money for necessities. Since you'll be staying here, you will need to take a train or a cab."

"I'm not getting my car back?"

"Negatory."

"What the hell?" Her hands flail in the air, making her tits bounce.

Dammit. Now I'm gawking at her again.

"I need my car, psycho," she follows up.

Looking back up at her face, I watch for a minute before I speak. "Maybe we can negotiate that if I decide you exhibit good behavior."

"Good behavior? I'm not a prisoner, Trent. I haven't committed any crimes, other than breathing, which you cannot seem to stand for some reason."

I'm a sick bastard because my dick hardens at the way she spits out my name with so much venom. It throbs against my pants. If she looks down, she'll see it.

Thankfully, she doesn't.

"Potato, potahto. You say prisoner; I say maid." A grin slices across my face. "Which brings me back to what I was saying. Money. You will help clean—"

"You want me to be your maid?"

"Why not? The more, the merrier."

"You don't need more staff."

"That's not for you to decide."

She swallows. "I don't understand."

"What's there to understand? One of the ladies who cleans my house is taking some time off. You will replace her."

She looks down at the floor and back up.

"I mean, if you don't want to go to school," I continue,

shrugging as if the situation cannot be helped, "I'm sure you can take online courses . . ."

"No. I want to go in person. Fine," she mutters, looking utterly defeated.

It's not as satisfying as I thought it'd be.

"Good." I nod. "With that settled, there are only a few more things."

"There's more?"

"Yes."

She lets out a long-drawn-out sigh. "What else?"

"I need you to prove you deserve this," I tell her matter-of-factly.

She bites her lip. "You lost me."

"I need you to prove that you deserve twenty-two million dollars."

She frowns. "And how exactly will I be doing that when I didn't know I *had* twenty-two million dollars?"

"You need to prove yourself to me. For example, you will need to prove you're smart."

Her eyes roll. "I'm in college."

"Yeah. And that means jack shit to me. Anyone can go to college. That doesn't mean you're smart. I need you to prove you won't squander the money. Prove you are deserving. Going to college and taking classes are only one part of an education. You need to be well-versed in life. Every week, I will expect you to read and study historians and philosophers."

"Um. Hard pass." She shakes her head. "I'm not doing that. I already have a full load with my business classes."

"This isn't up for negotiation. You *will* read what I tell you to read, and you *will* submit a paper on what you learned."

"This is ridiculous. I'm not doing that."

"You know where the door is." I shrug. "Your choice, princess."

There is no decision to be made. She will do exactly what I want. She knows it, and I know it.

I stare down at her, daring her to argue again.

She lets out a large huff. "Fuck, you need to check your cereal. I'm going to spit in every single one of your dishes."

"I'll eat out. The papers you will submit will be your homework."

"Homework? I'm not five."

The look I give her suggests otherwise.

"Yep," I say, popping the *P*. "You know, that thing teachers give to make sure their kids retained information. By completing the assignment, you're proving to me that you are, in fact, serious about your education."

I expect her to refuse, but I am shocked when she says, "Okay."

She never makes things easy. I'll give her that.

"There's more . . ."

"Of course, there is," she mutters under her breath.

"After four weeks of turning in papers, you will then report your findings and knowledge in front of my staff and me. Consider yourself the guest lecturer here. Once a month. For the next eight months."

"No. I shouldn't have to do this weird . . . public speaking thing as well."

"That's fine. Say goodbye to the money." I smile.

"You can't take the money." She raises her brow in challenge.

"Watch me." I move to walk out the door.

"Stop."

I do.

"Fine. I'll do it," she adds. There is no mistaking the bite in her voice. This is the last thing she wants to do.

Good.

I hope she's uncomfortable.

That's the whole fucking point.

Little does she know, I'm just getting started.

"I wouldn't agree yet," I say, turning back to face her. "There's more."

"Just spit it out."

"I will require you to do volunteer work. It's mandatory."

"You win." She throws her hands up in the air again. Clearly defeated and out of objections.

"You will learn, rather quickly, that I always do."

I turn, leaving her standing there, still naked. I walk into my office and slam the door.

What the fuck was I thinking when I decided having her under my roof would be a good idea?

Keep an eye on her.

Pressure her to work for me.

And, I don't fucking know, maybe *not* pressure me into looking at her naked body. Into spiking my desire to throw her on the bed and lick off the water.

Great. Now my dick is trying to break through my pants.

I'm never getting the image of Payton naked out of my mind.

CHAPTER FOURTEEN

Payton

THANKFULLY, TRENT TURNED ON MY PHONE BECAUSE I NEED to call Heather and check-in. But I'm feeling less than thankful when a horde of messages and voicemails turn the device into a vibrator for a solid minute. There are dozens of missed messages from Erin, accompanied by voicemails I'd rather not listen to.

On the plus side, no phone meant no prank calls.

I wonder if those will start up again, or if like I suspected, they were the workings of Trent Aldridge.

Grabbing my phone, I fire off a text to my best friend.

I'm not up for talking today, but I need her to know I'm okay. So I tell her just that.

Me: A ton of shit went down today. I'm okay, but I'll fill you in at school.

Heather: But you ARE okay?

I finger my hair, debating whether to tell the truth before settling with a quick answer that won't worry her.

Me: Yes.

Heather: Does this have anything to do with why you showed up at my house?

Don't get her involved with this, I warn myself.

I would never forgive myself if something happened to Heather.

Me: . . .

Heather: That's not an answer.

Me: I promise I'll talk to you, but I can't get into it yet.

Heather: Okay, just promise if you need me before class, you'll call.

Me: Promise.

The moment I stop typing, the phone rings again.

Erin.

Jeez.

The girl doesn't get a hint.

I sigh, answering because I know it won't stop until I do. "Hello?"

"Where are you?"

In Hell.

"It's a long story."

"I went to your house, and it's boarded up. What did you do?"

It's such an Erin thing to say, so laced with a venomous accusation that I can't help but laugh.

"God, Erin, why do you think it's always me?"

"Things go to shit when you are around," she answers, and I need to bite my tongue to stop myself from unleashing my beast on her.

As much as I want to tell her why that's not true, I'm too tired to fight right now. That's how it is with Erin. The victor in the argument is always the one left standing. Doesn't matter how wrong or right the winner is. It's about the stamina, and Trent Aldridge has just about drained me dry.

"Are you calling just to yell at me? Because I am busy."

I'm not busy at all.

I mean, unless you consider pacing the length of my gilded cage important. At the very least, it's more important than this conversation.

"Busy doing what?"

"If that's all, Erin, I have to go." My thumb hovers over the end button, my patience dwindling by the second. I can't believe I didn't want to live with her because SHE lives with a creeper. Irony at its best and all.

"Wait!" she shouts, and like a glutton for punishment, I do. "Just tell me you didn't get evicted because you did something stupid and lost my money."

"What kind of an idiot do you take me for?" I huff. I'm done with this right now. "I've got to run. I'll call you back."

Then, before she can dig into me some more, I'm hanging up, throwing myself on the bed, and closing my eyes. My day just started, and I'm already exhausted.

Two days have gone by since I've seen Trent. It's now Monday, and I don't know where I stand.

Do I go to school?

Class doesn't start for about five hours.

Fuck it, I'm going.

I spent the weekend in my bedroom and only came out to grab food, sneaking into the kitchen and raiding the stocked fridge as silently as I could.

A part of me expected him to storm in with a mop and bucket and have me cleaning already.

But color me surprised when it's completely radio silent where Trent Aldridge is concerned. There's been nothing from him.

Not a damn thing.

He hasn't even been here at the loft, I don't think.

I should count myself lucky, but instead of feeling relief, I'm on edge. It's a bit frightening. And perhaps by design. You never know with Trent. I'm starting to understand that. The hard way.

It's like I know there's another set of shoes about to drop soon, and now I'm waiting. It makes every second unbearable.

Way too many things are falling from the sky and landing on my head these days. I'm going to have to invest in a steel umbrella.

A knock on my door breaks me from my thoughts.

I'm already dressed and showered, so I get off the edge of the bed where I'm sitting and head over to open it.

A stout woman stands before me, dressed in a crisp pantsuit and pearls. She's wearing an expressionless mask, talking into a headset looped around her earlobe. When she sees me, she pauses and clicks a button on the headset.

"Hello." She nods her head in greeting. It's formal and stiff, like everything else about her. "I'm Gail. I work for Mr. Aldridge. He informed me that you will be helping out around the house while Christina is away."

The name tag pinned to her chest reads Gail Hanley, and below it, her title as house manager. It sinks in. She's treating me like I am her employee. And given my deal with Trent, I guess I am.

"Yes." I nod. "Did you need me now?"

If she finds my arrangement with Trent weird, she doesn't show it. She steps to the side, making way for me. "I do."

At her words, I follow her, closing the door behind me. "I have class in a few hours."

"Yes, Mr. Aldridge has made us aware of your schedule. This morning, it will only be light work. Just helping to tidy the kitchen for Chef."

We round the long hall, which spits us out in the living room. "You call the chef, Chef?"

I feel like I'm in an alternate universe. A universe where there are house managers, private chefs, and maids. A universe . . . in the eighteenth century?

I don't belong.

I don't *want* to belong.

Not even for a second.

Fuck, if someone puts a chastity belt on me, I'm going to scream.

Because I know, without a doubt, the only way Trent Aldridge would let me inside permanently is as someone serving him.

Hard pass.

Gail adjusts a painting as we pass. It didn't even look crooked in the first place, but she shifts it no more than a centimeter at the furthest edge and continues walking as if this is normal for her.

"Mr. Aldridge brought a chef in from a Michelin-star restaurant, and well . . ." She trails off, heeled toes pounding the hardwood floors at a pace nearly impossible for my short legs to keep up with. "Chef likes to be called that."

"Um. Okay."

She laughs, which is a sound I don't expect from her. So, naturally, it's the driest laugh I've ever heard.

"Believe me when I warn you," she says, stopping to blow away nonexistent dust from a nearby surface. "You don't want to piss off Chef."

"Got it. Don't piss off the chef."

My comment is met with a passive expression, and I have a feeling Gail doesn't do emotions. That's okay. Supposing she treats me fairly, we'll have no issues.

Maybe we can even be allies.

"How many people does Mr. Aldridge employ?" A hundred? A million? The entire state of New fucking York?

"There is Chef. Michael, the driver. His personal assistant, Allison. He also has Brandon, who runs security. Christina cleans the place, but she's on leave for personal reasons. There's also me and now you. Seven total. But often more. It really depends on where he is going or who he is working with. Sometimes, Brandon brings in more security, and it gets crowded." Her lips turn down at the end, like the idea of people invading her territory displeases her.

"Why does one man need seven employees?" I mumble under

my breath, and the moment I do, I realize that she could probably hear me. Meh, good thing I don't care.

We were getting off on the right foot. I would hate to ruin that. Maybe Gail can be a good person to have on my side in this house.

Sure enough, her response is fast—and in defense of her boss. "He's a very busy man, and he works with many important people."

"Sorry. That was rude of me to ask."

"It's okay," she says in a tone that implies it isn't. "I'm sure this is quite the change. I'm not exactly certain what landed you in this position but know that Mr. Aldridge is usually a fair man."

Fair.

My brows shoot upward.

I take what I said before back. Gail will never be my ally. Not with the way she waxes poetic about the devil that is Trent Aldridge. I want to roll my eyes at her, but I know that will not do me any favors with someone who is, technically, my superior.

I have to at least try to be friendly.

Also, it's not her fault. Truly, she probably doesn't know what he's done to me. I'm sure to the rest of his staff, he's wonderful. Not a manipulative ass who canceled my present and is holding my future hostage.

I follow Gail into the kitchen. The place is massive, like everything Trent owns and does. It's made of dark, earthy materials. Surprisingly welcoming. The ranges are top-of-the-line. All eight of the burners are in pristine condition. Every technological advancement I can think of seems to be here, from the newest blenders to a cutting-edge scale.

A set of shiny fridges line the opposite wall. An actual wall of machines. I've never met anyone who owned more than a single fridge.

One man.

Three fridges.

Maybe that's where he hides all the bodies.

I walk the row, realizing one of them is a freezer, another a fridge for food, and the final one covered with a clear glass door. I peer inside. Rows of drinks cover every space. Bottled water, seltzer, and pricey liquor that hammers in the fact that he doesn't need my inheritance at all.

He just wants revenge.

Revenge for something I had nothing to do with.

I sigh, turning back to the rest of the kitchen. From what I can tell, it's fairly clean, and I'm thankful it won't be hard work.

That's what I think until I round the island and find myself standing in front of the sink.

"Jeez," I say before I can stop myself.

"Chef uses a lot of dishes."

"You think?" How is this dude not five hundred pounds?

"This is from this morning's light breakfast."

Just breakfast? All this from one meal?

"How many meals a day does Chef cook?"

"Breakfast and dinner. Mr. Aldridge spends his lunch in the office, where I assume his assistant purchases his meals on his behalf."

Two meals a day.

A *light* breakfast, she said.

Fuck my life. I found the cure for world hunger, and it's in this guy's kitchen.

The sink must contain over ten pots and pans, and that doesn't even count spatulas, utensils, plates, and bowls.

Gail opens and closes cabinets, showing me where the cleaning gear is. "Let me preface your tenure by saying, Chef doesn't want anything in the dishwasher."

Of course, he doesn't. I'm sure this lady already must think I'm trash that Trent picked up on the street.

She certainly would balk at the fact that I'm doing this all for money.

Not just any money . . .

A twenty-two-million-dollar inheritance.

The truth is, I probably could fight him.

Over the past few days, unbeknownst to Trent, I did my research. I had no intention of taking this man's threats.

But it didn't take me long to find out his threats were not lies. He was connected. Very connected.

Not only did he rub elbows with Manhattan's elite, as evidenced by paparazzi photos, but he also ran in dangerous circles. With Cyrus Reed, the man who accompanied Trent's sister at the will reading.

That's the part that freaks me out.

The rumors of who his clients are.

Arms dealers.

Mafia.

Drug dealers.

Who is Trent Aldridge? The better question is, if he thinks his dad was the devil despite his association with men who legitimately are, then Ronald must have really been awful.

That's if I can take Trent's word on it. I never saw that side of Ronald, but what I have learned throughout my life is that everyone has a devil in them. Even my sister. So regardless of my feelings on Trent, I'll take his word for it.

Gail moves to leave, stopping just short of where the kitchen feeds into the open plan living room. "There's a schedule in the drawer to your left, which includes when you'll need to descale the appliances, instructions on how to care for specific items like the cast-iron skillet, and a list of Chef's things you are never to touch, the most important of which are his knives."

It sinks in that I'm in over my head. I've never descaled an appliance, I thought cast-iron skillets just get washed normally like everything else, and I don't even want to know what will happen if I touch Chef's knives.

With that parting warning, Gail leaves. I roll up my sleeves and start to wash each dish, aware I don't have long to finish this and prepare to leave for class. The man must have had a banquet.

It looks like fresh berries, yogurt, a homemade citrus sauce, granola, and something else that couldn't have required this many dirty dishes. Maybe fresh-pressed juices, too.

This man is so high maintenance he probably only dates super-models with a Ph.D. in dealing with bullshit.

What would he have thought if he saw my sister and me before his father pulled us out of the hovel and set us up in the lap of luxury?

When we were moving from place to place.

Squatting at Erin's numerous boyfriends' houses.

Or better yet, those weeks we lived in her car, which wouldn't run even if we had the money for gas.

If he thinks I can't handle a few dishes, he has another thing coming.

Trent Aldridge has no idea the life I have lived.

In comparison to the hell I have been through, his Michelin-star chef's dirty dishes are a slice of pie from heaven.

Whatever he throws at me, I'm ready.

CHAPTER FIFTEEN

Trent

"WHAT ARE YOU DOING?" CYRUS ASKS AS HE STROLLS INTO my office.

I'm surprised to see him here. Usually, he doesn't grace me with his presence. Normally, in typical Cyrus fashion, he orders me to his compound in Connecticut.

But not today.

Nope, here he is, striding into my space like he owns the place.

As per usual, a scowl has settled on his face.

The man never smiles. He always looks like he's plotting someone's murder.

As long as it's not mine, I'm cool.

"Making you money," I reply, not looking up at him from my computer. In reality, there's a game of online poker in front of me. I'm up several thousand.

"No, idiot." He lounges on the luxe leather chair on the opposite side of my desk, legs kicked up beside my nameplate like he owns the joint. "I know you're making money. A shit ton, by my calculations, and I'm thankful for that. What I mean is, what are you doing with that girl?" He snaps his fingers. "Paula."

The way he says "that girl" rubs me the wrong way. She's mine to play with.

Fuck.

I'm territorial.

I can't even stand her.

But if you asked me at gunpoint, maybe I'd admit that her in a towel is now my new favorite memory. That's neither here nor there. The truth is, I need to get over my weird obsession with her.

"It's Payton," I correct casually.

He snorts, picking up a metal Rubik's cube off my desk. None of the fifty-four squares share the same shade. There is no way of winning. But knowing Cyrus, he'd find a way.

"Are you sure it's not Phoebe?" he quips.

I shrug. "Might be Penelope."

It's a striking image to see Cyrus Reed here in all his glory. It's striking that this building—my building—exists at all.

It's been a long road coming.

My father left me with nothing but the clothes on my back and the desire to be successful. Yes, maybe I didn't set out to be the owner of the most ruthless hedge fund in New York City, but I fully enjoy the position I hold.

"I don't know why you keep this thing," he says, tossing it in the air and catching it just before it slips past him.

If his desired effect is to have me on edge, it's working. I'm not afraid of him. He's my brother-in-law. He wouldn't hurt me. But nothing about the man would make anyone relax. I don't know how Ivy does it.

"It's a reminder."

I don't elaborate.

He toys with the cube. It occurs to me that revenge is technically his right as well. Payton will be taking money that, in fact, should be his by proxy. He is married to my sister. Ivy's third of the multimillion-dollar estate is half his, entitling him to a little under four mil.

To us, that kind of money is pocket change. Him more so than me.

Sure, I'm worth a lot.

But Cyrus is in a whole other league.

I'm no billionaire. Pretty damn close, but not there yet . . .

After my next investment, I could be, though.

Which reminds me . . . I have more pressing matters than spending my time thinking about the money Payton is soon to inherit.

I need to talk with Cyrus about an investment I want to make. Using funds he and a few other clients are part of.

"Of?" he asks, tossing the cube back into the bowl, bored with it.

"Of life."

"The cube is unbeatable." He lifts his brow.

"It's supposed to be."

"Didn't take you for a loser, Aldridge."

"I am the cube in this situation, Reed." I mimic his flippant tone. "Life is the player."

A satisfied grin spreads across his face. He looks like a wolf, only more deadly. "Or, in this case, Priscilla."

His wanting to talk about Payton right now and asking these types of questions is grating on my nerves. We need to talk about work.

Not girls.

Sure. That's the reason you're annoyed.

It's not because thinking of Payton right now is a bad idea. Nor the fact that I'm fighting a very strong desire to see her naked again. The memory of those perfect tits popping up in my head every few minutes isn't doing me any favors.

Neither is the prospect of hate-fucking her all over the house. The idea holds great promise.

I shouldn't take it off the table just yet. Seduce her. Dump her. Leave her wanting. It's more appealing than it should be.

However, with her spine, I doubt she would be game for that. More like she will one hundred percent be against it. I'd have a better shot at convincing her that Santa Claus is real, and I play golf with him every Sunday.

Not happening.

I finish the online poker game, exiting out of the tab without enjoying the victory. "You're not here to talk about her."

"Maybe I am," he says, shrugging. "Ever think about that? Ivy wants answers."

"Then tell my sister to call me herself."

"She's been busy." *Lame excuse.*

"I'm busy, too, yet I would find time for her if I had questions."

"Give her a break. This is hard for her, too. Maybe harder." The rough edge to his tone offers no leeway. It's an argument I won't be winning, nor do I want to.

I exhale. "You're right."

We are both quiet in thought for a minute before Cyrus speaks.

"I hear you moved that girl in. Petunia."

"Petunia? Couldn't come up with something better?"

"Your mother would like it."

It comes off as a "yo mama" joke, but it's not. He's absolutely serious and so fucking right. Mom's thing is gardening. So is Ivy's, for that matter. Fitting, considering Mom named her after a flower and me, the Latin word for gushing waters.

Growing up, Mom would cement into us the fact that, like a flower and water, I need Ivy to see beauty in life, and Ivy needs me to grow. She failed to mention that we needed to depend on one another because our dad was destined to utterly and spectacularly fail us.

"My mother also thought it'd be a good thing to name Ivy after her favorite flower. Morning Glory. Could you imagine what that'd be like in school?" I shake my head, snorting. "Dad convinced her to go with Ivy, and that's about his only useful contribution to our lives."

"Saved you a bunch of fistfights while Ivy went through grade school," Cyrus points out.

"Yup."

"Then again, you could've used them. You fight like shit."

I hurl a pad of sticky notes at him, which he dodges easily. "Fuck off, Reed."

"Nice try, Aldridge." He settles in the chair, feet still kicked up. "Want to talk about the girl?"

"We aren't women, Cyrus. I appreciate your concern, but enough of this pussy pillow talk shit."

"Fine, then let's talk money." He straightens, lowering his feet, all business now. "Tobias is on my ass. He wants to know how much he's got."

"I'll get him the figures this week."

"He wants the figures now." His voice is calm and steady as if he's not commanding me to do something, but there's a threat beneath it all.

There is always a threat with Cyrus Reed.

If I were anyone else, I might fidget under his weighted stare. "What's the rush?"

"I think he's done," Cyrus declares, and I swear, you could hear a pin drop. "I think he's finishing the remaining shipments he's got en route, and then he wants out."

I lean forward against my desk. "Really?"

"Not sure. He was on the cryptic side. Per usual. But yeah, he wants to know how much money he's got. Think he's trying to see if it's enough to retire." He shakes his head. He knows as well as I do, there is no real retiring from this business.

"He's worth over seven hundred million. How much more does he need?" I grin.

Greedy bastard.

"Enough to never have to work again *and* afford his security."

No truer words have ever been spoken because that's the truth.

It doesn't matter if we are legit or out. We all will need security for the rest of our lives.

We have made too much money off the backs of others.

We have ruined and screwed too many bad men.

Men worse than us were sunk below for our rise to the top.

So, even though most of my clients are already semi-retired from whatever they did to become so powerful, there will always be a mark on their backs.

You don't rule the underworld, leave, and suddenly go back to living a regular charmed life with a white picket fence and a golden retriever more accustomed to greeting the mailman than biting him.

We all still have one foot in the door.

Legit or not.

Well, at least they do.

Me, I'm still all in.

I still work with men who run the mob, drug empires, etc.

And because of that, I need ways to make them money. Sometimes, it's just a way to clean the dirt from it. Other times, it serves a bigger purpose, and I need to find riskier investments that pay more.

Take my latest scheme.

I am about to short Torenzo Corp, a stock we all have been priming for the kill.

Due to a certain health code violation about to become public record, the stock will plummet, and we're set to make a huge fortune.

The assholes who own it won't know what hit them.

It's going to be fucking fantastic.

The best part is, Lorenzo will get his revenge, and in the meantime, until he does, my clients will earn a windfall.

Now, we just got to sit back and wait for the article I carefully placed to hit social media.

"I anticipate, by the end of the day, with the amount Tobias has in, he will be worth nine hundred million. Is that enough for him to retire?"

"Make him a billionaire, and I'm sure the answer will be yes." His voice is serious, but I still let out a chuckle.

These bastards and their money.

I'm not one to talk, but fuck. I would be happy with that gain.

Since Tobias came onboard, I have gotten him a return on his investment north of two hundred percent.

Again . . . *Greedy bastards.*

"You're a tough man to please, Cyrus."

"Good thing you're on my good side. Imagine how hard I am to please if I hate your ass."

"I'm not one hundred percent sure you don't."

"I tolerate you, at best."

Say what you want, but I know Cyrus considers me a brother, and not just because technically he is now.

We've gone to battle together. You don't live through the shit we have and not come out caring.

Regardless of how corrupt and ruthless you are.

The man is family, with or without my sister.

"When do you think the article will go viral?" he asks.

I lift my hand and run it over my jaw. "If I had to harbor a guess, within the hour."

"Paul is going to be pissed." He chuckles.

"Pissed is an understatement. His one chance at legitimacy is a complete joke. No one wants his damn sauce and taking it public was a dumb move. The second the story leaks about what is in the sauce, he will wish he never fucked with Lorenzo."

Lorenzo is a fairly new client for me. He took over the mob after another client of mine, the former mafia head Matteo Amanté, stepped down.

Paul made a play at him when he first took over and tried to ruin him before he even started, but that's a whole other story. One I don't even know the half of. Probably won't ever either.

Not my fucking problem.

But it is my solution to find.

Matteo came to me with the information that Paul planned on taking his family's business public.

With the help of a few friends, his product will be dragged through the mud.

A thought that makes me smile.

"You look way too happy."

"Just thinking of all the money I am about to make."

"There is more to life than money, Trent."

"Says the banker."

He shrugs.

I laugh.

Family, money, and revenge.

That is all I care about.

Nothing more.

CHAPTER SIXTEEN

Payton

I'M BACK IN THE SAME CLASSROOM WHERE ALL OF THIS STARTED. Heather isn't here yet, but as soon as my butt makes contact with my usual chair, I hear her speak from behind me. "You're alive after a weekend with Mr. McHottie."

"Barely," I admit on a sigh, turning over my shoulder to face her. "And don't rule out my murdering him, either. I'm keeping all the options on the table right now."

"So, you really were with him! What happened?" Her nose is scrunched as she moves to take the seat next to me.

"Basically, in a nutshell, he's blackmailing me."

She lifts her hand, offering me the half-drunk coffee in it. "White chocolate drizzled mocha latte. You need this more than I do. Now tell me what you mean. You're joking, right? He's not really blackmailing you, right?"

"No, not really. More like extortion."

Her mouth hangs open.

"Close your mouth, or you'll catch a fly," I say, laughing. "The truth is, he's actually bartering with me."

I think.

I'm not absolutely sure why he wants me under his roof, but I'm convinced it's a power play. Some way to drive me so insane, so I willingly want to give up on the twenty-two mil.

I've thought about it since I moved in. It's a shit ton of money, but his building itself is worth way more. He doesn't need it. His family doesn't need it. He wants me under his thumb, miserable, the only relic of his father wilted because of Trent's power.

I won't give him the satisfaction.

"It's your money." Heather sounds appalled on my behalf. It gives me a small measure of comfort. At least one person is on my side. "How is he even able to do this? We need to call a lawyer. This isn't legal."

"Well, technically, it's not my money until my twenty-second birthday."

"Not the point. He can't do this to you. I'm sure—"

"It's fine. I don't want to go to court. I just want to live through this and move on. Plus, I get to live in his bougie-ass house while finishing school. He thinks he's going to break me, but the way I see it, I'm winning."

"You got this. It's not too far away. What is it, like, eight more months?"

"Give or take." Bitterness is laced in my voice.

Dealing with Trent is hell, but I can't tell her that. It would lead to her worrying, and I'm worried enough for the both of us.

She nudges my shoulder, patting my hand. "So, you just have to hold out a bit longer."

"It feels like an eternity. I keep telling myself it will all be worth it."

"Hell yeah, it will be."

"I just don't know how I can do this." I shake my head, lost in the absurdity of his stipulations. "Living with him, the maid gig, going to college, and the extra work he's making me do. Add volunteering to the mix, and I'm fucked."

Heather's gaze becomes intense, and her mouth dips into a frown.

"Hold up. Did you say maid gig?"

"That's the only part you got?"

"Pretty much." Her hand squeezes mine so tight it turns white. "Oh, and what the hell do you mean *you are living with him now*?"

"Shh! Keep it down," I whisper-shout, paranoid someone's listening in. The last thing I need is rumors around our small campus. "I mean exactly what I said. Apparently, for him to pay for my school, I must live with him. Oh, and be his maid."

"Um." She nibbles on her lip. "That's really kind of creepy."

"You think?" I roll my eyes. "Brad has nothing on this dude."

"Do you think he's doing this to get in your pants?"

Her expression has changed from shock to something else. I can't put my finger on what, though. Curiosity?

"If so, he's doing a shitty job at it. Apparently, he doesn't find me pretty."

"So, you weren't handed a sexy French maid costume?"

"Heather. Come on. Like I said, he's not attracted to me. Although, I'm pretty sure he's lying." I giggle.

"Why do you think that?"

"I dropped my towel in front of him."

Cue the wide eyes.

Cue the open mouth.

Cue the gasp.

"Oh my God, you hooker." She leans into my side, and I just know she's biting back a squeal. "Details."

"No details. I was just trying to fuck with him the way he fucks with me. Prove he isn't so robotic and controlled as he thinks he is."

Heather looks at me like I'm a reality show she can't get enough of. "And—"

"And he definitely was affected. Whether or not it was in lust or disgust is the question."

If I'm honest, he stared at me like I'm a buttery steak he knows he shouldn't eat but can't wait to sink his teeth into. My heart throttles at the memory. Those damn eyes and smirk. Suddenly, it's hot in the classroom.

"Lust, obviously. Have you seen yourself?" Heather groans dramatically, making the shape of an hourglass with her hands, and fans herself.

I shrug. "Not to him. He is cold as ice."

"You would be hot to anyone, girl. The man is full of shit."

"He is that, for sure. He may think I'm hot, but he also thinks I'm trash. His pretentious ass wouldn't touch me with his maids' double-layered gloves."

"Your gloves," she corrects with a disbelieving shake of the head.

"I'm one of many."

"Damn. How rich is he?"

"Rich enough, he shouldn't care about my inheritance."

She lifts a brow. "Then why does he?"

"Good question." I look down at my hands and back at my friend. "It's weird that he wants me close. He says he wants to drive me insane. But something tells me it's more than that."

"Do you think he's trying to nullify the will?"

My upper teeth bite down on my lower lip. "A part of me does. There is no question he resents his father and resents me for being important to him. But the thing is, he's sketchy AF. He's crooked. If he wanted to steal my money, he could."

"Maybe it's really about making you live with him so he can see what will hurt you most, then he's going to strike."

I nod in agreement.

"I also think this has to do with what happened to his family. He holds me responsible for some reason."

"Crazy, since he doesn't even know you. Otherwise, he'd realize what a great person you are."

"You're obligated to say that. You're my friend." I'm smiling, but it fades as soon as my mind drifts back to Trent. "I can't even pretend to understand the motive. Nor do I want to. All I want to do is survive. If I clean some dishes, that's okay. I just can't let him ever have ammunition on me. That would be disastrous."

"Keep him away from your sister."

"Understatement of the year. Erin is likely to hit on him."

"I'm surprised she hasn't."

We both start laughing. Not that my sister is particularly funny, but when someone is this way, you just gotta laugh it off.

"She's not that bad."

"She's not good either."

Erin is a conundrum. There were moments right after our parents died that she was caring, but that version of my sister faded fast. Probably the moment she realized how hard it actually was going to be to raise me alone.

She went from being my sister to being someone I no longer knew. That and the biggest narcissist on earth.

It all depends on her mood.

Her ups and her downs.

Unfortunately, that mood is often dependent on her finances and whether she has a man in her life.

Right now, she's a loose wire.

Sure, she has someone, but I can't be sure about her finances.

I'm not sure how Ronald set her up.

If he gave her money before he went away.

It isn't my business to ask.

I'm trying to protect myself.

Now, I'm just trying to get as far away from everything, including Trent, as possible.

Eight months.

You can do anything for eight months.

"Listen," Heather says, turning to face me so she knows she has my attention. "Do what you have to do. Keep your eyes open. Don't ever let your guard down. Be careful and bide your time."

"I will."

"And know I am always here for you. Always."

"Thanks, I appreciate it."

"Come on. If we don't stop talking, we will never pass this

class. Especially after what happened last time you were here, you don't want to draw any more attention to yourself."

She's right.

Everything she said is true.

I can get through anything. I have already been through so much. I can handle a rich prick like Trent.

I just need to keep my wits about me.

Not pay attention to him.

Stay far away from him.

And certainly not allow myself to even look at him.

Because that's one thing I didn't tell her.

I might have told her how I stripped bare for him, but I didn't mention that a part of me wanted him to look. I wanted to get a rise out of him, and a small part, a part I don't want to acknowledge, wanted to see the hate in his eyes replaced by lust. And for the briefest moment, I got my wish.

CHAPTER SEVENTEEN

Payton

I HATE THAT I DUTIFULLY CAME BACK HERE.

I hate that I'm playing this game.

I hate that whenever I'm here, I feel as if he's won.

As if he owns me.

Put a smile on your face. Pretend to be happy.

It's hard to pretend I'm not bothered by Trent. The alternative, however, is letting him win. So, as I walk through the barren hall, I think of a time before. Before I lost my smile. Before the year I turned ten, when my sister moved us into yet another mansion. Before I met the boyfriend, Tony, who owned it. Before I realized he was beyond scary.

Okay, way to not think of depressing shit, Payton.

I shake my head and brush away my memories.

No place for them—here, now, or ever.

"You're late." I hear from behind me.

Turning, I see Trent standing at the other side of the hall.

He starts to walk toward me until we are inches apart.

I didn't expect him here. Doesn't he work?

I certainly didn't expect him to be dressed in casual clothes.

It's four thirty on a workday.

Yet here he is, standing in gym shorts and a T-shirt.

I take him in.

I might not be able to see his chest, but I don't need to in order to know his body is insane.

I can see that he is lean but cut, even with the shirt on.

Look away.

Don't allow him to catch you staring.

I lift my gaze from his chest, and of course, my perusal didn't go unnoticed.

"Enjoying the view?"

"Nope. Don't bank on making a dime on starring in postcards, honey," I fire back.

"The lady doth protest too much." *Jeez, what's up with everyone and Shakespeare.*

First Heather, now him. Is this some cosmic joke implying that my life is a tragedy?

"I wish your vocabulary matched your manners, Aldridge."

"You have drool on your mouth."

I almost lift my hand to swipe at my jaw. Almost. But thank God, I don't. I would never hear the end of it if I did.

"What do you want?" I ask.

"Is that any way to talk to me, your generous benefactor?"

I stand quietly.

Generous, my ass. The money isn't even his.

Trent continues, "I'm here to inform you that your first assignment is approaching. The books are in my library. On the desk. Remember, you will be telling the staff and me everything valuable you have learned from the stack of books in one month."

Stack?

As in multiple?

Dread builds in my stomach. I don't let him see it, pretending to be unaffected by his tyrant behavior.

"Thanks! Got it," I say in an overly sunshiny manner, turning away from him, bound for my room.

"I'm not finished with you." His voice doesn't raise, yet it manages to boom through the hallway.

I stop in my tracks. Afraid of what he will say next. Afraid of whatever way he's found to torture me this time.

"You need to clean my gym," he demands.

"Anything else, *sir*?" I spit out.

He grins, and again, I feel a pang of excitement when I can make him do that.

"Don't be late tomorrow."

"Why?"

"You're not to ask questions, Payton. You're to listen. Do you understand?" He speaks to me as if I'm a child.

I'm pissed off. So pissed off, it's hard to focus.

I nod, not trusting myself with words, but that's apparently not good enough.

His right eyebrow lifts. "Words."

"Yes," I bite out slowly, as sarcastically as possible.

"Yes, what?"

"Yes, I understand." My mouth is tight enough to make the words come out in a rigid tone that barely escapes the barrier of my teeth.

"That will do. Even though I did enjoy that last *sir* you used. I expect you not to be late tomorrow. I know you spent time with your friend today after class ended."

"How do you know that?"

"Your phone."

"My phone . . . ?"

The most genuine smile I've ever seen on him graces his face. Of course, it's at my expense. "When I turned the phone back on, I installed a Find My Phone app."

"You tracked me?"

"Are you surprised?"

My face must reflect horror because he laughs, and it makes me angrier.

I throw my hands in the air. "Are you insane?"

"Probably certifiable, but that's your problem, not mine."

"You're tracking me, asshole?"

"We've established this already." He gives me a look that suggests I am the biggest idiot on earth.

If he were a preteen, I would have expected him to roll his eyes at me.

But lucky for me, he's a grown-ass man because instead of dragging this conversation out any longer, he walks past where I'm standing and motions for me to follow him. Then I'm being led down another hallway and a hidden set of stairs.

How large is this place?

On the bottom level, a full gym covers an open floor plan. Boxing ring and all.

"Clean all the towels." The command rolls off his tongue, so easy for him.

He's getting used to ordering me around.

A part of me dares to challenge him, but I know it won't be any use. It'll only make things worse.

"Okay."

Translation: Screw you, jackass.

"And all the surfaces need to be wiped down."

With my spit? Don't mind if I do.

"Got it."

"Sweep, vacuum, mop, then hand clean the floors. I'm a fan of the four-step method."

Are you? I'm sure you've never had to clean anything a day in your life.

"Sure thing, boss."

My flippant tone must grate his nerves because there's the slightest shift of his hands. A reflex. As if he's holding himself back from clenching them. It makes me smile, and as I expected, his orders become worse.

"Christina uses non-toxic ingredients in her cleaning solutions, but I think I'm sick of lemon lately."

My cheeks hurt from smiling. "I'll be sure to buy a different scent."

Right after I dig your grave and bury you in it.

"No," he corrects, matching my smile with his own, and we must look ridiculous, grinning at each other like all is merry while venom seeps out of our eyes. "You'll have to *make* a different scent."

"Any preferences?"

Not sure you'll be able to smell it after I greet your nose with my fist.

"Lemongrass."

Is he serious? Lemon and lemongrass both smell like lemons. And he knows it. He may be a psycho, but he sure can smell.

But he's not done.

"You'll have to walk to the store to buy it. Chef doesn't like anyone touching his herbs." That smile hasn't slipped from his face. "Gail will hand you a few quarters to purchase it. I know your financial situation is tight."

It's official. If I don't get out of here fast, the only thing I'll be cleaning off these floors is a dead body.

He must know it, too, because he's already heading for the door. "Don't take too long," he calls over his shoulder. "I still need to go over tomorrow's schedule."

"Then you better stop talking and let me work." The bite is there, and I know I must take a breath and calm down. Going off on him won't be good for me.

He pauses at the edge of the staircase. "Always with the smart mouth."

"Better smart than stupid."

Yep. So much for listening to my own advice.

"It will get you in trouble someday."

"It already has. Nothing I can't live through again." The words leave my mouth before I can stop them, and I realize my mistake.

I gave him a glimpse into me.

I dropped a damn breadcrumb into my past that I never should have. Hopefully, he didn't realize what I said. Maybe he won't start digging around to understand.

Because that was a tiny thread of information. But if he picks at that thread long enough, it's sure to unravel.

I can't have that.

Trent Aldridge can't know my past.

He can't know anything I have done or had to put up with before.

If I ever want to get far away and start fresh, I need Ronald's money.

It's my only way to escape the demons that still haunt me.

CHAPTER EIGHTEEN

Trent

A LESS OBSERVANT MAN MIGHT HAVE MISSED IT.
Might have been too busy staring at her. The fiery woman as she barked back at me. The way her chest rose and fell with each restrained breath.

But I am not that man.

I miss nothing. I see everything.

And I certainly heard what she said.

She dropped a piece of the puzzle, and if she isn't careful, I will collect all the pieces and use them to ruin her.

I latch onto the clue like a detective, ready to unravel it, no matter how long it takes. And it will take a bit of time. The statement wasn't clear. It didn't point me in any particular direction.

So, her mouth got her into trouble once before.

Interesting.

In the meantime, I'm enjoying toying with her more than I'd like to admit.

Payton Hart is easily angered. Her cheeks flush red when she's upset. It quickly spreads down her chest.

Yes. I noticed that. Not something I'm proud of. To be fair, it's like I said . . . I do notice everything.

Gail greets me at the top of the stairs with her tablet in hand.

I plucked her from a top-tier service specializing in house management for military officials.

On the plus side, she cleared rigorous background checks with flying colors, knows how to keep a secret, and gets shit done without judgment. On the flip side, she possesses the humor of a five-star general preparing for battle.

"Mr. Aldridge."

"Do you have a report for me?"

She hands the tablet to me, watching as I scroll through the bullet-point write-up she prepared for me. "Ms. Hart spends most of her time in her room."

"And when you assign her the house duties?"

"She does them without complaint."

There's no emotion to Gail's tone. If there's any consolation to having a militant robot as a house manager, it's the fact that she is at no risk of befriending Payton. I think Gail would rather endure waterboarding than befriend anyone, let alone Payton Hart.

I hand the tablet back to Gail. "Does she eat?"

"I have Chef make her healthy meals and leave them in glass containers in the fridge, as you instructed."

"She has no idea they were made specifically for her?"

For the record, I'm not feeding her good shit out of the kindness of my heart. There is no kindness inside me. I'm an asshole. There's no prettying that up. But I'm not a dumb asshole. If this ends up going to court, preventing her from eating would be a nail in my coffin.

Her meals are well-documented, along with the fact that I ordered my chef to make fancy-ass meals specifically for her. Not my problem that he leaves them in containers, and she assumes they're leftovers.

I've never accused her of being smart.

"None whatsoever," Gail confirms. "She's under the impression the meals are leftovers, though I suspect she tries not to get caught eating them. She'll take a spoonful from each container so no one notices. The cameras inside the fridge and in the kitchen catch her each time."

"Perfect."

I dismiss Gail and head up the stairs, returning to my room. I can't wait until Payton is done cleaning so I can tell her our plans tomorrow. That's when I will find out the details I need to strip her of her inheritance.

Between commuting. School. Extra assignments. Cleaning.

And the next part . . .

Volunteering.

This girl will be hanging on by a thread.

The thread of that little towel she dropped.

I head straight to the bathroom and turn the shower on.

When I strip off my clothes, I see that I'm fucking hard.

Funny how that little vixen makes me hard. I'd be lying if I said she isn't hot.

She is.

But that's not what gets my dick like this.

Nope.

It's her fire.

It does it for me.

And those tits aren't bad either.

And now I'm back to thinking of those perfect tits.

I step under the scalding water. I'll need cold water to settle this, but my muscles are tense from the workout and the day in general.

Since it's not going to calm on its own, I fist my cock and start to work myself.

In my head, I try to imagine anyone but her.

And I fail miserably.

Instead, I picture her in my gym, cleaning my sweat from the ropes of the ring.

She's bent over. Her ass is on full display.

All it would take is one flip of my hand to expose her under the skirt she's wearing, pull over her thong, and sink into her willing warmth.

My hand moves faster.

I think of the way I would thrust inside her tight pussy.

In and out.

Reach forward and grab those perfectly round breasts.

Squeeze until she's coming all over my cock.

That's all it takes before I feel myself erupt in my hand.

After I'm fully drained, I reach for the soap and wash away all the memories of what I just did.

Better to fuck my hand than her. Either way, I'm going to need to call an old hookup because having this woman in my house is too tempting, despite the hatred I feel for her.

I spend the rest of the shower trying to think of everything and anything but her.

The news launched.

It went viral, too.

Rat droppings and E. coli in a tomato sauce are not good for business.

We made a killing when the stock plummeted.

Enough money that everyone can retire. Although I doubt anyone will. My friends, my colleagues, my clients, and who am I kidding, myself, love money too much.

Cyrus wasn't wrong. There's a good chance that Paul will realize it was us and come after our group. He's dangerous enough to make the threat real. It's a calculated risk, one that paid off, but still a risk.

All the stocks that I handle are set up, so the chance of him figuring it out is minor. All the accounts I used are shell companies, which are then rerouted through so many different IP addresses, so many different countries, and so many different banks that it would take a real fucking genius to figure it out.

And there's only one Jaxson Price.

Good thing the jackass works on our side.

But I'm still cautious. I have a meeting with Brandon later to discuss ramping up my security. Maybe even putting an extra guard on Payton.

I run the shampoo through my hair and wash it out. When I'm done, I shut off the water and grab a towel. Hopefully, she's done by now, and I can tell her the rest of my plan.

Once dressed, I head out of my room and down the hall.

Time to see what she's up to.

Her room is empty. I take that as an invitation to look around. It's my place, after all.

When we moved her stuff in, I already took the opportunity to peek, but now that her bag is here, I figure maybe I missed something.

I listen to hear if anyone is coming. It's silent in the hall, so I open the bag, pulling out her notebook.

Maybe there are some bank records or correspondences. Maybe there's something on her phone? I instructed the phone company to send me transcripts of her texts and records of her calls. But now that she knows I'm tracking her, I have a feeling if there is anything amiss, she is not going to put it in writing.

I consider having Jax install an app on her phone remotely. One that mirrors her phone calls and sends them to me, but even I think that might be a little invasive.

Probably highly illegal.

Definitely not favorable if push comes to shove, and we head to court.

Since I pay for her phone, it's not illegal to get transcripts, but duplicating and listening in crosses a line.

It's a slippery slope.

Nothing on her phone indicates she's texted anyone but her friend. I find it interesting and peculiar to see that she doesn't, in fact, call her sister, save for an incoming call from Erin that lasted less than two minutes.

That relationship is something I'm going to need to investigate.

Maybe, like me, she finds it interesting that my father left the money to his girlfriend's sister and not to his actual girlfriend. Then again, you'd think his wife and children would be the recipients but look how the fuck that turned out.

I wonder if Erin is reading between the lines and trying to figure out if Payton and my father were having an affair.

I realize that's what I'm looking for. Proof of her treachery.

But I find nothing in any of the stuff that she brought here. Her bag and her phone also don't tell me anything or indicate anything. I can't say I'm disappointed. It's a dangerous thought. One I have no business entertaining.

Being disappointed in Payton means I expected something from her.

Im-fucking-possible.

A month ago, I had Jax pull up all the information from the prison Dad was locked in, and Payton never called nor visited him, which begs the question . . . why leave her the money? What's the reason?

It makes no sense.

The only thing I can think of is that he didn't plan on ever allowing her to have that money. That something else was in motion, but unfortunately for him, he died too soon for his plan to come to fruition.

"What the hell do you think you're doing?" Payton hollers as she walks into the room.

I look up from where I am by the vanity, holding her notebook in my hand.

Clearly, I've been caught snooping. I have two choices: I can try to deny it, or I can admit it. Seeing as I'm an asshole, I go with the latter.

"Going through your stuff."

No reason to lie now.

"You can't do that."

"It's part of the stipulations," I say, opening the notebook again even though I've already finished skimming it.

It's not part of the stipulations. I just added that bit. But it works. I'm nothing if not flexible when it benefits me.

"You never, at any point, said that," she points out, crossing the room until she lands right in front of me.

"But it was implied."

"No, it wasn't."

"Very well. I guess we have nothing more to discuss. I'll have your belongings dropped off . . . where?" I smile at her. "Your sister's place?"

Her eyes are huge.

"No."

Interesting again.

Clearly bad blood between the two. *First the will reading, now this.*

"Then where? Your friend's place is the size of my closet. I saw the inside." I didn't. "It doesn't have enough storage . . ." I arch a brow, amping up the faux concern, laying it on her thick. "Would you like me to donate it? Sell it? Maybe it will get you enough for your first month's rent. Not enough for tuition, though. Such a damn shame."

"Fine, do whatever you want." She throws her hands in the air, face turning pink from her anger. "Go through whatever you want. I have nothing to hide. And if you think you will find something . . . Oh, well. You'll be S-O-L."

"S-O-L."

"Shit outta luck."

"I know what it means. I'm just shocked those abbreviations are being used by you."

"Why?"

"Because you are above the age of fourteen, Payton."

"Is there an age limit for a good abbreviation?"

The anger simmers beneath her words, but I have to respect

her. She's trying really hard not to let it out. The desire to taunt her, to unleash the fury she's holding back, is tempting.

"Yes."

"And what, pray tell, is that age?"

"Any age above high school. Actually, make it junior high. Regardless. This whole conversation is ridiculous. Yes. You agree to periodic searches. Now, let's move on to what I have to tell you. As part of my evaluation to see if I deem you fit to inherit my father's fortune, I need you to prove you are a good person."

"Pot, meet kettle."

I raise my brow. "Do you have something you would like to add?"

"Nope. There is something I'd like to deduct—myself. From this situation."

"Very well. Let's move on." I rapid-fire, tossing the notebook behind me, "Volunteer work. Tomorrow. After dinner. We'll be going together to start this new adventure."

"Where are we going?"

I lean against her bedpost. "Again, you'll find out tomorrow."

"Vague much?" she spits out.

"It's more fun that way. I enjoy watching you squirm."

She steps past me and walks farther into the room. "Basically, you want to keep everything as vague as possible to drive me crazy. I'm so happy I can serve as your source of amusement. It's an honor, *sir*."

"Sounds about right."

"I really hate you." She continues to walk toward the bathroom.

"Princess, I don't care what you think of me."

She halts and looks over her shoulder at me. "That name isn't very fitting."

"And what shall I call you then?"

"Cinderella."

"Yeah. I think not. No mice. No stepmother. And the most important part? There is no prince in this story."

"There certainly isn't."

Now that her body is facing me again, she boldly meets my stare. "Is there anything I need to know?"

"Be dressed and ready by five."

"You said after dinner."

"Yes, but just be ready. I'm not sure where we will be eating."

"You want me to have dinner with you?" She sounds repulsed by the idea.

"When you put it like that, no."

"Great. I'm not sure how I would swallow in front of you."

I quirk up my brow. Does she hear what she says? "Just be ready by five. Better?" I chide.

"Much."

She slips her shirt over her shoulders, letting it drop on the bathroom tiles. She's doing this on purpose. It's obvious. She wants to rile me.

I won't let her.

But fuck, her tits are bare to me, nipples on alert, pointing right at me. I haven't eaten all day, and I'm damn near ravenous for her. My dick is on its path to hard, and I just relieved it half an hour ago.

Fuck, this woman is dangerous.

"Anything I should wear?" she asks, fingers drifting down to her skirt.

"Clothes."

"Welp, since you specified . . ."

I shrug. "You asked."

"Fine. Clothes. Nice clothes?"

The skirt comes off, pooling around her feet. She's wearing a thong, just like I imagined. Just like I jerked myself off to. I could be in front of her in three strides, pushing the slip of fabric aside and sinking into her.

I'm so fucking hard at the thought, and I know it's obvious.

But she doesn't look. Her eyes are level on mine as she waits for my answer.

I give it to her.

"As opposed to rags?"

She lets out an exasperated sigh, tits bouncing at the movement. It's a lethal game we're playing. "You know what? Forget I asked."

"Forgotten."

I turn my back on her, officially done with this conversation.

"That's it?"

"Yes," I say over my shoulder.

"You are infuriating."

I am.

She isn't wrong. But everything has a reason, and this one is to drive her insane.

It seems the plan is working.

Unfortunately, so is hers.

She is driving me to the brink of action. Consuming my body with lust. I'm barely holding back each time we're in the same room.

I need a distraction.

I'm not sure what distraction I can have, seeing as half of my friends are married, but I still decide to go out regardless.

A drink and maybe another woman will take the edge off.

Drink? Yes.

Date? No.

Now I'm in a pissed-off mood and up way too early.

It's three o'clock in the morning, and I can't sleep. Normally, I'm up in an hour, but there is no point in sitting here if I'm just going to stare at the damn wall.

I step out of my bed, throw on a pair of sweats, and head to the kitchen.

Not much for middle-of-the-night snacks, but I figure I can eat breakfast now and go for my run a bit earlier than normal.

I'm not even halfway down the hall before I realize someone is in the kitchen.

Sure, I have a large staff and security, but it's not like them to be here in the middle of the night. Peter, who works the night shift watching the security cameras, would not come in here while on duty to snack.

Now I'm intrigued. I could make my presence known, but something tells me I know exactly who it is, and it will be a lot more fun if she doesn't know I'm coming.

Or I'm reading way too much into this, and I'm just so sick and twisted, I want to fuck with her. Even if it's not her I'm about to fuck with.

But it is her.

As soon as I creep into the room, I can see the silhouette of her body. What in the fuck is she wearing? She's bent over, looking into the fridge, and her ass is practically hanging out.

And what a fine ass it is.

She's got on these hot pink shorts that don't come close to covering the bottom of her ass cheeks. I can clearly make out the small of her back, seeing as her barely-there white tank top is cropped.

I should probably walk out of here. The idea of her turning around and giving me full visual access to her nipples through the thin white top drives me crazy. I have no doubt the sight will stay in my mind all day, and I really need to work out, not hop in the shower to beat off to thoughts of her.

Again.

Something is wrong with me. This girl has me all types of wrong. What does it say about me that, when she's around, I act like an idiot who can't control his dick?

The distraction I sought? Didn't work. I needed something

harder than liquor, which is not in the cards. Or I can just fuck her, use her as a distraction, and move on with my life.

This thought only makes me angrier. The possibility of double-dipping with my fucking father is disgusting. I shouldn't harden at the sight of her. If she had an affair with my dad, I am going to reanimate him from the dead and murder him, then I'm going to murder her, too.

I am about to turn around, avoid a double homicide, and walk out the door when she moves, and a scream ricochets through the room.

"Do you mind?" I yawn, pretending she doesn't bother me. "I don't want the whole house to wake up."

"Why are you here?"

"It is, in fact, my house and my kitchen, last I checked. What are you doing here is the better question."

"I was hungry."

"Okay . . ."

"I didn't eat dinner."

"Why not?"

She doesn't answer. A part of me wondered if she's one of those closet eaters. I noticed she never eats when I am around.

"You do know. So just spit it out."

"I was afraid eating your food would inspire you to add another stipulation."

"So instead, you scurry into my kitchen at night, like a nocturnal rodent, and raid my fridge?" I don't mention the fact that she's already been caught, on multiple occasions, by my staff and the many hidden cameras, which she hasn't seemed to notice. "Maybe Cinderella wasn't too far off point for a nickname. But it's not quite hitting the mark. Hmm . . . Maybe we should nickname you after the mouse."

"Ass—"

"Asshole. I know. I know. You have now said this a million times." I approach her, stepping beside her and ignoring it when

153

her hip brushes against my thigh. Fuck me. "I suggest you crack open a thesaurus. Your language skills leave much to be desired. And while you're at it, learn to act civilly. For someone who wants the money so bad, you really don't know how to behave."

"I don't want the money that bad," she lies.

It's written all over her features.

She does.

She needs it.

CHAPTER NINETEEN

Payton

DEVIL.
 Anti-Christ.

Lucifer.

All better names that are much more fitting than Trent Aldridge.

He is evil personified.

Okay, maybe that's dramatic, seeing as other than mess with my life, he hasn't killed anyone, namely me, *yet*. Yet being the operative word.

Something whispers in my brain that he has nefarious plans for me. Actually, not something.

Him.

He literally says this to me.

Which is why I don't trust him at all.

But there is something that doesn't make sense. I understand his anger. His dad neglected him and paid attention to me. His dad left his family for mine.

I represent the source of his pain.

Yet something else is simmering beneath the surface. Something I'm too afraid to identify.

Oh, I've identified a lot. Who am I kidding?

I know he was sporting wood when he left my room after I so smartly undressed in front of him.

Finally got him to shut up. But damn if he didn't turn the tables on me last night in the kitchen with nothing on but gray sweatpants. Those things should be outlawed.

Shit. I can't be thinking of him like that now. Not when I need to get ready, but instead am hot and sticky and in need of a shower, desperately.

Damn it.

I march into the bathroom, swing the glass door open, and turn the shower on. The water cascades down on me, engulfing me in its heat.

It reminds me of the type of rain that one would dance in as a child.

It awakens my senses and helps get me ready for the day.

The water is peaceful, calming, and I wish I could stay here forever.

But unfortunately, I need to get out, and when I do, I'll have to see him.

Those eyes.

They'll mock me. Tease me. Glare at me with hate. Why do they have to be the most beautiful eyes I have ever seen? And why, when he stares, does my body go warm?

When he touches me, every nerve ending comes alive.

Can I hate someone and crave their contact at the same time?

My body heats, but not because of the water that batters down on me, but from the way he makes me feel.

Needy.

So fucking needy all the time.

What would it be like for a moment to put away the animosity. To pretend we weren't enemies?

I reach my hand out, pouring the liquid soup onto my skin and scrubbing.

The suds of the soap trailing down between the valley of my breasts, making my nipples pebble.

Thoughts of Trent have my legs shaking with a pent-up emotion.

I close my eyes, imagining the man I hate is here.

Imagining him touching me.

My hand slips down my chest . . .

Past my navel. It slides to the place I wish he was, and with a flick of my finger, I pretend it's his tongue.

My touch is now his touch.

All rational thoughts leave my mind as I envision a world where Trent Aldridge worships me. Where I chase my high on his lips.

My hips buck, my pulse speeds up, and then I crash down from above, full sated.

Shit.

Looking down to where my legs are still parted, my back goes ramrod straight.

I did not just orgasm to fantasies of Trent.

You keep telling yourself that.

Grabbing a towel from the hook, I scrub at my body, trying to rid myself of the memory of what I just did.

How am I ever going to look at him?

You're not.

Once I'm dry, I get dressed.

Taking a deep breath, I place my hands on my skirt and straighten it.

He never did tell me the dress code for tonight.

I'm not sure where he's taking me.

It could be a soup kitchen. Or maybe he's taking me to a hospital to play with children.

I have no clue, which is why I am wearing a pale-blue cotton dress that falls right above my knee.

It's casual.

Yet cute.

It isn't dressy or showy and blends well with almost any situation.

On my feet are ballet flats in a bright white.

Again, simple.

I can run if I need to.

Ready for whatever the devil will throw at me.

He said five o'clock, but I'm ready at four thirty.

I have no desire to piss him off right now.

Been there. Done that. Have the receipts—or in my case, the callus on my palm from cleaning his gym—to prove it.

It's bad enough that he has me reading about Jung. It's not that I don't like his writings, but I am swamped with school, and the idea of presenting in front of Trent and his staff, people I see every day and technically work with, is humiliating.

Since I'm ready, I go in search of Trent.

First, I check the kitchen, but when that's empty, I walk down the hallway to his office.

Nothing.

Next, I find myself walking toward the room I think is his bedroom.

Heaven forbid I'm tardy.

I'm too tired to fight with him today.

It was a long day at school, longer with the new extended commute. I'm exhausted, and I didn't sleep.

Last night was a shit show.

Tossing. Turning. Anxiety.

And then *him*.

As much as he hates me, I see the way he looks at me. It's changed. There's lust underneath the anger. Pure need.

The worst part is, as much as I despise him, I like the way the looks make me feel.

It drives me insane.

I need to get my head out of my ass and stop enjoying his heavy, wanting stares while he destroys my life.

Shaking my head, I try to bring myself back to the present as I lift my hand to knock on his door.

Just as my hand is about to connect, the door swings open, and I stumble forward.

I lose my balance and fall.

I brace for impact.

Instead, I collide right into a hard body.

One that catches me and stops my descent with strong arms wrapped around my waist.

I'm frozen.

A large part of my brain tells me I must pull away. But another part welcomes the comfort of his arms. It feels safe. Right. Like two magnets drawn together, and it's exhausting to fight the pull.

But I have to.

Despite how good it feels.

Despite the fact that this goes deeper than lust, right down to comfort, and that should downright scare me.

One more second.

I want, no I need, one more second in his embrace. I'll store away the feeling, then I'll pretend it never happened and I don't like to be held by him. My eyes close of their own accord, and I give myself the time I need. Until I feel his arms go stiff.

I will myself to break away.

Move.

Move, dammit.

In a minute or three . . .

Finally, he coughs, and it breaks the damn trance I am in.

Using my right hand, I push off him. I try to fix myself, my dress, my hair, and my damn brain before looking up and catching his gaze.

His stare feels different.

It's as if he's shaking himself out of his own fog as well.

Which is weird.

Definitely unexpected.

It makes my heart kick up speed, like it's sprinting toward a finish line in a race I didn't even know it began.

"Crap. My bad," I whisper awkwardly.

"Watch where you're going." He grunts, and with that, any weird feelings of comfort quickly evaporate.

Why does he have to be such a jerk?

It's not even worth asking since he won't give me an answer anyway. Not one that doesn't involve a heavy dose of snark and misdirection.

That's one thing I've learned about Trent Aldridge. Ask him a question, and he just fires one right back. One that's even more confusing and makes no sense. Then, while you try to figure it out, he leaves you with a feeling like you have no idea what you're doing in life.

He's a condescending, arrogant jerk. Yet, despite this, I need to play nice.

Which sucks.

"I'm ready to go when you are," I say, taking an extra step away from him and feeling the distance like a punch to my gut.

"Did you eat something?"

"No." I raise my eyebrow. "Should I? Are we going to be out long?"

I thought we were eating together, but things are never clear with Trent.

"Only a few hours. When we're done, it'll still be early. You can eat after."

"You're coming with me?" I say, brows shooting up.

His steady gaze drills into me. "What did you think I was doing?"

"Why do you always answer a question with a question?"

"Because I don't answer stupid questions."

"Mm-hmm."

"No witty response." He laughs, and I think I freeze in shock. It's a pretty sound. Melodic, masculine, and just so . . . *him.*

My brain is too tired to keep up this back-and-forth banter.

"I give up," I declare. "No matter what I say, you always have to be sarcastic and completely intolerable. You never give me a real answer. You never say anything. You never engage. I'm sick of hearing the questions. I'm sick of the personal attacks. Again, you win. Tell me where we are going, and let's go."

To his credit, he doesn't gloat at my defeat.

Instead, he steps past me and says, "Okay. Let's."

I follow him as he leads the way to the underground garage and the fancy car I took, only to round the fancy Aston Martin beside it.

Of course, it's expensive.

Of course, it's super clean.

I bet my next task will be to wash it. Coupled with a ridiculous command like *clean it with your pinky finger.*

I'm shocked—mouth-hanging-open shocked—when he swings the car door wide for me.

It's not a date.

We are going to volunteer.

We don't even like each other.

Started out the evening with a mini-argument, to no one's surprise.

But I'm shocked by his manners. Usually, since he avoids me, fires sarcastic comments at me, and treats me with disdain, I assumed he would make me walk.

"No driver today?" I ask as I sit down in the passenger seat. "Not even a private helicopter? You're losing your edge, Trent."

"Michael has the night off. And I like to drive. It's calming to me."

File that away in the folder of random facts I find interesting about Trent Aldridge.

That being the only one so far.

Don't forget the gray sweats.

Trent starts the car, and we're off, weaving our way through rush-hour traffic.

The city is congested due to the time of day.

Before moving in with Trent, I never came to the city at five o'clock on a workday, but now, the terrible commute is the bane of my existence, too.

It doesn't seem to bother Trent. He just drives, not uttering a word, until he finally parks. There's something easy about the way he maneuvers the wheel. Like he's comfortable in control. I know this, of course, but it's another thing to see it without being on the receiving end. I find that I enjoy the sight.

Get your head straight, Payton. And whatever you do, don't think about how you just touched yourself to thoughts of him. Fuck. Head out of the gutter. Look at something else. Think of anything else.

I take in my surroundings as subtly as I can. I'm not familiar with this area or where we are. I don't know the West Side all that well.

But I'm sure he'll fill me in with whatever I'm about to endure. Something tells me this is the moment I have been scared of, that he's finally going to unleash hell on me. Because up until this moment, although it's been annoying, nothing has been bad.

Eventually, the other shoe must drop.

Something tells me it just did.

CHAPTER TWENTY

Trent

THIS SHOULD BE FUN.

Her eyes are wide.

There's something lurking within them. Suspicion, excitement, and something more foreign. Something I can't identify. I expected her to be nervous, to have her guard up, but this recent development throws me off. Especially the pinkish excitement lighting up her cheeks. Now that I think about it, she's been flushed since she showed up in front of my room.

"Ready?" I ask, taking inventory of her.

At my attention, her head turns away from me, fixed outside the window.

Now that's more like it.

"As I'll ever be," she mutters and latches on to the door handle harder than necessary.

"Come on."

Together, we walk into the building. She doesn't know I own it. That it's one of my many investments. Well, technically, since it brings in less profit than a fucking lemonade stand, it's a passion project. A piece of property I bought, renovated, and transformed for the sake of my mother. When the time came, I wanted to be ready. I didn't expect it to come so fast.

I built Cresthill to help older people who didn't have anyone to take care of them and who deserved to live a good life. Mom has Ivy and me, but back when she and Dad were still married, this would've been a good place for her, for *them* if he hadn't abandoned her.

It's like her dream retreat. Bouquet arranging, vast gardens, cooking classes, and more. Which is why she lives here now. Not because she needs to, but because she wants to. Cresthill gives her life a purpose. As a volunteer, as a worker, as a resident.

Payton pauses at the sign above the looming double doors. They're made of glass to look like water with crystals embedded in the shape of letters. Cresthill Home. Big, bold, and proud. Her mouth hangs open.

She can't take her eyes off it.

Can't even speak.

Honestly, I might be offended at this point.

Where did she think I'd take her?

Finally, eyes still glued to the sign, she speaks. "A senior living home."

"Yep," I respond, voice purposely flat.

But something about the way she said it spikes my adrenaline. The last thing I want or need is the approval of the woman at fault for my sister being fucking sold. Yet I can't help but feel instant gratification.

You've lost your goddamn mind, Trent.

She studies my face, probably gauging whether I'm serious. The disbelief is still etched across her face. Clear as day. "I wasn't expecting that."

I'm not exactly a peach to her, by design, but I've also been nothing but civil to everyone else—in front of her, too. She's seen me with Chef, Gail, Brandon, his team. Even Ivy and Mom at the reading. This shouldn't surprise her.

And now I'm completely offended.

"Really?" I deadpan, laying the sarcasm on thick. "From the

dislodged jaw and Bambi eyes, it seemed like you were totally expecting it."

"Sarcasm is the lowest form of wit," she points out, finally removing her eyes from the sign long enough for me to open the door.

I enter after her. "That would be stupidity, signs of which include glassy eyes and an inability to process information quickly. Remind me . . . How long did you stare at the sign for?"

"It's called surprise."

I drop the issue, leading the way to Margret's office. "This path will lead you to Margret. If you have any questions while you're here, she's your best bet at answering them."

Payton trails behind me, unable to keep up with my long strides. I slow a bit and peek at her from the corner of my eyes. She tracks every inch of the place with obvious fascination written all over her. I can't blame her.

Cresthill isn't like most retirement homes. It offers assisted living, independent living, and a custom mix of the two. It lacks for nothing as well. Anything you can imagine is here. Card rooms, shuffleboard, spa services.

I once caught Ivy in the movie theater, watching an unreleased film through our subscription deal with the biggest Hollywood distributors. (They agreed seniors should have early access to films given their age and the possibility they won't live to see the release. Well, after Cyrus showed up and made them agree.)

"Who's Margret?" Payton finally asks, glancing up at the chandeliers fixed to the high ceilings.

Cresthill was designed to resemble a luxury resort. Large, airy, and bright. A glass pivoting wall system stretches across the entire waterfront side of the building. It offers unfettered views of the Hudson. At any given time, you can watch the boats drift by.

Payton catches sight of one, pausing to watch it pass. It's peaceful and calming. Better than a vacation.

"The director of Cresthill," I answer, leading us through the common room.

In the corner, Nancy is playing the piano like always. A rowdy group plays cards in the center. Emily flops on triple aces. Henry wins a pot of fake chips on a wild bluff. I shake my head, a smile forming.

Always savage, Henry.

I turn to Payton to see what she's gawking at now.

Me, apparently.

I catch her watching me with a peculiar look on her face. Her pupils are wider than normal, and she looks confused. As if she's trying to reconcile the idea of why she's here with me. More accurately, of why I brought her here. Like, for the first time, she's considering the possibility of there being more to me than meets the eye.

I feel seen all of a sudden.

It's like a gut punch.

This was not what I had in mind when I rated this a calculated, controlled risk and decided to run with it.

My survival instincts kick in. I paste a scowl on my face and straighten my shoulders. I make myself larger, more consuming. It feels cowardly using my size like this, but the alternative is dangerous. Physical intimidation, it is.

But Henry catches sight of me and springs out of his chair with an unmatched agility that has me rethinking my decision to lowering Cresthill's age requirement from sixty-two plus to fifty-five plus.

He pinches my arms, then nudges me with his elbow. "Bringing out the big guns for your girl here, boy?"

Dammit, Henry.

Never in the history of humankind has anyone been taken seriously after being called "boy."

Payton knows it because she snorts and mouths "boy" behind Henry, a smirk gracing her lips. I should be thankful she didn't latch on to the "your girl" part.

"I read a study once that poker is bad for mental acuity in seniors. Maybe it's time to rethink Cresthill's policy."

It's bullshit. Well, maybe it isn't, but if it's not, I wouldn't know. I don't spend my time reading poker studies. I'd rather play it.

Henry guffaws, knowing I wouldn't. "Sure thing, kid. I interrupted your date. I can take a hint." He nudges me again with his elbow, despite the nearly foot-high difference between us. "Remember the hydro surfboard I requested next time you use us to impress your girl."

And then he's gone, moving on to his next victim.

"Whatever your intentions are, I think they're backfiring," Payton says, following me out of the common room.

No shit.

Thankfully, it's only a few more steps before we arrive at Margret's office. She spots me before we pass through the open doorway and stands to make her way to us, attention fixed on the thorn in my side, aka Payton.

At seventy-eight, Margret could be a resident here, and she is, but she also refuses to stop working. She's a triple threat. Sharp as a tack. Well-experienced. Well-liked. I put Cresthill in her care as soon as it opened a few years ago and haven't regretted it once.

"Trent," she greets, sizing up Payton. "Is this Ms. Hart?"

Payton reaches out a hand. "Pleasure to meet you."

As they shake hands, I send Margret a meaningful stare behind Payton's head, reminding her not to tell Payton I own this place. Margret rolls her eyes.

She releases Payton's hand. "Trent told me all about you."

"He did?" Payton asks skeptically.

"Only good things."

"Seriously?"

"Of course. He mentioned you need volunteer hours to pad your résumé once you graduate."

I said no such thing, but leave it to Margret to take it upon herself to create a cover story that makes things comfortable for everyone around here. Like I said. Sharp as a tack.

"I'll be sure to write you a nice letter of rec, should you need one," Margret promises.

Payton is taken aback. Frankly, so am I. This is not supposed to twist in her favor. Cresthill needs the help. I need Payton in an environment I can control. One where I can spoon-feed what she learns about me and how much she sees. It's as simple as that.

"Thank you," Payton says, and it's the most genuine I've ever seen her.

"No problem. Anything for Trent." Margret nods in my direction. "He's my favorite volunteer here, even if I think he's just doing it for the good PR," she jokes, returning to the cover story we agreed upon. The one she promised to have the rest of the staff on board with. Since the residents don't know I own the place, it works.

The last thing I need is for Payton to find out I have a heart.

"Margret," I greet, reminding her I exist. Not a position I'm often in. "Back to Ms. Hart. The one I told you all about on the phone."

I throw in the "all" for good measure.

Let Payton wonder what that means.

"As I said before, it's very nice to meet you. I'm Margret. As Trent, I'm sure, has told you, I run Cresthill House. Follow me, and I'll show you where you will be today." Margret turns to me. "Trent?"

"Yes?"

"You wait here. I have something I want to discuss with you."

The look she gives me tells me not to argue, which normally I would find comical considering our roles in this place. It occurs to me how often the women in my life order me around, from Payton to Mom to Margret.

Cyrus, the asshole, is right.

Women are my soft spot, and I need to harden it the fuck up where Payton Hart is concerned.

"No problem," I respond, walking farther into the room and taking a seat.

I fish out my phone after they leave and check my email to kill time.

Who knows how long I'll be here waiting. Could be five minutes. Could be an hour. You never know with Margret. She's a hardcore talker. Knowing her, she's probably shooting twenty million invasive questions at Payton faster than she can process them.

No new emails on the work front.

I made a shit ton on shorting the stock, and now I must figure out what to do with the earnings.

My money will go to Cyrus. But as for my clients, I need to come up with less risky investments to hold the funds until the right opportunity pops up.

I employ the best people in the business. They keep their ears to the pavement on upcoming product launches. I have no doubt the opportunity will arise soon.

There's a careful ecosystem in money laundering. Believability is key. With the meteoric rise of tech and crypto, they're safe investment bets. Realistic ones to clean dirty money through. Nothing too obvious to the SEC.

Most people find what I do risky, but it's the opposite. My clients are influential, their political friends equally so. They mitigate the risks. I had a higher chance of investigation before I went the dirty money route than after.

We have enough crooked politicians on payroll to make sure we're never the target of an investigation. That doesn't mean the companies we go after won't come after us, but at least the government is on our side.

As I fire off an email to Tobias requesting a meeting later this week, I hear footsteps approaching through the door. Margret is back.

"That was fast," I note as soon as the door swings open.

She settles in her little lounging couch, sans Payton. "I set her up in the rec room. She's helping paint pottery."

"Does she know anything about pottery?" I ask.

"I didn't say she was making pottery. I said she was helping paint pottery."

"Got it," I say, pocketing my phone.

"Now that we have that settled, why don't you tell me what this is really about?"

"I have no idea what you're talking about."

I smile. It's a crooked smile. One that tells Margret, who has known me for a long time, that I know exactly what she's talking about. I just don't want to tell her. I know she won't take the hint. Seventy-eight is long enough to learn to take no bullshit, especially when you have a spine like Margret's.

"Really, Trent?" She shakes her head. "You're going to play this game with me of all people?"

I pull out the itinerary she drafted for next month, skimming it without really paying attention to the words written. "All you need to know is that Payton will be coming three days a week to help you."

"How come I feel this is a lot deeper than that?"

"It is. But you don't need to worry your pretty little head about that." I straighten from her seat, setting the pamphlet down. "Just, from now on, give her the harder work. Serving food. Cleaning up the toilets." I beam at her, and she shakes her head at me.

"Trent?"

"What?"

"We have a large staff you pay to do that," she responds, and I shrug, staring at the floor long enough to make Margret shift in her seat.

Hear that, Dad? Your little princess will be cleaning up shit.

I return my attention to Margret. "So. Now you have a free hand, too," I add with a grin. "You've been begging me to reach out for volunteers for ages. Consider Payton ten volunteers in one. Treat her like it, too."

Margret studies me, her eyes narrowing before she speaks. "I'm not going to make her do hard labor precisely because I've been begging for more volunteers to entertain the residents. What will others think if I make our volunteers work like that? No one will want to come to sit and read with our clients."

"Not my problem."

"Actually, as the person who owns this place, it is exactly your problem."

"Cut that out, Mar," I say lightly. "No mentioning of my involvement here."

This fact is nonnegotiable. Everyone who works here already knows this. I held a meeting solely for this purpose. Lots of ironclad NDAs went around.

"Why?" Her voice softens. She meets me at the center of the room, forcing me to look at her. "You do a great service to everyone. We should be singing your praises, not hiding the fact you are a good man."

"I have a reputation to uphold."

Margret's hand reaches out, and she pats my shoulder, reminding me of my mother before Dad fucked her over hard.

"Fine," she says. "But I can't be held responsible for some of the people here. They love you. Eventually, this girl will find out the truth."

"Until then, keep a lid on it."

"Why are you doing this again?" she tries again.

I incline my head, giving her a look that tells her she's better off not knowing. "I told you not to ask."

"Just tell me," she presses.

"To drive her insane."

"Why?"

"The less you know, the better." I step aside and move to leave. "Trust me, she deserves it."

She lets out a sigh. "Very well. Toilets it is. But only when we are short-staffed."

With that, I leave the room.

Time to play cards.

CHAPTER TWENTY-ONE

Payton

W E'RE BACK IN THE CAR TWO HOURS LATER.
Trent speeds through the city as if he doesn't have a care in the world.

I, however, can't get over where we were.

I'm still in shock over it.

A part of me didn't believe he was serious that I would be volunteering, but the shocking part is that he was with me the whole time.

Not necessarily in the same room, but he was helping there, too, not just on his phone. And I don't believe for a second it's for the good PR. There were no cameras. No fanfare. Just a man doing a good deed for people he obviously cares about.

Trent Aldridge has a heart.

He is not a cold, callous villain.

It's just me *he hates.*

It's an ugly truth. One made uglier by the beauty I witnessed at Cresthill. When I finished cleaning the bathrooms, I headed back to Margret to see where I needed to go next, and I saw Trent with the same older man playing cards. The one who called me Trent's girl. Trent threw his head back, laughing with everything in him. Then he dipped to the floor, tying the man's shoes.

I can't reconcile the idea of Trent literally on the floor tying someone's shoes.

No matter how hard I try, it makes no sense. He takes away my place to live.

He takes away my money for food unless I work for him.

He looks at me like he wants to devour me, making it hard for me to even look at him.

But this . . .

Tonight.

The kindness everyone has toward him? It makes no sense.

Unless, and it's a big unless, he extends the same kindness toward them.

"You were serious about me volunteering," I whisper.

"I don't say things I don't mean."

We fall back into silence. I still can't believe it. We zip past cars at breakneck speed. This is the Trent I'm more familiar with. In control. Living fast and hard.

Fast and hard.

God. My cheeks flush. I'm disappointed in myself for touching myself thinking about him. And we're right back to square one, only I know he has a heart. One that beats for everyone but me.

Why do you care, Payton?

"Volunteering," I blurt out, forcing the embarrassment out of my head.

"Is that a question or a statement, Payton?"

"I'm just surprised," I answer honestly.

"Yeah, well, happy to keep you on your toes during our time together."

I turn my body to face him. "Why do you have to be such a dick?"

"That's an upgrade from asshole." The corner of his mouth twists . . . up? Down? I'm not sure. He looks both pleased and annoyed. Quite a feat. "What can I say? I was born that way. I get that trait from dear old *Daddy Ronnie*." He keeps his eyes on the road as he answers.

"He wasn't like that with me," I mutter under my breath, and I realize as soon as I do, I shouldn't have.

"No, he sure didn't try to sell *you* to pay off a debt." His shoulders rise and fall fast. He's forcing back his anger. It's sad that I consider that a development.

I decide to feed the beast. I can't help it. "No matter how many times you tell me that, I have a hard time believing it . . ."

"Go speak to my sister," he deadpans, switching lanes with speed and precision. "She can tell you all about it."

My heart leaps. I'm not used to driving, let alone at speeds like this. I can't wait until we get back into a congested part of the city, where there's traffic to slow him down.

"I'd rather not," I mutter.

"You'd rather pretend he was a good guy. It wipes the blood from the money. I get it. I don't respect it, but I get it. Cowardly as hell," he adds with so much derision, the temperature in the car rises in an instant. "Well, I'm sorry to break it to you, princess, he wasn't good."

"It's not about the money," I start before giving up. It's not like he'll believe me when I say I actually cared for Ronnie, and the desecration of his memory is difficult to stomach. I pivot to his last sentence. It's the only thing I have undoubted grounds to attack. "If you knew me at all, you would know your nickname isn't fitting."

"Twenty-two million dollars says it is." He scoffs and slams on the brakes.

The car jerks to a stop. That's when he finally looks at where I'm sitting beside him in the passenger seat. The expression on his face tells me a lot. None of which I want to hear.

I know you think very little of me. You're not exactly high on my Christmas card list, either.

"Yet, I don't have that money." I give him a pointed look,

refusing to avert my gaze, even when his attention is almost sickening. My stomach churns faster than a laundromat spin cycle.

Trent returns his eyes to the road. "You might never have it either."

The anger this man has for me is palpable.

Like a noose tightening around my throat, never failing to remind me it's there.

I've had it. "What is your deal?" I throw my hands in the air. Months of anxiety, anger, grief, and heartbreak burst out of me with my words. "I get it. You hated your father. But what the hell did I ever fucking do to you?"

"Change of plans," he announces, making a U-turn that has me reaching for the center console.

My fingers brush against his thigh with the movement.

Both of us freeze.

Then Trent grits out, "We're going back to my house. You can eat there."

I shrug, returning my hand back to my half of the car, where it belongs. "I didn't want to eat with you anyway."

We continue to drive, the air in the car thick with tension.

This man makes no sense.

A conundrum I have no hopes of unraveling.

The perfect treatment he gives to Ivy and his mom makes sense. They're his family. The one that didn't abandon him. But the center? It's obvious everyone at Cresthill loves Trent Aldridge. It's a difficult pill to swallow, mostly because the label's warning reads: HE ONLY HATES YOU, PAYTON.

I stare at his profile, not bothering to hide it.

Why are you treating me like I'm the one who hurt your family? Yeah, you're pissed at your dad, but what the hell? Can't you just yell at me, get it off your chest, visit one of those expensive Manhattan therapists? Literally anything but this . . .

If my attention bothers him, Trent doesn't show it.

"You don't even need the money," I finally say.

"You're right, I don't."

He changes lanes with ease, then we're back in his part of the city. The part full of men like him. Rich, savage, and privileged.

Who are you kidding, Payton? Those men are minnows. He's the shark.

"Twenty-two million is pocket change for you," I state the obvious. "So, what is this? A big middle finger to Daddy? Grow up, Trent."

"The money is blood money, princess."

"Well, maybe it doesn't have to be . . ."

"What is that supposed to mean? There is no changing what it is. If you have a time machine that can take you back to the moment that bastard made the money, do share. Maybe while you're at it, I can end him before he chooses to sell Ivy."

I swallow. A lump in my throat formed with his rage. By my own, too. The part of me that believes Trent is angry. Stewing at Ronnie.

Some lines should never be crossed, and hurting your family is one of them. It makes Ronnie just like Erin.

Actually, it makes him worse.

At least Erin never sold me. I mean, I don't doubt that she's tried, but she's not the type to succeed at things.

So, there's that.

"That's not what I meant."

"What are you going to do, donate it all?" He snorts. "Doubtful. I have seen your bank records. Or lack thereof. You don't have two pieces of shit to rub together."

"What the hell! What do you mean you've seen my bank records? That's a huge invasion of privacy!"

I have a whopping twenty-five dollars in the bank. I set it up when I turned eighteen, never used it, and let it sit with the minimum deposit. I kept it open to remind me of the choices I've made. Instead of eating that day, I opened a savings account.

I chose to hope for a future.

"Cry me a river."

"You can't just go about meddling in people's lives."

"Yet . . ." He trails off with a shit-eating grin on his face.

Even though half his face is out of view, the side I do see is obnoxious enough that I want to remove my shoe and throw it at his face.

Seeing as he's driving, and I don't have a death wish, I'll refrain. Barely.

"I'm not your dad." I glare out the front windshield, hating the city for the first time. Every inch of it reminds me of Trent. "Making my life hell won't fix what he did to you. And despite what you think, I never knew about your family. I was kept in the dark. So hurting me doesn't change anything."

"But it will make me feel better."

"It will be a short-lived pleasure."

"What do you know about that?"

"I know a lot more than you'd expect." The double entendre isn't lost on me. I flush, reminded of the shower. Gosh, I really screwed myself with that one.

Figuratively and literally.

"You think you've had it rough," I pivot. "Try living in a ca—" I stop myself before I finish.

The vehicle rolls to a stop, and Trent looks at me.

"You lived in a car?"

"Not everyone grew up in a gilded castle."

"So, basically, that means your sister really is a whore."

Of course, that's what he got from that.

"She did what she had to do to survive and keep us both alive." I don't like the defensive edge to my voice. It makes me feel like my life is a game. One in which I'm always on defense.

I don't know why I bother to even tell him this. He knows nothing of the suffering that comes from poverty. His privilege is so thick, not even an obsidian knife could cut through it, and that shit is volcanic glass.

"And you . . ." He looks me up and down. I think it's disdain, but I don't trust myself to get an accurate read on him right now. Not when I'm so on edge. "Did you do *who* she had to do, too . . . ?"

"Oh, fuck you," I spit out.

"Princess has claws." Mockery invades his stare.

"Only for assholes." My words escape through clenched teeth, but it only seems to entertain him some more.

He basks in my misery.

"You never answered the question." His tone is light, but I know this is the big unknown plaguing him. "Did you spread your pretty little thighs for Daddy?"

"That's disgusting."

He makes a noise at the back of his throat. One I can't read. I'm unsure whether he believes me, but if I had to guess, I'd say no with a capital *N*.

The light turns green. Trent starts to drive again.

This time, as the car moves, neither of us speaks, and this time, I'm completely okay with it.

I'm not going to say anything to break the silence.

I have no desire to hear what this man has to say.

He's vile . . .

But . . .

I shake my head.

No, don't read into it.

Don't read into the depth I see in his eyes when they aren't filled with hate toward me. When he makes other people smile, and it brings one to his face in return.

The thing is, no matter how hard I try not to, deep down, I can hear the hurt that lives inside his voice, and I wonder more about how it got there.

I need to find my sister.

There is so much more to Ronald than I know, and I'm starting to wonder if she knew the real him or not.

And I'm afraid of the answer.

CHAPTER TWENTY-TWO

Payton

I'M NOT GOING TO CLASS TODAY.

I should go, but no matter how much I try, I can't get past the mystery and drama surrounding Ronald Aldridge. I need to know how much my sister knew.

Did she know about what he did to his daughter?

Why he was in jail?

Did she even talk to him about anything of substance?

The only thing she told me came the day before the funeral and will reading. She admitted, point blank, with no remorse, that Ronald Aldridge had a family. It sounded like she'd known about them for a long time. That I was the only one left in the dark.

Instead of taking the train to where I normally get off to go to school, I take it one extra exit to where my sister's house is located.

This is the house she moved into after Ronnie stopped paying her bills a few months before he died.

I haven't been here since he died, come to think of it. I haven't really been here very much since I found out the new scumbag showed up. He was in prison for his hand in some scheme, and God knows what that was really all about because Erin won't talk. Finding out she had known him through her ex—Tony—is enough for me to never want to get to know him, though.

Seems like a pattern . . .

I walk up the driveway to the door and knock. It swings open. My sister looks like a mess.

Her normally beautiful blown-out hair appears greasy.

Her face has sunken in.

Is she eating?

Is she sick?

I hate myself for the instant pang of worry that festers inside me, but she's my sister. No matter how she treats me, I can't help but worry.

"What brings you here?" She narrows her eyes at me.

"Can't I just want to stop by to visit my sister?"

"You haven't given a shit about me since you found out all the money is going to be yours." She huffs as she lifts her hand up to rub her nose.

Is she using again?

My sister has been clean for years, but she's been spiraling ever since Ronnie cut her off, so it does make sense.

"Can I come in?"

She rolls her eyes but steps aside, allowing me to pass.

There are empty bottles of wine, beer, and vodka everywhere. If I didn't know better, I would mistake this place for ground zero of a rave. After the lights come back on, and the people left with the mess realize how utterly fucked they are.

Erin might not be doing drugs, but she certainly is drinking. The scent of alcohol invades my nostrils. I can't even pinpoint a single type. It just smells like the air is eighty proof.

Brad's lying on the couch in the living room. No shirt on. Beer in his hand.

Charming.

This house looks like a squatters' paradise. Not the beautiful, seven-figure home Ronnie once purchased.

"Why are you here?" Erin glares at me, temper flaring.

"I want to talk about Ronald."

"What about him? Isn't it bad enough that he left me nothing?" Her voice sounds shrill, reminding me of nails on a chalkboard.

He gave you a home for years. Money for years. Food and safety, too.

It's more than most people ever have.

She's forgotten so much of our past, so much of what it felt like not to have a roof over our heads, that I want to point it out. I also want to live, and in the interest of self-preservation, I pocket the comment.

"I didn't ask him for this."

"You did *something* to get it."

"That's ridiculous."

She looks me up and down. "Really? Because you were just his type."

"Erin!" I shout because the idea is not only gross but absolutely ridiculous. And offensive.

"What? It's true." She nudges a beer bottle, watching it roll and hit the wall. "I was around your age when I started dating him. Maybe a few years older. Not so hard to believe, huh? Maybe you seduced him."

"I never touched him, and he never touched me."

"I don't believe you." Something sinister flashes across her face, and then she's prowling toward me in slow, steady steps. "If you never touched him and you didn't ask Ronnie for the money, why not leave it to me?"

I force myself not to back up when she closes in on me, and all I smell is the vomit-inducing scent of booze and sex on her. "I don't know why he gave me the money, Erin."

She sags, looking a foot smaller. "What am I going to do?"

It feels like I'm being sucker punched as I watch her.

Erin can be difficult, but she's had it rough. With her shoulders slumped, she appears younger. It reminds me of when she first took me in. The girl who lost her parents and put her own dreams aside to take care of me. Erin hasn't always been the woman she is now.

It's why I still put up with this new version of her.

"Don't worry. I'll take care of you." The moment I say the words, she visibly stiffens. "Do you think I'd leave you with nothing?"

She took care of me for years, best she could.

Does she think so little of me?

Instead of reassuring her, she rears up at my promise. "I don't need you to take care of me."

"I know you don't. Consider it a thank you for everything you did for me."

And I mean it.

Although she's made my life difficult the past few years, it doesn't negate that she took me in. That she once tried her best to be there. That, in truth, she saved me.

"You'll give me the money?" She leans closer. "When you finally get it, give it to me like it was never yours, to begin with."

"Yes."

She worries her lip at my answer, then nods. "It's the least you can do for me raising you."

I nod. I'll figure out another way to escape. To achieve my dreams. To be free. The money is worth this fight with Erin. And I meant it when I said it's the least I could do for Erin raising me.

"But I'm not here to talk about the money," I add.

"Fine." She motions to the kitchen chair. "Sit. Now that I know you aren't forgetting about me, you can stay. Hang out."

That's the last thing I want to do, but instead of making this awkward, I do.

"Did you know about Ronald?"

"Know what?" She laughs as the question clicks. "About him having another family? Hell yeah . . ."

"No, not that. Did you know about Ivy?"

That Ronald sold her . . .

Erin looks everywhere but at me. First at her hands. The ones tapping her thighs. Then she glances down at her feet. Both shake, moving her legs in a frantic rhythm. I don't know if she's having withdrawals or just nervous.

Finally, her gaze lifts, but instead of looking at me, she looks over my shoulder. Something in the way she holds her body and the lack of eye contact makes my heart sink, and I don't want to know, but I have to.

"Did you know what he was planning for his daughter?" I press.

She doesn't answer, and her gaze never meets mine.

"How could you stay with him knowing he'd sold his own—"

She cuts me off, "Don't judge me, Miss Perfect. You have no idea what it would have been like without him to save our asses."

"I do. I remember."

"If you remember, then shut the fuck up. If it weren't for Ronnie, you would have been on the streets. Everything I did, I did for us," she hisses. "That fancy college cost a lot more than money. So did the food you ate. You have no idea what I had to do to keep you fed. To keep you safe all this time."

Her words sting. Because they're true.

I know it in the bottom of my gut that, if it weren't for Ronald, I'd probably be dead. Or worse . . .

A shiver runs down my spine for a reality I know would have been mine, had Erin not intervened.

My sister might not be the best person, but she did make sacrifices for me.

"I'm sorry, Erin. You're right." Despite my desire to rid myself of her toxic presence, I do know she kept me alive.

"It's fine. You'll make it up to me like you promised."

I nod. "I will. Just need to get through these months."

"Maybe if you try to butter up the son . . ." She licks her lips. "Maybe *I* should . . ."

"He would never go for that."

"What are you saying? I'm not good enough for Trent Aldridge? Or are you already spreading for him now?"

"No. I don't do"—I shake my head—"That's not what I said." Not even close. I hate that her thoughts are so binary—defend and attack. Sex and pride. "And I don't want to fight with you. He hates us. There is nothing we can do to get the money faster."

"Fine, whatever."

We sit in silence, then Brad moves to stand and walks over to me.

My body instantly tenses.

He looks down at me with a look in his eyes. One I know too well from seeing them replicated on Erin's past creeps.

"I'm sure you can think of a way to convince him not to hate you . . ." He dips his chin down.

His gaze lingers too long over my chest, and I feel dirty. Not the first time a man in my sister's life has made me feel this way. But now I'm older, stronger, and use my voice.

I get up and move toward the door. Away from him. "I'm not going to do that."

"Well, bills are due soon, so you might need to reconsider it," Erin adds into the conversation.

With a sigh, I look at her and ask, "How much do you need to tide you over?"

Before Erin can give a number, Brad walks closer again. "Three grand, minimum."

"I don't have access to that kind of money."

"Then find a way to get it, dammit. If there is nothing else, you can fuckin' go," Brad says. "The bills are due in four weeks. Tell your boy toy you need money for school. It's yours, right?" He doesn't wait for me to answer. "Then there ain't no problem asking for it."

"Fine." I head out the door.

The trip was a waste of time.

My sister gave me no information I needed.

Not true.

She knew what Ronald tried to do to Ivy.

She knew what a monster he really was.

Trent is right.

It is blood money.

I'll give my sister her share and keep a little for me to use to leave. Then I'll get as far away from all of this as I can.

There is nothing salvageable here.

My mind is all over the place when I head back to the loft. It feels like everything inside me is twisted up. I can't think straight. Sometimes seeing Erin will do that to me. Talking to her brings me back to the past. Especially today after what she said.

I don't need her to remind me what my life could have been like had she not been there.

Those thoughts live in my brain whenever I'm alone at night and allow my thoughts to wander.

Normally, I would hit the gym at Ludlow. A good forty-five-minute run does wonders to clear the cobwebs of the past from my mind.

That's what I'm missing.

The release of endorphins. Those bad boys will get my brain in the right place in no time.

As I'm about to enter the loft I notice that across the street there's a truck. I halt my steps, my eyes narrowing to look at it.

It's just sitting there. Across the street. But that's not the part that has my back going straight, it's the person in the driver seat.

He's staring at me. Not moving. Just looking at me.

I can't see who it is, he's wearing a baseball hat and sunglasses. That's the thing that bothers me, it's not sunny out.

I'm still staring as the door behind me opens. I jump at the movement, turning my body to see Gail.

"Are you okay?" she asks.

"It's just the truck across the street."

"What truck?" she asks, confusion evident in her voice.

"The one over there." I turn to point at the truck, but it's gone. "That's so strange—I swear . . ." I shake my head. "Forget it, it was nothing." Not wanting to make a bigger fool out of myself. Obviously, it was nothing and I'm being dramatic. No reason for Gail to know I'm being paranoid. That's all I would need, Gail telling Trent. I would never hear the end of it.

I enter the loft, and then I head straight for my room and change into my workout clothes. Then I'm off in search of Trent.

He might have something he expects me to do. So, before I leave again to run, I need to let him know where I'm going.

After I come up empty-handed in the main level, I head to his gym.

That's an option.

Would Trent mind if I used it?

Probably, but it's not enough to stop me.

As I turn the corner, my feet stop, and my mouth drops open. My brain stutters for a moment at what I am seeing.

Better yet—who.

It's him.

Electricity courses through my body.

I feel warm and tingly in an instant.

Trent is naked.

Lying in his sauna. The glass foggy from the heat, but not enough to block my view of him.

And I see *everything*.

Every inch of his perfectly formed body.

My eyes trail over his exposed skin . . .

Lower.

Lower.

Holy hell.

I want to fan myself. Or better yet, lie on top of him.

He is hard, thick, and long.

I wonder what he's thinking. If he's thinking about someone.

If he's thinking about me.

My tongue feels heavy.

My cheeks are burning.

I'm on fire.

Move. Payton.

The last thing I want is for this man to catch me staring.

I will myself to take a step back.

Then another.

I retrace my path backward until I'm out of view.

Until I can retreat to the confines of my room.

As soon as I'm sure he can't hear me, I take off and run up the stairs, dashing across the hall and slamming the door shut.

Once it closes behind me, I slide down it, resting my back on the heavy wood.

Head in my hands, I finally exhale.

Now that I've seen him, I don't know how I'll ever speak to him again.

The unbelievably sexy image has branded itself in my brain.

And something tells me no quantity of cold water, or even holy water, will rid me of it.

CHAPTER TWENTY-THREE

Payton

D AYS HAVE PASSED, AND JUST AS I SUSPECTED, THE IMAGE haunts me.

Trent naked.

Yeah, it's all I think about.

I'm doing a crappy job of studying. Heck, I'm doing an even crappier job at just existing with his picture in my mind. If Trent really wanted to kill my academic career, he should've skipped the chores and extra homework and gone straight to the nudity.

The only saving grace is he hasn't been around much to taunt me further.

Like this moment.

I'm back at the Cresthill facility. But unlike most days that I'm here, he's not.

He dropped me off and left me standing on the corner of the street to find my way in. My cheeks colored red, but I stood tall. This would mean there would be no toilets to clean.

Without Trent here to micromanage me, I'm able to spend time with the residents instead of burning my hands with cleaning products.

I look around the room, searching for someone to talk to. A conversation will help me stop thinking of lickable abs. Okay, that's not the body part I'm thinking about.

Sue me.

That's when I see the man who called me Trent's girl. Henry. I've since seen Trent with him. Often.

Maybe he knows something useful about the man who holds my life in his hands.

Any piece of information will help me.

There's a deadline looming. I need to ask Trent for money to give to my sister today. Maybe, just maybe, Henry can give me info I can use to barter with Trent.

I cross the space and take the empty seat across from him.

"I hope it's okay I sit here."

"Pretty lady like you is always welcome." He smiles, and that makes me laugh.

I never knew my grandparents, but in my imagination, mine would be just like him.

A flirt like my sister.

Not like me.

She's the only family I remember well.

Our parents died when I was only six years old. Payton was eighteen and raised me.

I can't imagine how hard that must have been, which is why I am now trying to pilfer information off Henry to get money for her. Even if I have to use the fact that he thinks I'm Trent's girl to get the info.

"Henry, right? I'm Payton. I just started helping out here." My voice is soft as I flash him a smile.

"I saw you," he says, chocolate brown eyes finding mine.

They are deep. Probably filled with great stories and anecdotes only a person of his age would have. Probably the reason Trent spends so much time with him. From what I can tell from Trent, he didn't have a relationship with his dad. Maybe Henry was the father figure he went to.

I'm banking on it.

"You're Trent's girl," he finishes, and I nod, forcing the guilt to roll off my shoulders.

There is no need to correct him. If I do, I run the risk he'll clam up.

I place my elbows on the table and lean in.

"So, you've known Trent for a while . . ." I lead, hoping he divulges some useful information.

"Pretty long. About two years, maybe. However long this place has been open."

"Oh, wow, really?"

It comes as a surprise to me. I didn't realize Trent had been volunteering here this long.

"Yep." His lips part and he grins widely at me.

It's obvious this man cares deeply for Trent. That Trent is important to him. My stomach drops at the thought. I'm a horrible person. How can I try to take advantage of him?

"I didn't realize he's—" I stop myself.

I don't want to say anything that will make him think I don't know Trent well. I may feel bad pressing him, but I also don't want to upset him by making it obvious what I intended to do.

I change directions. "I didn't realize he comes here so much. That's nice."

"It's more than nice. He's here almost every day, visiting."

That is news. But instead, I keep smiling and pretend I know all of this.

"It's amazing of him that he finds time. He's so busy at work," I say.

"He says the location is close to his office, but I'm not geographically challenged. I know Cresthill is at the very edge of the city, and he's not. That traffic is a bitch when he comes. I'm thankful that he tries to stop by every day for a game of cards."

I cock my head to the side.

"You like to play?" I ask.

He beams at my question. The deep lines on his face grow larger. "Love it."

"That's how you and Trent bonded?"

"Yeah, Trent plays poker. He's good. But not as good as me."

"Do you guys play for money?"

He narrows his eyes on me. "Nope. Trent doesn't believe in gambling for money."

My spine goes ramrod straight. What a dumb question. Of course, Trent doesn't play for cash, not after what his father did. I should have known this, and Henry is probably wondering why I didn't.

"Doesn't matter," Henry finally says. "It's still fun, regardless. I'm simply happy for the company."

He looks away from me. A faraway look consumes his eyes.

"Are you okay?"

"I was just thinking."

"Do you want to talk about it?"

He tilts his head and stares. "I guess . . . Trent trusts you after all."

I feel like I've been stabbed in the gut with the lie that's lodged in my throat, threatening to choke me, but my instincts tell me it's worth it for Henry to open up to me.

"You can tell me anything." I pause, feeling so much guilt but laying it on thick anyway. "That's what I'm here for."

"My son," he whispers. It's a haunted, broken sound.

"What about your son?"

"We had a falling out, and my son"—Henry shakes his head— "he won't talk to me."

"Have you tried to reach out to him?"

He nods. "I have, but I don't know where he is anymore. We lost touch, and every day I'm here, I wonder how much time I have left. I'm not the same man I once was . . . I have regrets. I don't want to die without righting my wrongs."

I reach for his hand and squeeze it, gentling my voice. "Tell me about your son."

And this time, I forget about my mission.

This is one hundred percent about the broken man in front of me. The one I find a kindred soul.

Henry spends the next hour telling me all about his son. The good times. The tough times. The falling out. Every now and then, he stops, and it looks like he will cry.

It breaks my heart, and I know I must do something.

Tell someone.

An hour later, I settle on an answer. One that isn't my first choice but is the best option we have.

I get back in the car with Trent when he picks me up.

"Can we talk?"

"Sure." He sighs.

If it were up to him, I'd probably never speak.

Well, that's not true.

In a couple of weeks, he expects me to speak in front of his staff on the information I have turned in.

I can't believe I'm going to have to do that.

Not the point.

"It's about Henry."

"What about him?" He glances quickly at me while he navigates traffic.

Now that I have his attention, I can see the concern. It's obvious that he cares greatly for the man.

My gut tells me after Ronald showed his true colors, Henry replaced him as a father figure in his life.

"He doesn't seem okay."

Trent pulls over, double-parking in front of a cop car without a care in the world. His head turns to me fully. His jaw is tight, and his eyes are wide.

"Why? Did he look sick?"

"Um, no." I try to stay calm. "Is he sick?"

Trent looks away, and I think maybe Henry is, but that's not why I'm talking to Trent about him. And if he is sick, then what I have to say is even more important.

"He misses his son," I blurt out when it's clear Trent isn't going to talk. "He doesn't know where he is. I think we need to find him."

He looks back at me, relief sinking into his body for a moment. His shoulders relax. He leans against the plush leather seat. There's a softness to him I've never seen before, one that I'd consider fondness if I weren't so unused to any positive emotion from him.

Then all at once, his brows raise, and he looks back at the road with wide eyes. He starts the engine again, veering onto the road so fast, it's like he's crazed.

"We?" He speeds. "There is no *we*. Henry is not your problem."

I'm not sure why he snaps at me, but it does shut me up. Too bad it can't stop my heart from wanting to break free of my chest. It wants to run straight to Trent and fix him.

He isn't yours to fix.

CHAPTER TWENTY-FOUR

Trent

THIS WHOLE SITUATION IS FUCKING STUPID.

This woman drives me completely insane.

The worst part about it?

This is all my fault.

I forced her to stay at my place.

To volunteer at the one place I feel most like myself.

If anyone is to blame, it's me. All me and my dumb fucking ideas.

Now I can't decide whether I want to bash my head against a wall from her questions or stroke my cock from the way she looks at me.

Both, I decide.

What the ever-living fuck is wrong with me?

Like clockwork, I hear the bell-like sound of Payton's laughter. It reaches my office and is enough to force me out of my chair and into the hall. I round the corner to the living room and spot her immediately. She's on the floor, knees on the hardwood, ass in the air.

This is not the first time I've wanted to sink my teeth into it.

Or flip her skirt up and sink into *her*.

Payton Hart is more dangerous than every weapon in the secret arsenal behind my closet.

She is a pain in the ass.

She asks too many questions.

She interferes in my life.

She always wants to talk about something.

She makes a mockery of the term peace and quiet.

And she's a goddamn distraction because it takes me too long to realize it isn't Payton laughing. It's Gail. Militant, came-with-recommendations-from-Pentagon-officials Gail. Gail, whose closest proximity to humor is the fact that she has a humerus bone.

Payton broke Gail.

There is no other explanation.

Gail doesn't laugh.

She doesn't even smile.

But she's doing both right now, and I don't know how to process it. I think I'm shocked still for the first time.

I watch from my perch at the corner as Payton straightens and launches into an animated discussion about her adventure making the new cleaning solution she's using. Gail follows the story, even when Payton cracks a dumb joke, and they both sink into a fit of laughter, clutching their stomachs.

What. The. Fuck.

It's time to accept the fact that I didn't think this through. Because the alternative—that I did think this through and Payton Hart managed to crack through my barriers, my plans, and my perfectly contained life—is downright frightening.

Living with me? A horrible idea.

Volunteering where I do? A worse one.

And let's not forget that she is always around me. That's the final straw of all the idiotic fucking things I have done. Instead of finding things to hate about Payton now, I'm finding things to like about the woman.

What the fuck is wrong with me?

The fact that Henry spoke to her doesn't bode well. I don't like that Margret likes her, too. She broke Gail. The only way this could be any worse would be if my mother liked her. No way in hell that'll happen. I'll keep them as far apart as possible.

I creep back into the shadows and make my way down to the garage, forcing the image of Gail and Payton laughing from my head. Including the fact that I didn't exactly hate the sight. Not even close.

But this all takes a back seat to Henry.

I want to drag myself into the street and kick my own ass. I see Henry almost every day. I didn't realize he missed his son. Guess I have a mental block when it comes to father-son relationships, but if what she says is true, then it is imperative I find him. Henry's getting old. There's no way around death.

However, I don't want Payton involved.

I don't want her help.

I hop into my car and take off without warming up the engine. Needing to get as far away from her as possible. As fast as I can.

Baker told me having Payton live with me was a stupid idea, and I brushed him off.

When I first met her, I was sure she would be a spoiled brat. She was supposed to be a money-grubbing gold digger like her damn sister.

Instead, she's anything but that. She seems to live off nothing. Other than the train tickets and cab fare, she asks for absolutely nothing.

I don't even know how to handle it. I need Jaxson's help to find out what skeletons lie in her closet. He should've found something on her by now.

I've got nothing, too.

Not a single damn thing.

Zilch.

Speaking of Jax, he's exactly who I need to talk to again.

This time, I'll make him help me.

Unannounced, I roll up to the meatpacking district, to his warehouse.

He will be here. He is always here.

Not many people know about this location. Only a select few. I consider myself lucky. After I park my car halfway up the block, I get out and walk the rest of the way.

Protocol.

There is no point in announcing myself or even ringing the bell, not that he has one. The door is opening as soon as my feet touch the concrete tiles. His state-of-the-art surveillance system is doing the job, opening like magic. It blends with the street, understated, to give the illusion of nothing beyond a run-down building, but inside tells another story.

"You don't even call anymore," he says, eyebrow raised. He's still seated behind his monster of a desk, not bothering to stand to greet me.

"Who are you kidding? You wouldn't have answered," I chide.

"You're right. I wouldn't. Now get in here before anyone sees you."

With that, I step inside, and the door slams behind me. As I walk into the cavernous space, no matter how often I come here, I'm still shocked. I saw the before and after of the building. Saw each step in the transformation process.

It's no longer the crumbling warehouse with questionable infrastructure.

Concrete, stainless steel, and metal are now entwined to mix the urban feel with cutting-edge design. Flat-panel computer monitors are the only thing on the walls, but not just one or two. There are dozens.

These monitors display the outside of the warehouse. Hence the door opening for me.

And standing there, in front of millions of dollars' worth of equipment, I tell my best friend exactly what I need.

CHAPTER TWENTY-FIVE

Payton

I'M RUNNING LATE. AGAIN.

This is officially the story of my life since I moved in with Trent.

Every morning, I wake up and clean this asshole's loft. Wouldn't bother me if I got to pick the time, but for some reason, he now wants me to do it after he leaves for work, but before I go to school.

I wake up at five in the morning now, which again wouldn't be a problem alone, but I'm up until two every night, studying.

Worst part? I'm not even studying stuff for my major. I'm studying things '*Trent deems appropriate.*' Gail's words. Not mine. Though she gave me a heads-up on the next curriculum Trent set up, and I'm pretty sure that's a major breach of procedure for her.

On the train, I find myself muttering the same sentence to myself

"What doesn't kill us only makes us stronger."

It's my mantra these days. It's either that or "Fuck. My. Life."

And I'm still secretly comprising a list of all my grievances against Trent Aldridge.

What started as a way to prepare myself for a court case has now become therapy journaling. I pull out the journal and spend the entire train ride reviewing the list, debating what to add to it.

It reads like this:

- Without written notice that the Trustee would no longer pay my bills, all services and tuition payments were canceled.
- Without warning or legal timing to find alternative housing, I was evicted from the home that should have been paid for by Trustee.
- My mode of transportation payments was canceled by Trustee and vehicle repossessed.
- Without telling me the rate and penalty ahead of time, I get charged two thousand per minute from the trust when I arrive late to meetings the Trustee requested.
- Trent is a giant dickhole to me for no reason, except his father decided to be nice to me and an asshole to him. (*Fine, I don't know what to say about this one . . . but I feel like a court would need to hear it.*)
- He's making me write homework assignments and volunteer at a retirement community. (*Again, probably not a big deal in the grand scheme of things, and I really do love going to the retirement center every day. Maybe I won't bring that to the court either.*)

Normally, when my journaling is done in the morning and Trent leaves, I begin cleaning the apartment one room at a time as quickly as I can. Once I put down the mop, I have to shower, dress, sneak food out of the kitchen without Chef cutting off my hand, and catch the train to get to school on time.

With the new schedule, I save the journaling for the train ride and catch as much sleep as I can manage. The thing is, no matter how much it sucks (and it does), I know I'm lucky.

I have a roof over my head.

A bed to sleep in.

A tyrannical chef feeding me, even if it's behind his back.

Plus, even if I don't take all that into consideration, I know this is not the worst Trent Aldridge can do. He is going easy on me. Soon, he will turn up the heat on the amount of work he requires of me. And these days will be ones I look back on fondly.

In comparison, at least.

I hop off the train and sprint to catch a cab, all while telling myself that I'm not scared. That I'll be able to handle it.

And I believe it.

I've lived through worse.

My bag slaps against my back as I run. The air chills me where my shirt is wet from my hair. I didn't have time to dry it before I left. The strands still cling to the back of my shirt, little droplets of water saturating the material.

I pull my bag higher on my shoulder when I hear, well feel, it vibrate. I'm already late, but I pause in my dash to take out my phone.

I look at the screen. It's a number I don't know.

Normally, I wouldn't answer an unknown number.

Especially after the creepy hang-ups months back, and the strange music always playing.

I *know* I shouldn't answer it.

But I'm waiting for some information for grad school, so I really don't have the luxury of sending any calls to voicemail.

The thought of not getting into a grad program after everything I have endured to get here is not something I want to think about, so I pick up the phone, still not convinced it isn't one of Trent's mouth-breathing lackeys again, trying to scare me.

"Hello," I answer, but I'm not expecting anyone to respond, so when I hear the rough voice on the other side of the line, I stop walking.

"Payton," a gravelly voice says.

"Yes—who is this?"

"It's Brad."

It takes me a few seconds to realize who Brad is, but when I do, my stomach clenches tightly.

He's never called me before.

Why is my sister's boyfriend calling me?

"Is everything okay with Erin?" I reply, my voice tight with dread.

The air in my lungs spills out with relief that it's not a prank call, followed shortly by momentary panic. It's rooted deep inside me, just from speaking to him. His mere voice sets me on edge.

"She's fine," he grits out, and his tone is enough to tamp down my fear and replace it with annoyance.

Typical.

The man is calling me, obviously wanting something from me, and he gives me attitude.

"Oh, okay, what can I do for you, Brad?" I'd rather do more chores for Trent than lift a single finger for Deadbeat Brad.

I also have a feeling I will not like whatever he says. It's not just that he's rough around the edges.

There's something else about him that I don't like, but I can't put my finger on it. It's not that he's ever hit on me, but it's the way he looks at me. I know I'm being paranoid.

Not every man wants you, Payton.

Still. I don't like him. I remind myself it's okay not to love everyone I meet.

"Did you get our money?" he asks without a lick of shame.

A part of me isn't surprised that my sister has her boyfriend doing her dirty work. Erin keeps asking and texting, looking for the money that I don't have.

I don't know what more I can say to her.

I tell her all the time that the moment I turn twenty-two, I'll get it, but it doesn't matter.

She still wants me to ask Trent for it now. I'm supposed to, according to her, tell Trent I have expenses I didn't anticipate.

The problem is, she doesn't know that it's hard enough to get money from him to pay for my train tickets at this point.

I haven't told Erin what's going on with Trent.

I have too much going on in my life right now to deal with

her on my case. Freaking out about the situation. Being all dramatic about "how this is cozy." How she thinks I'm lying about my situation. How I cannot be trusted. How I'm the worst family she could ever ask for.

I can already hear her ranting how this isn't fair to her.

It's easier for me just to pretend that everything is all right and that I've just been busy, but I know I'm going to have to come clean and tell her that he is giving me hell.

My teeth bite down on my lower lip.

"I don't have it," I respond, knowing full well, Brad won't be happy.

But I'm sick of this.

Frankly, I don't deserve to be hounded by them when she hasn't even bothered looking for a job.

"You gotta get that money," he warns. I'm not sure if I'm imagining the threat there, but it puts me on edge. "We need it now, dammit."

I flinch at the tone of his voice, but I steady mine and respond, "It's not that simple, Brad."

"Make it that simple." I hear his pants. Like he's pacing. Working himself up. "Your sister is driving me insane. She's freaking out."

"What is the cash for?"

"Our fucking bills," he spits out. The panting intensifies. If anything, he should use that money on a trip to the doctor's. That doesn't sound healthy at all. "I already told you once, Payton, and I ain't telling you shit again."

They told me the same thing when I was at their place, but I am still cautious. Honestly, I don't believe a thing that comes out of either of their mouths. Ever.

"How does Erin not have any money left?"

"Not everyone is living in the laps of luxury, little princess."

When Brad says that nickname, it feels like spiders are crawling up my arm. Although it rubs me the wrong way when Trent says it, it's nothing like when Brad does. Trent might hate me, but Brad makes it sound dirty.

"There is no part of me that is a princess, and you of all people should know that," I snap. Inhaling, I forge on, "You'll get the money for the utility bills, but it won't be three grand. I'll call you when I have what I can get. Pass that on to Erin."

I hang up the phone, annoyed.

He's not kidding. I'm sure Erin is driving him crazy. I know she has some money, but she's probably just used not to having to pay for her own utilities and credit card bills.

In the past, everything was automatically deducted from a fund Ronald made for her. An allowance of sorts. Even for the first year that he was gone, he paid for everything.

Shortly before Ronald died, the money just stopped getting sent out. Which was why Erin started freaking. Even with my suspicions about Ronnie's undesirable behavioral traits, I have no doubt Erin is at fault. She must have done something for her to lose access to the funds.

And instead of owning up to her mistakes, I'm the one being forced to go to Trent and beg for more.

Which I know will cost me so much pain and suffering from him.

I'm so sick of all this bullshit.

I turn around and walk faster, my anger and frustration pouring out of me in tears.

The train ride back to Trent's is a blur. Literally. I can't see past the rim of hot, unshed tears coating my eyes. I swipe at them before I reach his office.

I should wait until I'm alone to cry, but I can't hold them back. I don't even know why I returned here. Why I didn't say fuck it and go to class like I should've. But I know I'm weak right now, and I need to get out of here before anyone sees.

By the time I make it to the front door, I'm practically sobbing, and if my day isn't bad enough, I walk into a wall.

Except it's not a wall.

Walls don't smell this good.

"Hold up, princess."

Trent's arms wrap around my shoulders, steadying me so I don't fall over.

I feel like crawling into a hole and dying. It's not bad enough I had to see him, but I have to see him when I'm crying and sobbing like an idiot.

With his hands still holding on to my shoulders, I continue to look at the floor, refusing to meet his eyes. But then his right hand drops, and I feel it touch my jaw. He lifts my head.

"Wait. What's wrong?" he asks.

The care and concern in his voice is enough to give me pause.

"Nothing."

He looks into my eyes, and it unnerves me. It makes my body fall forward, wrap around him, and cry.

Sob.

I'm freaking holding on to the enemy and sobbing into his arms.

And as much as I want to pull away, I can't.

I physically can't move.

Instead, my body slumps forward even more. A muffled cry escapes my lips. I let out all the emotions. The pain of the past twenty-one years. The fear of what's to come. The heartbreak of having family that doesn't love me.

And during my episode . . .

Trent Aldridge holds me.

That's the most shocking part.

He holds me as I cry.

He holds me as I breathe.

He holds me as I try to pull myself together.

This man who hates me rubs his hands up and down my arms to comfort me.

A part of me knows I should pull away.

But this feeling is scarce.

Not readily available to me.

I'm not prepared to let it go just yet.

The need to bask in it for a little longer weaves its way through me.

I don't want it to end.

Not when I know the feeling won't be back.

I can't remember the last time I've been comforted like this. Maybe never.

Eventually, and after a few deep breaths, I wake up from the dream I'm in and pull my head back to look up at him.

Blue eyes meet mine.

A million questions staring back.

I think he's going to press and ask me why I was crying, but instead, he stares down at me before blinking. The look from before is gone, replaced with a look of confusion.

I don't think he's confused about me. More at himself.

Neither of us moves for a beat.

Then he drops his hands, turns, and walks away.

What the hell just happened?

Time passes way too fast. I get busy with schoolwork and the dumb papers I'm required to turn in every damn week. Buried in books, I almost forget that we are going to Cresthill today.

When I leave my room and head to Trent's office, he's not there.

Next, I go to the kitchen.

Nothing.

Where is he?

However, his driver, Michael, is waiting for me in the foyer after I have searched the whole damn loft.

"Mr. Aldridge won't be riding with us, ma'am."

A part of me is annoyed that he didn't tell me himself. Another part is happy because I feel a bit awkward after he held me when I cried. Couple that with still remembering him in his birthday suit . . . well, maybe not being trapped with him in a small space is a good thing.

When his body was pressed against me, I was too upset to think about it, but the moment he left me, it was all I could think of. The heat dissipated too quickly when I lost his touch. His warmth was something I couldn't understand craving.

Once in the car, I let myself wonder where he is.

I tell myself it's not worry I feel, but it doesn't change the ugly truth. Trent is religious about his volunteer work. There have been a handful of times he hasn't gone, and it's usually planned out ahead of time. Not sudden like this.

The drive takes less time than usual, or maybe it just feels quicker because I don't have to deal with Trent giving me dirty looks.

Technically, it's way more peaceful—and spacious. His large presence and ego in a car are almost too much for the space. But it's also a stormy experience, with my brain working in overdrive to convince myself I'm not worried.

We arrive about twenty minutes later.

Doesn't matter how many times I've come here, my breath still leaves my body from how beautiful this place is.

It's not a home.

It's a sanctuary.

Peaceful and calm.

Flowers and fountains greet me as soon as my body leaves the car.

Even the fragrance is different in Cresthill.

It's as if I'm walking through a field of lilies. A floral scent, rich and sweet. Too strong to be anything but natural.

Like always, my coiled-up muscles relax as I make my way through the large lobby. I head straight in and see Margret.

She doesn't spot me at first.

No, her gaze is looking in the opposite direction.

I follow it.

That's when I see Trent.

He's not alone.

Nope.

He's with a man who looks to be in his late thirties.

I'm confused. He's way too young to be a resident, and I've never seen him visiting or volunteering.

I continue to watch them walk, and it's when they walk up to Henry that my heart starts to rattle in my chest.

Oh, Trent. You didn't . . .

They stop at the table in front of Henry. Henry hasn't seen them yet, but when he does, my world shifts on its axis.

He did.

Henry's jaw trembles first. Then his hands. They shake uncontrollably as he reaches out to the man. Small tremors wrack out of him until a pair of strong arms reach out and help him stand.

Tears roll down his cheeks, and then the man, the one I don't know, is hugging him.

"W-who . . ."

I can't speak.

My throat feels like it's closing.

I know who it is, but I refuse to believe it.

Margret steals the words from my mouth.

"His son." Her voice cracks. She, too, is feeling the weight of this moment.

My own eyes start to feel heavy, and I know what's coming.

"I'll be right back," I blurt out, needing space.

Without another word, I walk out and head in the opposite direction. The tears I have been trying to hold back fall regardless.

I finally stop in an enclosed garden.

The ceiling is high and made of glass. I didn't even know this was here. The last light of the day shines in the space with three clear walls. During the full light of day, I can imagine that it's bright and refreshing with all the greenery. A planned, repeating design to the plants turns into a sort of boxed garden I've seen in movies with English houses. A private oasis in the middle of a building surrounded by the city.

My tears start to dry as I take deep inhales of oxygen. It's fresher in here. I have the plants to thank for that. The calming space relaxes me, offering me a connection after feeling unmoored after seeing Henry with his son.

That's when I realize I'm not alone.

In the corner of a space, kneeling next to a plant, is a woman. She must hear me because she turns over her shoulder.

Then she's walking toward me.

Her face has mud on it. Her eyes are a crisp shade of blue. She looks familiar, but I can't place her.

"Are you okay?"

"Yeah, I just—" I stare at a freesia nearby, unable to meet her eyes. I finally turn to her. "Have you ever wondered if everything you know about a person is wrong?"

She looks at me with sad, knowing eyes. "Yes. All the time."

"How do you deal with that?"

"I find that gardening helps."

"How can a garden help me figure out what I'm missing?"

Her fingers trail along the path of flowers. I follow her.

She stops at one, adjusting the stems. "Do you know that, to most people, a dandelion is just a weed? Something to be plucked and pulled from the yard and flower beds. But in the spring, when the flowers are just starting to wake from winter, the dandelion is the first bloom available for the bees." She looks off into the distance like she can see that bee now.

"I had no idea."

She plucks the flower she's holding and offers it to me. It's a dandelion. "A weed is but an unloved flower. And people are the same way until you can see around their mistakes and watch them bloom."

A small gasp leaves my lips as the implication of her words hit me in the chest. I swallow, take the flower from her, and stare at her in astonishment. "Thank you," I say, and I mean it.

This woman said exactly what I needed to hear at the exact moment I needed to.

Not everything is black and white.

Shades of gray make up the world.

Weeds are flowers, too.

I turn to walk away when she speaks once more. "Trent wasn't always hateful like this, you know."

Trent . . . ?

I never mentioned his name.

I turn and look back over my shoulder.

My heart begins to sink before it kicks into high gear as I remember her eyes. A crisp blue I've seen before.

That's when it hits me.

She's Trent's mom.

Ronald's wife.

"He was the sweetest boy," she continues. "I loved the fact that he was too kind, too soft, but his father knew that wouldn't do. He made it his goal to harden Trent. It's not Trent's fault that he goes about things the way he does now."

And then, with a sad, small smile, she turns back to her plants.

I leave the little garden in a daze, stepping out a back door and edging myself to the waterline. A gust of wind hits me. The puffy, white seeds fly from the dandelion between my fingers, streaking across the air until they're too far to track.

When I look back down, all that's left is a stem.

Trent's mom was right about the wrong thing.

Nothing in this world stays the same.

CHAPTER TWENTY-SIX

Trent

TODAY IS A SHIT DAY.

I went for a run, but that didn't help.

Ever since I saw Henry and his son together, I've been off.

Don't get me wrong, I'm happy for them, but my own wounds are still fresh and making it hard for me to concentrate.

Now, I'm fucking around on my computer.

Story of my life.

Work. Work. Work.

The only time I play is when I'm giving Payton a hard time.

I lock my gaze on the screen in front of me, but I swear the words are blurry as I stare.

I'm not looking at the numbers. I'm looking past the numbers. Basically, I am one hundred percent useless today.

No matter how hard I try, I can't clear my thoughts.

I should answer emails, but I'm just not in the mood for anyone's bullshit.

Instead, I close out the screen and open a new one.

Solitaire.

Yep, it's that kind of day.

If one of my clients saw me right now, they would probably put out a hit on me. I'm supposed to be making them money, not fucking around on my computer, passing the time, because I have the motivation of a five-year-old asked to read a math book.

Just as I'm about to start the game, the door to my office swings open.

It's not hard to guess who it could be.

Not many have the balls to roll up on my place without an invitation, which leaves Cyrus, my mother, or a pissed-off, straight-outta-the-underworld victim.

At first, I can't tell who's walking in, but when I look up from my computer, I instantly know.

Ding, ding, ding.

I'll take pissed-off victims for five hundred, Alex.

Although I have never seen him in person, I am well aware that the man standing in front of me is Paul, the most recent recipient of my shady practices on the stock market.

The first thing I can tell as his feet stomp on my marble floors is that he isn't happy. But I guess I wouldn't be either if I lost hundreds of millions of dollars in one day.

That's the consequence of pissing off one of my clients. I refrain from smiling. That action will get me a bullet in my head. I have to assume the only reason I don't have one already is because security cameras are all over this place, and Paul is trying desperately to go legit.

When he stops moving, I inspect him.

He's an older man, probably close to my father's age, had my father lived. I'd guess late fifties or early sixties. His hair is salt and pepper, and his forehead is creased with lines. Crow's feet edge his eyes, but it's what's under them that gives him away.

He's barely hanging on after my attack. The dark hollows tell the tale of many sleepless nights.

Probably my doing.

Yet I can't seem to find it in me to care.

"Paul, good to see you." I meet his eyes.

"Oh, so you do know who I am," he responds tersely.

"Of course. Your name *precedes* you." Adding a little flair is certainly going to piss him off, but I'm beyond caring right now.

The dick isn't going to kill me in my office.

"Or it could be the fact that you've chosen me as your enemy."

I shrug, pressing start on my solitaire game. "I don't know what you're talking about."

"Oh, no?" he challenges, his face serious, his brow lifted.

"No, I'm sorry. I don't." I nod to the seat in front of me, not really looking, focused on matching up numbers and suits on the screen. "But if you'd like to take a seat, I have to assume you would like to invest with me."

His hand hits my desk while the door opens again, and this time, security decides to step in. I make a mental note to figure out why Paul was able to get this far. To figure out whether my security officers need to be changed.

"Do you need me to escort him out, sir?"

"Give us a minute," I say to the guard before continuing back to Paul, finally looking away from the solitaire game. "Now that you have my undivided attention, why don't you get to the point, seeing as you've made it very clear you're not here to invest?"

"Cut the shit, Aldridge. You know why I'm here."

"Spit it out. I don't have all day, I'm busy."

Busy playing solitaire.

But I don't say that.

Instead, I pretend that I'm looking over something important.

He rounds the table and moves closer as though his presence will rattle me.

It doesn't.

"I know what you did," he seethes out.

"I do a lot of things. You're going to need to be specific with me."

Leaning back in my chair, I make myself comfy. He wants to intimidate me. I'll show him he can't.

"You tampered with my product!"

"Your product?" I offer a small shake of my head. "Oh, you mean your special sauce. I heard about that ordeal. Sounds like you got screwed. Sorry. Can't say that I tampered with anything. Plus, I don't eat your shit. I'm more of a Rao's guy myself."

There is no missing how his hands clench.

"I don't know how you did it, but you fucked with my report."

I tsk. "Again, that sounds like something highly illegal, and I am simply a man who likes to invest. I wouldn't know the first thing about tampering with a recipe."

"I don't think *you* were the one to tamper with it."

Another step closer.

"Isn't that what you just said?" I tsk again. This one says, *you've lost it, dude.* "Paul—I can call you Paul, right?" A vein on his forehead pulses. I ignore it. "I think you're confusing me with someone else. I said I wouldn't know what to do, and you agree." I turn to the guards hovering by the door and lift a brow. "Right?"

One of them nods, and Paul is straight-up seconds from losing his shit.

"Fine. Maybe it wasn't you." And another step. "But Lorenzo tampered with the sauce, and you shorted my stock."

"Do you have any proof of this supposed plot . . ." I trail off because if he had anything, he wouldn't be here, and I would already be in jail.

I spare a glance down at the floor.

Dad, you could have had company.

Paul's fists land on his hips. "Of course, I don't have any proof."

"Slandering is beneath you, Paulie." I shake my head. "I would leave before I have to throw you out."

"I know it was you." He points a finger at me. "I know it was Lorenzo. I know it was all you guys and your idiot friends making money off my back."

"I don't get involved in this type of shit. I can't imagine that Lorenzo is your only enemy. However, that being said, you have no proof, so you should keep your mouth shut."

And he's finally around the desk, right in front of my face. "I don't need proof to go after you."

I lift a casual hand, stopping my guards from spurring into action. "Is that a threat?"

"No, Aldridge, it's a promise."

I lean forward, placing my elbows on my arm rests and leveling him with my stare.

"Your time here is up, Paul."

Lifting my hand, I signal the security guards to take him away. He sees them approaching him right before he spots the solitaire game on my desktop. He lunges for me, but I casually kick my chair to the side and watch as he loses his footing, toppling to the wooden planks.

"Oooh." I fake a wince. "You scratched my floors. That's African Blackwood. Expensive stuff to replace. Tell you what," I say as the guards flank either side of him. "Since I'm sure you can't afford it at the moment, I can put you on a payment plan."

Paul lunges for me again. I make sure he's on camera, clear as day. This is great evidence, should I need it.

The guards stop him just before he reaches me.

Shame.

A bit of blood and a bribe would've done the trick, landing him in jail.

The guards grip either side of his arms tight.

He shrugs them off and points at me again. "I will come after you. I will come after all of you. I will find the things you care about, and I will dismantle them the same way you dismantled my company."

My security guards lead him out.

Once, not so long ago, he had power.

Then Matteo and Lorenzo squashed him like a bug.

A part of me feels bad. After all, he was trying to go legit. But a bigger part knows he's full of shit.

Like most of my clients, men like him might say they are trying to go legit, but it's really a front.

Take Tobias, for example. No way will he ever really be out of the game.

Look at Alaric, Matteo, and Cyrus. They're married and starting families of their own. They still get involved with illegal shit all the time, even if they technically aren't working in the same capacity anymore.

Pulling out my cell, I call my brother-in-law.

He answers on the first ring.

"What?" the prick says.

"Hello to you, too, Cyrus."

"I'm busy, Trent." He sighs. "Unless this is important—"

"It is," I cut him off.

My relation to his wife is the only reason he allows me this luxury of speaking back to him and keeping my life.

"Speak."

"Paul was here. He's on to us. He knows we shorted his stock." Standing from my desk, I begin to move to the floor-to-ceiling windows.

"How?"

I take in the city. As if New York will have the answers I need.

"Not sure."

He groans, clearly annoyed by this new information. "I thought you handled this."

"I did. I bought everything with our offshore accounts. It's not traceable."

The line is silent.

Cyrus is probably thinking about what I said.

Finally, he says, "Well, obviously, it is."

I nod despite him not being able to see me. "That's for sure."

"Tell me what he said."

"He said he knows everything."

"Do you believe him?"

"Yes." I know his next question will be *how*, so I beat him to it. "Honestly, I don't think it stems from my office. The shorting of the stock is pretty obvious if you know who tampered. If he thinks it's Lorenzo and has proof of it, it's not a far jump to make the conclusion that the men in charge of Lorenzo's finances shorted the stock."

And that unlucky fucker is me.

"We need to tell Lorenzo and Tobias someone spoke within their ranks," Cyrus says.

"Yep."

"Fuck!"

The sound of a glass hitting a table echoes through the line.

"Exactly."

"There's a traitor in their house."

Not a question. A statement.

"Seems that way."

"Talk to Lorenzo. I'll speak to Tobias." There's a pause as he talks to someone. My sister. He assures her it's okay, even though we've just made her life a hell of a lot more dangerous. "Make sure nothing is traceable," he orders, returning to our conversation once Ivy leaves. "He can speculate all he wants. As long as it doesn't trace it back to us, it will be fine."

He hangs up, and now I have to make a phone call I dread.

Lorenzo Amanté is not a friend. He's a client who I took on after Matteo Amanté stepped down from his role in the family business.

His role being straight out of *The Godfather*.

The man ran the whole mafia.

But after Matteo stepped down, his cousin Lorenzo took his place.

Now he runs the whole fucking show while Matteo runs the legitimate side of things.

I can barely believe that this is where my life went after what my father did, but I don't regret it.

I like the power.

Even if it comes with scary motherfuckers on speed dial.

I hit the call button and wait for Lorenzo to answer.

"Aldridge."

"I need to see you."

We're a lovely bunch, us two. Full of manners and good vibes.

"Well, that sounds ominous," he clips out, and I think I hear a muffled gunshot in the background before he returns to the conversation at hand. "Did you lose all my money? Because if you did—"

"I know. I know. You won't be happy," I taunt, knowing full well he would probably cut off my hands if that happened.

"Understatement of the year. I'd be lethal." His comment would be funny if it weren't accurate. Death would be too easy for the man or woman who stole from this man.

"Got it. No. The money's still there."

My mouth twitches with amusement. This is one sick fucker. I'm happy to have him on my side.

"So, spit it out." His voice is the usual cool tone that I've grown used to over the past few years since Matteo introduced us.

"I'll tell you in person," I say to him.

"Even more ominous."

He laughs, figures he would—again, sick as fuck. The sketchier or more dangerous a situation is, the more entertained Lorenzo is.

"When are you free?"

"Tonight. Seven. Meet me at the dock."

He doesn't have to tell me which dock he means. It's the main one they have been using ever since they switched locations after that shit went down with Salvatore, Matteo, and Lorenzo's cousin.

"I'll be there."

I hang up first. Looking down at my watch, I see it's only four, which means I can't go home first.

It's fine.

There is plenty of work for me to do before I make this

meeting. When I add in the commute, I don't have that much time at all.

I pick up my phone and dial Gail's number, calling to inform her of the list of chores I want Payton to do. I honestly don't give a crap what she does. My house is spotless, but I like to keep her on her feet. So, tonight, instead of the gym or my bathroom, I'm going to have her redo my pantry.

It's not a nice task to thrust upon her.

Chef will be pissed.

I'll tell Gail to skip on the laundry and let Payton do that, too. Yep.

Gail can throw in some extra towels and sheets for good measure. Maybe I'll tell her to make them extra dirty beforehand. Spill some ketchup on it or something. That thought makes me smile.

With a shake of my head, I focus my attention back on the call. Gail isn't happy with my tasks. She's officially joined the dark side. Actually, for a second, her change in loyalties makes me consider the possibility that my side *is* the dark side.

But I push that thought out and hang up the call.

I stare at the computer screen in front of me.

My fingers hit the keyboard. The tapping drowns out everything else.

I spend the next few hours researching companies I think would be a good investment.

Then when it's time, I get up, head to my car parked under the building, and leave to meet Lorenzo. I trust my men, as I hired them all from Jax, but you never can be too careful. After all, they let Paul past them earlier.

Traffic is a bitch today, and it takes a good forty-five minutes for me to get out of the city. When I'm pulling onto the docks, it looks to be in its usual abandoned state, but I know better.

I pull up, shut the car off, and get out.

Heading inside, I throw open the heavy metal door. In the corner, I can see that they have a massive shipment a few men are currently going through. I imagine it's one of Tobias's shipments of pills.

He's trying to get out.

Well, he's gotten out of most.

No longer selling cocaine or heroin, the only thing he still has his hands in is Molly.

I imagine, by the time next year comes, he'll be fully out.

Or that's the hope, at least.

Like I said, no one really leaves.

Since he knows I'm coming, Lorenzo is already waiting for me. He's sitting at the table, a tumbler of scotch in his hands.

I walk over to him, take a seat, and reach for the glass he left for me to use, pouring myself a few fingers.

"Well," he drawls, leaning back, "since you reached for that drink pretty fast, I have to imagine this isn't something good."

"To be honest, I'm not sure what this is," I admit with a sigh. "Talk."

"Is there anything that can lead Paul to the tampering?" I ask. Point blank.

It's probably not a smart question to ask Lorenzo, seeing as he can easily kill me and find someone else to invest his money for him, but I ask anyway.

Glutton for punishment and all.

"There are no loose ends," Lorenzo responds, brushing the offensive accusation off with a sip of his scotch.

"Are you sure?"

"Really, pretty boy? Do you want to question me?" He laughs.

There's no question I think Lorenzo likes me, but that doesn't mean he appreciates me questioning him.

"Well, someone said something to him." I shrug.

"What do you mean?"

"I had a visit."

"From Paul?"

I nod at his question.

"Interesting," he says, leaning forward in his chair. "Go on."

"He accused me of not only shorting his stock but also of tampering with his product to short his stock."

"Wow." His head bobs up and down. "I'm impressed."

"Yet I'm not," I fire back, setting aside my glass because I need to keep my wits. "This was never supposed to get out. How does he know? Who spoke?"

"None of my men said shit." His tone has lost all sense of humor. Now it's replaced with an edge to it. Cold and direct.

"Okay, well, it had to be someone," I respond, trying to tone down the accusation in my voice.

No part of me wants to get killed today. But the way Lorenzo has narrowed his eyes, I've done nothing to calm him.

"Are you questioning the people I work with, Trent?" he bites out as a vein throbs on his temple.

Two choices present themselves to me at this moment. Stand my ground. Sure, I might get stabbed. But the other option is to backpedal like a son of a bitch and risk losing his respect forever.

Is my pride worth it?

I decide that it is, mostly because ego is vital in my industry. My clients need to see me as the cocky son of a bitch who's so skilled, his confidence cannot be breached. Lucky for them, I'm a special type of full-of-myself.

"I'm saying I said nothing. We covered all the tracks on my end," I say, choosing to stand up to him.

Time will tell if it was a mistake.

Lorenzo stares at me for a minute. Lines form on his forehead. He's assessing me, but he smiles. Not one that says he's about to gut me either, which is nice.

"That might be so," he allows, "but let's be honest here, Trent. It doesn't take a rocket scientist to know it was me, and if it points at me, it points back to you."

He has a point.

"You're right."

"Is that all you got? Or did you have something else to talk about?"

"Nope, that's it. I just wanted to double-check that there were no loose ends."

He lifts his glass, takes a swig, and places it back down. "There are never loose ends."

"Do I even want to know what you did?"

"Haven't you figured out by now that you never want to ask me that question? No one is talking, Trent. Anyone who was involved, anyone that could have been a possible liability, is in the ground. You got me?"

He winks.

A fucking wink.

Shit.

"I got you."

"Good." He slides my glass back toward my hand, and it slams into my palm with more force than necessary. "Now, let's drink and forget this shit. It's been a shit day, and I need to get drunk."

My fingers curve around the scotch. "I'm driving."

"Stop being a pussy and get drunk with me."

And seeing as that wasn't a question, I decide to say fuck it.

I grab the decanter and pour myself another.

This is going to be a long night.

CHAPTER TWENTY-SEVEN

Payton

I HURRY OUT OF CLASS.

If I don't, I'll miss the train.

Missing the train will bring a long list of other problems for me.

Namely, one named Trent Aldridge.

His lectures are not something I'm in the mood for right now. It's bad enough I still have to stop by the library before I head back to the city.

I make my way across campus, but I don't get very far before that familiar feeling of being followed creeps up on me. Stopping to turn around, I come face-to-face with a man standing a few feet away from me. He's around forty, with a baseball cap . . . again.

Is it the man from the truck? This time, however, he has a camera in his hand. It's pointed at me.

Snap. Snap.

What the hell.

I march right up to him before I can stop myself. There is no doubt in my mind this is the work of Trent. He's probably having me followed. Taking pictures of me for god knows what?

"Give me that camera!" I shout. "It's not cool to take pic—"

"I don't know what you're talking about."

"You're taking pictures of me."

"No—actually, I'm not, I'm taking pictures of my kid."

"Dad, is everything okay?" I look behind me, and there is a kid my age.

Shit.

My cheeks begin to warm.

"I-I'm so sorry," I mutter out. I have never been more embarrassed in my life. My paranoia is officially getting ridiculous.

No one is following you.

No one is taking pictures.

With my head down, I whisper I'm sorry before sneaking off, but I don't get very far before I hear a familiar voice calling my name.

"Accusing someone in public. That's a new low for you," Erin says.

"What are you doing here?" I ask, looking around her to make sure Brad isn't with her.

The only thing worse than a surprise visit from Erin is a surprise visit from Brad.

"Well, since you don't answer my calls . . ." She trails off, being ambiguous on purpose.

She's right.

I don't answer every time she calls. What's the point? Every time I speak to her, she asks me what's going on with Ronald's money.

Nothing.

Nothing is going on with the money.

The answer is still the same answer I have had for months.

I have to wait until I'm twenty-two. No matter how often I tell her this, my sister never seems to grasp it.

A part of that is my fault. I didn't tell her about the deal I made with the devil. I didn't tell her he's basically blackmailing me. I'm going to have to at some point, or she will never leave me alone. Period.

I decide that moment is now.

"I don't answer your phone calls because there's no point," I say, shifting my textbooks into my other hand. "I have nothing new to tell you."

Her eyes open wide at my tone. "What do you mean, nothing *new*? You said you would get me some cash. Cough it up, Payton."

"I know what I said, but that doesn't mean it will be easy."

"Can't you just ask for it? It's yours."

"If only it were that easy," I mutter under my breath. It's now or never. Time to spit it all out. I sigh, going for it. "The thing is, I can't. It's already hard enough for him to pay for anything else."

She narrows her eyes, clearly not believing me. "What's that supposed to mean?"

"There's something I didn't tell you—" I start, but she cuts me off.

"You're having sex with Trent Aldridge, just like you did his father," she hisses under her breath.

"Are you fucking kidding me!" I grip my books to my chest. Tight. My head shakes so hard it leaves me dizzy. "No. Nope. Never. Why do you think that?"

"What else can I think, Payton? Ronald left you all the money. The money that should have been *mine*." She grinds her teeth.

"I didn't ask for that."

"Yeah. Okay. Whatever." She doesn't believe me. It's clear in her voice. "Why don't you tell me your excuse for screwing me over this time?"

"I can't get Trent to give me the money early. I can't even get money to pay for rent near the college."

"Sure." She nods her head. It's condescending as hell, and she knows it. "That's why you're on campus right now. I highly doubt that. Cut the crap, little sis."

"Do you really think it was that easy? That Trent just took over the bills, and I lived happily ever after? A piece of shit like him?"

The words feel dirty coming out of my mouth, mostly because

he's nice to everyone but me, and it's hard to call him names like that after he reunited Henry with his son.

I pummel forward, feeling dirtier and dirtier each second. "It wasn't that easy. He doesn't want to sleep with me. He *hates* me."

"Probably because you were banging his father," she deadpans.

I take a deep breath. Bite my cheeks and try to calm down before I lose it on her. That will do me no good.

"I wasn't." I shrug. "I don't know what else I can say to prove it to you."

"Why should I believe you? You've always wanted what I had."

I shake my head back and forth. "What are you talking about? I've never—" I stop myself. Take in a deep breath. Exhale it once I'm calm enough to. "You know what? No. Let's not do this here. What you don't know is that Trent is extorting me. There's no other way to say it. He's extorting me."

"For sex?"

I shudder at her inquisition. "Not everything is about sex."

"Well, what else would he extort you for?" Her curt voice lashes out at me.

I turn up my chin. "Money to pay my bills. He kicked me out of the house. He canceled my college tuition payment. He had my car repossessed. The only reason I'm even going back to school is because I caved to his demands."

She stares at the expensive textbooks in my arms, full of disbelief and accusations. "What exactly are these demands?"

"I'm his cleaning lady." It's the ugly truth. I almost shrivel inside myself as I say the words. "He calls me his maid, but really, I'm on call for every demand beyond cleaning. I clean his house. I do random tasks in his house. I live in his house."

She narrows her eyes as if she's not sure she believes me. "You're staying at his fucking house, but you really aren't sleeping with him."

"Jesus! God! No!" I tuck my textbooks under one arm and

throw up my free hand. "What more do I have to say to make you listen?"

She tosses her brown hair behind her shoulders. "Maybe I should sleep with him, then."

"Erin." I hold back a snort, unable to even imagine Trent caving. "Trust me when I say he hates both of us."

"Fine," she says, but she obviously doesn't believe that any man could hate her. "Make another deal with him for extra cash. It's the least you can do after everything I gave up because of you."

Her words hang heavy in the air.

All I can do is nod.

I don't know what else to say to her. A part of me wants to tell her to leave me alone, but another part knows that she did take care of me.

There's truth to her words.

I do owe her my life.

When I get the money, I'm going to give her half, and then I'm going to leave.

Start fresh somewhere.

"I'll talk to Trent," I tell her.

Just as she opens her mouth to say something, my phone starts to ring. I pull it out, but before I can see who's calling, she grabs it from my hand.

"Why the fuck is he calling you?" she snaps. And the accusations never end.

If I weren't holding hundreds of dollars' worth of textbooks, I'd rub my temples to stave off the burgeoning headache.

"He's asking the same question you are," I groan out. "You both keep asking the same questions."

"I'm sure that's not all it is,"

"Trust me, it is."

"Mmm," she mutters.

I want to shout: I DON'T WANT YOUR BOYFRIEND WHO GIVES ME THE CREEPS. I DON'T WANT YOUR EXES. I

DON'T WANT YOUR MONEY. I DON'T WANT ANYTHING.
I JUST WANT TO BE LEFT ALONE.

But I say nothing.

I'll get her the money.

Then after that, maybe I will finally be rid of the guilt.

Erin tosses my phone at my feet, hikes her purse up on her shoulder, and walks away. More like stomps. If there was a door nearby, I'm sure she would slam it, too.

Luckily for me, there isn't.

I stare down at my phone.

A violent crack slashes across the screen.

What a metaphor for the state of my life if I've ever seen one.

CHAPTER TWENTY-EIGHT

Payton

THE PAST FEW WEEKS WERE NOTHING LIKE I EXPECTED MY
life to be under Trent's roof.

I'm so confused, I can barely think.

And now, I'm sitting in my bedroom reading about Carl Jung
before I leave for class.

The worst part is, I only have one week until I perform in
front of the staff, and I can barely concentrate.

None of the Trent parts of my situation is as bad as I thought
it would be. It's just confusing as hell. Especially the last time I
was at Cresthill.

Trent.

He's different than I imagined.

And then there's the talk with his mom. Every day, I become
more and more confused over who he is.

The angry son of Ronald Aldridge.

The caring friend to Henry Wian.

The benefactor—*cough*, torturer, *cough*—of yours truly.

The hot guy in the sauna I wouldn't mind seeing naked some
more.

Thinking about Trent in all of his forms, clothed and not, has
become something I'm doing far too frequently.

And right now, I can't.

I have too much to do.

I need to get through a grueling day of classwork, but more studying first. I had too much work for my actual business major before he assigned this damn presentation on top of it.

I pray he'll let it go, not make me do this silly book report and presentation, but I know he won't. There is no point in wishing when I am certain this man is going to take every opportunity available to make me suffer through his "homework" regardless of my coursework.

No amount of begging and pleading for him not to will work.

Placing the book down, I stand from the bed and fix my dress before heading out the door.

It's late enough in the morning, so Trent won't be around.

I step out into the hall, and like I expected, it's clear. Walking toward the front of the loft, I bump into no one.

Just the way I like it.

I can finally breathe when I step out into the city air.

It's cold today. Winter is officially in the air.

I didn't bring a coat, but I guess it will be okay.

The subway is only a few blocks away, and then I'll be hot.

I am halfway up the street when I hit a proverbial wall. My body lurches forward, my hands shooting up to brace for something to catch my fall.

There is nothing there.

My hands grasp air.

The next thing I know, I'm falling to my knees.

The air in my lungs is pulled out of me on impact.

What the hell did I hit?

Knowing my pattern lately, it has to be a person.

And sure enough, when I look up, it's just in time to see not a what but a who.

A man.

I can't see his face because his head is down, and he's already off in the opposite direction. The man hit me and didn't even apologize. And he turned the opposite way, back to where he came from.

He's in a rush, on the phone, and I was the casualty.

Stupid jerk.

The least he could do after almost making me roadkill is say he's sorry.

Two muscular arms reach out and lift me up from the ground, and I'd startle, but the familiar scent of his cologne grounds my insecurity.

"Are you okay?" Trent's gruff voice asks.

His brows are drawn together in anger.

Is he angry with the man or with me?

"Thank you," I say sincerely as I straighten back to my full height.

His jaw goes tight, and he stiffens at my comment. He doesn't want my thank you, that much is clear from the way he looks down at me like I'm a pesky little mouse.

"You need to be more careful," he grits through clenched teeth.

"Did you not see what just happened?" I think I've reached my threshold for bullshit because my voice is way harsher than I intended. And still, I don't stop. "He plowed into me. Not vice versa."

He lets out a huff. His head tilts down, breaking our eye contact. I welcome the peace from his scrutiny.

Until he sighs. "Did you hurt yourself?"

"Yes, just my leg. I'll be fine."

His gaze pulls back up, and our eyes meet. There is a softness to him now. One that I'm not used to.

"You should clean it," he says, and that's when I finally look down.

How I didn't feel the cut is beyond me. My leg hurts more than my knee.

I can't believe I hit the concrete that hard. Embedded in my knee is dirt and debris from the New York City sidewalks.

Gross.

I don't even want to think about it.

Trent's eyes look dark when I return my gaze up to his. The blues of his irises are almost all gone, replaced with black pupils. As to be expected, his jaw is tight.

I'm not sure if he's angry with me still, but he doesn't seem to be. Not really. At least not more so than usual.

"Come on, let's go."

I shake my head. "I have to get to school."

"You don't have to be at school for two hours."

"I forgot you know my schedule."

My eyes roll of their own accord.

He glowers down at me. "I know everything about you, Payton."

"Not really," I mumble under my breath.

We're both silent for a minute, staring at each other before Trent takes a step toward the direction of his building.

"Come on." His fingers brush against my elbow, nudging me forward. "I need to clean your leg, and then you can go to school."

"I don't have time. The next train isn't for two hours. I'll still miss class."

"I'll drive you."

"Don't do me any favors, please," I mumble.

They always come with strings attached. The kind capable of choking.

"Want to say that louder?"

"I said don't do me any favors." I tip my chin up and cross my arms. "I know you're just going to have a damn attitude about it later."

That shuts him up.

Together, we start to head back in the direction of his place, but I'm slow on my feet. It's not that it hurts a ton, but it stings, and because of the blood trickling down my leg, I'm limping.

I'm shocked when his hand reaches out, stopping us. The next thing I know, I'm in the air and resting tight in his arms.

Cradled to his chest.

Like the day I cried into him. Only this time, I'm able to enjoy it.

Dammit, Payton. You are not supposed to enjoy this.

"I can walk," I say, sounding more breathless than I wish to.

"This is faster."

He can't hold me like this. Not when I am embraced so tight I can feel his heartbeat.

I hate him.

Fine, maybe not hate him, but I have strong feelings against him. Feelings that will certainly be confused if he's nice to me again. The last time he was, I was torn up inside for days, not sleeping and playing over the moment on repeat in my head.

And that was merely a hug.

This . . .

This is so much more.

He has to put me down, or I'm destined to be the next star of a *Groundhog Day* sequel, and this is the day that I will choose to re-live. That, or the one when I spotted him enjoying his sauna nude.

"You can't just pick a girl up on the street like this," I plead, hoping he will come to his senses before I allow myself to melt into his warmth.

Because if I close my eyes right now, his presence is enough to soothe me. To help me forget all my problems . . . except he is the problem, so I can't allow this.

"Yet . . . I did." He tightens his grip on me. "What are you going to do to stop me? Just be quiet. The faster we get home, the faster we'll have you cleaned up, and the faster I can get back to my day."

"Again . . . Don't need your help." I realize I'm leaning into him and shift away, sucking in a breath when he just pulls me closer. "And I didn't ask to be knocked over by that guy."

"You're still going to get my help."

"You're impossible."

"Rich coming from you," he says, and I bite my lip to keep from saying an obnoxious retort.

He's helping me.

And he is right.

At the speed I was walking, it would take all day for me to get it cleaned. I would never make the train.

This might be completely embarrassing, but it certainly does help.

In his arms, I feel strangely at peace.

I don't want to read into these feelings.

Nor do I want to think about the way he smells.

Or the butterflies that are flying in my stomach.

Nope.

Keep your thoughts on something that doesn't make your body warm.

Socks.

Yep.

That's what I'll think of. Smelly socks . . .

He takes a step, and as he does, he pulls me even closer to him. His hands that are wrapped around me dig into my exposed flesh.

Shit.

Socks.

Socks.

Socks.

It's not helping.

Nothing is helping.

His fingers are too close to my upper thigh . . . and not close enough to where I've wanted him for weeks. Touching my skin under the hem of my dress, wishing they would move higher.

My eyes flutter closed.

My senses reel with sensations.

Conflicting emotions swirl inside me.

As much as I want to deny it, I can't. The feeling of him on my skin has me hoping for more. With each step he takes, his fingers move ever-so-slightly, a gentle massage that sends currents of desire pooling in my core.

If he moved his hand a little higher, he would touch my . . .

"Socks."

"Socks?" he says.

My cheeks burn.

I said that out loud.

"Nothing."

He sends me a weird look, adjusting me against him to open the door to his office.

He places me on the couch, and I'm left alone with my thoughts and a pounding heart. When he's near, I'm overwhelmed with want and desire I've never felt for another man before. I take a deep inhale, hoping to regulate my pulse that is still skittering erratically.

When he reenters the small office, he feels too big for the space.

My face isn't the only thing hot. The skin on my neck, down to my chest, and across my collarbones starts to heat as he moves closer and closer to me. When he drops to the floor in front of me, I think I might pass out.

The man has seen me naked, and I've seen him naked, but nothing feels as intimate as this.

"Give me your leg." He huffs.

I look down at him and pucker my lips. "It's fine. I'm a grown woman. I can do it myself."

I have no desire for a showdown right now. I am hurt and not in the mood.

"Give me your leg." His voice is rough around the edges. Leaving no room for disagreement.

I'm afraid if I don't, he will do something rash. Reluctantly, I move back on the couch, and my knee is now directly in line with where he is crouched in front of me. I can see his eyes are staring down at my bruised and bleeding leg.

I'm not sure what is wrong with me, but the sight makes me feel tingly all over.

Like I have pins and needles across my body.

My heart hammers in my chest as his hand reaches out. Even though I am watching him, I'm not prepared for my reaction when his palm wraps around my calf muscle to steady my leg so he can clean it.

The second his skin touches mine, I think I might faint.

It's not that this is the first time he has touched me.

Most of the time, it's by accident, but there is something about this position.

Him kneeling in worship before me.

His head angled toward my thigh.

His fingers on my skin.

My heart feels like a pinball. Or at least, like it will certainly combust from all the pent-up pressure building inside me.

As he wipes me with a wet rag. It feels like my skin is on fire. It ignites under his ministrations. Not even the cold compress can cool me.

His gaze is intense as he mends my wounds. It roams lazily over my leg, following the path of his hand as he works up to my knee.

With each caress, the fire grows inside me. It's a blazing heat I can't comprehend, and at this moment, I don't want to.

Instead, I just watch him.

His palm is so big, he grazes my upper thigh as he cleans the wound.

He never looks into my eyes. It's like he refuses to see me. See me for the woman I am. Not the miserable reminder of what his father did to him. Did to both of us, really.

I'm torn about how this new situation makes me feel.

Part happy. Part relieved.

But a bigger, hungrier part is desperate for him.

I feel so much right now.

Lust. Desire. Need.

I *need* to see the look that is reflected in his eyes. To see if he feels it, too.

Has this all been a figment in my mind?

No. This has to be a two-way street of excitement. The way he swallows when I'm close. The way his gaze follows mine, and just now his touch . . .

I'm not making this up.

There must be something he feels for me besides this hatred.

Something is there. I'm sure of it.

It lingers beneath the surface, but I sense it in every look.

It's the same way I think I must look at him. Confused. But still with desire. Conflicting emotions. But that's okay.

People can feel two different things.

They can be two different people, too.

Desire and hate can coexist.

Just like Trent can be an asshole, yet . . . he's not.

His actions are never black and white. There are shades of gray in every move he makes.

The way he treats me is in complete contrast to the Trent who volunteers at Cresthill.

It's like his father.

Good and evil.

Trent's touches have me looking back down. His forearms flex as his large hands clean and remove the rag.

What will he do next?

I think my heart might beat out of my chest as he leans in and gently blows on my skin.

"W-what are you doing?" I finally croak out.

"Drying it," he grits through clenched teeth as he works.

Everything inside me feels warm and tingly.

His hand creeps higher. His fingers bracket my thigh.

He waits there for a beat as though asking permission.

Time stands still. The warmth of his fingertips playing havoc on me.

Melting me.

Toying with me.

Searing me with a desire I can't understand, nor do I want to.

When I look at him this time, I find that he is looking back at me.

His eyes are hooded, giving him away as he breathes out through a clenched jaw.

Then he pulls his gaze from me and slaps a bandage on my knee.

The pain that radiates from the sudden movement is enough to make me hiss out an "ouch."

It breaks the spell.

I shake my head, and he stands and steps back.

"Meet me down in the garage in five minutes," he grits through his teeth.

Then he leaves the room as fast as he can.

But it's too late.

Something has changed between us.

Shifted.

Morphed into something more lethal.

More dangerous.

Slipping easily past the iron cage of my heart.

What the hell just happened, and where do we move on from here?

CHAPTER TWENTY-NINE

Trent

I STORM OUT OF THE ROOM.

Acting like a pussy is not my usual schtick, but fuck, I needed to get out of there.

For so many reasons:

1. Why was she wearing that dress? It's the middle of goddamn November.

2. Why did I think it was a good idea to clean and bandage her knee?

3. We can never have a future while I'm actively trying to ruin her life.

4. The biggest one . . . I'm a dumbass.

I had to leave because if I didn't, I would have hit on her.

Or worse, propositioned her.

Or even worse, closed the distance and kissed her right then and there.

I'm trying to break this girl down, and instead, she has the upper hand. I've tried everything, but all my assumptions about her have been wrong. I thought she would balk at the toilet cleaning, the laundry, the extra studying.

She didn't.

Even volunteering didn't garner the reaction I wanted.

She freaking smiles the whole damn time.

Every punishment I dole out is the same thing.

I see her on the surveillance videos; she can't stop being happy, doing all the asinine things I come up with for her to do without a complaint or issue.

This is fucking annoying and drives me motherfucking insane.

The only time she scowls is when she's talking to me.

Which is quite telling.

After I clear my head, I make my way back down the hallway and to the garage. She better be in the damned car waiting for me. This whole thing is a massive imposition.

Truth is, even though I didn't want to admit it to her, it wasn't her fault.

I watched the scumbag plow right into her.

She's actually lucky she didn't get even more hurt.

It was almost deliberate.

And the truth is, as much as I hate to admit it, I don't really want to hurt her.

Ruin her, sure.

Physically hurt her? Not so much.

I might spend time with the most ruthless men in the world, but I've never had a bloodlust.

Thankfully, when I make it into the garage, I see her sitting in the front seat of my car. I already sent my driver off on another errand, so it's just us.

It's up to me to get this woman to school on time.

Opening the door, I get into the driver's side. Her lavender fragrance hits my nose. Fucking son of a bitch.

Does she have to smell good, too?

I tear out of the garage. Driving way too fast. But I'm pissed. I need her out of my car ASAP.

The faster she is out, the faster I can get myself in check.

I pull out into the New York City streets and start driving around to get us to the island. I take the bridge, weave my way through traffic, and the whole time, the car is silent. I have nothing to say to her, and she probably has nothing to say to me.

When we're finally over the bridge, she proves me wrong. "Thank you for driving me."

I grip the wheel tighter. "We aren't there yet. You shouldn't thank me."

"That implies we may not ever make it."

I shrug, speeding up for kicks. "You never know."

"That's true." She grips the oh-shit handle. "I rescind my thank you."

"Nope, it's already been thrown into the world. You can't take it back."

"That's not very fair."

I spare her a glance before changing lanes. "Life isn't fair, princess."

"You don't have to tell me," she mutters, not for me to hear.

But I do.

I hear her every damn time she hints that her life hasn't been all sunshine and rainbows.

I can't help the curiosity that rises, but in my typical fashion, I make sure to express it in the most condescending tone possible. I really can't help myself.

"What do you know about suffering?"

A sound emanates from her mouth, and I can only imagine what she must be thinking.

Her life before my father.

She crosses her arms. "I let you belittle me. I let you say a lot of things to me . . . but do not tell me what I know about life. Unlike you, Trent, I didn't grow up with a silver spoon in my mouth."

"Touché, *princess*."

"Stop fucking calling me that."

"Why would I do that?" I stop at a light and fix my entire attention on her, enjoying the pink flush of her skin. "It's fun to get a rise out of you."

"Maybe because you're a decent person."

"I'm not."

"But I think you are." She turns to face me. "You took care of me when I was hurt and bleeding after all."

I didn't think this through.

I am so fucked in this argument.

"Don't delude yourself to think that meant anything." I stare straight at the light, willing it to turn green and give me an excuse to drown out this conversation with the sound of my engine. "I was protecting my investment."

"Sure, tell yourself that. We both know you are full of shit."

The light finally puts me out of my misery.

I keep driving.

Instead of answering her statement, I reach my hand forward and turn on the radio.

I'm done listening to her speak.

Music blares through the speakers. Angry lyrics and long guitar solos.

From the corner of my eye, I glance over at her.

She's uncomfortable. Fidgeting beside me. Staring out the window.

She wants to say something else.

Probably wants to tell me what a prick I am.

She doesn't need to. I already know.

No point in stating the obvious.

Luckily for me, traffic is nonexistent. A huge plus, because before long, I'm pulling up to the building she told me her class was at.

"I'll pick you up after class."

"You don't have to."

"Yeah. You're right, but I will. You're in no condition to walk to the train. Then, on top of that, take the subway back to my place. I'll pick you up."

She opens and closes her mouth, reminding me of a fish. Then eventually, she must think better of it because she nods.

There are no goodbyes.

Instead, I turn to look out my window, and she slips out of the car.

Once she's gone, I'm left alone in front of her building with nothing to do to kill the next two hours.

I throw the car in park and just decide to work from here.

I have plenty of calls to make. Plus, I do have my laptop in the car.

I use my car as a hotspot, and then I start to look at the figures for the day.

After about an hour of work, I close out my computer and dial Jaxson Price.

"Now what?" he answers.

If I didn't know him as well as I do, I would think he's actually pissed, but since I do, I know he's just messing with me.

"Can't I call to chat?"

"Nope." He chuckles, and I laugh back.

"Not cool."

"Speaking the truth, bro. No one ever calls me to just shoot the shit."

"You know I love ya, man. You're practically my brother." My voice is serious now.

Over the years, Jaxson has had issues with feeling this way with his family. I hope he's not actually upset. It doesn't sound like it, but I say it anyway.

"Nope, you're confusing me with Cyrus."

Of course, he minimizes the sentiment.

"I could never confuse you two."

"He's much grumpier." He laughs.

"You think?" I chuckle. "But you're right. I am calling you for something. But I promise after this one favor, I'll stop being a complete selfish prick and ask you about your life."

"Doubt it. Prick is the only character trait you have."

"Not true."

"Oh, you aren't calling me in some ridiculously concocted plan to further ruin an innocent girl?"

I'm silent, and he laughs again.

I can picture him shaking his head.

"Just as I thought," he says. "You need to get over this, bro. She's getting the money. Your father, prick that he was, left it to her for some crazy reason and was a complete dickbag to you and your family, but that doesn't mean she had anything to do with it."

"Mmm."

"You know that, right?"

"Maybe. But—"

"No buts. Let the woman live her life. Leave her alone."

I'm silent for a moment. "Well, that might be hard now."

"What is that supposed to mean?"

I don't answer him.

"Trent," he says my name in a way that tells me I have no choice.

If I don't answer, Price will probably hack into my surveillance system and see what's going on at my house, and the last thing I need is for him to see how much I've jerked off to the thought of her. Not that he'd know it's her I think of, but the timing isn't a coincidence.

Payton in a short skirt, kneeling? Hand, meet dick.

Payton reaching up to dust my highest shelves, her shirt rising? Hand, meet dick.

Payton eating a banana in slow motion because she's distracted by Carl fucking Jung? Hand, meet dick.

There's a pattern here.

Doesn't take a rocket scientist to put two and two together.

Jax's company set up my surveillance camera, so it wouldn't be very hard for him to invade my privacy. Actually, come to think of it, it's probably a good thing he doesn't know Payton is living with me. That means I can trust my security team not to tell him. He found me the men I employ. If I ever wondered about where their loyalties lie, this proves it. My loft is as secure as Fort Knox, unlike my office building. Take Paul's unannounced visit. He took the service elevator, a well-paid bribe to a building employee granting him access. That breach has been taken care of.

Nevertheless, I have to say something because this is Jaxson Price. If he wants to find out, he will. It's better if it comes from me.

"I moved her in with me," I admit.

"What the fuck, Trent?" His voice is loud enough that, if someone were near my car, they would hear him.

Also, damn, my ear hurts.

I shrug, even though he can't see it. "It's just easier this way."

"In what universe is keeping her locked in your house easier?"

"This is different."

He groans over the line. "How?"

"She's not locked up."

"Oh, do tell then . . . What cartoon-level genius plan do you have? Please, I'm dying to know." His voice drips with sarcasm.

"Well, for one, Christina took a vacation—"

"Jesus, Trent, please do not tell me you moved her into your house to clean for you. Please don't say you are hoarding her money because you want a maid."

"Fine. I won't."

Doesn't make it any less true.

"Are you fucking her?"

"Nope."

But I want to.

"So, you aren't trying to live some hot maid fantasy, right?"

"Um, no."

But now that you mention it . . .

"Even worse," he says, and he sounds appalled, which is rich coming from the guy with absolutely no sense of privacy. "If this is some creepy fantasy of banging your maid, at least I would understand. As long as she is willing."

"Of course, she would be willing. And I would fucking ask first. But that's not the point. I don't want to bang her."

Ha.

"Yeah. Okay," Jax says as if he has a direct line to the bullshit in my mind. "Then why else is she there?"

"I want to get to know her."

"Go on. Because I'm not buying any of this shit. Real reason, please."

"I want to make her life hell for what she's done. Plus, if I keep her close, I can see if she has any skeletons in her closet that I can—"

"No."

"I haven't even asked you for anything."

"Trent," he says, and it's in that *bitch, please* tone. "I have known you my whole fucking life. I know what you will ask me. And the answer is no. No fucking way."

"Dude. You fucking do shady shit all the time," I say.

"Yes, Trent, I do. To awful men. Not to innocent girls who just happened to piss you off because you have daddy issues."

"I don't have daddy issues." I scoff.

"Yeah. You keep telling yourself that. You're acting like a little whiny-ass bitch. Get your head out of your ass and drop this shit. Give the poor girl her pocket money, and leave her alone."

"Twenty-two million is not pocket money."

"You're right. It's pocket *change*," he corrects.

"Does that mean you won't help me?"

"Of course, it means I won't help you!" he exclaims in irritation.

Over my stupidity, probably.

"But I can still come over when I'm bored, right?" I chuckle, trying to change the tone of the convo.

"That, you never have to ask. You're family."

"Thanks, I appreciate it."

The line goes silent, and I can hear him breathing.

Then he sighs. "Let her go."

"I promise I'm not keeping her."

"Are you at least feeding her?"

"I'm not a complete animal. Actually, if you must know, I'm playing chauffeur for her today because she hurt her leg. She got knocked down by some asshole on the sidewalk and tore up her leg pretty good. Oh, and I also cleaned and bandaged her," I add as if my little show of kindness negates all the bullshit I've done.

"What you are telling me is you . . . *played doctor*?" he says it like it's another kink of mine he's discovered, and honestly, I'm not as against the idea as I should be.

I'm so fucked.

"What?" I say, going with the denial route. "No. No. No fucking way."

"Sounds like you have a thing for this girl, after all. Why don't you bring her over? We can have dinner."

"Fuck no."

"Fiiiiiiiiine."

I hang up the phone.

Jaxson is a pain in my ass. But he's not wrong.

That doesn't mean I'll listen, though.

CHAPTER THIRTY

Trent

TONIGHT, I AVOIDED HER.

I've been doing that a lot recently.

The thing is, despite avoiding her, I find myself heading down the halls of the center and looking for her.

It makes no sense what I'm doing, yet I can't stop my feet.

I find her in the library. She's not alone. She's with Anne, a resident here at Cresthill. My feet stop short, but it's not her companion but what's in front of her that has me halting my steps.

Even here, she found time to read the book I gave her this morning. The one she has to report back on this week.

This woman is impossible to bring down. No matter how much work I throw at her, she rises to the challenge.

If I weren't actively trying to ruin her, I'd probably hire her.

"Let's go," I huff out.

She looks up from the table, confused. A cute line forms between her brows.

Not cute. It's just a line.

"Where are we going?"

"I'm hungry."

Payton still doesn't get up.

I step closer and glare down at her.

"Well, maybe I'm not," she states, crossing her arms over her chest.

"I didn't ask."

When she still doesn't move, I let out a sigh.

"Are you hungry?" I begrudgingly ask.

"I can eat."

Before I can think better of it, I'm reaching out my hand, offering it to her to help her up. If it weren't for everything between us, I would swear I feel a spark when we touch.

Once we're in the car and out of the lot, I weave my way in and out of traffic. When I pull to a stop, it's in front of my favorite hole-in-the-wall diner. I finish parking my car outside.

"This place looks nice," she says with a laugh, taking in the dilapidated front of the building.

The awning is hanging on by a thread, and the name of the restaurant has been worn off by time. Three of the letters don't even light up anymore. The vowels, too, which I hear are important.

"Trust me when I tell you, it's the best food you'll ever eat."

"Oh . . . I believe it." She unbuckles her seat belt, reaching for the door. "It's always the places like this that are the best."

"Agree."

"Can never judge a book by its cover, right?"

I turn to look at her, and I see how she looks back at me. Probably insinuating that I'm an asshole, even though I probably look like a nice guy.

She's not wrong.

Or maybe it's the opposite. Maybe she thinks she sees something more in me, even though I look like an asshole. Who knows with her?

But I don't care, so I'm not gonna ask.

I get out of the car, and she follows suit. This is not the kind of establishment in which you wait for a hostess. You just take a seat. So, I lead us to an empty booth in the corner.

Normally, when I come here, I know everyone who works in

this place, but tonight, I don't recognize anybody. That's when I spot Tanya, one of my favorite servers. She waves over to me and comes to greet me.

"Are you having your usual?" She beams at me.

"Yes. What about you, Payton? Do you need to see a menu?"

"What's your usual?" she asks me.

"At this time of night . . . pancakes."

Payton's lips spread into a large smile. One I have never seen on her. Probably because I am the asshole who never gives her a reason to do it.

"Pancakes for dinner . . . I like it." She turns to Tanya. "I'll have the same. Can I add extra-crispy bacon?"

"Who doesn't love a woman who orders bacon?"

Fuck me. I did not just say that out loud.

Tanya walks away, leaving Payton and me to sit in silence.

"How long have you been volunteering?" She breaks the still air with her question.

"A few years."

"Can you elaborate?"

"Nope."

Mature.

Her brows furrow. "Can you ever just answer a question honestly?"

"No."

I could, but this is more fun. Like I said . . . mature.

Payton leans forward, her elbows now resting on the table. She places her chin in her hands. "Is there a reason for that?"

She's analyzing me. Trying to understand what makes me tick. If only it were that easy.

I'm all types of fucked up. Ain't that right, big guy?

My head tips up to the sky as if he can hear me better at this angle.

"Yes," I finally say.

"Are you going to tell me said reason?" she presses, pulling out a packet of brown sugar from a sticky white box, emptying it on the table, and playing with the mess.

Lowering my gaze, I meet her stare. "Negative, Ghostrider."

"You're intolerable." She grins, and I love the way it looks on her.

"Absolutely."

She looks frustrated from across the table, but that last smirk is still there, and I can't help but enjoy it. I love messing with her. I love getting a rise out of her. I'm surprised when she continues to fire off questions. She's not surprised when I continue to vaguely answer.

Until the food gets there.

Then I'm rewarded with a soft moan that falls from her lips.

Just that one little squeak, and my cock stirs to life.

Watching her eat pancakes is turning me on.

Who the fuck am I?

I don't say a word further. I can't be thinking this kind of shit. I don't even trust myself to speak. Not with my little comment earlier.

I eat my pancakes; she eats hers.

That's when I see him making his approach. He's by the front door. He must have followed us.

Paul.

I don't know what he wants, but I don't think it's a coincidence that I'm eating dinner at a low-traffic, obscure, hole-in-the-wall dive that he happens to be walking into.

Pretty calculated.

If I were by myself, I would approach him, but I don't know what he wants, and my gut tells me, at this time of night, whatever it is, it's nothing good.

Right then and there, a protective instinct snaps through me.

Payton.

Despite my hatred and animosity toward her, I don't want to see Payton die.

I quietly stand from the chair, throw down a hundred, and then lift my finger to my mouth, telling her to be quiet, and pull her up from the seat.

Where we're sitting, I have a view of the door; however, he can't see us, so I quickly steer her out the back way.

"Why are we—"

"Shh," I cut her off

She listens to my advice and is quiet as we get back into the car.

"What was that all about?" she asks, her voice laced with confusion.

"Nothing that you need details of right now."

With her eyes locked on me, she watches me. "You rushed me out of there, but I didn't finish eating."

She pouts, and I sigh.

"Fine. I'll get you some dessert."

Pulling the car onto the street, I weave my way through traffic until we are back on West Broadway, heading to my place.

"Then why are we headed home?" she points out.

"Because, believe it or not, Chef makes homemade ice cream for himself."

From the corner of my eye, I catch her mouth falling open. "How did I not know that?"

She sounds more appalled than when I ordered her to give presentations to my staff, and I shouldn't be amused, but I am.

I shrug, changing lanes. "Because it's a secret."

"And you know this then?"

"It's my house."

"But it's his ice cream."

"Well, technically, it's mine. Duh. My house."

There's that cute grin on her face again, and damn if my cock did not get the memo.

I make a few rounds through the area, checking for tails. It's not a secret where I live, but I'd at least like to know if I have someone following me. If Payton notices that we're driving in circles, she doesn't comment.

Finally, I pull up to my building, park the car in my spot, and lead her upstairs. My hand touches the small of her back. I feel the warmth radiate through it.

This need to protect her tonight was overwhelming. I have to keep her safe. It's one thing for my father's will to chain us together and another for my sins to do so. My world shouldn't touch her life, no matter what my father caused me to do.

We're very quiet as we tiptoe into the kitchen, and I take her to a secret freezer hidden behind a cabinet door in the butler's pantry.

I browse through our flavor options. "Chef has a personal stash here."

I grab one of his pre-scooped jars, filled with homemade mint chocolate chip ice cream, and collect two spoons from a drawer.

"Taste it," I demand.

She takes the spoon out of my hand, dips it into the ice cream, and swallows.

An honest-to-God, full-on moan escapes her mouth this time.

Dammit all to hell.

That moan.

That will haunt me for the rest of the night.

Then she fucking licks her lips. I watch the movement. Track it with hungry eyes.

Great. Just fucking great.

I find myself taking a step closer, a moth to a flame.

She has ice cream on her lip, and I need to taste it.

I know I shouldn't.

I can't help it.

Before I can stop myself, my hand reaches forward.

I close the distance.

My body is almost touching hers.

I lean closer, my hand touching her lips.

She stops breathing for a second.

Then I wipe the ice cream.

She exhales, her chest heaving, and she moves a step closer.

I want to kiss her.

My lips hover over hers.

We are so close I can feel her exhale.

"Why are you making a mess in my kitchen?" Chef shouts.

And just like that, the moment is ruined.

I remember who I'm standing with.

I remember why I shouldn't do this.

I remember both our sins.

And I internally scold myself for thinking with my dick when it comes to her once again.

This won't end well, I remind myself.

No shit.

CHAPTER THIRTY-ONE

Payton

I SIT ON THE EDGE OF THE BED, HEAD IN MY HANDS.

What the hell was that?

Did we almost kiss?

Why is it that I hear the venom from his lips but still want to feel them on mine?

He hates me. He hates how his father cared about me but not his own daughter. He hates how his father sold his sister when he had the money and instead spent it on me.

For fuck's sake, this is not how I should feel.

But as I step out of my clothes to climb into bed, I wish the door would open. I wish he would come in, grab me, and kiss me. Hard and unapologetic. A wall kiss, like you read in romance books and see in movies.

Again. Why?

Why do I have this feeling that he could be more than my tormentor?

Payton, you need sleep.

After the week I have had, the last thing I want to do is perform for Trent Aldridge.

Not only am I in a crap mood because I'm not doing too hot in my classes, but I'm also so fucking tired.

Commuting sucks.

Yeah, sure. Trent gave me a ride a few days ago, but since the ice cream, he's been missing in action.

He didn't even come with me to volunteer.

I found the address on the counter in my room and a note reminding me of my obligation to him.

Ass.

His place is big, but I still haven't seen him anywhere.

Does he even sleep here?

Does Trent have a girlfriend?

The idea of it makes my stomach hurt.

I shouldn't care.

I don't want to like him. Not with the way he is vindictive, then caring, and then ghosting me the next second.

He can be with anyone he wants. But for some reason, I want to know if he has a girl in his life.

And if he does, is she going to be here tonight to mock me?

I feel ill at the thought.

There is not one part of me that wants to read a book report to the gorgeous model he's probably dating. It occurs to me that I know nothing of this man. Never had the chance to pry into his life.

I don't even know if he's seeing someone.

Ugh.

This is going to be awful.

Well, if she is going to be here, then I'm going to make myself look hot, too.

It's such a petty, shallow thought. I hate myself for thinking it. I hate myself for acting on it, too.

I walk over to my closet, throw off the sweats I have on, and put on a tight-fitted skirt and blouse.

Then I fluff my hair with a brush and put on a light dusting of makeup. Squaring my shoulders, I head out into the hallway.

There is a gathering in the living room.

Most of the faces I know.

And I'm happy to see there is no sexy woman.

God, what is wrong with me?

I shouldn't be happy.

I shouldn't care.

Get your hormones in check, girl.

The man is a major asshole.

Just because he is hot and makes you feel tingly inside when his blue eyes find you doesn't mean you have to act like a complete idiot.

"Payton," he drawls, lifting a glass to his lips.

It's full of mahogany liquid. He's drinking, and I'm his entertainment. Got it.

He sets his glass down, gesturing to a space set aside for me. There's a little box there. The type kids stand on to reach the sink to brush their teeth. And he is exactly the petty type of asshole to send his staff out to buy something like this for tonight.

Actually, I'm surprised he didn't ask me to do it.

He continues, "Tell us something you have learned this month and how it is relevant to this household. Impart some learned wisdom . . ."

Shit.

His question is open-ended, and it means I need to use my own interpretation to reference him and the other unfamiliar people around. So . . . mainly me.

This isn't good.

I studied Jung.

But having to pull from my brain something relevant to Trent . . .

Yeah, I am not prepared for that. I'm prepared to talk about history.

About the theories he's most famous for.

Which is what I read and made flash cards for.

But this . . .

I don't know Trent.

How am I possibly supposed to do this?

That's when he smiles.

He knows he set me up to fail.

There was no part of him that wanted me to succeed. He knew I would memorize facts. Facts that anyone could recite.

The bastard had this planned.

To make me look like an ass in front of everyone I have to see day in and out.

A Barbie struts into the room

And my fear is brought to life.

A tall, gorgeous blond woman walks up to Trent and smiles at him. "Am I late?"

"No. Just in time. Payton is going to give us some impactful words of wisdom on Carl Jung, and then we can have a cocktail before the party tonight."

She is still smiling at him.

I feel sick.

He hasn't taken his eyes off me.

Not for a minute.

She's here exactly for the reason I think she is.

To throw me for a loop.

He knows it's not bad enough to have me make a fool of myself in front of his staff.

He brought in a stranger to seal the deal.

Why does she have to be perfect?

She's as beautiful as he is, and not an imposter like me.

No.

I won't do this.

This is his plan, and I won't let it work.

He won't get a rise out of me.

I smile back.

Smirk is more like it.

One that says "well-played asshole, but you haven't seen how I throw down."

Taking a few steps forward, I kick aside his makeshift stage and take my place in the center of the room. My back straightens to my full height, and I shrug off my blazer, allowing only my black lace camisole to stay on.

I toss my blazer toward the couch.

It lands right on the intended target's lap.

Trent's.

He is staring at me.

More like shooting daggers with his eyes.

He's pissed by my outfit of choice.

The way his jaw is locked makes me want to laugh.

Allowing my brain to empty of all the BS, I think of everything I read this past month. I think of all the things I know about this household. About this man.

A man bitter and angry.

Hurt.

And probably lonely.

A little boy whose father probably wasn't there for him.

A man who had no role model.

I think about it all, and finally, I open my mouth and speak.

As I do, I never tear my gaze from his.

"Carl Jung once said there is no coming to consciousness without pain. In life, the only true obstacle we face is ourselves. We must face our pain. Address our faults. Stop placing blame on others." I stop, take a deep breath, and continue, "We must face our demons. Even if we know the process won't be easy, we need to step forward from the shadows. The things that hurt us can also shape us into remarkable people. When I was a child, I was homeless . . ."

I then talk of forgiveness. Of strength. I talk of things I probably shouldn't.

I speak from my soul. From my past. I say things that make me bleed. But when I do, I hold my head high and never break eye contact.

Not even when I want to.

Not even when his forehead pinches.

Not even when I steer the topic to fathers and sons.

Not even as he looks like he might kill me.

When I'm finished, I smile broadly, turn, and walk away. I head toward my room. Needing air. Needing to compose myself.

As strong as I appeared, this whole escapade has hurt me.

I didn't just allow myself to feel for this man hell-bent on hurting me, but I also allowed myself to be a pawn again.

Because that's what I am.

A piece to play with in his little twisted game of revenge on a man who is dead and no longer here to play.

I'm halfway down the hall when someone grabs my arm.

Then, before I can comprehend what is happening, I'm thrown against the wall, and his mouth is on mine.

The heat sears through me.

Need, want, and desire buckle me right to my core.

I should *not* kiss him back.

I shouldn't let this happen.

There is no way having his mouth on mine is a good idea.

He's an asshole.

He wants to ruin my life.

But for some insane and crazy reason, I can't help myself. I allow myself this one blip of stupidity and kiss him back.

Just once.

We have been dancing around this crazy waltz of hate and desire for weeks. From the moment I saw him in the lawyer's office till today, I have been fighting my desire.

One kiss is okay.

Only one.

And it will be enough.

We're all teeth and tongue.

Hate and lust.

My arms wrapping around his neck.

I pull him closer.

It's a desperate kiss.

Frenzied. Urgent. Primal.

But as fast as it starts, it stops. Then he pushes me off him and wipes his lips with the back of his hand as if he's ridding them of something dirty.

The moment is shattered.

I crash back into reality.

"Put clothes on," he hisses before turning on his heel and storming back down the hallway.

CHAPTER THIRTY-TWO

Trent

WHY THE HELL DID I DO THAT? I have done a lot of stupid things in my life, but this . . . ?

Yeah, this takes the cake.

Kissing Payton.

Her soft, sweet lips.

Fuck.

I can't even form a sentence as I barrel back into the living room.

My jaw is locked. My hands are clenched.

I need a drink.

Now.

I don't make eye contact with anyone.

Over my shoulder, I bark orders, and Mia, my pseudo date, follows me, judging by the clicking of her heels.

She was supposed to be here early to give me the edge.

Instead, Payton turned it all around on me.

Her words resonated inside me.

For the first time in my whole miserable existence, I felt seen. Of all the people in my life, Payton broke down the wall I formed around my heart and fucking saw me. She saw me for more than the trust fund kid.

More than the funny friend.

More than the corrupt investor.

More than the angry son who inherited a shattered dynasty.

She had a first-row seat to the Trent show, and she didn't miss a beat.

I should have stayed put.

But I couldn't.

Words had to be said, so I followed her.

Then . . . I don't know what my plan was. To say something? To tell her she was wrong? That she didn't know me? That everything she said was a load of shit?

All of the above?

Instead, I kissed her.

Big mistake.

I still taste her on my lips.

She tastes like strawberries.

Sweet yet tart.

I can't even allow myself to think about it because the more I do, the angrier I get. How this woman managed to mind-fuck me, I can't possibly begin to understand. I am so pissed at myself. Pissed I let her get to me when this whole scenario was designed to rattle *her*.

Her.

The one my father dearest left money for when he couldn't be bothered to save Ivy.

I don't hassle with opening the door for Mia. I walk around to the driver's side and fling my own wide before taking a seat and revving the engine to life.

"Where are we going?" Mia asks.

I never noticed how annoying her voice was before. "Nowhere. You are going home."

Her face crinkles faintly next to her eyes, where the Botox has dissolved a bit between injections. "I thought—"

"I don't care what you thought."

"You're such an asshole."

"Tell me something I don't know," I mutter, drawing out the sound with another rev of my engine.

I was supposed to get laid tonight.

I have been so busy that I have not been with someone for a long time. I thought this plan of having an old prep-school class-mate come with me would kill two birds with one stone. One, I would throw Peyton off her game and be happy to piss her off, and two, I get my dick sucked.

Neither of which happened.

Or will happen, in Mia's case.

I really played this one wrong.

"Why are you in such a bad mood?" she asks, pouting.

"You want to talk to me? After calling me a dick?"

"Um."

"That's what I thought."

"I just don't see why we can't have fun." She leans over the console, hands resting on my thigh. "You seem stressed. Do you want me to help?"

Her hand starts to creep up, but it's not the hand I crave.

I imagine Payton sitting in that seat, moving her hand onto my leg.

Finally, my dick starts to spring to life.

Fuck. How do I fix this runaway Payton train in my head? I look down at Mia's hand. Being anywhere with her, let alone fuck-ing her, is a terrible idea.

Right now, the only thing I want to do is grab a drink alone.

I lower my hand to my lap, and Mia's perfectly veneered smile lights the car. She thinks I'm about to say yes, but she is grossly mistaken.

"Remove your hand, or I'll remove it for you."

When she doesn't move, I do it for her and put it back into her own lap.

Then without another word, I start to drive her back to her apartment.

Never call an ex. Too complicated. It's never what you truly desire . . .

I keep driving until I pull up in front of her high-rise.

She pouts. Again. "I don't get you. You tell me to come over and say we are going out. That you just need to hear some presentation you didn't even explain. Then you make me listen to some woman ramble on in some speech on Carl Jung. One—who the hell is Carl Jung? I still don't know. And two—are you fucking the help, Trent?"

"Not that I have to explain myself to you, but no."

"Then why are you not taking me out?"

"Because I realized I don't want to."

I also don't want to have this conversation, so why are you still here?

"Does that mean you no longer want to fuck?"

"I never wanted to," I growl.

"Could have fooled me."

She stares at my dick, but it's no longer hard. And it was never hard for her, but I don't tell her that. That would require admitting aloud that Payton Hart gets me hard.

I turn to face Mia more squarely. I'm too tired for this shit.

"Just get out," I say, tired. "I'm not in the mood."

I never was.

"Never call me again," she fires back as she swings open the door.

"Trust me, I won't."

And, for the record, Mia called me first. I accidentally answered, caught sight of Payton, and succumbed to my need for a distraction. Sue me.

Mia storms from the car, and before the door is even fully closed, I'm pulling away down the street.

I'm not sure where to go.

Who to speak to.

A drink is what is necessary at times like this, but I can't bring myself to go alone.

Instead, I find my car driving uptown.

Heading in the direction of my mother, believe it or not.

Heading to Cresthill.

The reason I bought the building and transformed it into a luxury retirement home in the city was for my mother.

I didn't tell Payton my mother lives there.

But Mom needed something to do.

Yes, she has gardening that brings her joy, but she needed a purpose.

So, I gave her one.

It doesn't take me long to arrive.

I go in through the back entrance, then look for her. She lives here, too, but at this time of the day, she's working.

Either helping someone learn how to plant in the garden we built in the rotunda for her or just talking to someone. Obviously, I didn't get my inability to give a fuck from her.

Although everyone is here by choice, sometimes the tenants' families don't come often. Mom knows a thing or two about being alone. When she found out I was building Cresthill, she volunteered to live here and help manage it with Margret and keep the residents company.

I see what the purpose does to her.

Gives her something more than just Ivy and me to live for.

After being with Dad for so long, she needed to fill the void he left in his absence.

She's made great friends and is happy.

Just as I suspected, I find her in the rotunda.

She's kneeling on the floor, gloves on, looking at her plants. With her hands pressed together at a stem, she almost looks like she's praying to them.

"Everything okay?" I ask.

"I'm afraid this one has rust."

"What does that mean?"

"It might spread and harm the rest."

I sit beside her, staring at the thing, not sure what I'm looking at. "What will you do?"

"I'll try to separate it." She fusses with the stem. "See if I can heal it on my own."

"And if you can't? What if what infects it . . . can't go away?"

Her hands stop, and she turns to look at me. The blues of her eyes meet mine. "Why are you here, Trent? It's late."

"Can't I just be here to see my mother?"

She raises her brow.

She knows me too well.

"Is this about the girl? I saw her here. Apparently, you want her to clean toilets."

Margret. The blabbermouth.

"It's not about her," I lie.

She nods. But I know she doesn't believe me.

She goes back to her plant. "We can remove the plant. Distance it. Allow it time to heal on its own."

"And if the time away doesn't help?"

She sighs. "Then there is no helping the plant . . ."

"And then what happens?"

"It dies alone."

CHAPTER THIRTY-THREE

Payton

I'M BEING A BABY, BUT I'VE NEVER LEFT A PLACE FASTER THAN I left Trent's.

I don't know what part is driving me out of my mind more—the fact that he kissed me or the fact that he pushed me away so fast as if I was something disgusting.

He treats me like a gnat that is buzzing around his head, annoying him. Like his only objective is to swat and kill me.

It sucks.

Majorly.

And the killing blow is when Gail told me Trent left with *her*. The blonde. Who knows where they even went? Did they go for drinks? Is it a date?

Since I have no clue, I refuse to be there when he gets home.

Sure, the loft space is large, but it's not large enough that I wouldn't know if he brought a girl home.

The sound in this place echoes, too.

I would die if I had to hear him sleep with her.

I don't know why I care.

Correction: I shouldn't care, but I know why I do.

It's because he's weaseled his way past my barriers in ways I vowed never to let anyone do.

How can I give a shit about what some jackass does (or whom

he does) when he's been trying to make my life a living hell for the past several weeks?

Add up the time from the day we met, and it's been twelve—no, not twelve. It's been fourteen weeks since this man began his quest to ruin me. The fact that I care about him is an insult to the word self-respect.

So, why do I?

Once the adrenaline of finishing his task faded, why did it gut me so much to see his reaction to my presentation?

Because you saw inside him. That's why.

I saw a piece of him that he didn't want me to see, and now I understand.

Or maybe, you understand nothing.

Maybe the truth is, everything was a façade. Maybe he really is a jerk, plain and simple, and there is no good side. Maybe he's not a lost little boy looking for his dad's approval, even after his death. Maybe his mom's words were mere ramblings of a biased woman who can't help but love her son.

Get a grip, Payton.

As I ride the train back to Long Island, the hairs on my arm stand like someone is watching me.

I know I'm being paranoid. It's the residual effect of the phone calls, the break-in, the strange truck that I swear was following me. These weird things, things I should confront Trent about but keep forgetting to, make me on edge. Twenty-four seven.

I feel the adrenaline spiking.

Is this Trent's doing still?

Wouldn't put it past him. There is a very good possibility he is doing things to drive me insane.

That's probably the goal.

Has it all been about money this entire time?

If I am deemed insane, if I have a mental breakdown, he will petition the court so that I am not able to get the money, or maybe even worse.

He will position himself in a way to hold the money over me throughout my life.

It's fine. You're fine.

No one's following me.

No one knows I'm even gone.

Trent doesn't know where I am.

I don't believe my bullshit, palming my phone just in case. But knowing Trent, he probably had one of his goons deactivate it again.

And this is a man you kissed back.

I force myself to relax. I'm not doing anything illegal. I can take a little break. Trent never said I have to be at his place every minute of every day. He just said I have to live with him. Not one time did he state that I cannot stay with Heather for a few days.

Or at least tonight.

As long as I maintain everything else, it's totally reasonable.

A sleepover, a little girl time, is exactly what I need.

Throughout the rest of the ride, I still feel as though something is wrong. Maybe Trent is having me followed.

I wouldn't put it past him.

He has the money to. And the astounding lack of boundaries.

Of course, he would.

Anyone who has gone through betrayal from a father would not be above having me followed. I know because if I had the money, I would have someone track Erin. Make sure she's still alive. That whatever sicko she's dating isn't getting her into something dangerous and destructive.

But you don't have the money. And whose fault is that?

My stomach growls out of nowhere.

I forgot to eat.

Maybe I have a protein bar in my bag. Normally, I carry something to munch on since I'm always running around.

I start to go through my bag to look for a snack. When I get to the small side compartment, my finger slips through a hole in the bottom.

Dammit. This is a new bag, and it's already torn.

It feels like something is stuck in there, too.

Carefully, I probe the hole to see what it is. When I find the small object, I fish it out.

I stare at it, brows furrowed. It's some kind of weird black metal device in my grasp. Never held one in my life before. It reminds me of a USB flash drive.

Lifting it up to get a closer view, I realize that's not what it is at all because there is no plug for the computer.

That's when I realize where I've seen it . . .

Every stupid spy movie I ever watched flashing before my eyes.

It's a tracking device.

Trent isn't having me followed; Trent is fucking tracking me.

He already mentioned his access to my phone. Now I realize he put a tracking device in my bag as well. Probably because he knows if I don't want him to find me, I could turn my phone off. This, I can't get rid of, because I didn't know about it.

A great idea forms.

That's exactly what I should do. I should turn my phone off, but first, I keep it in my palm and head down the aisle. Normally, I would never go in a train's bathroom, but I find my sense of humor at the idea of one of his men going into the public bathroom of a train to locate me.

I can't stop laughing at the thought. I can't stop laughing until I bump into someone.

"I'm so sorry," I say, but the man just grunts, his head down as he walks away.

It reminds me of the jackass who bumped into me on the street the day that Trent cleaned my leg.

The day he touched me. *Really* touched me.

The day a part of me ignited and lit a fire that has yet to be put out.

His lips.

It's as if I were branded.

I can feel his mouth on mine.

No, don't think about that.

He's not a good guy.

He's a jerk.

He's the reason I left tonight.

I need to remember this every time I think of his lips on mine . . . Trent Aldridge walked out after kissing me to go do whatever it is he is doing tonight with his date.

Finally, in the bathroom, I look at myself in the mirror. It's dirty, and my reflection looks cracked.

It makes me look as sad as I feel.

Removing the tracking device from the palm of my hand, I search for a place to leave it.

A place where it won't shut off, then he will have to search for it.

I decide to place it on the floor behind the toilet. Holding my breath, I kneel and drop it.

My gag reflex kicks in, and I'm sure I will vomit, but I hold it in.

Pushing the feeling down, I stand.

Good.

Take that.

I hope he's the one who looks.

I hope he vomits all over himself.

It would be the best karma a girl can have.

CHAPTER THIRTY-FOUR

Trent

TWO DAYS.

Payton has been gone for two damned days.

The first thing I did when I got home that night was try to find her. I called her a bunch of times, but she never answered. She's ignoring my texts too.

A part of me, a very big part of me, wants to call Jax, but seeing as he's been clear on his feeling about tracking her, I know he won't help me on this.

I'm sure she's okay, but with everything happening with Paul, I just want to make sure. That last time anyone has seen her was at the presentation. Apparently, she stormed out of there. Which makes sense, seeing as I kissed her and then left her standing in the hallway like a dick.

I'm trying to give her space, but at the same time, my mother's words unnerve me.

Pacing my room, I grab my phone and dial the one person I haven't wanted to burden with all my Payton shit because deep down, I know she wouldn't approve. I call her anyway because the truth is, she is the only person who's always been there for me and will be able to help.

"Trent. Took you long enough to call," Ivy answers.

"Hey, sis."

"You've been avoiding me."

"Not true. I've just been—"

"Trent Aldridge," she scolds, and I'm transported back to elementary school when she used to mimic Mom's tone whenever I got into trouble. Which, admittedly, was a lot once Dad thought it was a good idea to *make me into a man* and *toughen me up*. Apparently, kindness is for pussies. "You're my big bro. Don't you think I know when you're lying?"

"Fine. I've been avoiding you."

She laughs at my brutally honest answer. "Spill."

And I do. I start from the beginning, rushing through the entire ordeal because I'm desperate to get to Payton. Sue me.

"I knew you wouldn't approve," I say when I finish.

"Oh, really? You thought tormenting an innocent girl would bother me?" She's laying on the sarcasm heavier than I appreciate, but my actions asked for it.

I shrug. "Yes."

"At least you have the decency to sound sheepish."

We settle into silence.

She breaks it with a soft sigh. "Why are you calling, Trent? I know it's not just because you miss me."

"I don't know what to do . . . about *her*."

"You need me to tell you it's okay that you like her."

"No," I respond, too fast.

"Then what?"

I clear my throat, scratching at the skin of my neck. "I need you to forgive me."

"You did nothing wrong."

"I didn't protect you."

It's the big regret of my life. The one I'll feel every morning when I wake up. And every night when I go to bed.

I didn't protect my baby sister.

How fucked is that?

"Trent," Ivy whispers.

I can hear the tears in her voice. It drives the guilt deeper.

"No," I interrupt. "Let me talk." I clear my throat again, trying to figure out what apology would be adequate for something so unforgivable. "I never protected you from Dad."

"Stop, right there." Her voice is firm. An unbreakable barrier. "It wasn't your job to protect me."

"I'm your older brother. Of course, it was." The damn lump in my throat won't go away. I swallow, and swallow, and swallow again. "Ivy, I failed you . . ."

"Is that what this thing is with Payton?" She quiets. All I hear are sniffles on the other line for a few minutes. "Are you doing this for me?"

"Ivy—"

"No, Trent, you've gone too far." Her strength is back. That's how I know, without a doubt, she means what she says. "I love you for thinking of me, but this is not her fault. Whatever Dad did was not her fault. Nor was it yours. Be better than Dad. It's time to let this guilt go."

"But—"

"There's no room for a but here, Trent."

I'm taken aback by the hard edge of her tone.

I open my mouth to apologize again, but she blazes forward. "I didn't ask for you to do cruel things under my name. I'm actually mad about it, and the only reason I'm not full-on pissed is because I know you did it out of love for me. It doesn't make it okay, but I understand. Apologize to her, Trent. She deserves an apology."

I know she's right.

Worse, it's the answer I've been hoping to hear.

Hating Payton while craving her is so taxing I've spent the past several months exhausted. I can't even imagine how she feels. And now the guilt is hitting harder, only this time, it's over what I've done to Payton.

"Okay," I promise. "You're right."

"Of course, I am."

"I love you, sis."

"Love you, too. Now go," she urges, and this is the demanding sister I know and love. "You have a lot to make up for, but not to me. Never to me."

I hang up the phone.

The truth hits me hard, like a forecasted storm I should've seen coming.

Mom is right.

Ivy is right.

My grudge is unfounded.

My hatred misplaced.

I have been basically torturing an innocent woman.

I glare at the floor. At the dark hardwood that smells of the fucking lemongrass cleaning solution Payton made.

You listening down there, Dad? I'm no better than you. You raised an asshole. Just like you.

Maybe I didn't sell Payton to a Russian trafficker, but I was holding her prisoner with blackmail.

There might not be any chains, but the monetary ones I wrapped her wrists with still cut deep. They tethered her to me. I used her hopes and dreams of financial security—of a life different from the one she was raised in—against her.

I need to speak with Payton. To tell her she is free to go. It doesn't matter what she did to get that money. I need to call Baker. Get him to make the changes to put her in charge of the money as soon as possible.

I don't care about any of that shit anymore.

Pacing my office, I try to think of what I will say once I find her.

Maybe she went back to school.

She could be with her friend, Heather.

Now the question is, will she let me see her, will she speak to me, or will she tell me to go fuck off?

I deserve to be told off; I can stuff it.

Hearing my sister's disapproval, the way that she compared me to my father, I know she is right, deep in my bones.

There is only one thing left for me to do.

I pick up the phone and try to dial her cell phone number, but it goes straight to voicemail. Ever since my talk with Jaxson, I lost my okay to look her up and see where she is, but I am certain she's at school. I still remember her schedule from before.

I try her phone again and again; it goes straight to voicemail. This time, I decide to text.

Me: I want to talk. I know you're getting my texts. Please, Payton. I'm begging you, respond.

I'm surprised when the phone chimes right away.

Payton: And you haven't figured out I don't care what you want.

Me: Please.

She doesn't answer.

Although I can see that she read it.

Me: We need to talk. Can you come back home?

Fuck. I'm calling it home like it's a place she belongs. As much as I want that, she won't. She will want to be free from me.

Payton: No.

Me: It won't take long.

Again, she doesn't answer right away, and I'm sure she is going to tell me no.

I could use my power over her money to make her.

But I don't.

Blackmailing her into meeting me would defeat the whole purpose of the conversation.

Payton: Why?

Me: I owe you an apology.

I don't mention what for, but it's pretty obvious.

Payton: Don't worry. It was just a kiss. I haven't thought about it since.

Her response is not what I expect, but rather than give a witty retort, I shrug it off.

That's my MO.

Get insulted. Fire back.

This time, I'm going to shut up and not say anything

Me: Just meet me, please. I'm serious. Please.

I stare at my phone for a second and wait for her to respond, but after a few more, I realize she won't.

Walking back toward my desk, I pull out my chair and take a seat.

My emotions are still conflicted.

I know I have to let this whole thing go, but at the same time, I don't want to.

My phone chimes as I'm about to tip the glass back into my mouth.

Payton: Fine. But you get five minutes.

Me: Deal.

Payton: Where?

Me: Meet me by the library. The parking lot?

Payton: Fine. What time?

I put the glass down. Can't be drinking right now.

I shoot back a time, then go back to work for a few hours, distracted by the upcoming meeting with Payton.

My phone rings again, and this time, it's Tobias. I send him to voicemail. Not a smart idea, but I still haven't figured out what to tell him. Once I have an answer, I'll call him back.

Tobias has made it clear he wants out. He's in the process, with the help of Cyrus, of brokering a deal to sell his business. That means an influx of money I need to invest. That also means I have all my feelers out for any tips of something that's going to be hot.

Or something that's going to fail miserably.

After the last scheme, I have to be careful. Although every relevant politician is in my pocket in one way or another, I can't make it so blatantly obvious. This time, I'm going to have to rely on insider info.

I'm going to be active about it, placing a few phone calls and seeing if anybody knows anything that would be worth investing in rather than waiting for my people to bring the info to me.

I spend the next hour speaking to a handful of people.

One of Lorenzo's men has the most information that will be useful. He owns a garbage and sanitation company, and after hours, they sift through and send me anything I need.

That will work for now.

But I'll need something bigger for Tobias soon.

Standing from my chair, I walk toward the door.

It's time to bury this hatchet I have with Payton once and for all.

CHAPTER THIRTY-FIVE

Payton

I TOLD MYSELF NOT TO ANSWER. I PROMISED MYSELF I WOULDN'T. Yet I did.

The tone of his text threw me off.

A tiny voice I've been trying to shove away started whispering in my ear to find out what he wanted.

I have an angel and demon on both my shoulders when it comes to Trent Aldridge. One of them tells me to meet him. The other is adamantly against it. I don't know which one will win, and that has me hyperalert.

Either way, this could be the biggest mistake of my life.

I don't want to go back to the way things were. However, I do miss living at Trent's place.

I felt safer there.

His security is state-of-the-art, and with the phone calls and creepy feeling I get of always being watched, I feel protected in his loft.

Unless it's him, of course, which it very well could be.

If this is all his doing . . .

I shake my head.

No. That makes no sense.

I'm perplexed, that's for sure.

Maybe he'll give me the answers I need for peace of mind.

Or maybe he won't.

To be honest, I expected one of his text messages to tell me that I had no choice. That I had to come home.

I've actually been waiting for that text message for these past two days.

Had he said I had no choice, I would've returned, so a part of me wishes he did.

Which should make me sick, but it doesn't, and that thought actually does make my stomach turn.

I officially am the most confused person in the whole entire world. I can barely concentrate in class as the teacher drones on and on because all I'm thinking of is seeing him.

Will he want me to come back?

Is he bringing my stuff to me and leaving me hanging again?

Will he want to kiss me like that all over again?

Finally, the professor announces that class is over. She rambles off an assignment, and I don't hear a thing.

Luckily for me, Heather does.

She's been great about letting me crash on her couch. Although not ideal, for both of us, it is better than the alternative.

Seeing my sister was awful, so the fact that I can stay somewhere else in the interim is a blessing.

Erin keeps trying to call me, too, wanting to discuss the money.

I have nothing to say to her.

It's a moot point right now since I have no control over the money, and I have no idea why Ronnie left it to me.

That's the part no one understands. Everybody wants me to tell them, but how can I say anything if I don't even know?

I stand from my chair and turn to Heather. "I'll meet you back at your place."

She reaches out and touches my shoulder. "You're not coming with me?"

"No."

Her brows furrow. "Where are you going?"

"I have to meet someone."

"You're being shady."

I inhale deeply.

"Come on. Spit it out," she says.

"I have to meet Trent."

"Seriously?"

"Yeah."

"Is he making you?" she asks casually, but I can see how her face is clouded with unease. It's her eyes that give her away. They're sharp and assessing, dragging over every visible inch of me.

"No."

"Are you sure?"

Now they narrow.

She doesn't believe me.

"Yeah," I promise, still feeling weirded out that he isn't demanding anything of me. "He said he wanted to talk, so I'm going to let him."

"Are you sure that's safe? You said you don't trust him . . . maybe you should trust your gut."

She's right. I don't.

There is something off, and I can't figure out if it's him or something else. Between Trent and Erin, I feel unsteady all the time.

I'm going to trust my gut.

Stop the paranoia.

Stop the dramatics.

I keep that thought to myself. If I tell Heather I think Trent has had me followed and is tracking me, she'll freak out.

She would certainly freak out if she knew he did check my phone regularly.

The only things that she knows about are the superficial little things that are pretty harmless.

I'm certain I didn't tell her about the tracking device.

"I'll be fine. He's a rich trust-fund boy. What harm can he do?"

"I don't know . . . Maybe make you debate in front of Congress?"

That makes me laugh, not because it's a ridiculous thought, but because knowing Trent, it's actually something he would make me do.

"Imagine." I laugh.

"Actually, I can, and from the stories you tell, you would be debating something hysterical, too."

"If you ever meet him, don't give him any ideas."

She leans forward, nudging me. "Oh, will I meet him?"

"Maybe one day, if he forces me back."

"Do you want me to come with you?" she asks, the sincerity deep in her voice.

Her chocolate brown eyes are full of warmth and friendship, and I realize that she is the only person I have, and I'm lucky for that.

Lucky to have her in my corner.

And that's exactly why I cannot bring her into this.

I need her far from the nuclear fallout.

"No. I'll be okay."

"You sure?"

"Positive."

"See you later . . . ?" She doesn't sound convinced.

"Obviously." I laugh before turning to head to where we are set to meet.

The parking lot next door to the library.

Makes sense, seeing as it's my home away from home. I would have preferred a coffee shop.

But I understand why he chose this. It's a convenient location, plus it won't be as loud. Looking around, it won't be loud at all, seeing as there are no cars. I also notice that Trent is not here yet, so I'll be waiting a few minutes.

I wait for the crosswalk to indicate it's my turn, and I head toward the parking lot.

Standing in the first space, closest to the street, I wait.

I pull out my phone to see if he sent a text telling me whether he's going to be late or not, but as I do, I hear a sound. A screech. Tires?

I pull my gaze up, and that's when I see the car. It looks familiar, barreling its way in my direction. It takes me too long to react because I'm convinced it's Trent. It looks like his car.

But the car is driving fast. Too fast.

And Trent wouldn't . . .

I'm standing, almost frozen, and then I *am* frozen when I realize the car is not slowing down. *The car is not slowing down.*

I try to move out of the way, but my feet don't work, and when they finally do, it's too late.

I'm too late.

CHAPTER THIRTY-SIX

Trent

I SEE IT AS IT HAPPENS.

I'm powerless to stop it.

Fear, harsh and vivid, streaks through me.

I'm in my car, half a block away, watching in slow motion as the car heads in her direction.

There is nothing that I can do.

Panic like I have never known before wells in my throat.

Before I can think twice about my actions, I'm throwing my car into park, dashing out of my car, and running.

Chest heaving. Arms pumping.

In front of me is the crumpled body of Payton. My heart lurches in my chest as I pick up my pace to reach her in time.

Her body in an unnatural position.

I drop to the ground beside her, moving closer, but I'm careful not to touch her in a way that could hurt her.

First, I check her pulse.

There.

Then I fish out my phone and dial 911.

When they answer, I rattle off the information.

"Payton. Princess?" I try to see if she is okay.

Her eye cracks open.

"Y-you . . ."

"Shh. It's okay. Help is on the way."

"You d-didn't do this," she mutters through a cough, and then her eyes close.

"No. Payton. Wake up." I want to shake her awake, but I don't. It's too risky.

Her chest is still moving.

She's still alive.

I take her hand in mine. Holding it. Rubbing it. Telling her she will be okay. She has to be.

A pool of blood spreads beneath her.

Where the fuck is the ambulance?

How long has it been?

It feels like an eternity as I wait, but then I hear the familiar sirens, and I know they're almost here.

I continue to speak to Payton.

She doesn't answer, but I feel her pulse on her wrist. She is still alive.

Her pulse is still there.

I count its beats as I wait. Pray with each one that she's okay. That she doesn't leave me.

It doesn't take long before the paramedics are rushing over. They start to work on her.

And the next thing I know, they are lifting her onto a stretcher, then rolling her into the ambulance.

By the time I realize what's happening, they are gone and off to the hospital.

Now that I'm alone, her words ring back in my ears.

"You didn't do this."

Like a punch to my gut. It feels like a brick has been placed on my chest. She knows it wasn't me. Despite everything I've done to her in the past.

She trusts me enough to know I would never hurt her.

From where I am still sitting on the ground, my gaze spots the blood.

The car was similar to mine.

I told her to meet me here.

Someone wanted her to think it was me.

Paul?

But whoever it was didn't succeed.

Payton saw through the ruse.

Because to her, I'm more than a criminal. I'm more than the rich playboy who skirts the law.

She sees past every wall I ever erected, and somehow, despite what I put her through, she sees the real me.

The man who feels heartbroken right now for every mistake I made with Payton.

It feels like I'm free-falling at the realization.

"Excuse me," someone says from above. I look to see a campus security guard standing above me. "I'm going to need to take your statement."

"I'm going to the hospital." I don't have the time for this shit, not when Payton needs me, but I know if I don't cooperate, campus security will tell the cops, and then I won't be able to be with Payton. "A car, black. It looked like mine . . ." I point at my car where it's still parked. "It wasn't the same make or model, but it certainly looked like it was. It barreled into her. Listen, that's all I know right now. But I will find out who it was." I reach into my pocket, grab my wallet, and then pull out a card. "Here's what I need. I need you to send me the footage from the security cameras in the area."

"I can't—"

"Trust me, you can. Send everything for the incident."

I stand and then head to my car. As soon as I close the door, I hit the button on my phone to call Jax. I forgot to ask the EMS which hospital they took her to.

"What's going on?" he answers.

"I need you to help me with something," I rush out so fast that my words blend, and I'm not sure he will even understand me.

"Calm down, man."

I take a deep breath.

"Someone tried to kill Payton."

"The fuck?"

"I need you to tell me what hospital she went to, and after, I'm going to need you to look over the footage, but first, the hospital for Payton Hart."

"On it." I hear his fingers hitting the keyboard. "How're you holding up?" he asks as he continues his search.

"Not well."

"She'll be okay."

"She better be." I grunt because I won't even humor the idea that she won't be.

"Found her. Mercy General. It's five miles from where the GPS on your car says you are. Make a left on Franklin, and you're there."

"Thanks."

I call Cyrus next, and before he can even say hi, I'm speaking.

"I'm on my way to Mercy General by Ludlow University. There was an accident."

"Shit," he grits out. "What's going on? Are you okay?" The worry in his voice is palpable.

"Not me. Payton." It feels like ice is spreading through my chest as I tell him about the accident. When I'm done, he inhales deeply.

"Is she okay?"

"I'm not sure yet, but I need a favor. Fuck, I need all the favors."

"What can I do?"

"I need you to call whoever you know at the hospital and pull some strings. I want to be able to see her. Also, whoever you know on the police force. I want all the info on Payton's accident sent to Jax."

"Done and done."

"Thanks, man. I owe you." I hang up the phone and continue

to drive. Cyrus knows everyone. If anyone can get me in to see her, it's him.

Because I will see her. Today. And then when the time comes, I'll take her back home and take care of her.

No matter what she says. Because I won't give her a choice. I'll make her.

Once I arrive at the hospital, I pull up right in front of the building. I don't bother going to the lot. I just throw it in park. They can tow my ass for all I care.

They won't, though, because Cyrus will take care of that.

Barreling into the waiting room, I head straight for the front desk, slamming my hands down on it, startling the poor girl behind it.

"A girl, Payton Hart, was just brought in. Car accident. Where is she?" I don't have to see myself to know my eyes are wild.

"Please, sir." The woman clicks away at her desktop. "Can you slow down?"

"Payton Hart."

She looks down at her computer and starts to type.

I can hear the way her fingers hit the keyboard in slow, spaced-out movements. It's driving me insane with how long it is taking.

I'm probably better off walking away and having Jaxson hack the hospital. Then I would know exactly what is going on.

After another second, she looks up from the computer.

"I'm sorry, sir. She's in triage right now, I'll be able to find out—"

"I want to see her now."

"I'll see what I can do."

And I know without a measure of doubt, Cyrus Reed will come through for me *again*.

I start to pace as I wait for her to update me. My feet hitting the floor heavily.

Fear and anger knot inside me. The thought of her broken on the ground, blood pouring out of her head, has me shattered.

I feel like a piece of glass that just got hit with a hammer.

No matter how hard I breathe, it's impossible to calm my erratic pulse.

Hands clenched at my sides.

I can't rid myself of the image of her lying there.

Who did this?

Paul.

He's the only one who makes sense.

A commotion has me turning to the entrance of the hospital.

Cyrus.

He's striding toward me.

When he's in front of me, he places a hand on my shoulder.

"What are you doing here?"

Cyrus doesn't answer. Instead, he gives me a look that tells me all I need to know.

We are family.

Family takes care of each other.

"Let's go," he says, and I shake my head in confusion, but I follow anyway. We walk past the woman, straight through the doors that lead into the restricted part of the hospital. We're only a few steps inside when a man in a suit approaches us. He's not a doctor, that's for sure.

"Mr. Reed. Mr. Aldridge. I'm Steven Rigsby. I am in charge of this hospital. If you'll follow me, I'll bring you to Ms. Hart. She's being worked on right now, so you'll be right outside her room, but as soon as you can see her, you'll be right there."

I nod, and he turns around to show us the way. Down the hall and through corridors, we keep moving. Finally, he leads us to a small waiting room in front of a door.

"This room is private, Mr. Reed. No one will disturb you." Then he steps out, leaving Cyrus and me alone.

"Cyrus—" I start, and he lifts his hand to stop me.

He's not one for words or emotions, but him doing this, him being here, means something.

Both of us are quiet.

The door to Payton's room opens a crack, and from my angle, I can see her. Or at least what I think is Payton. I see a bed, an elevated foot. I see a machine.

I watch it.

Watch the graph. Watch her breathe.

Listen to the sounds of life.

Beep. Beep. Beep.

Neither of us speaks. But we don't need to.

Having him here is enough.

The door to the room opens, and the doctor walks toward us.

My pulse picks up. Standing, I walk toward him, Cyrus right behind me.

I swallow hard. "Is she okay?"

"She will be," the doctor says, and Cyrus places a hand on my shoulder. "She was very lucky. She has a concussion. Cuts and bruises. A sprained ankle and wrist and she bruised her ribs, but she was very fortunate not to have broken anything."

"Thank you."

"You'll be able to see her soon."

I let out a deep breath, and my body vibrates with relief.

"Come on, sit," Cyrus says, leading me back to the chair. "She's going to be okay."

"It was my fault." I bury my head in my hands. "Our fault."

"You think this was Paul?"

"Who else could it be? Especially since I am fairly sure this is about the shorting of Torenzo Corp. As soon as I get Payton home, I'm going to call a meeting to figure this out. But first, I need to make sure she is okay."

"It could have been an acc—"

"Cyrus. You didn't see it. It was no accident."

His jaw tightens. "All you have to do is worry about Payton." He pulls out his phone and starts typing out a text. "We will handle it. All you need to concern yourself with is your girl in there. You understand?"

I nod, too emotional to speak.

That's when Ivy walks in, clothes in hand.

She throws her arms around me, hugging me tightly.

"Thanks for coming, sis."

"What can I do to help? Have you called her sister?" I pull back and look at her.

"You can't be serious."

"Trent . . ." She inclines her head. "She's her sister."

"Fine, call Baker, have him contact her."

Ivy nods her head and walks toward Cyrus. I turn away from them, granting them privacy.

Time goes by. One hour, to be exact. I know because I studied the clock on the wall as if it would tell me the secret of life.

Finally, the door opens, and a nurse smiles at me.

It's my time to go in.

I take a step inside where Payton is lying on the bed unconscious, hooks and wires attached to her.

She looks so helpless.

Fragile.

It feels like I'm being stabbed as I look at her.

My emotions are all over the place.

I want to scream. I want to punch something. But most of all, I want to pull her into my lap, kiss her, and tell her I'll take care of her.

Bruises litter her face.

Red welts, scrapes, and cuts from where her head hit the pavement.

I continue to look at her.

My heart lurches in my chest with each bandage I see. There is one on her head. Her wrist. Her leg is elevated and wrapped as well.

With the concussion and bruised ribs, I imagine she will be holed up for at least a few weeks in my place.

Payton doesn't open her eyes as I make my approach.

I'm sure whatever drug they gave her for the pain has knocked her out.

I take the empty chair beside her bed. Again, I'm surprised that she doesn't wake up and am slightly unnerved as well, but I sit by her bedside.

Her hand is in mine, my gaze glued to her face when I hear a groan.

Her eyes are still closed, but they start to blink.

With confusion still heavy in her gaze, she stares up at me, and when her eyes go wide, the machine next to the bed starts to beep faster. Her heart is beating rapidly.

"Payton, you're okay," I promise. "You're safe."

She tries to speak, but her words don't make sense. It's as if she's gargling rocks.

"It wasn't me, Payton. I was still in my car across the street. I ran to you as fast as I could."

"The-the car."

"It looked like mine, but it wasn't my car."

"I-I . . ." She coughs to clear her throat. "I know, Trent. I know you would never hurt me." She inhales, and when she does, she cringes from the pain.

"You have to take it easy," I tell her. "You hurt your ribs. They gave you something for the pain, but I imagine it still hurts."

"Water."

"Let me just check with the nurses," I say because I'm not sure what she's on and if she's allowed. "I'll be right back."

I stand from the chair and make my way into the hallway. I flag down the first nurse I see and ask her to check on Payton.

"You stay out here. I'll get you when she's ready," the nurse says to me.

I stand in the hallway as I wait for them to talk.

After a few minutes, she leaves the room and motions for me to re-enter.

Payton still looks hazy, but at least she isn't backing away in fear again. I head to the chair and sit down.

I grab her hand again, unable to help it.

She looks down at our joined hands, then back at me for a minute. Her eyes widen, but she doesn't say anything. There is no witty retort. No fire I never realized I crave.

"How did this happen?"

I brush my thumb over her knuckle. It's the only one left untouched by rocky scabs. "I'm still trying to get to the bottom of it."

Without thinking of what I'm doing, I take her other hand in mine, too. I'm holding them both now, stretching my arm out so she doesn't have to move a hair on her body to accommodate me. Hope flashes across her face. Brief. Like a firework.

"I promise you, Payton. I know I told you I want to hurt you. That's why I wanted to talk to you. I finally realized that what I was doing is no different than what my father did to Ivy. I swore I would never be that man, and that's what I was coming to tell you. I was coming to tell you I'm not going to fight you anymore."

"You were going to give me the money."

"Yes. I put in a call to Baker to meet. Then once you are allowed, I'm taking you home, and I'll take care of you." I hold her hands steady, unable to bear breaking contact yet.

"You don't need to take care of me."

"I do. I don't trust anyone else. I upped security. You will be safe in my place. It's my fault you're here, but I'll make this right."

"What do you mean?"

I lower my voice. "I can't talk about it here."

Her hand is still in mine, and I squeeze it very gently to get her attention.

"I promise, I'll make it up to you." I reach up and pull hair away from her eyes, hating the bruises there, wishing I could've been the one in front of that car instead of her. "I promise I'll tell you everything."

"What if I don't want you taking care of me?" she teases, and I'm happy to hear the sound of it.

"Nonnegotiable. Your safety is my only priority," I respond. "Listen to me, Payton. You have a concussion. Sprained wrist. Sprained ankle. You can't walk. You can barely breathe. You can't be alone. Heather can't help you. So that only leaves your sister."

Her jaw tightens at that suggestion.

Just as I'm about to open my mouth to say more, the door to the room bursts open.

Speak of the devil.

Erin runs into the room.

"Oh, Payton." She sprints to the side of the bed, looking genuinely concerned. "Are you okay?"

"Erin," Payton croaks.

"What happened to you? Who would do this?" Erin asks.

"They don't know."

"Why would anyone want to hurt you?" But then Erin turns to me, brows furrowed. "You're the only one who would want to hurt her," she hisses in my direction.

"I can assure you, I had nothing to do with this." I don't have to justify my actions to her nor my relationship with Payton, but it still pisses me the fuck off that she is doing this right now.

"I see the way you look at my sister. I saw the way you spoke to her. You want her dead."

"Erin—" Payton groans.

"What?" She lifts a defiant brow, crossing her arms. "It's true."

"Please, stop."

Erin gives a reluctant nod and takes the seat on the other side of the bed. The side furthest from me. "When can I take you home?"

Payton turns her head toward her sister and stares at her for a second. "I'll be fine, Erin."

"You won't be fine. You need someone to take care of you, so you'll come home and stay with me."

"And Brad? Will he be there?" she asks her.

"Of course, he will be," Erin chastises. "He lives with me."

Brad. The boyfriend . . .

"I'm not going home with you, Erin." There is an edge to her voice, and I want to smile at how tough she is. Even in a hospital bed, she has a spine of steel.

"That's ridiculous. I'm your next of kin. I'm all you have. You need to come home with me. No one else."

Payton's eyes beg me to save her with a million unsaid words.

"She's coming home with me," I interject. "I've hired staff to take care of her."

I'm not sure if this is what Payton wanted me to say, but this is the answer I've come up with, mostly because it's nonnegotiable. I have round-the-clock security, and after this, it'll only be tighter. There won't be anywhere safer for Payton.

"You can't possibly be serious," Erin says, crossing her arms with a scowl.

"Seeing as I'm the executor of Payton's estate, and I need to pay bills for the staff, it makes the most sense for me to oversee the staff in my own house." My pragmatic answer will win me no favors with Payton, but it speaks to a language Erin knows . . . money.

"She doesn't need staff. She has me, and you just need to turn the damned money over to me so I can take care of my family."

I take a deep breath, trying to calm myself from saying something I will regret about the fucking money.

"Payton"—I pause—"what would you like to do?"

This might not be the right course of action. Her sister might railroad her into going back with her, but at the same time, after everything I've put Payton through, I feel strongly that I need to give her the choice.

She turns to her sister, and for a brief second, my heart races a little bit faster. *What that means, well, I can't read into that right now.* Instead, I wait for her answer.

"I'm staying with Trent."

"What?" Erin shouts, and I take a protective step closer to Payton.

"Erin, this makes the most sense, seeing as he's in charge of my money," she points out. "He can get me the best help. Round-the-clock nurses. I just feel like my healing would be better off at his house."

"You're making a mistake. I can guarantee when the cops look into this, they will see he's the one who hit you." She scoffs.

Payton visibly shakes at the accusation.

Payton's eyes dart back to me, boring into mine. Unspoken words are said with her gaze. I trust you.

"Erin, it's final. I'm going to go home with Trent."

"Fine." Erin stands and snatches her bag off the seat. "But don't say I did not warn you about what can happen to you."

"What does that mean?"

"Nothing."

With nothing more to say, the room goes quiet, but the threat still lingers.

CHAPTER THIRTY-SEVEN

Payton

T RENT ALDRIDGE HAS A HEART.

It is big and vibrant, and hidden behind ironclad walls he erected himself. I'm not sure how it took me so long to realize it, but now that I have, I can't unsee it.

Ivy and Trent bicker over the next steps of my recovery near the door to my private hospital room.

I wave a little. "Right here, guys."

They ignore me.

Meanwhile, Cyrus has his phone out, growling orders into the device in a language I can't identify, let alone understand. I only know they're orders because it's Cyrus. I don't even have to have known him long to know what that means.

I agreed to continue staying with Trent, what in the hell did I say yes to?

Now that Trent is no longer ignoring his sister (something I gathered over the past few days through contextual clues), she's all up in his grill. I think he likes it. I also think it's a recipe for disaster. The kind that tastes like chocolate and gooey marshmallows but is all sorts of messy.

"She needs a wheelchair," Trent insists, already pulling up his phone, presumably to order one.

"The doctor didn't mention that at all." Ivy snatches his phone from his hands. "Actually, he did mention her legs. To say they'll be fine. They just need to be elevated."

"If they need to be elevated, she needs a wheelchair."

"A wheelchair is flat."

"Hello?" I cut in.

Still nothing.

If I'm being honest, I want the wheelchair. I tried walking with the crutches the hospital offered and failed miserably. But I understand what Ivy's been trying to do since she showed up—cement into Trent that I am not fragile. I will not break because of one accident.

I have no illusions that it's a favor to me, and every impression it's for Trent. Ivy doesn't want her brother to feel guilty over my condition, even if it means she has to point out how intact I am. And I agree with her. Dealing with Trent's guilt is uncomfortable. I never know how it'll manifest.

I end up in a hospital wheelchair, being pushed by a gentle-handed Ivy. We descend a private elevator and are led out by the staff to a small, empty parking garage. Cyrus pulls his car beside Trent's. Ivy waves goodbye, and then they're gone, leaving me alone with Trent.

He helps me into the car even though I don't need it. I think it's guilt, but he's going overboard. I don't want this to be awkward. Especially if I expect to hide out at his place. We need to find some way to let the past stay in the past and move on.

The problem is, this peace is so tentative, so fresh that I fear broaching the subject is like poking a bear.

Trent sits beside me in the back seat as his driver steers us into the city. My leg is elevated like the doctor ordered. I guess it's a good thing Trent owns a Maybach. I can't imagine that many cars would allow me to do this.

We still haven't pierced the silence since his sister left.

I won't be the first to do it.

Trent's profile is the only thing visible to me as he stares out of the window, watching the scenery change from rural to concrete.

I wonder if he regrets his decision to bring me back with him.

Yeah, he feels guilty for what happened to me, but he could have pawned me off on my sister. Despite our differences, I'm thankful he asked me to stay with him.

Since all my stuff is already in Trent's loft and his is the most secure place I've been to, this plan makes the most sense.

However, the closer we get, the more I'm not sure.

The drive is eerily quiet.

No music plays. Neither of us speaks.

I just want to get home already.

Home.

What a strange word.

Is his place my home?

No. Not really.

But I have lived there for over a month and feel safer in the loft, under Trent's wings, than I ever felt in any house or apartment with Erin.

Maybe it's not my home, but it sure does feel good to be going back.

After the accident, I just want normalcy.

That would never have happened with Erin and Brad. The man gives me major creep vibes.

Something's off about him. Beyond the drugs, the booze, and the penchant for dealing.

At first, it was the way he looked at me.

It wasn't sexual necessarily.

Just off.

I shake my head and pull my focus back to the outside landscape. We approach the bridge and cross over it.

It won't be long now.

My bed beckons me, and I stifle a yawn at the thought.

That makes Trent shuffle in his seat.

I turn to see what he's doing.

He is staring at me.

Blue eyes that have no bottom.

"Tired?" His voice is low as if to keep the conversation strictly between the two of us.

"Yeah. It feels like I got run over by a car," I joke, trying to lighten the mood.

It has the opposite effect, though, and instead, little lines form between Trent's brows.

"I'm so sorry about that."

It's not the first time he's apologized, and it probably won't be the last. I thought I'd enjoy the moment, but I don't. It lost its novelty after the first time, and now, I just want things back to how they were, minus the animosity.

"It's really not your fault," I point out.

"But it could be," he admits on a sigh.

This is the second time he's made a cryptic comment like that.

"What does that mean?"

His eyes dart to the front of the car. "Not now. But I'll explain back at the loft."

I give him a little nod to show him I understand. Whatever he has to say or confess shouldn't be done in front of his driver.

Makes sense.

I know that Trent rubs elbows with some powerful men.

This could be about that.

Maybe he pissed someone off.

I shiver at the thought.

"Cold?"

"No."

He moves in his seat, and his body slides closer. Our legs touch. His hand grazes mine.

The shifting makes it more pronounced, and I wonder what he is doing, but then he pulls his coat off. He's making sure I'm warm.

And at that gesture, I thaw.

Soon, the car slows down. I peek out the window and notice we're pulling up to the loft building. When the driver throws the car in park, Trent turns to me and signals with his hand for me to stay. Then he is up and out of the car, walking around to my side.

He opens the door and reaches his hand in to grab me. I shake my head, but he just frowns.

"No way am I letting you try to walk."

"What are you going to do?"

"Carry you, of course."

"You are not carrying me." I cross my arms over my chest.

Petulant child in aisle one.

He leans into the car doorway and almost whispers, "It wouldn't be the first time."

My face starts to warm at the implication. The last time I got hurt, he carried me. I remember his arms, the way he held me tight, and the smell of his cologne. It feels like it was just yesterday.

Yeah, no, I can't let him carry me.

It's hard enough being attracted to a man you hate.

Oh, shut up, Payton. You don't hate him.

Tolerate. You tolerate him.

Even I am getting annoyed with my lies.

It's more that he makes you feel things you don't want to think about. Which means you can't be held in his arms.

Because that will confuse me even more.

However, his narrow eyes tell me there is no getting out of this, so I pivot my body to the right, extend my leg out, and move to stand. Before I can, he's reaching in and pulling me carefully into his arms.

"Can't you just get me crutches or a wheelchair?"

"No."

"Seriously?"

This is unbelievable.

"Yes."

301

"Why do you have to be so difficult? I am perfectly capable of handling myself."

"Yet you're not. You said you would stay with me. You said you would heal in my place. You sprained a rib, sprained your foot, and don't get me started with your concussion. Can you just not argue with me?"

"Fine," I say on a huff.

He chuckles, and this time it's a happy laugh. A sound I'm not used to hearing come from his lips. I really like it. It's contagious. I stop the matching smile from spreading across my lips.

In his arms, he pulls me tight, but he's careful not to hurt me. I'm having a hard time reconciling the two versions of Trent.

The one who treated me like a servant, forced me to write papers, and had me volunteer.

That Trent was nasty, cruel, belittling. Yet the one I see now . . . This is the same man who brushed an old lady's hair and helped Henry find his son. He tied shoes, cleaned, and stayed with me in the hospital every day . . .

It's hard to figure out who the real Trent is.

I don't think he knows either. I think he's lived in a dark world for too long, and he doesn't remember what it's like to grow in the sunlight anymore.

I want to show him the light. I want to remind him what he has to be grateful for.

My mind says that would be dangerous.

But my heart? It's beating like a drummer, begging to see him shine.

If I let those walls down, if I stop protecting myself and it turns out I'm wrong . . .

If the gamble isn't worth it, if Trent turns out not to be the man I think he is beneath all the practiced hatred?

He can use that against me.

All the things in my past before his father stepped into my life, he can use against me.

Trent's driver must've called ahead to let the staff know we were arriving because as Trent walks up the sidewalk to the door, it swings open, and everyone in the house greets us.

Each one of them approaches us, trying to make sure I'm okay, but Trent doesn't want to stop. Instead, he walks down the hall.

To his room.

"What are we doing in your room?" I ask when he swings the door open with me still in his arms.

"You'll be staying in here for the time being."

I take in the grandiose space for the first time. It's oversized, dark, and neat. Just like I expected. It also only has one bed.

"And where will you be staying . . . ?" I trail off.

He steps into the room with me and shuts the door behind him with his foot. "I took the liberty of moving your stuff in here and placing my stuff in your room, temporarily."

"Why would you do that?"

I think I need him to spell it out for me because I'm not computing. Is this really the same man who makes me mix custom cleaning solutions for him?

He swallows, adjusting me in his grip. "Because you need more space."

"I don't need this much space."

He walks toward the bed. "If you decide you want to use a wheelchair while you heal, your room is not adequately shaped for it. Also, your shower doesn't have room for a chair."

"You are being ridiculous. I don't need a chair, and I am not staying in your room."

He looks like he wants to argue. His Adam's apple bobs in his throat, but with obvious reluctance, he nods. He retraces his steps and carries me to the room I've been living in.

I breathe in the familiar space, but all I catch is Trent's scent. It's overwhelming how much he consumes every space he enters. He places me on the bed, taking special care to avoid putting pressure on my injuries. Then he turns and storms out of the room before I even have time to process that I pissed him off.

What in the world did I do?

I don't see what the big deal is about me not sleeping in his bed, but I can't deal with a thirty-something-year-old man having a tantrum. He may as well lie on the floor, kicking his feet. It's obvious what this is. A tantrum.

At least he closed the door behind him because I need a minute by myself.

My ribs ache. My leg aches. Hell, my wrist even aches.

But I don't like to ask for help.

So I lie on my bed, try to get comfortable, and close my eyes.

I don't know what time it is when I finally flutter them back open, but I'm met with darkness despite the curtains pulled wide open. My cell phone sits on the other side of the bed. I scoot over to look at it, moving extra slowly thanks to the haggard state of my body.

It's three in the morning.

Wow. I fell asleep for twelve hours.

I still don't feel rested.

At the hospital, the nurses woke me up so often for tests and drugs and who-knows-what. Then they told me they wouldn't discharge me until I proved I felt well-rested, which was downright impossible with how dead set they were on keeping me awake.

There's dirt and grime on me. I can't see it, but I can feel it. I look around the room and wonder what I should do. The bathroom is an en suite, but it feels particularly far right now. I eyeball the distance between the bed and the entrance to it.

Fuck me.

I'm wide-awake. There is no way I'm falling back asleep. It feels like spiders are crawling all over me. I can't ignore it. Luckily, I don't have a hard cast, so I shouldn't need help taking a shower.

But getting there?

Trent is right. I do need a chair. I also don't want to admit he's right, nor wake him up.

I place my good foot on the floor. With all my strength, I hobble to the bathroom, keeping pressure off the bad foot. When I reach the toilet, I sit down on the closed lid and unstrap the boot I'm wearing. I place it to the side, remove the arm brace, and strip off my clothes.

I'm slightly winded from hobbling, but it wasn't impossible. Definitely doable. And something I can repeat again. But my ribs ache, and I wonder if I'm straining myself by doing too much.

But it's a shower.

I can't exactly ask for help.

I open the shower's glass door, grasp the handle on the wall to steady myself, and turn the water on, stepping under it.

There's nothing like getting washed clean after days without. It beats taking off your bra after a long day. A midnight taco run. Acing a test. I groan out in bliss, ridding myself of the past few days.

The water is a bit warm for my normal liking. Actually, it's scalding hot and probably burning my insides alive. But it wipes away the grime and all the disgustingness of what happened.

I try to lather my hair up with my bad hand once while my good hand stays occupied holding the shower handle. I fail, of course, suds running into my eyes. They burn. I blink fast, shoving the water over my face.

Dammit. This is more difficult than I wanted it to be.

I grasp the outside of the shower door, trying to find a washcloth, but I lose my footing. Luckily, there's a shower bench. I grunt as soon as my butt makes contact with the hard marble.

I steady myself on it before I fall, but it's inclined downward and not large enough for me to sit on for long.

Who built this thing so it would only fit a foot and not a butt?

I would be lying if I said that showering while standing didn't hurt like a sonofabitch. My ribs begin to burn from the pain. At least I didn't fall again.

I need to get out of here as soon as possible.

This isn't a smart idea.

As I wash the soap out of my eyes, the door to the bathroom swings open.

"Are you fucking kidding me?" Trent hollers.

"Are you fucking kidding *me*?" I respond, trying desperately to cover my exposed body with my bad hand while trying not to let go of the handle with my good one.

"What are you doing taking a shower?"

I shrug. Or try to. My hands are otherwise occupied. "It's my bathroom, and I felt gross."

He stalks toward me. "You can't take a shower by yourself."

"And what am I supposed to do when I wake up like yucky?"

"Let me set you up in my bathroom."

He's fuming, his shoulders rising and falling with the ragged intake of oxygen. I turn off the water, planning my escape. The air is cold. It elicits a shiver. I'm still naked in front of him, and it must hit him because his eyes go wide.

Then his gaze dips down.

Not that it's something he hasn't seen before, but goose bumps rise along my arm.

"Stop right there, buddy," I scold. "Hand me a towel."

He crosses his arms. "I'll hand you a towel if you agree to let me carry you back to my room."

I tip my chin up. "I'm perfectly capable of being by myself."

"Says the girl who didn't listen to me. Didn't ask for help, and very possibly could have face-planted in the shower and sprained or worse, fractured her other wrist."

"None of that happened." I wave my good wrist, internally groaning when my breasts sway with the motion.

His eyes darken, but he fixes his attention on my face. I don't think I would have the same restraint.

"But it could have," he says, stalking forward again. "So be a good girl, take the towel, wrap your body, and let me take you to my room. Tomorrow, I will make sure everything is set up. That way, you don't have to move unless you have support."

I let out a giant groan.

"Fine." I hold out my good hand. "Just hand me the damn towel. I'm cold, and I'll do whatever you want just to shut you up."

He wears his smile like a trophy. He won, and now he's basking in his winnings.

He hands me the fluffy towel that was out of reach. I quickly wrap it around my wet body as best I can. I don't miss the way he trails his gaze over my skin, and if I were in my right mind, I would probably relish it and taunt him.

But after all this movement, I've exerted too much energy, and I'm exhausted. I have no fight left in me.

So, I don't do anything.

There's no witty rebuttal.

I allow myself to be picked up, yet again. I close my eyes once I'm in his arms. His cologne lingers in my nostrils. It makes me feel safe. It is a complete contradiction to how I felt earlier.

We walk back into the room, and he places me on his bed.

"I'll be right back."

I adjust the towel around my chest. "Where are you going?"

"To get you something to wear to sleep."

He walks into the closet, then a moment later, he returns holding a black T-shirt.

I lift a brow. "That's not mine."

"You're right. It's not. Great detective skills, Sherlock." He clutches it tight in his grip, eyes drifting to my collarbone. "You need something to wear. It's late at night, and I don't want to rummage through your stuff."

"That kind of makes sense," I mutter under my breath.

Trent crosses the space and stands in front of me. His hand

reaches out with the shirt at the same time I do. Our fingers touch. A heady sensation washes over me, but I push it down.

I can't think of him this way.

I can't read into the way he looks at me.

I can't remember our kiss. Or the way he held my hand throughout my time in the hospital.

This is stupid, Payton. Get your act together.

"Everything okay?" Trent interrupts my inner rambling.

"Yeah, why wouldn't it be?"

"Maybe because you were shaking your head."

"Oh." I fumble for an excuse. "I must be more tired than I realized . . ."

"Or, knowing you, you were fighting with me in your head." He starts to laugh, and I realize I probably made a face that gave me away. "You were. What were we fighting about?"

"Doesn't matter."

I take the T-shirt from his hands and slip it on over my head. As soon as it covers the towel that is wrapped around my body, I shimmy it off.

And that's when I realize I'm missing one thing . . .

"Um . . ."

He gives me a *go on* look. "Yes?"

"I, um, need underwear."

He looks down at my exposed legs, and a slight smirk spreads. "I don't have any women's underwear in here. Guess you will have to go without."

"This is total bullshit." I groan, tilting my head up to the ceiling as if it holds all the answers. "I knew it was too good to be true."

"What?"

"Your good behavior." I drop my gaze back to him. "You're back to being a jackass."

"I hardly call refusing to rummage through your underwear a jackass behavior, but tomato, tomahto. You say jackass; I say princely."

"It's not that. It's that damn smirk on your face."

His smile grows bolder at my claim.

"See?" I nod toward it. "There's the brat."

"Again, I have no idea what you're talking about." He shrugs. "Go to bed, Payton."

"Give me a pair of boxers, Trent."

He reaches into another drawer, tosses me a pair, and turns his back to pull down the covers on the bed.

I huff and struggle into the boxers. When he's done with the bed, I expect to hear his footsteps announce his exit. Instead, I'm shocked to still hear him walking around in the room. I refuse to ask him what he's doing because, obviously, I'm very mature at this point in our arguing.

Climbing into the soft bedsheets, I grit my teeth and wait . . . and wait.

And wait some more.

Finally, it's too much to bear.

"Why are you still here?" I ask him.

He takes a seat in the chaise lounge opposite the bed, just staring at me.

"What are you doing here?" I ask again.

He lifts the throw blanket he tossed on top of himself. "Isn't it obvious?"

"Jeez, stop with the damn question-for-a-question and just tell me."

He adjusts in the chaise. "I'm sleeping here."

The hell he is.

I try to pop my body up, but it hurts too much.

I just shake my head and tell him, "No, you're not staying."

"I am staying."

He uses a growly tone that sounds so pompous. So arrogant, yet so damn sexy.

Ugh, I want to hit myself for these thoughts.

I shake my head. "You can't sleep here."

"Someone has to watch you."

"You weren't watching me before, and I was perfectly fine."

"That's where you're wrong." He tsks. "I was watching you before I went to go get water. In the time it took me to go downstairs, get water, drink it, and come back up, you managed to get yourself stuck in the shower."

My mouth opens and shuts.

"You were in the room the whole time?"

"Yep." He smiles. "FYI, you talk in your sleep."

"I do not."

"Okay, sure, princess."

Maybe I do, and by the way he's grinning, it can't be a good thing.

There is no way I'm going to get him out of this room. I let out a deep, audible, dramatic sigh.

"It's really not that bad, Payton."

"Which part?" I lift a brow. "The part where you spy on me when I sleep? Or the part where I can't actually do anything to get you outta here?"

"The latter." He kicks one foot on top of the other, getting way too relaxed for his own good. "Think of it this way. For the night, you have a personal butler. If you want a drink, I'll get it for you. You need help getting up? I'll help you." He says it like he just offered me the best gift in the world.

"How about you go down the block and get someone else to watch me?" I grumble.

"That's not going to happen, princess." He shakes his head. "But if you keep playing your cards right, maybe I'll ask your sister." He lifts a challenging brow.

"You wouldn't dare."

"Yet . . . I think I would."

That is all he has to say for me to fall in line.

Point to you, Trent.

In the morning, I awake to the sight of Trent sitting on the side of my bed. Just looking at me with concern on his face.

"Good morning, princess."

Normally, the moniker bothers me.

But today, when he says it without venom, when he uses that deep rumble of his morning voice, I want to melt.

Wow.

What changed since the accident?

Maybe that concussion did something.

"Morning. Did you get much sleep in the chair?" I ask him.

"It was fine once I got used to the snoring."

My mouth drops a little. "You woke yourself up with your own snoring?"

"No, silly, yours woke me up," he says with the devilish look back on his face, mischievous eyes matching it.

I sit up in the bed to smack him, but as I reach forward, the movement pulls on my sore ribs, and I wince. Trent reaches forward to grab my shoulders and help me sit up.

"Thanks."

His face is only inches away.

I can't help but look at those lips.

Lips I want to kiss again.

He shifts and stands fully off the bed, one arm around my back to hold me upright. His other hand works to rearrange the pillows until I'm supported again.

"There. That should help. Sorry." He pats at the pillow. "I didn't mean to make you reach and hurt more."

The furrow is back on his forehead again. He looks worried; the concern creeping back into the space between us.

I reach up and touch his arm.

"It's okay. I just forget I can't move like I want to sometimes. This is still all a little new, right?"

So is him taking care of me.

But it feels good. Better than it should.

Trent's eyes bore into me. I take in the emotions shining from them. Determination. Sorrow. And something more tender.

He cares.

Or is it just guilt?

As if he can read my mind, he says, "I'm truly sorry for all this. It's my fault. If I would have just left you in your rental house, if I would have just talked to Ivy in the first place and left you alone, none of this would have happened."

"But it did, and we can't take it back."

"What if I want to?" he says, sitting back on the edge of the bed. He reaches out and touches my cheek with the slightest of pressure. "What if we start a different path?"

I can feel it.

The swirl of desire building between us.

Intensifying when we touch.

"You never know until you take that first step," I whisper.

Trent reaches forward, arching toward me.

I can feel his warmth.

Feel his breath as his lips close the distance to mine yet again.

I close my eyes.

I want to savor this moment . . .

His phone rings.

CHAPTER THIRTY-EIGHT

Trent

I'M NOT SURE WHETHER IT'S A GOOD THING OR A BAD THING, but my phone rings.

Payton's eyes pop open.

Again, I get lost in Payton.

I want to kiss her.

Pull her close and erase all the shit from the past.

Even the last kiss, because when that happened, I pulled myself away. Hatred rushed at me like a giant tsunami. Sudden, brutal, and disastrous. I'd gotten lost in the moment. Blind to anything but Payton.

My own personal tunnel vision.

All I could see was red where she was concerned. My anger channeled straight into her.

This moment would have been different. There was no anger as I held her in my arms last night. Just a desperate desire to protect her better.

Softer, gentler kisses.

Not just because of her pain. Because I want to show that side to her. Show her the man I think I could be for her.

The phone rings again.

Payton's eyes dip down to it. She licks her lips, her voice coming out husky. "You should probably answer that."

"Probably," I say, but I don't move.

If I'm going to be that man for Payton, I need her to be well. I need to know that I'm not confusing my emotions with guilt. And the truth is, she needs to know that, too.

But later. She's right. I need to answer the phone.

I do, and all it takes is a few seconds for the grin to consume my face.

Looks like the crew is back.

It needs to be said that Tobias is an asshole. Even when the dickwad is technically the source of my problems, we end up catering to his schedule. To his needs.

Apparently, he had other pressing matters.

So, here I am, driving to Connecticut in my car.

Despite the fact that Matteo lives closer.

That Jaxson lives closer.

This long-ass drive? Totally unnecessary.

We could've stayed in the city.

I sound like a whiny bitch again.

The truth is, leaving Payton with a nurse, even if only temporarily, doesn't sit well with me. I'd be much happier if it were me there, watching over her, making sure she's comfortable and safe.

I slow my car, driving the speed limit for once. I need the time to think about what I'm going to do with her. Also, the idea of causing a crash like Payton's, even if I'm one hundred percent confident behind the wheel, sickens me.

Great.

I'm one step closer to being a normal, boring, law-abiding citizen. Society can thank Payton Hart for that. Now that I'm no longer lying to myself, I can admit that I'm attracted to her. I can also admit that I like her, too.

I want to build her up instead of crushing her life and pissing on the rubble. Which is a welcome first. I'm going to use this time to get to know her.

I sound like a love-sick puppy.

Next thing I know, I'll be braiding her hair and singing her lullabies to sleep.

Spending some time with Lorenzo and Tobias should help me put my brain back in order. Matteo and Cyrus, on the other hand, are useless. They're pussy-whipped.

Maybe I'm no exception, except for the fact I am not actually fucking her.

Traffic is on my side. Before I know it, I'm in Connecticut, making the approach up Cyrus's long, elegant, and very private driveway. I park my car in the circular roundabout, get out, and head to the large mahogany doors.

I don't even have to knock. Gerald, Cyrus's butler, opens the door for me as if he's been waiting for my arrival.

No one needs to announce me or tell me where to go.

I have spent more nights and weekends here than I can even count over the past four years. I head straight into the parlor, where we normally play poker.

I'm not the first one here.

Tobias sits at the table that's now empty of chips.

I nod to him. "I see you're the first."

"That I am." He lifts his glass to me. "I had other business to discuss with Cyrus. I got here yesterday and stayed the night."

"Anything I can help with?" I ask.

"Not yet, but I'm sure Cyrus will contact you when he needs you to do something with my money."

"Looking forward to that phone call," I say, the sarcasm eliciting a snort from Tobias.

No matter how much we tell Cyrus to retire, he hasn't. Sure, he's taken a major step back and only works for certain clients now, Tobias being one. But Cyrus is ruthless with his money. Always seeking ways to grow it.

Not a bad thing, but also not exactly a call I look forward to receiving. I like Cyrus best when business is not involved, and we just drink cognac and play cards.

Cyrus doesn't gamble when there's money on the table. He might run a card game with a six-figure buy-in, but he will only play with friends.

The sound of footsteps draws my attention. Lorenzo, Matteo, and Cyrus enter the room and take their respective seats around the poker table. Cyrus, naturally, sits at the dealer's end.

Matteo breaks the silence. "So, what did you need to discuss with us?"

I run a palm along my jaw, considering how to approach this. "I'm not sure how much you all know about Payton . . ."

"The girl you have living with you." Lorenzo smirks as he speaks.

"Yes."

"Are you banging her?"

"Not your business, Lorenzo."

"That's not a no." His smile broadens like a pig in shit.

"What I do with Payton is none of your business," I snap.

The bastard tilts his head, and I know he won't let up.

I'm right.

"Since you aren't, maybe I could," he drawls. "Dating as the head of the mafia is difficult these days."

"The fuck you will." I jab my finger in his direction. "Don't even step foot near her."

"So . . . you *do* want to bang her." Lorenzo's smile never drops. Bastard.

I walked right into that one. But I'm on edge when it comes to Payton. Overprotective and reeling from what happened.

"Jesus, Lorenzo. Give the guy a break," Jax says as he enters the room and takes a seat beside Cyrus. "Did I miss anything important, or are we here to break Romeo's balls?"

"Nothing other than the fact that Trent is hard up for the

girl living in his house. His stepsister." Lorenzo, apparently, has a death wish tonight because if he doesn't shut the fuck up, I'm going to kill him.

Would that make me the new head of the mafia?

"Dad fucked her sister, so at best, that would make Payton my aunt, which she's not since Dad and the sister were never married," I inform him, my voice curt and to the point.

Cyrus cracks his neck. "As much as I want to chitchat with all of you pussies, which I don't by the way, I have better things to do. Can we get to the fucking point? No more interruptions."

Not surprisingly, Cyrus is the serious one.

"Someone tried to hurt her, and they wanted it to look like it was me," I tell the men at the table.

"She's going to be okay?" Matteo asks.

"Mercifully, she is. Concussion. Bruised ribs. A sprained ankle. That's it, and she got lucky. She didn't get the brunt of it, but still, not the point. The point is, someone tried to kill her, and I have a feeling I know who it is."

"Paul," Jax finishes.

I nod.

"That fucker," Lorenzo hisses.

Matteo leans forward in his chair. "Why do you think he went after her?"

"As much as I hate to say it, I think it's because he thought she was important to me."

"Well, she is, right?" Matteo assesses me.

"I have no idea. My feelings are complex, to say the least. All I can tell you is it didn't start this way."

"Welcome to the party, brother." He laughs, and I'm happy Matteo finds my suffering so entertaining.

"The thing is, from an outsider's point of view, I was always with Payton. She lived in my house. He must have thought that she meant something to me. That we're involved. So, he went after her to hurt me."

I care about her.

It's obvious at this point.

I can deny it, but it won't do me any good. Paul wanted to hurt someone I care about. Mission fucking accomplished. To be honest, he's not that nostalgic. Emotional connections don't exist to him. Hurting Payton was a means to an end to disrupt my life, thereby disrupting my business.

But I don't care about my business.

I'm not gonna admit that in front of a room full of my clients, who trust me with their billions . . . but going after Paul isn't about the hedge fund.

It's about revenge.

I won't let him get away with what he did to Payton.

I lean forward, placing my elbows on the table. "We need a plan."

"Fuck the plan. We need to grab that motherfucker and torture the hell outta him." Angry Lorenzo has replaced the annoyingly playful version. For once, I welcome it with eager arms.

"Or we could try to do this in a more civilized fashion," I answer him, but only because I think torture is temporary.

"Civilization is for pussies. We took his money. We fucked him out of everything. The man doesn't want civilized."

Lorenzo has a point.

"Okay, so we take him. Then what?" I ask.

Normally, this is where I step back and let the guys do their thing, but for Payton, I'm all in.

"We torture him, obviously."

"Guys—" Jaxson chimes in, but Lorenzo lifts his hand to silence him.

"Nope, you have no say in this," Lorenzo tells him.

"Then why am I here?"

"For someone so smart, I thought it would be obvious."

Jaxson shoots Lorenzo a nasty look. "You need someone to locate him? Great."

I turn to Jax and incline my head. "Oh, cut the shit. If you didn't want to do this kind of work, you wouldn't be here. You get bored of all that government crap you do."

"Yep, that's why I keep coming back," he says, playing it off as sarcasm, but we all know it's the truth. "Because all the government crap is boring, and I miss you guys."

"He loves us." Lorenzo grins at Jax like an idiot, and I'm pretty sure Jaxson will one day have his revenge. He'll probably hack his computer and give him some crazy bug.

Jax leans back against his seat. "Okay, I'll do it. Once I get the intel, who do you want me to send it to?"

"Me," I tell him, rapping my knuckles on the velvet table. "Encrypted files on a hard drive with instructions for us on where and when to meet you."

He rolls his eyes. "Or I can just send a text asking you to grab drinks with me, and I'll tell you in person."

"That does sound simpler." I turn to the rest of the guys. "Okay, and once we get Paul, where are we holding him?"

"My island is out," Cyrus says. "Ivy lives on it."

"Unfortunately, my place is out, too," Matteo chimes in. "Viviana might be pissed if she hears the screams."

"I have the perfect place," Lorenzo adds, a grin on his face.

By the way Matteo cringes, I have a feeling things get ugly there.

"Thanks, Lorenzo," I tell him, and I mean it.

Even though he's talking about torturing a man (and killing him, most likely), this is for Payton, and I owe him.

"It's the least I can do. You did make me a shit ton of money last year."

"And it was clean," I add.

"True."

CHAPTER THIRTY-NINE

Payton

THE LOFT SEEMS COLDER WITHOUT TRENT HERE.
The room is empty.

My pen hovers over my journal, my mind consumed with thoughts of earlier this morning. I truly thought he would kiss me, but then his phone rang, and the moment vanished.

The good thing about being alone—despite the nurse situated in this house to watch me—is that I have time to think about this morning. She set me up with a tray desk so I can do schoolwork without leaving my bed.

Instead, I have my list out. The one full of anti-Trent scribbles. It seems absurd now that I look at it, and I struggle to add to the tally, my mind straying elsewhere.

Do I want him to kiss me?

I skim over the list, reliving the past few months. The scenes run through my mind in slow motion. His strong arms around me. The feel of his hands on my skin. The way he looks at me. When he laughs . . . the sound makes my heart beat a little faster.

Every second leads to the ultimate realization.

Yes, I do.

I want him to kiss me.

I want him to do *more*.

On this emotional roller coaster, I've gone from hating him, to tolerating him, to understanding him . . .

And right back to hating him again, only to realize that despite everything, he has a good heart . . .

Mostly for others. He did try to ruin your life, remember?

But his mom's words stick with me. Trent is misunderstood. Designed by Ronnie to be as cruel as possible. And dammit, I see him.

I see the good.

I want to unwrap him like he's a gift and keep what's inside for myself. I want to act on my attraction. On every base, animal-level instinct I have had toward him since the moment I thought he was Mr. Baker.

You can't fake chemistry like ours.

His personality, his confidence, even his arrogance—none of those put me off.

Granted, him being a complete douche canoe doesn't help. It's funny how you can hate someone and want them at the same time. Well, maybe not; love and hate are two sides of the same coin.

But . . . truth be told, I don't hate him anymore. Not now that I've seen the other side. The one that took care of me, looks out for me, and seeks to protect me. The other shit doesn't matter anymore.

Trent's mom is right. I need to peel back the layers and understand the gray area. Our awful beginnings and the way he treated me are byproducts of his pain. Transferring it to me wouldn't help him, but it was what he knew from Ronnie.

Trent isn't evil.

He doesn't get a free pass either.

He needs to grovel—to be held accountable for his actions—but there is beauty in life's shades of gray. I'm willing to let him show me his.

His good qualities replace the other stuff I dwelled on.

And that's a problem as I try to add to my list but find myself starting a new one. A list of reasons I should want Trent.

It is scary long.

Those butterflies he gives me.

The way his fingers feel when they touch me.

I almost died, but when he touches me, looks at me deep in my eyes, I feel alive. As if he sees me, too. If that doesn't mean something, I don't know what does.

The fact that I miss him right now means something, too.

I want him to come back, sit on my bed, and finish what he started.

If I told Heather the crazy thoughts running through my head, she'd try to convince me to check myself into a hospital because I'm obviously still suffering from the concussion I sustained when I was run over.

She'd say I am still confused.

But she doesn't know him.

She didn't see him with Henry.

She didn't see him at Cresthill.

She didn't see the way he makes everyone smile.

How contagious his laughter is.

How he makes *me* smile—even under these circumstances.

I stare at the door, willing Trent to come back.

There's something between Trent Aldridge and me. I'm finally ready. I'm not scared to see what it is. Naturally, with my amazing luck, he isn't here when I come to the realization.

Hours pass.

There is literally nothing for me to do.

Yes, there is a TV in the room, but I can't binge-watch Netflix right now. The screen makes my head throb.

It hurts to read.

It hurts to watch.

And not to be rude, but I really don't like the nurse.

Okay, fine . . .

It's not the nurse. She seems kind.

I just want Trent.

As if summoned by my desire, the door opens to the bedroom, and he walks inside.

My eyes go wide.

Holy wow.

He's handsome in a white thermal long-sleeve shirt and ripped jeans.

Jeez, this outfit should be illegal. He just looks so damn sexy.

He smiles broadly at me as he walks in, as if he knows he's hot, and my reaction to him is something he's used to.

The way he looks at me makes me feel hot, and all I want is for him to cross the space and resume what he started earlier.

"How're you doing?"

I try to answer. Try to play it off as if I haven't been sitting in a bed all by myself for the past four hours, counting down the minutes until he returned.

"You know." I shrug. "Same old, same old."

"Keeping busy, I see?" he jokes.

A little laugh follows, and again, I melt.

I like this playful side of him.

It's sweet when he's funny.

Yeah, he's sexy, cocky, arrogant, and condescending, but I don't even care. All I want is to kiss him. I have been dreaming about it every day since the last time he placed his mouth on mine, and now I can't stop staring at his lips.

I shake my head and answer him, "You've missed quite the morning. Some of the best clubs in New York couldn't hold a candle to all the fun I've been having."

"Go on . . ."

"Well, I'll tell you what I haven't been doing . . ." I trail off, dipping my voice conspiratorially, "Believe it or not, and I know this might come as a ginormous shock, but I have not gone dancing."

"No?" Feigned shock echoes in his voice.

"No." I nod to my leg. "Apparently, I have a bum foot."

"Then what did you do?" He sits on the bed, a safe distance from me.

"I also didn't watch TV."

"No binging Netflix?" he teases.

I lift my brow. "I also didn't read Carl Jung."

"Well, aren't you the party animal?"

"I am. I stared at the paint," I deadpan.

"Interesting."

"I found it fascinating." I lift my index finger. "Were you aware that you have a mark in the top left corner by the far wall?"

He turns to look at where I am pointing. "Nope."

"If I could stand, I would show you."

His playful expression turns serious. I press on, letting my tone turn teasing so he understands my game.

"I would like you to help me with the prison break because that's what this is, by the way. A prison."

His eyes light up with understanding, and the humor returns. "And I'm the mean prison warden?"

"If you break me out of here and do something fun with me, then you won't be," I tell him, my voice taunting him, hoping he rises to the challenge.

It occurs to me that we've built up a kinky fantasy. Roleplay. My cheeks flush, and his eyes narrow on the color.

"I don't really think there's very much you can do," he murmurs, hungry eyes fixed on my lips.

I lick them. "Don't sell yourself short. I bet you can imagine something . . ."

His eyes twinkle. "I can definitely come *up* with something."

My cheeks warm again at his innuendo. My heart picks up its pace. "Not *that* something . . ."

"What about a picnic?" he suddenly offers.

"I highly doubt I'm up for walking in the park."

"Why don't you let me deal with that?"

"I am certainly not going to allow you to carry me through a park!" I give him a pointed look.

"Why do you keep saying park?"

"Where else would we do this?" My eyes roll.

"Again, let me handle this." He stands, straightening from the bed. "I'm going to send your nurse in. You're going to take a shower, and then you're going to rest. Once you're ready, I'll come and get you."

Great.

I love being showered by a stranger.

I'd rather be showered by you.

I shake my head, forcing the thought from it. "This sounds so much fun." Sarcasm drips off the word fun.

"You have no idea what I can plan." He heads toward the door, stopping just short of it to stare at me.

"I'm a little scared. Not going to lie." As these words come out, I realize there's truth in them.

I am trying to be playful, but a part of me is scared.

He did say someone's after me.

That they will try to use me to get back at him. Does that mean they can find me? What if, next time, they succeed?

Trent must see the change in my eyes because he crosses the space to sit next to me on the bed, in the same spot he was earlier today.

Then he's directly in front of me, and he looks at me with the same warmth and kindness that he radiated this morning when he almost kissed me.

He takes my hands in his.

"I promise you, Peyton. I will never let anyone hurt you."

"Why do you care now?"

"We talked about this."

His blue eyes darken with emotion. They pierce the small distance between us. A tense silence envelops the room. Neither of us speaks for a second as we stare at each other. The memory of everything that has happened over the past few months fills the space.

Gently, his thumb rubs the palm of my hand, melting away the tension.

"The way I treated you was wrong," he says on a heavy sigh, his voice filled with anguish.

"Being wrong and caring are two separate things."

"You're right. They are. I did what I did, and I was wrong, and I apologize. The other part . . . Why do I care?" His eyes shut, and when they open again, they find mine with precision. "I don't know. That's the honest truth. But I do. I just care. I don't know when I started, but it doesn't change the fact that I don't want anything to happen to you. I don't want anybody to hurt you."

I stare into his large eyes, probing their sincerity. I see nothing to make me doubt him. He holds my hand and stares back into mine, the truth between us hovering just beneath the surface.

After a beat, he lets go, and then he's standing. "I'll be back in an hour."

I shake my head, trying to bring the playfulness back. "You're giving me far too much credit."

"Payton, I know it won't take you an hour to get ready."

I raise a brow. "And how do you know that about me?"

He sobers, and he's one hundred percent serious when he says, "I know a lot more than I've ever let on about you."

I know I've lost it when his words send butterfly jitters all over my stomach.

I've officially lost it.

I clear my throat. "From your spying?"

"There was only that one time."

"No, that's not true."

"I never really spied on you."

"Sure."

He shakes his head and moves toward the door. "Be ready. Jen will be here in a minute to help you."

I want to say I don't need help, but that's a blatant lie. The tracking device I found can attest to that. It sours my mood a bit, especially when Jen, the nurse he hired, walks into the room a moment later, and I remember I have to let a total stranger shower me.

She helps me up and into the bathroom.

This is overkill.

I'm sure I can walk a bit. The problem is, Trent is babying me. That's why I allow this, but I'm not letting her sit in the bathroom with me when I shower.

That's where I draw the line.

It takes way too long to convince her I can shower by myself. When I step into Trent's bathroom, my breath hitches in my chest.

Not just because it is gorgeous.

White marble.

Rain shower.

Large, free-standing, modern-looking tub.

Nope, that's not what does me in.

What does is in the middle of the two-person shower . . .

It's a chair.

A chair I can sit on until my ankle heels, rather than hobble or worse, must have someone in the room with me.

He was right. I should have listened to him, stopped being stubborn earlier, and not showered in my bathroom. I should have always used his. This is amazing what he's done for me.

Trent has given me my dignity back.

And I can't help the smile that spreads across my face.

When Jen has me settled, she leaves me alone in this beautiful space. I know she's going to be right behind the door in the bedroom, but that's fine, as long as I'm by myself.

I strip all my clothes and hobble the two steps until I reach the open shower door.

Once I'm sitting down, I turn on the warm water.

It feels amazing. It feels even better than yesterday's shower because I don't have to worry.

Trent set up everything so I can reach all the items I need. They're lined up in rows in front of me. It feels like my heart will explode with all the time he took to make this possible.

Normally, I'd think someone on his staff did this, but my gut tells me this was all Trent.

Trent did everything.

He went out of his way to make me feel comfortable and safe.

And now I'm supposed to go on a picnic with him.

Excitement bubbles in my chest.

When all the soap is gone from my body, I turn the water off, and that's when I notice he even has a towel set ready inside the shower. I don't even have to reach. He thought of everything, and I melt over it.

Once I'm dry, I let Jen know I'm ready. Her help is needed, seeing as my feet are wet now.

She helps me walk over to the vanity, and I take a seat. I blow out my hair with a round brush. I'm not going to put makeup on because there's no point. I don't know where we're going, so there's no reason to get fancy.

The truth is, we really can't go anywhere since, technically, I'm still on the mend.

Everything hurts, but I still want to get dressed.

Trent is probably just going to bring the food into my bedroom, but that's okay. At least I won't be alone.

An hour later, I'm sitting on the edge of my bed, my ankle and ribs wrapped, with leggings and a T-shirt on.

The door opens. Trent strolls in, handsome in the same outfit as before, and he stops to look me over.

"You might be cold. Let me grab you a jacket."

Cold? Where are we going?

I don't ask any questions, though. Instead, I wait for him to get me one and come back.

"Let's go." He hands me the jacket. "Do you want to go the fast way or the slow way?"

"Obviously, the fast way." I playfully roll my eyes, and he picks me up again. "You seem to like picking me up a lot."

This close, I can smell his cologne. Fresh and crisp. It reminds me of nature. Intoxicating. A warm fall day. A walk in the park. Whatever the scent, I wanted to immerse myself in it and get lost.

"This is the fast way," he points out.

"I wouldn't have said that if I knew that this was the fast way."

"Shh." He tightens his grip on me. "Be quiet."

I close my mouth, and I let him take me for a ride. I expect us to go to the garage, but instead, he heads toward another door, one I have never opened. It's skinnier than the rest, so I always assumed it was a closet.

He presses a button hidden slightly behind a floral arrangement. It dings a moment later, and the door slides open.

My mouth drops. "You have an elevator."

"Yep."

"I didn't know." I stare at him, heart pounding at the proximity. "Why didn't you just use the elevator instead of carrying me up yesterday?"

"That wouldn't have been as much fun."

I shake my head at him.

He steps inside with me still in his arms, turning sideways so we can fit through the opening without my ankle banging against anything. As soon as the door closes, the elevator starts moving.

In a flash, it feels like we've stopped again.

The elevator door opens, and I expect to be in another room on another floor, but instead, the New York City air hits my face.

It's an outside patio.

"Is this yours?"

"Yes."

"Wow."

If I thought that was "wow," I gasp when I see what he has actually created.

After a few steps out of the elevator, I see not only the New York City skyline and all the buildings higher and lower but also the picnic he set up.

Correction: Picnic 2.0.

There's a canopy with woven lights. Underneath, a blanket is spread out in the middle with a basket settled on top, too. Since I can't sit on the floor, Trent even set up little reclining chairs.

Trent Aldridge went all out.

There's even an outdoor space heater.

He thought of everything.

Of *me.*

He lowers me to the chair, and then he sits in front of me on the ground.

"Ready to see what we've got?"

"As ready as I'll ever be."

At my words, he opens the basket and starts to pull out French baguettes, a cheese platter, pastries, champagne, and strawberries.

It's like a date.

Is that what this is?

CHAPTER FORTY

Trent

I MAY HAVE GONE OVER THE TOP . . .

The roof deck of my building is fully decorated.

It's straight out of a romantic movie, with whimsical decorations and flowers, but instead of this being in the park, I built all of this on the top of my loft.

I googled how to build a canopy with the materials I had on hand, for fuck's sake.

This is one hundred percent too much.

It's also the first time I've spent real time up here, so my only memory is this. With her.

Payton is quiet for a beat. The clear city sky reflects in the blues of her eyes. They remind me of a day at sea, clear and wondrous.

I've made her speechless, and although this isn't the first time ever, it might be the first time she's not simultaneously planning my death.

"This is . . ."

"Over the top," I finish.

"No. Well, yes. But, wow!" She looks awestruck.

"Wow, good?"

This is more self-conscious than I've ever been, and I don't like it. But the novelty of it grows on me, probably because it's with Payton.

Who the fuck am I?

What has this woman done with me?

"Wow, amazing! I can't believe you did this." Her voice sounds far away. "No one has ever done anything like this for me before."

I let her take in everything in silence, not bothering her as she oohs and aahs over the details. After a moment, her small hand reaches out toward the picnic basket, and she traces the wicker with her fingertips.

"Why?" she finally asks.

"Why, what?"

"Why did you do this for me?" She meets my eyes. "Guilt?"

"No." I shake my head, and she cocks her head as she assesses my face.

She's scrutinizing me, trying to figure me out. I have no doubt she will. Even if I haven't myself. Payton gets me. At first, I hated it. But now? I don't know. I just know I don't want to go back.

"It wasn't really because of guilt," I allow.

"Not really?" She lifts a brow. "That's not a denial."

Her nose scrunches, and I know she's thinking about what to say. Whether she should be upset or not.

This isn't going as planned.

Before she can speak, I move closer.

I'm on eye level with her from where I am perched on the floor.

"This has nothing to do with guilt," I respond, firmer so she won't get the wrong idea this time.

"Then why?"

"Because . . ." I run a palm down my face and groan. "Goddammit, Payton. Because I wanted to."

"Why?" she presses, unrelenting. It's one of the things I like about her. Just not right now. At my expense.

"Because I want to see you fucking smile," I blurt out.

"Why?"

Dammit, what's with this girl?

Then it dawns on me that she's goading me. Pressing me to answer. To speak my truth.

That she already knows it.

She just wants to hear it.

Payton Hart wants me to cut myself open and bleed my emotions all over the floor.

And fuck it, I will.

"Because I fucking like you," I say. Simple as that. "That's why. And I want to make you happy."

"But why?" she challenges, and I shut her up.

I pull her toward me, wrap my arms around her back, and fuse her lips to mine.

Moving my hand, I cup her face as I kiss her. The kiss starts off soft at first with me testing the waters, seeing how she responds. When she lets out a soft sigh and arches her back, I deepen it.

Pressing my lips more firmly to hers, I kiss her faster.

I slide my tongue in her mouth.

Minutes pass, or maybe just seconds, but I'm lost in this woman.

I want more.

I will always want more where she's concerned.

Then she's pulling away and looking at me with confused eyes that are hazy with lust.

"Um . . ." She shakes her head as if to clear it. "What was that?"

"A kiss."

I'm unapologetic.

This time, I don't regret even a second of it.

Payton's cheeks are colored red, but it's the way she observes me through hooded eyes and thick lashes that makes me wish I had done that sooner. Fuck, she stares at me like I'm everything.

"I should have done it weeks ago," I admit.

"Oh"—She blinks back at me, stunned—"Okay."

I pull back and start going through the basket. "Now, let's eat."

"I can always eat."

"Me, too. What do you want first?" I ask her.

"Sandwich?" She scrunches her nose.

"Not cheese?"

She grins, rolling her eyes at me. "If you want to start with cheese, why bother asking me?"

"Not sure." I tilt my head. "Maybe to fuck with you. Creature of habit. I have a compulsive need to do the opposite of what you say."

I smile as I reach for a small sandwich and hand it to her. Then I grab one for myself.

She takes a bite and moans. "This is amazing."

"I made it all by myself."

"You did?"

"Hell no. I don't even know where my kitchen is." I laugh.

"Har, har. You do, too; we had ice cream."

"Chef made them," I admit, picking one up and staring at the perfectly cut square. "Scowled the whole way through."

"I'm not surprised." She shakes her head, throwing it back in laughter. "This is amazing regardless."

"Good, enjoy. There are plenty where that came from," I tell her as I pick up another bite-sized sandwich.

"I'm not used to this," she says right after she swallows. "I don't know how to handle this side of you."

I lift my eyebrow, telling her to continue. My mouth is full, so I can't speak. Wouldn't know what to say even if I could.

"You being so nice to me," she says. "You taking care of me. You kissing me." She bows her head, and guilt tries to invade the picnic.

I won't let it.

I know she hates it. She's said so herself a few times already. And we agreed to put the past behind us and start fresh . . . But damn, if that guilt doesn't sucker punch me.

"Listen, I was a real asshole."

"I'm not going to argue with that."

I set my sandwich down and give her the full force of my attention so she knows I'm serious. "It took me a long time to get my head out of my ass, but this isn't something that just happened overnight. I knew I was acting poorly. I knew you didn't deserve my malice for a long time."

I shake my head, wishing I'd come to the realization sooner, so she wouldn't be here like this. Injured.

"That's what I was coming to talk to you about that day," I add.

"When did you realize?" she asks, her voice dipping lower than normal.

"When you kept showing up."

She looks confused.

"Every time you showed up at the center," I explain. "When you spoke with Henry. When you helped my mom in her garden. When you took care of the people who mean so much to me. It was everything."

I was so stubborn, I didn't want to admit it.

I couldn't see past my own pain, my own ego, myself.

I continue, "That's when it started to happen, but I refused to see past my own anger. There were little things along the way, but then I finally realized I wasn't angry with you. I was angry with myself."

Her hand settles on mine, comforting me.

I squeeze and press forward. "I was angry I had put so much hope in the idea that my father would change and do better. I wanted to believe that even after what he did to Ivy. Even after all of that, I still held hope things would change. That he would change." I shake my head. "It doesn't matter."

Her hand picks up mine, interlocking our fingers. "Did you think if you hurt me, you'd be hurting him?"

I nod. "But the truth is, you have nothing to do with that. Nothing to do with any of it. My father purposely did this. He purposely left the money to you, knowing I would be in charge because he wanted to torture me. He had no shame."

"Are you sure?"

"Yes—"

She gives a dry, bitter laugh. "It's funny how he was such a different person for you than he was for me."

"It's sick, actually." I stare at the ground, wondering if there's an afterlife and if Dad's there right now. "Sometimes I talk to him."

"What do you mean?"

"I stare at the ground, and I talk to him. I taunt him. Because I'm alive, and he isn't. Because he isn't here to fight back."

She plays with my fingers, taking her time to explore each one with her fingertips. "Does it help?"

"No." I close my eyes, enjoying her touch. "It never does." I repeat my words, knowing it's better this way, knowing he's evil and hating that part of me is still that same kid holding on to a piece of his father in hopes he'll change. "Because I'm alive, and he isn't. Because he isn't here to fight back."

Payton's hands still, and she moves them to my face, brushing over my eyelids so gently, I barely feel them. "Did you ever read the letter he gave you . . . ?"

"No."

"I understand."

And I know she does.

Because Payton Hart sees me.

All of me.

CHAPTER FORTY-ONE

Payton

WE REMAIN IN A STATE OF LIMBO.
The days pass and turn into weeks. He never kisses me again.

I find that I dream about it.

Think about it.

Fantasize about it.

It's all that occupies my brain.

Sure, I'm plenty busy.

Between the appointments with the pricy in-house physical therapist he hired, Trent helps me do exercises to strengthen my ribs and foot. I'm always exhausted. Pushing my body to recover.

My concussion is gone, which is good, and I'm healing nicely.

I'll probably even be able to stop wrapping my ankle soon. I'm lucky it isn't a break, just a sprain.

The truth is, I don't need to work with a physical therapist, but Trent wants to make sure I'm strong, and I humor him.

Although he's made no attempt to be physically intimate with me again, he spends a lot of time with me. Whether we're eating, reading, or watching TV together, he's by my side often. He works in his home office instead of driving to his company's building. If I need him, I know he'll be at my side within seconds.

Reading to me is one of those things that he started to do after the concussion, but I've grown so accustomed to it now. Every night, as I settle into bed, he sits by my side, and I curl in close to his body, and he reads in that gravelly, deep voice of his.

It's sheer perfection.

The only thing that would be more perfect is if, after this chapter is done, he made a move. But I think he's trying to prove his self-restraint first—I'm just not sure if he's trying to prove it to me or himself.

Tonight, I wait for him to finish before I pounce, ripping the book from his hands and throwing it across the bed.

I am tired of waiting.

The kiss is slow at first.

His lips on mine, my mouth parting his.

Then we start to move together. It reminds me of a very slow dance. One you spend months preparing for, and as you finally start to move, your heart beats faster, and you feel like your eyes are closed, and you are left spinning.

It's exhilarating.

Our tongues circle.

The kiss deepens and becomes desperate.

Months of pent-up emotions pour into it.

I allow myself to become lost in the kiss. I allow it to wash over the past. To erase the pain and hurt I felt at the hands of this man. At the hands of everyone else, too.

I get swept away in the moment.

I think only of the good things.

The things about Trent that make him a good man. The tenderness in his eyes right now. Every piece of him I see that others don't.

I bask in that feeling, in that warmth.

He tightens his embrace around me, pulling me closer to him, wrapping his arms tighter around me.

There is no separation between our bodies now.

A moan escapes my lips.

"Are you okay?" he asks against my mouth.

"Yes," I mutter back.

"Does anything hurt?"

"No."

He loosens his grasp as if he is going to let go, and I tighten mine.

"Don't you dare stop kissing me," I basically growl.

I'm desperate for this man.

"Are you—"

"Shut up and kiss me."

He chuckles against my lips, and then his hands move below my ass, holding me tight.

Finally, after a few minutes, he pulls back and looks down at me with hungry eyes.

They devour me.

They tell me all the things he wishes to do to me.

I want all of them, mine beg back.

When he doesn't do anything, I speak, "Please don't end this."

"I'm not sure," he mutters to himself.

"But I am." I grip onto his shoulders tight like I'm afraid he'll part from me. "I'm sure. I want you. Don't deny me this. I need this."

His head inclines into a nod.

But he doesn't say anything, so I'm not exactly sure what he's doing when he steps back.

Is he leaving?

Staying?

He must see my confusion because he smirks at me.

That smirk drives me insane.

Then his hand lifts the hem of my shirt until I'm left in nothing but a skimpy lace thong.

His sexy smile deepens as he removes it, too.

"Now that you got me naked . . ." I trail off with a lifted brow, gesturing to him.

He begins to undress, too.

Both of us are fully naked. Admiring each other.

I will never get enough of this man.

The look he gives me makes me feel like I'm on fire. A raging inferno.

Ready to combust.

He drops to his knees in front of me.

My heart flutters with excitement.

My limbs begin to shake as I wait for him to touch me.

It feels like this moment has been in the making for so long in my mind, and I'm busting at the seams to feel him.

He presses a kiss to my knee, and then he starts to trail his mouth up my thigh.

Finally, after what feels like the longest, sweetest torture, he answers my prayers and places a kiss where I need him the most.

His tongue licks.

It's slow. Too slow.

I wiggle my hips.

He laughs, and I want to smack him, but then he presses a finger inside me, and all thoughts of beating him up are long gone.

I'm mindless now.

A quivering mess.

Breathless.

Needy.

He quickens his pace, and I'm falling over the edge. An ecstasy-filled moan escapes my lips.

I'm fully sated, but I still crave more. He's an addiction. I whisper his name as I come down from the high. It's a plea for more.

Then he's moving, and I watch through hooded lids as he rips a condom open and slides it over his length.

I shimmy back up the bed and wait for him.

He moves like a predator, stalking, ready to devour me whole, crawling up my body. When he reaches my face, he frames it with his hands. His touch is gentle. Caring. I swallow hard at the movement, breath hitching when his thumb brushes my neck.

He returns it to my cheeks, rubbing just before the corner of my lips.

Our gaze meets.

"Are you sure?" he asks.

"Yes, please."

I'm basically panting.

I know it sounds desperate, but I'm not embarrassed because he is too. I can feel his hardness pressing against my thigh. It throbs.

Trent laughs at my tone, but then he is kissing me, and I part my legs wider in invitation, allowing him access.

"Trent," I groan as he makes me wait. "Fuck me already."

He groans.

When he does nothing but smile against my lips, I scold, "Now."

This is just like us, to fight even when in bed.

Slowly, he guides himself deep inside me. He doesn't move for a few seconds, probably allowing me to adjust to his size, but when I'm about to open my mouth and tell him to move, he does.

He pulls out.

Thrusts in.

Pulls out.

Thrusts in.

He continues this slow and steady pace.

In, out.

The feeling is too much, yet I hope it never ends.

It's amazing. Like him.

With each press of his body within mine, I moan and wiggle against him to go faster.

Harder.

His movements pick up. He answers my pleas until both our breaths accelerate as we chase our release together.

Together, with a gasp, we find it.

"Don't move," he orders once we both come down from our euphoric high.

"As if I could?" I laugh, and he walks away.

A few seconds later, he returns with a soft towel and cleans me off.

He's so tender.

I hope this never ends.

CHAPTER FORTY-TWO

Trent

"Morning, Sleeping Beauty," I mutter against her hair.

I know she's up because her breathing has changed. It's no longer rhythmic and peaceful. No, the change indicates—in true Payton fashion—she's overanalyzing this. It stops and holds before picking up again.

She yawns, stretching her arms. "I thought I was Cinderella."

"If I'm not mistaken, we decided you were the mouse," I say in jest, and she turns her body around and swats at my chest.

I stop her hand, bring it up to my mouth, and place a long, soft kiss on her palm.

"Not so fast, Prince Charming." She pulls her hand out of mine, grinning. "None of that . . ."

"None of what?" I say innocently, knowing exactly what she is talking about.

"None of that—" She gestures to the raging hard-on I have under the blanket. "Not before I brush my teeth."

I roll my eyes at her, but I allow her to pull away and get off the bed. I give her a few minutes' head start before I'm jumping out of bed and heading straight toward the bathroom to be with her.

I find her at the sink with my T-shirt covering her body. I like how she looks in my clothes, just as much as the first time I had her in my tee. I wait for her to turn the water off, stepping up beside her. When she's done brushing her teeth, I'm leaning down and placing my mouth on hers.

Her breath now tastes like mint as I devour her in a kiss. She moans into it, her hands looping around my neck.

Without separating, I pick her up and walk her back toward the bedroom.

As much as I want to fuck her in this bathroom, I'm not sure she can stand that long, but then another idea hits me.

I move toward the counter.

As soon as I place her down on top, I lift my shirt up over her head. I'm thankful she never put underwear back on because this makes it so much easier.

I, however, still have pants on.

Something I need to remedy right now.

My hands work to remove them.

Our kiss remains unbroken as I lower them.

Her legs are wrapped around my waist, and I rummage around the counter to see if I can find the box of condoms.

Still kissing her, still looking, I mutter a curse against her lips. She moves her face away from me.

"I'm on the pill and clear."

"Thank fuck," I mutter, grabbing each side of her face. "I'm good, too."

The next thing I do is align myself with her core.

With one quick thrust, I'm inside.

She gasps into my mouth at the sudden movement.

Then groans as I slowly pull back out.

This is my favorite thing to do.

Tease her.

Pushing myself in.

Slowly retracting.

It's torture.

Not only for her but for me, too.

The way she wiggles into me makes me want to draw this out. I stop my movements on the brink of re-entry and hold.

She's lifting her hips, wordlessly begging me to bury myself deep inside her again.

I thrust deeply, impaling myself inside her, then pull out. My movements speed up.

In. Out.

In. Out.

Her breathing becomes frantic as I thrust myself inside her over and over again.

I'm so close.

She's close, too.

I pick up the pace, lower my hand to where our bodies meet, and press my thumb as I need her to reach the other side of this frenzy.

My hips rock up. I thrust up one more time, hard and fast. I circle my thumb, bringing her closer and closer. Then she buries her head in my neck, and she tightens around me as she moans my name.

My speed increases until I'm joining her in sweet release.

CHAPTER FORTY-THREE

Trent

WE HAVE BEEN LIVING IN A HAPPY BUBBLE FOR THE LAST three weeks.

Payton's foot is healed, as is her rib.

She was damn lucky.

I'm even luckier.

Having her here has been the best time of my life.

I have to put a damper on it, though. I need to ask her a question I don't want to ask.

She once made a comment about all the things that happened to her, and I need to know exactly what they were because today, we take Paul.

Payton is watching me. What she sees makes her brows furrow.

"What's got you so stressed?" she asks.

I continue to stare at her, hating to disrupt the peace we have cocooned ourselves in. "I have something to ask you."

"Okay." Her voice is low, belying her concern about what I'm going to ask.

Maybe, like me, she doesn't want the real world brought into my room.

"You mentioned I was stalking you . . ."

Her eyes go wide at my words.

I gauge her reaction before continuing, "Why did you say that?"

"I don't want to talk about before. We're good now." She goes to move away from me, but I place my hand over her stomach.

"Stop, Payton." I take her hand, hoping it gives her the strength she needs. "I need to know. This is important."

She frowns, then huffs. "My stuff."

I shake my head. "Not following."

"In my house. Before you took everything . . ." Her hands tremble in mine. I squeeze them, encouraging her to continue, and she does. "I thought someone was in the house. Going through my stuff."

My teeth clench. The idea of anyone harming or stalking her puts me on edge. I'm not dumb. I know I have a role in her hiding it from me. She probably thought it was me and didn't want to show her fear.

You're a fucking asshole, Trent.

I school my features. I need to know everything, and if I lose it, on myself and the stalker, she won't tell me any more.

"Go on, please," I say softly.

"My computer was opened. I know I left it closed. It was on purpose. I didn't want to drain the battery, it was dying, and I couldn't find my charger. I went to search for it in my car, but when I came back fifteen minutes later, I saw someone I knew from class and got to talking." Her free hand palms her face before dropping. "When I finally walked back into the house, the computer was open. A decoration was misplaced. My computer bag was open, too, but my wallet wasn't missing, so I thought I was being overdramatic."

"Was anything used?"

"No, that was the weird part."

"What else?"

"I always felt eyes on me." She clears her throat. "Then there was the time I found the metal tracker you left in my bag."

I pull my hand from hers, rearing back a bit.

What. The. Hell.

"What?" She shrugs, looking away.

I reach my hand out, touch her jaw, and make her look at me. "Payton, I never left a tracker in your bag."

"Then how . . . ?"

Her mouth drops open, and her eyes go wide.

"Did anyone ever have access to your place?" I ask, more urgent this time.

She's been in danger this whole time.

Her nose scrunches. "No."

"Did anyone ever bump into you, maybe—"

She gasps, snapping her fingers. "Yes. It was that time I fell by your apartment. That man."

It wasn't an accident.

Payton starts to chew her lip, nervously. She's come to the same conclusion. He bumped into her to drop the tracker.

"Did you see the man's face?" I stare into her eyes, studying her. "Would you recognize him if you saw him again?"

She shakes her head, frowning. "No."

I grab her hands and bring them up to my lips. "I have to go, but I promise I'll be back soon. I have to go take care of something."

A man I must kill.

"Can I come with you?"

"No." I stand and press a kiss to the crown of her head. "I can't have anything happen to you, princess."

It doesn't take long to pull up the address of Lorenzo's warehouse.

It's located on the dock.

Cliché as fuck.

But since he now runs the mafia, I'm not sure what else I should have expected.

As I pull up, it doesn't look like anyone is inside. It appears to be abandoned.

But I imagine this is exactly the idea Lorenzo is going for, and since I know Lorenzo, I also know there are snipers on the roof. He doesn't fuck around. Not when it comes to the safety of him and his men.

I'm not involved in this part of the business.

The guys gave me a way out. They texted, saying they could do this without me. That it's nothing they haven't done before.

In the past, I probably would have agreed to that offer. But after what happened to Ivy and now Payton, hell yeah, I'm all in.

I make fantastic money, and this violence comes with the territory. It's why I pay a shit ton for my security system and the security team Jax recommended. But despite all of that, I'm not okay with any of the women in my life involved with this shit.

I trust Cyrus to take care of Ivy and even my mother.

But Payton? She's mine to care for.

And I failed.

It won't happen again.

Ever.

Throwing my car in park, I step outside. It's cold and dark out. The perfect setting for what we're doing. I stroll up to the building. The door is shut, but I know before I turn the handle that it'll unlock for me.

Someone is always watching the cameras hidden around the property. Lorenzo is too careful not to take every precaution. Dozens of his men guard the building in addition to the technological security measures, probably put in place by Jax.

So, I'm not too worried about our safety as I swing the door open and walk inside. It slams shut behind me, and I find it exactly how I thought it would be.

Unlocked and heavy as shit.

I can only imagine this warehouse stores Tobias's drugs, and now it holds one more thing.

Our enemy.

I'm taken aback by what I see when I walk farther into the warehouse. But then I straighten my back and let the bile settle.

It seems the men were already having a bit of fun before I arrived.

Paul is naked, other than welts and bruises.

His arms are locked behind his back and tied behind the chair. He took a beating before I came. Blood is caked all over his body, some fresh and some dried. It looks like a combination of fists and knives. Then cuts meant to extend his torture as long as possible.

Cliché again, but I guess this is what happens in the underworld.

I would have settled for blackmail.

Nudity?

Not my cup of tea, unless it's Payton, and we're both about to reach an orgasm or ten . . .

But I'm sure it's needed here.

Lorenzo doesn't do anything without a reason.

Entertainment is a reason.

He's a sick bastard like that.

But this time, there's a reason for his cruelty.

I think they're searching for a tracking device on Paul's body because the cuts are strategically placed and only deep enough to find the type of devices he's known for using—close to the surface. A small metal rod implant, as Jax mentioned in the meeting leading up to today.

Paul must hear me because as I stride closer, out of the shadows, my footsteps echoing around us, he lifts his head.

Can he even see me?

His eyes are swollen and basically glued together with blood.

I walk over to where Lorenzo is standing.

"What did you find out?"

"Nothing yet, but you're here just in time." He flashes a sinister grin. "The fun is about to start."

Paul's trying to appear strong, but he's not fooling anyone.

Not with the way his hands shake beneath the rope that ties him to the chair.

He's fucked, and he knows it.

He's a dead man.

No matter what he says, Lorenzo will kill him.

How painful will it be? Well, that's yet to be decided. I'm sure if he cooperates, maybe (and that's a big maybe) Lorenzo will take mercy on him and give him a quick and painless death.

Doubt it.

I nod to Lorenzo to begin, and then I move to get closer.

When I'm standing directly in front of him, I look down at his mangled, bloody body. "You can make this easy or hard. Your choice."

"Fuck you, pretty boy," he responds.

He spits out blood, barely missing my shoe.

"Very well. Hard it is." I nod again, and this time, Lorenzo steps beside me with a cleaver.

"For every question you don't answer, you lose a finger," he says casually as if he's talking about what he plans on eating later.

Paul spits toward us again. He's so weak right now, he misses for a second time. The blood and saliva hit the floor.

"Did you try to kill Payton?" I ask. Hard. Tense. Waiting for his answer.

When he doesn't give one, the cleaver is lifted.

The instinctual urge to turn away and let Lorenzo handle this grips me, but I don't. In the corner of the room, Matteo, Tobias, and Cyrus stand. They are here for support, but this is my girl.

My plan.

My revenge.

I need to go all the way.

With a quick look to me for confirmation, Lorenzo steps up. He's ready. The cleaver raises right over Paul's hand.

"You may want to hold the finger out," Lorenzo drawls. "I can't promise I won't chop off more otherwise."

Within a second, a bloodcurdling scream rings through the air. Blood splatters everywhere. I look down.

Paul chose the middle finger.

"Did you hire someone to stalk Payton?" I ask.

Again, he doesn't answer.

"Guess he loses another one," Lorenzo says, and my friends laugh. It is loud and raucous. Borderline obnoxious.

The sound echoes across the warehouse. It sounds like there are more than us here. Like a viewing room to Paul's pain.

"Tell us what we want to know," I press.

"Maybe you should ask better questions," he spits back.

"Or maybe we should try better forms of torture." Lorenzo walks over to the pliers on the table, and I know he's about to rip Paul's fingernails out one by one.

Then after, he'll probably cut his fingers off.

Fuck.

I should never get on Lorenzo's bad side.

I widen my stance, crossing my arms. "Just tell us what we want to know."

"I didn't try to kill your bitch," Paul snaps with a dry laugh. "That would have been too easy."

"What the fuck does that mean?" I kick his chair, stepping on the bottom leg to straighten it just before he starts to fall.

He shakes his head. "I know all about your girl, but I wasn't the one to run her stupid ass over."

I walk over to the table and reach for the gun. I'm sick of this shit.

"Talk." I check the chamber and cartridge for bullets, finding them exactly where I need them. "Tell me what you know about Payton's accident."

"Running her over isn't my style. What I had planned for your whore after what you did was way worse."

I'm not much for violence, but this asshole . . . He deserves the worst hell can deliver. I can't help it as I reach out and smack the fucker in the face with the butt of the gun. His head rears back from the impact.

"Yeah, big guy, what plan is that—"

"I would have used the goods, hard, before selling her sorry ass to the highest bidder." He grins despite the blood staining his teeth.

I act, moving back toward where he's tethered and punch him. My fist connects with his face. A loud crunch is followed by a rush of blood as I break his nose.

Turning to Lorenzo, I look at him for what he thinks. I might not know Paul, but it doesn't add up. He's quick to tell us what he wanted to do, proud even, so why won't he admit to running her over?

It doesn't make sense.

It isn't him.

Yeah, he still needs to die for even thinking about hurting Payton. But maybe he's not the person we're looking for.

I nod at Lorenzo.

He knows what he has to do.

Without another word to Paul, I walk out of the warehouse and toward my car.

I don't need to see him die.

He was planning on torturing Payton.

I'll sleep just fine tonight, knowing I helped rid the world of that man.

Knowing I helped keep my girl safe.

CHAPTER FORTY-FOUR

Payton

IF I TELL TRENT I'M BETTER, WILL HE KICK ME OUT OF HIS BED? My ankle doesn't hurt anymore, and to be honest, I'm almost fully recovered. At this point, I'm just milking it.

Am I just a passing fancy?

An itch he needs to scratch?

Is this part of his guilt?

No.

I stave off the insecurities that have no place inside me. This is more than that. I can feel it.

I get dressed and make my way into the kitchen.

No one is here right now, which I'm cool with.

Trent sent everyone but security away. Said he wanted to be alone with me. And well, I'm famished from our alone time.

Opening the fridge, I grab an apple and sit down on one of the high stools at the kitchen island.

As I eat, I hear the sound of his shoes before I see Trent.

He looks a little rough around the edges. His hair is a mess. It's the circles under his eyes that have me worried. He looks like he hasn't slept in days, which is weird because we sleep in the same bed.

Except for last night.

He was gone when I went to bed and gone when I woke up.

As he gets closer, I also notice something else . . . Red splotches of blood darken his right hand and sleeve. Whatever he did, I have a feeling it wasn't good. I also have a feeling it had to do with me.

"You have . . ." I trail off, nodding to his sleeve.

For some reason, I can't find it in me to say what he has on him, and he must realize it because he looks down, and his face grows sullen.

Lines form along his brows.

"I'm going to shower."

I don't object.

I let him walk away, but for some reason, I feel like he needs me, so I get down from the chair and make my way to his bedroom.

I find him in the bathroom staring at his hands.

He's in a trance.

"I've never taken a life before . . ."

Shuddering inwardly at the revelation, I don't let him see my reaction. Taking a life must be devastating, but this isn't about me. I heard from Mr. Baker that Trent deals with bad men. I know this. I have no doubt, whoever it was, he deserved it.

But I'm not the one who needs to hear this.

These are his demons, and I need to comfort him.

I place my hand on his arm. "I'm sorry."

And I am.

This is one hundred percent about what happened to me.

"Maybe I wasn't the one who pulled the trigger, but I'm the reason he's dead." His hand reaches up to squeeze mine where it's placed on his arm.

Dried blood transfers to my skin.

"Did he deserve it?" I whisper, staring at the dark red.

"Yes."

"Then you have nothing to regret."

I step closer to him, taking his bloody hands in mine.

Most of it is dried.

But still, it's there.

And even after they wash away, the stains of blood will linger.

Maybe not enough to see, but the traumas of our past never really go away.

It's okay, though.

I see that now.

Pain makes you stronger.

"Let me help you," I whisper, standing on my tiptoes to press a soft kiss to his cheek.

I pull him with me, and then I turn on the water to the shower.

Together, clothes on, we stand beneath the hot streams.

"You did what you had to do," I reassure him.

"How did I become this man?" he mutters to himself, steeped in regret.

"You are a good man."

"I cheat people out of money for a living."

I know him well enough to know his "victims" aren't good people. That they did something to fall onto his radar. Something bad.

Vigilante justice is still justice.

Sometimes, the underworld has its own rules. Its own jury. Its own judges.

Its own sentence.

"You do what you have to do to survive." I hold his hand under the water, letting the crimson wash away and swirl down the drain until it disappears out of sight. "This wasn't of your making. You did this to protect the people you love. Not just your family, but all the people in the senior living home. You're a good man, Trent Aldridge."

"You barely know me."

"I see you."

I think he's going to say more, to fight me on this. To tell me I don't.

But instead, his mouth latches on to mine.

Then his tongue sweeps in.

All words are lost.

All feelings swept away.

All we have is now.

I kiss him back.

I tell him with my mouth all the things I know he will never let me say.

Without breaking away, I feel his hands on me. He rids me of my soaking wet pajama pants. I do the same, helping him out of his ruined clothes. The air is foggy with the steam and our lust mingling together.

Then he lifts me.

I feel him hard against my skin.

We continue to kiss as he aligns himself with my core. Our mouths never separate as he thrusts inside, and I gasp at the sensation.

It's everything we both need.

It feels like he fuses himself with me.

Like we're one.

Our bodies say everything.

Confess everything.

They say the words we're not ready to say.

He works himself in and out.

Pulling and pushing inside me.

It's too much.

The emotions fill me, bringing tears to my eyes.

They are masked by the water streaming down from above, and I cry out in climax with his name, which he quickly follows with mine, breathlessly, against my lips.

We stay entwined for a few more seconds before he places me back down on the steady ground.

It doesn't feel the same, though.

It feels like everything has changed.

CHAPTER FORTY-FIVE

Payton

TIME HAS FLOWN BY.

Weeks of it.

We have fallen into a routine.

I'm back at school.

He's back at work.

The days jet past us, and we are no closer to understanding the accident. Trent told me about Paul. That he planned to hurt me but didn't get the chance. That he wasn't the hit-and-run driver.

I'm starting to think maybe it was just an accident.

Not a crazy plot.

Just a hit-and-run.

Some maniac who decided to drive recklessly, right at me.

That's what the cops think it is.

A drunk driver who almost killed me.

Trent seems to agree with them.

The one good thing that came out of all this is Trent. Now that I'm better and healed, I should probably leave, but I don't want to, and he hasn't asked—yet.

I'm not ready to go.

I'm torn whether or not I should even speak to him about it.

He walks in. I'm in his office, sitting behind his desk, working on an assignment. Not something he gave me. He told me to stop those after the accident.

The ass.

"Almost done?" he asks, peering over my shoulder at the bar graphs I've compiled into a PowerPoint.

"No. But I'll finish it up later." I save the file and exit, turning to face him. "What's going on?"

Don't let your past drive your insecurities. Trent is not Erin. He won't turn on you. He is not your parents. He'll be there when you wake tomorrow.

Still, my heart quickens as I wait for him to speak.

"Let's go out to dinner," he says.

"Okay."

I stand from the chair to leave the room. He stops me with both his hands, grabs me on either side, and places a kiss on my lips. I barely kiss him back, my mind still moving at a million miles a minute.

"What's wrong?" he asks, breaking through my thoughts.

"Nothing."

"It doesn't seem like that." His right eyebrow arches.

"I'm fine."

"Now I know you're not." He takes his hand and places it under my jaw, tilting it up, forcing me to look into his eyes. "Talk to me."

"I was just thinking about the accident."

"You're safe, Payton."

"Am I?"

"Yes. You are." His voice never wavers. He believes it, and I want to believe it too.

"Then if I'm safe. . . it's time to call off the dogs."

"What do you mean?" he asks.

"Security. If I'm safe, I don't need them to trail me." I lift my brow. Challenging him. If he says no, it means I'm not safe.

"Fine." He throws his hands up in defeat and I smile, throwing my arms around his neck and kiss him. Now, without the tail, maybe I'll start to feel normal again.

"I do have a lot of work to do later," I say, remembering that I'm still behind after my accident.

"Then let's eat at home." It comes out of his mouth casually. Like this is normal. Referring to his loft as our home.

CHAPTER FORTY-SIX

Payton

THE FIRST THING I NOTICE AS MY EYES OPEN IS THAT THE bed feels empty, but as they adjust to the light gleaming into the room, I confirm my suspicion.

Trent is not here.

I've gotten used to him being around, so it feels odd when he's gone.

I miss Trent.

For the past few weeks, I knew I was falling for him, but right now, as I think of the way he makes me smile and the comfort I feel when he's in the room, I realize this is more than that.

I *have* fallen for him already.

Completely.

I need my best friend to talk to.

I'll go to Heather's. I haven't spoken to her in ages. A few texts here and there, but we haven't been alone since before my accident. Although she has come to visit, eyes nearly popping out of her sockets when she first caught sight of this place and Trent strolling shirtless out of his gym, someone is always around, so I never feel like we can talk openly.

Wistfully removing myself from the comfort of Trent's bed, I cross to the bathroom.

I need to brush my teeth.

Shower, too.

My reflection stares back at me in the mirror. I look like a mess.

A fully satisfied mess.

Even I can see the difference in my eyes.

They no longer look tired.

No, now they beam with emotions I haven't felt in forever.

A smile spreads across my face as I think of what I want to do today . . . See Heather.

Me: I'm coming over!

Heather: Maybe I'm busy.

Me: Never too busy for me.

Heather: No truer words have ever been spoken. See you soon.

I finish my morning business and head into the closet to get dressed. All my clothes are still here, and I rustle around until I'm pulling on a chambray button-down, leggings, and a pair of boots. It's cold out, so I grab a coat, too.

Once I'm dressed, I go in search of Trent to tell him I'm leaving, but no matter where I look, I come up empty-handed.

With a shrug, I sit on the couch and pull out my phone to call him, but as I'm about to, my phone rings.

Erin.

I have no desire to speak with her, but if I send her to voicemail, she will just keep calling or show up here on Trent's doorstep, demanding I speak to her. She's persistent when she wants something, and since I never came through with the money, I imagine by now, she's desperate.

Answering and hanging up as fast as possible is the move.

"Hello," I say.

And through the line, I can hear the sound of my sister crying.

I can't remember the last time I heard her like this.

She's gasping into the phone.

I'm instantly back to when we lived in her car, how she would sob.

The sound makes my stomach hurt.

All the memories from my past are front and center in my mind.

She's still my sister.

Of course, I care. No matter how horribly she treats me, she will always be the girl who raised me when no one else would.

"Erin? Are you okay?"

She doesn't answer, but I can hear her hyperventilating.

"I need you—"

The phone goes dead.

I'm out of the house, on the subway, then heading to the train in no time.

Once seated, I pull out my phone to fire off a text to Trent, telling him I'm going to Heather's.

He cares about me.

I know it in the bottom of my soul.

I'm lost in my thoughts as the train rolls up to the station. I realize that I've spent the last thirty minutes obsessing over what happened to my sister to even think of what Trent will do when he finds out I'm gone without his security team.

I knock on Erin's door as I dig through my bag, looking for my phone. Once in my hand, I hit the button to call him, and as the other line rings, I think about what I'm going to say if he doesn't answer.

Should I just blurt it out?

Trent, I'm in love with you.

Too much?

But I realize that it's the truth.

I love Trent Aldridge.

I have fallen in love with the man who tried to ruin me but instead, showed me so much more.

The voicemail picks up, and as I hear his familiar voice, a

smile spreads across my face. I open my mouth to say every-thing I need to say. I'm too distracted with my own thoughts to hear the steps.

I'm too distracted to hear anything.

All I know is one minute I'm about to speak . . .

And the next, the world goes black.

CHAPTER FORTY-SEVEN

Trent

WHEN I ARRIVE BACK HOME, THE HOUSE IS QUIET. I'm not sure where Payton is.

Maybe she's still working? Earlier today, she said she was going to Heather's.

She could still be there.

I pick up my cell and see I missed a call from her. I try her back, but the phone goes to voicemail, so I call Brandon.

"Where's Payton?"

"She went to her friend's."

"Did anyone follow her?"

"No."

I had said they didn't have to anymore. Once I knew it wasn't Paul, I decided to respect her wishes.

Now I wish I didn't.

Walking toward my office, I check all the rooms I pass, but she's not in any of them.

Maybe she's at Cresthill?

I call Margret.

"Hi, Trent," she answers.

"Hey, Margret. Any chance Payton is there today?"

"No, I'm sorry. She doesn't normally volunteer on Fridays."

"Yeah, you're right."

"Everything okay?" she asks.

I can't put my finger on it, but I feel like no, it's not.

"Did you upset the poor girl?" Margret takes Payton's side in an instant, but I don't mind. Payton is lovable like that. She has that effect on people. "Why don't you just tell her how you feel?"

"What are you talking about?"

"You know what I'm talking about."

In the background, I hear my mother's voice say, "Put him on speaker."

Jeez. Now what?

"Trent Aldridge."

"Hi, Mom."

"What did you do to Payton?"

"What? Nothing." I groan over the line.

"Then why does it sound like something is wrong."

"She's just not here. It's nothing."

"Or maybe she left. You were an ass when you first moved her into your house. Anyone with eyes can tell she loves you."

"Mom. I appreciate the dating advice, but that's not why I'm calling. I did nothing but care for her. I'm calling because I wanted to check to see if she was there."

I hang up quickly and try Payton's line once more. But again, she doesn't answer.

Not speaking to her makes me realize how I feel.

There is no right moment to tell someone you love them because every moment is right. Love is something you grasp when it's there. People don't realize it's a blessing. That if it's taken for granted, it might not be there to appreciate later. Seize every moment. Tell people you love them when you feel it. Life is too short for anything else.

Payton has changed me. I see it now.

Opening my desk, I see it.

The letter.

The letter I received months ago and never read. I had thrown it into my drawer, hoping to never see it again.

When I was first handed the envelope, I knew there was no way I would ever read it.

For so long, I have hated my father. There was just no point in reading anything he had to say to me.

But now, after letting Payton in, after getting to know her, something has changed inside me.

I pick up the envelope.

The familiar handwriting stares back at me.

With a deep breath, I pull it open.

I need to know what he said.

Inside is the kind of lined paper a kid uses at school to draft an essay. I imagine my father in the prison library with a pen and paper, looking down at the lines and thinking about what he was going to write.

The ink looks to be thicker over the T . . . As if he placed the pen down and couldn't find the words to continue.

Or maybe it was the strength.

Could that be it?

Was he searching for the strength to contact me?

I shake my head.

There's no use speculating. I have never understood my father. And now, I never will. Instead, I read it.

Trent,

You probably won't open this. I don't blame you. I don't deserve your attention. I don't deserve anything from you.

Another family visitation week passed today. I was alone, watching from the corner of the rec room because I couldn't bring myself to miss it. Just in case you came. In case Ivy did. In case your mom did.

I'm a sick bastard for holding on to hope I haven't earned.

I sat there, just watching. Seeing everything I missed out on and knowing I damn well deserve the misery. I was getting ready to leave after it got to be too much. Had one foot past my table in the corner when a rubber ball rolled forward and hit my shin.

A kid came up to me, hand out. I gave him his toy back. He asked me why I was alone. For the first time, I told the truth.

It's my fault I'm alone.

It's my fault I have no one.

It's my fault I hurt my family.

I am sorry for everything I did to you and your sister. You will never understand the pain I feel knowing I ripped apart my own family.

All I have is time.

Time to think.

Time to regret.

I realize now, I was every bit the monster you said I was. I wish I could go back. I wish I could take the blinders off and realize what I was doing, how warped my view was.

I thought I was in love.

But I was blind.

Blind to the truth.

I have no excuse for what I did to Ivy. Or to you and your mother.

I was a fool.

It's the honest to God, ugly truth.

I'm so sorry.

I hope you will find it in your heart to forgive me one day. I know it's not fair that I'm asking you to forgive me.

But I need to try.

Some things are happening. Things I'm afraid to put in writing. I don't think I'll make it out of here.

Erin isn't who I thought she was. I saw her talking to Brad, my cellmate. I think there is something going on between them. I don't trust either of them.

Something feels off.

I'm going to try to reach you, but if I don't, please protect Payton. She was my second chance. When I met her, she was a scared little girl. She looked at me like I hung the moon from the sky, like I was her savior, and in a way, I was.

They were homeless, dirty, and destitute. I fell in love with being the dad I could never be to you and Ivy. It was too late by then. You both were older, and I had royally fucked up, but with her, I had a second chance.

I need you to put aside your feelings for me and take care of her. I know that's a lot to ask, but I know you are a good man.

You are a better man than I'll ever be.

I used to think your kindness was a weakness I needed to drill out of you.

I was wrong.

I'm sorry.

Love,
Dad

My heart rattles in my chest.

This is his dying confession.

Emotions I'm not used to gnaw at me.

Guilt.

Sadness.

Regret.

I read the letter over and over again.

What did he mean, Erin isn't who he thought she was?

I keep reading it, and every time I do, more questions arise.

My father knew he was going to die.

He left the money to Payton because he didn't trust Erin . . . but he also said to protect Payton, so that means she's in danger.

Then it hits me . . .

The last piece of the puzzle falls into place.

Dad's cellmate.

Brad.

I rack my brain for anyone I know with the name, coming up with only one.

Erin's boyfriend.

Could it be the same person?

Is that why Dad wanted me to take care of Payton? Why didn't he trust Erin?

A sinking feeling weighs heavy in my stomach as the pieces of the puzzle fit together.

It's got to be.

All the threats. The accident.

Is it all connected?

I pick up the phone and call Mr. Baker.

"Mr. Aldridge, how can I help you?" he asks.

"Who gets the money if Payton dies?"

"Her sister, why?"

I hang up. I need to find her and warn her.

Pulling out my phone, I try to call her, yet again, her phone goes straight to voicemail.

Something isn't right.

Before I can think twice, I'm racing down to my garage, guilt and fear running through my veins. I need to find her.

I dial the one person I know who can help me.

When I hear him say hi, I'm already speaking. "I need you to track Payton."

"Trent, jeez, you're a dog with a bone," Jax says. "We already went over this . . . How many times do I have to tell you? I won't trace her phone, dude."

"You don't understand!"

"Calm down." He must sense the urgency, the sheer panic in me because he relents in an instant. "Come to my warehouse, and we can talk."

"I'm already on my way."

"Figures."

I hang up and hop into my car, weaving through traffic at breakneck speed. It takes me ten minutes before I'm throwing my car into park and stalking toward his warehouse.

He throws open the door the moment he sees me on camera.

"Did you find Payton?"

"Kind of," he answers.

"What do you mean, kind of?" I storm past him into the large, cavernous space and turn around to look at him.

He types at one of the many computers, pulling up something that looks like an address and GPS beacon. "I tracked her last call to you. Her phone has been turned off since. Are you going to tell me what the hell is going on?"

"I think it was her sister's boyfriend."

"What did he do?" he asks.

"Everything."

CHAPTER FORTY-EIGHT

Payton

A WAVE OF NAUSEA HITS ME.
I push it down, holding back the vomit. It won't do me any favors.

Where am I?

Everything around me is black. I'm bathed in darkness. My lids feel heavy, and my head throbs.

I blink a few times before colors finally start to stream in. My surroundings hit me like an avalanche. The darkness is hard to adjust to, but when I finally do, I immediately realize where I am.

Erin's basement.

The questions threaten to crack my head open. It throbs everywhere. Someone hit me on the head. I don't know why I'm here, or why it's so dark, or why I can't move. I just know it's bad. That I should've told someone where I was headed before I left.

That I should've told Trent I love him.

I close my eyes, forcing myself to think. To remember what happened.

It's difficult past the splitting headache that comes from all angles, starting from where I was hit in the back of the head.

I went to Erin's because she was crying, sobbing . . .

Someone knocked me out.

Then I ended up here.

In her basement.

The couch is sticky and uncomfortable beneath me. I stare down at my lap. My hands rest on it, bound together by a rope. My feet are in the same state. If I try to move, I'll fall over.

Who did this to me?

The answer comes at once.

That sicko Brad.

There's no one else.

Paul is dead.

Erin has no history of physical violence.

Is she also tied up somewhere nearby?

This has got to be about the money.

Maybe he thought my sister would get it, but now he thinks he can get it from me?

It's the only thing that makes sense.

Around me, music starts to play.

Goose bumps break out on my skin.

It's that song again.

Bile rises in my throat.

The same song that played on my phone.

The same song I couldn't place how I knew.

But now, I know everything is because of him.

Brad is the one who tried to kill me.

I hear a footstep, and I search for who's coming.

That's when I see my sister. Her face is lit up by a single stream of light wafting from the door she left cracked open.

"Erin, thank God!" I jerk against my binds, trying not to fall over. "Get me out of here!"

She cocks her head and stares into my eyes. Her gaze is void of emotion.

"Why would I do that?" she asks.

"Because Brad might be coming back . . . I think Brad's the one who is trying to kill me!"

A laugh rings through the air.

A sinister one.

"You think this is Brad?" She shakes her head as she stares at me, unhinged. "This was never Brad . . . this was all me."

I want to scream.

I want to deny it.

I want to be someone else for once. Someone whose parents aren't dead. Whose sister loves her. Who's brave enough to tell the man she loves her feelings before it's too late.

"What?" I shake my head and begin to rapid-fire questions at her. "What do you mean? Why? Why am I here? What do you want from me?"

My brain swims in too many unknowns.

They come pouring out of me.

"I want you to admit it!" Erin screams. Her hands wave around her. She is losing it. Or maybe she's already lost it, and this is all that's left.

"Admit what? What are you talking about?"

"Admit that it's all your fault!" The anger on her face morphs into sadness. "You took them all away from me."

"Erin, calm down." I lift my tied hands, trying to reason with her. "Took who?"

"Everyone." Erin points at me. "You took everyone and everything from me."

"What are you talking about?"

"First, you took our parents . . ."

I shake my head, confused.

"They were going to pick you up. You called them, sad." Her face turns into a sneer, and she mocks.

My brain tries to remember. I was homesick. The girls were mean. They were teasing me. I called my parents.

"Poor Payton. At a friend's house and oh, so sad. Never happy no matter how many people you bend to your will. It's always about you. Always about Payton. You just had to beg them to pick you up and take you home," she snarls out. "They died going to

374

get you. They died trying to make you happy." Her nostrils flare with fury.

"I'm so sorry, Erin, but I was a kid—"

A hand slaps against my face. The skin on my cheek burning hot.

"Shut up, you little brat! Everything. You took everything from me." She swipes away an angry tear. "I had a life before you. I was going to go to college. I was going to make something of myself, but then I was forced to raise you. I was forced to take you in."

"You didn't have to. You could have—"

"What? Put you in foster care?" She scoffs. "Then I wouldn't have gotten my parents' money . . . Because obviously that was in their damn will."

"What money? Our parents didn't leave us money."

"Of course, they did, you little idiot. But you were a minor. You didn't know anything I had to do for you." She stalks forward. I edge back as far as I can with the binds. "Unfortunately, it wasn't enough. But by then, I was already saddled up with you."

"Again, why didn't you get rid of me?"

"I was going to. But then I saw how men looked at you." She shrugged. "I thought I could use it for my benefit. Until you took *him*, too."

I shiver at her words. "What the hell does that mean?"

"I was going to sell you." She spells it out for me, her tone condescending, betraying how dumb she thinks I am. "Tony was going to help me . . . We would have gotten a pretty penny for you, but you had to mess that up, too."

Tony. Her ex.

Her horribly abusive ex.

The music gets louder, and suddenly, I'm back there.

On the couch.

His warm breath on my cheek.

His hand on my lap.

The music playing on the stereo in the room.

"He was going to hurt me," I whisper, remembering everything now. It slams into me, harder than the car did. "You saved me."

"Saved you?" Erin's dry laughter pierces the air. "I didn't do it to save you. I did it because he was mine, and you couldn't have him."

The memory of that day plays in my mind.

My sister was screaming . . .

They fought.

Then she pushed him.

He fell down the stairs.

An accident.

She was protecting me. It was the thing I clung to in my worst moments—how she'd been there when I needed her most. It was why I never left her. It was why I kept the loyalty even when she treated me like dirt.

I thought she saved me.

That she loved me.

But now?

Now I know the truth.

After that day, we lived in her car. We left before the cops came and moved from city to city . . . until Erin met Ronald.

"It's always been you." She reaches forward and slaps me again. My head flies back. "You have always taken everything from me."

My cheek stings. I push it down, croaking out, "He was going to rape me."

"You seduced him, you whore!" She looks downright unhinged.

This is not my sister.

This is . . . a monster.

"Probably like you seduced my Ronnie," she accuses. "Is that how you got him to give *you* my money? It was all supposed to be easy. I knew about the account. It was supposed to be in my fucking name. Mine." She jabs her thumb against her chest.

"I never asked for the money," I say, knowing she's beyond logic.

"When Ronnie went to jail, I thought he would give me access to the money, but he still wielded it like a sword. Brad was easy to convince. You know that's the funny part?" She laughs. "I saw him when I was visiting Ronald. Tony's old friend Brad. When I found out he was Ronald's cellmate, I knew what I had to do. I got Brad to handle it all . . ."

"Brad killed Ronald," I finish.

"Not by his own hands. He got out before, but he made sure it happened. And what was it all for?"

She shakes her head, and I realize there's something in her hand. I can't see without the light, but fear pulses through my veins.

"I still didn't get what I deserved," she continues, closing the distance between us. "Yet again, you fucking won the prize."

"It was never about winning, Erin. I never seduced him. I was a child! I never seduced anyone!"

"Oh, keep telling yourself that. I'm sure that's exactly why you are spreading your legs for his son. Acting like you're better than me, you worthless bitch."

My head spins.

It feels like I'm free-falling off a cliff.

"You should have died when Brad hit you," she tells me, standing right in front of me now. "It would have been so much easier if you had." She tilts her head, staring down her nose at me. "What do I do with you now? Well, not me. Brad . . ."

She reaches toward me, gently strokes my hair, and makes me a promise.

"I'll make sure it's painful."

CHAPTER FORTY-NINE

Payton

Erin storms out of the room and up the stairs. Adrenaline rushes through me. I force as much of it out of me in a quick breath. I need to clear my head. I can barely think clearly.

What the hell am I going to do?

Erin killed Tony, and now she's going to kill me.

It was always her.

My heart hammers in my chest.

Pulse thumps erratically.

I need to get out of here.

Need to find something to use.

I must break free and fight.

A vision of Trent flashes before me. Of the last conversation we shared in his office. How I never told him I loved him.

I can't die without telling him how I feel.

I need to survive.

For Trent.

For me.

My hands move around, trying to loosen the rope. It's tight, but it's not tight enough that I can't budge my hands a little. I take advantage of the little gap and push harder, even when my skin burns and muscles strain with the effort.

Luckily for me, my hands are tiny because if I keep doing this, I'll probably be able to shimmy it off.

I hope I have enough time before she comes back.

I rub my wrists back and forth, trying to get the right angle. Almost there, but not quite. Footsteps ring through the air as I work to gain some wiggle room to get my hands free.

There's no way I'll get my hands or feet free before she gets down here.

But this time, when my sister steps into the basement, regardless of my tied hands, I intend to charge her.

I would rather die this way than see what Brad has in store for me. He's a monster. They both are.

As Erin walks closer, I wait until she's within range before I jump off the couch and plow my body into hers.

It's one swift hop.

I can't manage more with the way my ankles are bound together.

Erin is taken off guard.

She falls to the floor, yelling when her arm hits the floor at a weird angle. "You fucking bitch!"

She's howling, calling out, cursing me, and fighting back.

I don't care.

She's no longer my sister. She doesn't deserve mercy from me.

I jump on top of her. I still haven't gotten my hands free, but I use the fall to my advantage and hit her on the head, repeatedly, with my tied hands that are now clenched together to form a fist.

I'm kneeling on top of her stomach with all my weight. It's brutal, and her dominant hand is too broken to lift and block my blows. She fights back with her left arm, but this is a fight I refuse to lose.

My knuckles burn. My wrists feel like they are being torn apart, but I keep going. I keep thrashing. I keep hitting.

I go for every inch of her flesh I can make contact with.

I do anything to stop her, to help myself, to escape so I can tell Trent I love him.

Erin wrestles against me.

Muscles flex, bodies collide.

Neither of us is willing to give up.

Her unbroken hand tries to grab at my bicep, but I never stop pounding her with my tied fists.

I only stop when her blood seeps onto my fingers.

It comes from her face, escaping in slow drips.

She's not dead, but I knocked her out.

Now I just need to get out of this house.

Using the knife she dropped when I charged her, I cut the rope around my ankles first, then put it between my legs for leverage and jimmy at the binds around my hands.

When they are loose enough, I break free and rub at my red wrists.

Then I run.

I take the stairs two at a time and am almost out the front door when I hear the click of a gun cocking.

"Not so fast."

I turn.

Brad is here.

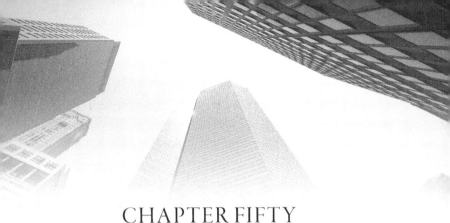

CHAPTER FIFTY

Trent

I WASTE NO TIME GETTING TO ERIN'S HOUSE.
As soon as Jax gave me the address, I was in my car on the phone with the police.

They weren't as eager to help me, seeing as I had no way to tell them whether she was in the house or not.

That's when I called Lorenzo.

I don't know what I'm walking into, so I need to be prepared, and having an army of men is the best way to do that.

The drive feels like it takes forever. But Jax fires off directions through the car speakers as I race to get there.

Throwing the car in park, I hang up and head toward the house.

I'm supposed to wait for my backup.

But if Payton is in there, she might not have enough time.

Then I hear her, and I know I don't have the time to wait.

I bust open the door and charge.

I allow the full weight of my body to collide with Brad's, knocking us both over. The sound of the gun falling to the floor echoes around us. His shock wears off as soon as it clatters to the hardwood.

We start to struggle for it.

I throw the first punch.

He throws the second.

Blood sprays all around us.

Payton moves across the room, her hand stretching out to grab the gun.

Brad's hands loop around her ankle. He pulls her back out of range of the gun.

She hits the floor with a thud, and I want to make sure she is okay, but I don't have enough time.

Brad is back on me, heavy, tall, and built like a tank.

He moves to grab my head, an attempt to kill me, I'm sure.

But I'm too fast.

I head-butt him, knock him off me, and charge for the gun.

I can feel the metal in my hand. Brad shakes his head, bringing himself back to the present, and charges me.

I only have a second to move.

A second to think . . .

And I don't.

I just lift my hand, and the gun goes off.

Brad's body slumps to the floor. Payton is lying on the rug, not moving. I drop beside her in a second, leaning over her and pressing my fingers to her neck, searching desperately for a pulse.

"Please wake up, princess," I beg.

I plead.

I cry.

"I can't do this without you, Payton." I chant her name against her temple. "I don't want to be without you. Please. I love you."

"You do?" she whispers.

"Oh, thank fuck." I lean down and kiss her mouth, pulling her body to rest on mine. "Are you okay?"

"I'm fine, I think."

I move her up and place my hands on her jaw, forcing her to look me dead in the eyes. "You swear you're okay?"

She nods, but she groans as she does.

"Don't move," I order, holding her still so she doesn't hurt herself. "Don't move until I know you're okay."

Her wrists are raw, bruised, and cut in places. Red-hot anger fills me. Death was too quick for Brad.

But Payton, my Payton, is too fixed on me to think about him.

"You love me?" she asks again.

I press my forehead to hers. "I do."

"I love you, too."

"I know."

She chuckles at that, and I'm sure if she were feeling better, she would fire back a witty retort. Instead, she leans into my body and lets out a sigh.

As she does, Lorenzo strolls into the house.

He takes inventory of the dead body beside us, followed by the pool of blood slinking our way. "I see you couldn't wait . . ."

I lift a brow. "Nope."

He takes stock of the rest of the room, fixing on an open door with a bloodstain in the shape of Payton's tiny hand on it. "And now I have to clean up your shit."

"Yep."

"Ass . . ."

"My sister, Erin, is in the basement." Payton looks sheepish. "I think I kind of knocked her out."

Lorenzo looks at Payton and nods at her with appreciation.

"I like her. She can stay," he says to me, and I narrow my eyes before he laughs loudly and moves to find Erin.

"What will he do?" she asks after he disappears down to the basement.

"We're better off not knowing."

She nods.

I'm not sure how this will end yet, but I know Payton will be by my side.

And I know I wouldn't have gotten here without that letter.

I forgive you, Dad.

EPILOGUE

Payton

TWENTY-TWO.

I'm finally twenty-two.

Guess I made it.

The past few months have been a hell of a ride.

Not just because I almost died, twice, but also because in the end, I didn't let Lorenzo just cover up the crime.

That would have been too easy for Erin.

We decided this pathway was for the best. We needed to move through the events as they happened. Not bury them deep and let the lies fester like they had in both our lives before we met.

Similar to what his mom said in the atrium the day I talked to her for the first time, we needed all the secrets we found after Ronnie's death to come out in the daylight. That way, we could now start fresh and clean.

No secrets.

It wasn't easy telling him about how Erin had wanted to sell me, nor was it easy having to relive the day Tony died. I admitted to years of guilt I had for my sister having to take his life. I always thought she had done it to protect me, but now knowing the truth, I have made my own peace with what happened that day. It was never my fault.

It was always Erin.

And we were lucky because Erin confessed to everything.

There would be no pain of a trial.

She will be in jail for the rest of her life.

Today, the calendar says another fresh start.

Today is the day the money transfers into my name.

I'm sure Trent is wondering what I'm going to do with it, but I already know, and now I'm off to tell him.

It's Tuesday, so I know exactly where he is right now.

When we were at the lawyer's office earlier, I didn't mention my plan.

It didn't seem right to talk about this big step in front of Mr. Baker.

It takes me only twenty minutes to get to Cresthill. Cresthill, the place I now know Trent owns. Yep. That came out too, this year.

A fact that made me fall even more in love with him.

When I walk through the doors, I smile broadly to myself.

This is the right decision.

I find him where I knew I would.

In the atrium, kneeling on the ground with his mother.

They're in the middle of a row of plants, fussing over the leaves.

She sees me first, stands, and wipes her dirt-covered hands on her pants before waving to me.

The movement makes Trent stop what he's doing and look in my direction. He places a small shovel down, stands, and strides to me. The moment he is standing in front of me, he looks down at me and places a kiss on my lips.

His thumb lingers on my lips, tracing the bottom one. "I thought you were going to the bank."

"Been there, done that." I smile coyly.

"You're a very rich woman now."

"Nope. I'm not . . ."

He lifts a brow, clearly not understanding what I am trying

to say. I reach into my purse and pull out the check I made out to Cresthill.

His eyes go wide, and his mouth drops open.

It's all there.

All twenty-two million of it.

I'm not even sure I can, technically, write a check this big. I've never had access to money like this in my life. But whatever I need to do to get it into Cresthill's accounts, I'll do. With a smile on my face.

I love this place.

I love *Trent*.

"I don't need money, Trent." I press a small kiss to his thumb, cheeks burning when his mom leaves to give us privacy. "I only need you."

His eyes look glassy, and then, before I can say another word, he shuts me up with a passionate kiss.

"I'll love you, forever," he promises against my mouth.

"Forever is a long time."

"Are you arguing with me, princess?"

"Who? Me? Would I do that?"

He presses his forehead against mine. "Hopefully every day for the rest of our lives."

Our lives.

And then, just like that, in dirty jeans, with a smile on his face, he bends down on one knee. He reaches into his pocket, pulls out a tiny velvet box, and opens it up. An oval-shaped diamond winks at me. It's set high on a pave band.

"I was waiting for today to give you this," he says, box raised up to me. "Will you marry me?"

Tears fall from my eyes. "Yes."

I chant it over and over.

"Yes, yes, yes."

Rising to his feet, he pulls me up with him, looping his free hand around me. He lifts me off my feet and seals his mouth to mine. When he drops me, he slides the ring on my finger. It's a perfect fit.

And then his lips are back on mine, and he's claiming me as his in ways words could never deliver.

There, in the garden, my life once again changes.

It was here, in this same place, that I learned Trent is more than I thought.

I learned that shades of gray do exist.

Your enemy can absolutely be your soul mate.

And a single moment can change your life.

The End

ACKNOWLEDGMENTS

I want to thank my entire family. I love you all so much.

A Special THANK YOU to Paige, you know why . . .

Thank you to the amazing professionals that helped with Shattered Dynasty.

Suzi Vanderham

Jenny Sims

Tamara Mataya

Marla Esposito

Jaime Ryter

Champagne Formats

Hang Le

Jill Glass

Kelly Allenby

Grey's Promotions

Thank you to Jason Clarke, Vanessa Edwin, Kim Gilmour and Lyric for bringing Shattered Dynasty to life on audio.

Thank you to my AMAZING ARC TEAM! You guys rock!

Thank you to my beta/test team.

I want to thank ALL my friends for putting up with me while I wrote this book. Thank you!

To the ladies in the Ava Harrison Support Group, I couldn't have done this without your support!

Please consider joining my Facebook reader group Ava Harrison Support Group

Thanks to all the bloggers! Thanks for your excitement and love of books!

Last but certainly not least. . .

Thank you to the readers!

Thank you so much for taking this journey with me.

Made in the USA
Monee, IL
09 October 2021

79691428R00229